A Wicked Persuasion

KAREN FOLEY
CARA SUMMERS
DEBBI RAWLINS

MILLS & BOON

First Published in Great Britain 2016
By Mills & Boon, an imprint of HarperCollins*Publishers*
1 London Bridge Street, London, SE1 9GF

A WICKED PERSUASION © 2016 Harlequin Books S. A.

No Going Back, *No Holds Barred* and *No One Needs To Know* were first published in Great Britain by Harlequin (UK) Limited.

No Going Back © 2012 Karen Foley
No Holds Barred © 2012 Carolyn Hanlon
No One Needs To Know © 2013 Debbi Quattrone

ISBN: 978-0-263-92060-4

05-0416

Our policy is to use papers that are natural, renewable and recyclable products and made from wood grown in sustainable forests. The logging and manufacturing processes conform to the legal environmental regulations of the country of origin.

Printed and bound in Spain
by CPI, Barcelona

NO GOING BACK

BY
KAREN FOLEY

Karen Foley is an incurable romantic. When she's not working for the Department of Defense, she's writing sexy romances with strong heroes and happy endings. She lives in Massachusetts with her husband and two daughters, an overgrown puppy and two very spoiled cats. Karen enjoys hearing from her readers. you can find out more about her by visiting www.karenefoley.com.

This book is dedicated to our men and women in uniform; thank you for your service!

1

AN IMPERIOUS KNOCKING on the door of the opulent hotel suite startled Kate Fitzgerald from her disturbing thoughts. Hurrying to the door, she peered through the peephole and then opened it wide to the man who stalked inside, dragging his hand through his long hair.

"Keep your voice down," she said without preamble, closing the door behind him. "Tenley is sleeping in the next room."

Russell Wilson might look like a British rock star with his skinny jeans, necklaces and leather jacket, but he was one of the most coveted talent agents in the country. Kate could see he was angry, and she couldn't blame him.

"The video of Tenley's meltdown has gone viral," he snapped. "It's only been three days, and every social media and video-sharing website is promoting it. Even the major news networks have picked it up. Bloody hell, what a train wreck."

Kate chewed the edge of her thumb as she watched him pace. Behind her on the flat-screen television, the evening news was running yet another clip of Tenley Miles's anti-military rant, caught by several fans on their cell phones and provided to the media. Kate cringed as she listened to Tenley scream about how the military was medieval in its enlistment tactics, brutal in its treatment of new recruits and uncaring of the young men and women who gave their lives to feed its ravenous appetite. But worst of all, she'd concluded her shocking meltdown by stating she was ashamed to call herself an American. Was Tenley overdramatic? Certainly. But even knowing her sister's tendency toward extreme emotions, Kate had to admit it looked bad.

"I'm more concerned about Tenley than I am about her fans," Kate said. "She's emotionally fragile right now."

Russell gave a snort. "When isn't she emotionally fragile? Whatever possessed her to run off with a complete stranger and get *married* is beyond me. At least you had the good sense to have it annulled."

Kate sighed and moved to the window to gaze out at the lights of San Antonio. Tenley would perform at the AT&T Center later that night before heading to Dallas for two shows, and then finally home to Nashville. Had it really been only a week since they'd spent three nights in Las Vegas? Since her sister had met Corporal Doug Armstrong, a young soldier who had scored backstage tickets to meet her, and had run off with him? She'd hated hurting Tenley by using her role as legal guardian to have the marriage annulled, but she wouldn't let anyone take advantage of her sister's soft heart—or her substantial bank account—no matter how handsome or charming he might be.

"I didn't have a choice," she said tonelessly, staring through the glass at the neon lights of the strip below. "They barely knew each other, and he's stationed in California. What did she think—that she and Doug were going to move there and they would live happily ever after?"

Kate closed her eyes against the memory of Tenley telling her she had just gotten married, and her own reaction to the news. If it had been anyone else, Kate might have been inclined to let the newlyweds discover for themselves that they'd made a terrible mistake. But a failed marriage would destroy Tenley, and if they were to have a child…

No, she'd made the right decision. The annulment might cause Tenley pain now, but that pain would be far worse if Kate had allowed the marriage to continue. She only hoped her sister would forgive her for interfering.

"Well, so long as the public doesn't learn about the elopement, then no harm done," Russell finally said. "Although it will be hard to keep the information quiet after that public display. People will want to know what caused her to act so out of character, and we can hardly tell them her bitterness toward the military is because her husband—to whom, by the way, she is no longer married—has just been shipped off to Afghanistan for a year." Russell gave Kate a smile. "That was a great move, by the way."

Kate compressed her lips but didn't immediately say anything. If Tenley ever discovered that Kate was the one responsible for having the young man peremptorily shipped overseas, she'd never forgive her. All it had taken was a couple of phone calls, and the deed was done. Kate didn't regret her actions. She had acted in Tenley's best interests.

As the daughter of two famous singers, both of whom had been killed in a bus accident when she was just a child, Tenley Miles was the darling of the country-music scene. She'd grown up in the public spotlight and her sweet disposition and naivety, combined with the obstacles she had overcome, had helped to fuel her popularity.

Kate still remembered the day she had gotten the news that their mother and her fiancé had been killed. She'd been just two months into her freshman year of college and the news had changed her life forever. She'd wanted to become part of the exploding internet industry and had been excited about the prospect of designing programs that would connect people with others around the globe. But when she learned that her mother had died, she'd left college to care for her then six-year-old sister. That had been twelve years ago. She didn't regret her decision, and if her own dreams of becoming a web designer weren't progressing as quickly as she'd hoped, then she had only herself to blame. She'd made her choice and she told herself that she didn't regret any of it. Besides, she'd been able to help Tenley achieve her own success.

At just eighteen years old, Tenley Miles was the biggest thing to hit the country pop scene in more than three years. She'd signed her first recording contract at just fifteen years old, and her debut single had spent eight weeks in the number-one spot on the country charts. A year later, she had released two albums and won five Grammys, along with a dozen other awards. By the time she was seventeen, she was filling music halls and stadiums around the country and each of her four albums had gone platinum. Her anti-military rant could definitely have a negative impact on her image, especially if the news got out about her elopement with a soldier. The last thing Kate needed was for Russell to drop his young client just when the country singer's career was skyrocketing.

"Look, I'll do damage control, I promise," Kate said to Russell. "We'll figure this out."

Russell whirled on her in disbelief, his eyebrows nearly disappearing into his hairline. "Damage control? Are you freaking joking?" He gave a laugh of disbelief. "Katie, darling, do you realize her little diatribe cost her nearly half of her audience attendance at last night's concert? Her recording label called this morning to say that she's already receiving hate mail. They can't afford this kind of negative publicity and are actually considering dropping her. What kind of damage control can you possibly do after *that?*" He stabbed his finger in the direction of the television, where a fan had caught the country pop star having her very public, very ugly meltdown. "It's bad enough that she eloped during a concert tour with some soldier, but now this? It's like she's deliberately trying to sabotage her own career."

Kate bit her tongue and forced herself to remain calm. "You know Tenley," she replied. "She's impulsive. That's why she has me."

"And what are you going to do about this?" Russell snapped in irritation. "In less than five minutes that girl has managed to destroy everything we've worked so hard to create. She's alienated every patriotic and uniformed person in this country. Christ, there's a public outcry to boycott her music. Even the liberals are lambasting her."

"Keep your voice down," Kate admonished, glancing toward the bedroom door. "I have an idea, one that will demonstrate her goodwill toward the troops."

"It had better be good," Russell snarled. "If she has to cancel the rest of her tour—which is looking more likely with every passing hour—this is going to get very expensive, very quickly."

Kate pulled her cell phone out of her pocket and began scrolling through her extensive list of contacts. "I've been thinking about the huge Independence Day concert tour taking place in Afghanistan next month," she said, slanting Russell a quick look. "Everyone is talking about it. In fact, I believe several of your biggest clients are participating. Let me make a few calls and see if we can squeeze Tenley into the lineup."

"You can't be serious," Russell groaned. "Do you know the hoops I had to jump through to get my other clients on that tour? Even if you could pull it off, it's too late! Tenley can't just cancel her scheduled performances to go overseas."

Kate arched an eyebrow. "To hear you tell it, she'll be

lucky if her remaining performances aren't canceled due to lack of interest. But I'm not buying it. Tenley is a box-office juggernaut, and I can't imagine that the USO won't be thrilled to have her join the tour."

"And what makes you think Tenley will agree to go over there?"

Kate gave a tight smile. "Are you kidding? She'll jump at the opportunity to be in the same country as her lost love, even for just a few days. Not that there'll be any chance of seeing him, of course. My understanding is that he was sent to one of the remote outposts in the northern part of the country."

Russell was silent for a moment as he considered Kate's words. "That might just work," he mused. "Of course, the USO may not agree to finance her trip, especially at this late date, so we could have to pay for it out of pocket. That's disappointing, but if it works…"

"I'll make it work," Kate promised.

Russell raised his eyebrows. "You've always been so protective of Tenley. Are you sure you want to send her to a combat zone?"

Kate gave him a tolerant look. "If Carrie Underwood and Faith Hill can do the tour, then so can Tenley. It's not as if she won't have ample protection. Besides, I'd rather send her to Afghanistan for a week than see her career crash and burn."

Glancing toward the bedroom door, Russell lowered his voice. "I've always thought you were too easy on her, and I'm glad to see you finally take off the kid gloves."

Kate looked at him in exasperation. "I'm not doing this to punish her. I'm doing it because I care about her. After all, she's my baby sister."

"Half sister," he corrected.

"The point is," Kate said carefully, "I'm all she has. No-body else is going to look out for her, and she's certainly not capable of looking out for herself. The fact that she ran off with the first guy she met is proof of that. She *needs* me."

"Hmm," mused Russell. "Still, it *is* Afghanistan."

"This is a huge Independence Day event," Kate said. "Trust me, if there was any danger, the USO wouldn't allow the concert to proceed. In fact, my plan is to arrive a few days ahead of Tenley, tour the various bases where the concerts will take place, and ensure the proper security measures are set up." She smiled at Russell. "She'll have the entire United States Army to protect her. What could possibly go wrong?"

2

Bagram Airfield, Afghanistan

"WHAT DO YOU MEAN we've been told to stand down?" Chase Rawlins growled at the uniformed man standing behind the desk.

Colonel Decker planted his hands on the surface of the desk and leaned forward. When he spoke, his voice was hard. "Major, we've known each other for a long time, but I'll advise you not to forget who you're speaking to."

Chase stared at the other man for a long moment, trying to rein in his frustration. Compressing his lips, he straightened and stared at a point over the colonel's shoulder. "Yes, sir."

He and his men had been in the middle of a critical operation when the stand-down order had come through. The team of special-operations commandos had been relentlessly tracking a top Taliban leader through northern Afghanistan for nearly a year. They had finally discovered him hiding out in a heavily fortified village in the mountains, and had been preparing a nighttime raid to capture him, when they had received the order to stand down and return to Bagram Airfield.

Immediately.

He and his men had literally been positioned on the bastard's doorstep. Chase had reluctantly acknowledged the order and signaled his team to retreat. The fact that one of his men had chosen to disregard that order and had attempted to singlehandedly storm the compound where the target was hiding was proof of the sheer frustration they all felt. Chase had managed to stop the soldier before he actually gained entry to the building, but not before their position had been compromised. The ensuing firefight was intense, but Chase's team had escaped to the west and made their way to the extraction point, where a Black Hawk helicopter had picked them up and returned them to Bagram Airfield. Two members of his team had stayed behind to maintain surveillance on the target.

But the knowledge that they'd let Hamid Al-Azir get away pissed him off on a level so deep that he hadn't stopped to fully consider his actions. As soon as the helicopter had touched down at Bagram, he'd stormed over to the Special Ops commander's office to find out what the hell was going on. He hadn't even stopped to clean himself up and still wore the dust and grime of fourteen days in the field.

"I understand your frustration, Major," Colonel Decker said. "Vital operations have been disrupted across the theater, but the Pentagon has demanded a full investigation into the U.S. air strike that occurred outside Kandahar two days ago. Until that investigation is complete, your orders are to stand down."

Chase hadn't read the reports, but by all accounts the Special Ops air strike against the summer retreat of a top Taliban leader had been a complete disaster. The local population claimed that dozens of innocent civilians had been targeted, and Washington's response was an abrupt and complete halt to all special-operations missions.

Chase blew out a hard breath and looked at Colonel Decker. "How long?"

The Colonel shrugged. "The Pentagon says at least forty-eight hours, but my guess is a week. Maybe longer."

Chase bit back an expletive. At least with a two-man team in the region, they could still keep tabs on Al-Azir. The months spent tracking the Taliban leader wouldn't be completely wasted, but Chase didn't think he could relax until they had the bastard in custody.

"Sir, I'd like to rejoin my surveillance team ASAP."

Colonel Decker picked up a folder and pinioned Chase with a hard look. "Before I let you do that, why don't you tell me what happened after the stand-down order was issued? My report states gunfire was exchanged at the compound, and your team requested air support."

The Colonel's expression was grim and Chase knew it didn't bode well for him. "Sergeant Morse was unaware of the stand-down order," he lied, "and attempted to take the target into custody."

"Uh-huh." The dry tone clearly said the Colonel didn't believe a word of Chase's story. "And as their leader, your responsibility was to ensure your men not only heard the order, but heeded it."

"Yes, sir."

"In light of your inability to control your team, Major, I have a new assignment for you. Here, take a look. This should keep you busy for the next week or so. How well you perform this duty will determine whether I send you back into the field."

Frowning, Chase took the file from his superior and opened it, quickly scanning the contents of the dossier. Along with the usual personal information, the folder contained several glossy media photos of a young woman with a guitar. She was attractive in a sexy, teenybopper way, with wild blond hair and heavy eye makeup. She wore a pair of tattered jeans and cowboy boots, paired with a red camisole top that laced up the front like a corset. Scanning the dossier, he saw her name was Tenley Miles and she was some kind of country-pop singer. And she was coming to Afghanistan.

"What is this?" he growled, but he had a sinking suspicion that he already knew.

"Your new assignment," Colonel Decker announced cheerfully. "She'll arrive in three days as part of the Independence Day concert tour, and you will act as her escort while she's here."

"Her babysitter, you mean," Chase muttered, flipping through the photos. A quick appraisal of her personal information confirmed that she was barely eighteen years old. "Why isn't the USO handling security? This isn't something we do."

While Chase and his men routinely provided protection details for VIPs and dignitaries during their visits to Afghanistan, they had never been asked to act as bodyguards to celebrities. The USO had its own contracted security personnel for that purpose.

"The USO staff is stretched thin with the other entertainers who are coming over. Besides, she's not here on a USO ticket," the colonel added. "She's here on her own dime to make nice with the troops and, as I understand it, try to repair the damage she did at a recent concert when she publicly lambasted the U.S. military."

"Christ, leave it to the celebrities," Chase said in disgust. He pulled out a news article that provided the details of Tenley Miles's anti-military rant. He gave a disbelieving huff of laughter as he quickly read the column. "I think I'd rather take my chances with the Taliban."

"Are you telling me you can't handle one girl?" The colonel arched an eyebrow.

"That depends," Chase said absently, thumbing through the remaining documents. "Is water-boarding still allowed?" Picking up a black-and-white photo, he studied it for a moment before turning it toward the other man. "Who is this?"

"Her personal assistant."

There was some writing on the back of the photo. "Katherine Fitzgerald," Chase read aloud. "Publicist." He gave a snort of disgust. "Great. Tell me I don't have to babysit her as well."

Turning the photo over, he studied the woman again and something fisted low in his gut. She was slender and her face boasted beautiful bone structure, although her baggy cargo pants and cardigan sweater effectively hid any curves she might have. Her hair was an indeterminate color and style, having been pulled back into a ponytail. Her eyes were hidden behind a pair of sunglasses, and Chase let his gaze linger for a moment on her full lips and the determined set of her chin.

"Actually," the colonel said, "her flight lands in about two hours and I'd like you to be there to meet her and get her settled."

Chase frowned. The last thing he wanted to do was pander to some entitled celebrity and her publicist. "I thought you said she wasn't coming for another three days."

"Tenley Miles won't be here for another three days," the Colonel clarified. "Her publicist arrives today to scope things out. So...you have three days to tour three of our bases—Bagram, Camp Leatherneck and Kandahar, where you'll rendezvous with the entertainers upon their arrival."

Chase frowned. "Is that typical protocol for these kinds of events? To send a publicist or personal assistant—or whatever the hell she calls herself—over early to scope things out?"

"I guess that depends on the star power of the celebrity,"

Colonel Decker said wryly. "And I'm not into the country-pop scene, but my understanding is that Tenley Miles is a very big deal."

"So if the USO has run out of room, where am I supposed to put her?"

"I'll leave that up to you. But keep in mind that how well you perform this assignment will determine how quickly I allow you to return to the field with the rest of your team."

In other words, if he couldn't handle these two women, there was no way he'd be allowed to oversee a covert Special Ops team.

"Just so that I'm clear," he said carefully, "I have complete responsibility for this woman while she's here, correct?"

"That's right."

"And if she's not happy with the, uh, accommodations?"

"Then she goes home. Same thing for the singer. I won't compromise their safety or the safety of the troops, so if either of them is unable to follow your rules, Major, then they're on the next flight out. But you won't let that happen. They *will* follow your rules, do we understand each other?"

Chase read the unspoken message loud and clear. If the women ended up leaving early, it would only be because he had failed in his assignment. And if that happened, he could expect to spend the remainder of his deployment chained to a desk somewhere. He considered the factors involved in the first phase of his assignment: one woman, three bases, three days. No problem. He hadn't failed a mission yet, and he wasn't about to start now.

KATE DECIDED THAT planning a trip to Afghanistan was a little like planning a trip to the moon. She had no idea what to expect and, therefore, little idea what to bring. In the end, she'd packed lightweight, practical clothing. She still believed that allowing Tenley to visit the troops in Afghanistan was the right thing to do, although seeing all the uniformed soldiers on the last leg of her trip had admittedly given her pause. They'd both be lucky if they didn't get themselves killed, and after Tenley's public meltdown, Kate thought they were probably in as much danger from the troops as they were from terrorists.

She had known it would take a long time to reach her destination, but she'd been unprepared for just how exhausted she'd be when she finally reached Bagram Airfield, more than forty-eight hours after leaving Nashville. Additionally, since she had been forced to make her own travel arrangements, there hadn't been anyone to meet her at each location and direct her where to go next. At least when she traveled with Tenley, they had Russell to lean on. But after assuring Kate that she'd do splendidly on her own, he'd left her at the airport. Even Tenley hadn't been overly interested in any of the travel plans, although she'd perked up a bit when Kate had told her they would be going to Afghanistan. But after breaking the news that there would be absolutely no likelihood of seeing her young soldier, Tenley had retreated to her bedroom in tears, preferring to be alone until she received word from Kate that she'd okayed the security setup and Tenley could fly over. For the first time Kate could recall, she was traveling completely alone.

She'd arrived in Kuwait the previous afternoon and had waited nearly fourteen hours for a military flight to Bagram Airfield. Now she watched as the base came into view on the ground below. From a distance, the place looked enormous, but for as far as she could see there were only unrelenting shades of brown, from the desert to the distant mountains, and even the base itself. Opening her shoulder bag, Kate looked again at the information that the Army Morale, Welfare and Recreation department had sent to her.

Over the course of a week, Tenley would perform concerts at three different American bases in Afghanistan, as well as conduct meet-and-greet sessions with the troops. The USO had assured Kate that someone would meet her upon her arrival, and escort her to each location. Kate had spent most of the flight writing Tenley's speech, in which her sister apologized for her thoughtless rant and pledged her support for the men and women in uniform. Kate only hoped it would be enough.

The big jet touched down on the airstrip at Bagram Airfield, and Kate was surprised to see they would disembark directly onto the tarmac. Peering out the window of the plane, she couldn't see any building that looked remotely like an airport terminal. The airfield seemed to be nothing more than an enormous airstrip alongside a cluster of tents and makeshift hangars, and a hodgepodge of other small buildings. Maybe this wasn't the airfield at all. Maybe the plane was making an unscheduled stop at some remote base and then they would head on to Bagram.

The aisle of the plane was quickly filling with uniformed soldiers waiting to disembark. Leaning forward, Kate tugged on the sleeve of the nearest man. He turned and looked at her expectantly.

"Excuse me, but is this Bagram Field?"

"Yes, ma'am."

"Are you sure? I mean, have you been here before?"

"Yes, ma'am," he assured her. "This is my third deployment."

"Oh. Well, where exactly is the terminal? I mean, where do I pick up my luggage?"

Ducking his head to avoid the overhead storage bins, the soldier leaned across the seat and pointed through the window. "See that hangar, there? That's the terminal. This is an airfield, ma'am, as in air*field*. They're not really set up like you're used to at home. Look, they're bringing the luggage out now."

Kate watched as a group of soldiers began systematically dragging baggage from the cargo hold of the plane, only instead of stacking the items on a small trolley to be transported into the terminal, they literally threw the bags into one enormous pile right there on the flight line. When the mountain of duffel bags threatened to fall over, they started a new pile right next to it.

"Oh, my God," she breathed. "How am I supposed to find my bag?"

The soldier gave her a grin and straightened. "Well, ma'am, that's half the fun. Welcome to Afghanistan, and good luck."

Kate watched helplessly as he departed, then scooped her shoulder bag up and fell into line behind the soldiers. As soon as she stepped out the door of the aircraft, the heat slapped her in the face like a hot brick. To compound the discomfort, the air itself was filled with a fine, powdery dust that immediately infiltrated her mouth and nose and sent her into a fit of uncontrollable sneezing.

"Oh, my God," she gasped, when she could finally catch her breath.

The soldier in front of her turned around and gave her a quick grin. "You'll get used it."

Kate doubted it. She'd never experienced heat like this. It seemed to suck the very moisture out of her skin and left her gasping for breath. Even Las Vegas in the summer hadn't been this oppressive. At the bottom of the airplane steps, she automatically turned toward the piles of luggage, but found her way blocked by a military police officer.

"Just follow the line for processing, ma'am," he said briskly, indicating she should continue toward the nearest hangar. "You'll be notified when all the baggage is out of the aircraft."

In dismay, Kate saw that the line snaked across the tarmac and disappeared inside one of the makeshift hangars. It was moving at a snail's pace, and Kate knew she would die of heat stroke before she ever made it into the building. She could almost feel the sweat evaporating from her skin as she stood under the baking sun.

Hefting her shoulder bag higher, she looked around her, astonished at the sheer number of men. There were men *everywhere*—soldiers who seemed to be waiting for transportation, soldiers sleeping or sitting upright against their gear, soldiers reading books, standing around in small groups, playing handheld video games or listening to music on their ear buds. There was a handful of female soldiers, but they were hugely outnumbered by the men. Kate couldn't help but notice that all of them—male and female—carried some sort of weapon.

She was acutely conscious of her own vulnerability. She carried no weapon, unless you counted the Montegrappa pen that Tenley had brought back from Italy as a gift for her. She didn't even possess a helmet or bulletproof vest. Who would protect her in the event of an attack?

"Miss Fitzgerald?"

Kate turned to see a soldier striding toward her—a tall, muscular soldier who looked like he kicked ass for a living. He had the easy, loose-limbed gait of an athlete, and as he drew closer, Kate swallowed hard. The growth of beard he sported couldn't hide his square jaw or detract from the chiseled cheekbones and proud nose. With his broad shoulders and powerful arms, he looked more than a little dangerous. The thought flashed through her head that given a few spare hours, this guy could singlehandedly end the war.

"Yes?" Her hand went self-consciously to her hair, and she tried to ignore the way her pulse kicked up a notch.

As he came forward, he yanked his sunglasses off and she saw his eyes were a translucent green, startling in his tanned face. Her breath caught and she found herself helpless to look away. He was the stuff of heroic action movies, a combination of masculine strength and confidence all wrapped up in a mouthwatering package. She'd never had this kind of immediate reaction to a man before. Her heart raced, and her knees were actually wobbly. Feeling a little panicked, Kate tried to recall the last time she'd eaten. Her blood sugar must be low. Either that or she was dehydrated.

The soldier extended his hand and his eyes swept over her in sharp assessment. "Ma'am. I'm Major Rawlins. I'll be your military escort for the duration of your visit."

His hand gripped hers, and she barely had time to register how warm and callused his palm was against her own before he released her.

"If you'll follow me, please."

Without giving her an opportunity to respond and without waiting to see if she would do as he said, he turned and walked toward the hangar. Kate watched his retreating back, feeling as if she'd had the wind knocked out of her. Then, realizing her mouth was hanging open, she snapped it shut and stepped out of the line to hurry after him, her oversize shoulder bag bouncing uncomfortably against her hip.

"Major Rawlins," she called as she caught up with him.

He glanced over at her but did not slow down. "Yes?"

"My understanding was that the USO would provide a civilian representative who would be my point of contact." As he strode briskly along, Kate tried to simultaneously walk and fish through her bag for the paperwork she had received from the USO, but the task was nearly impossible given the pace he set. Maybe she'd misunderstood him.

Maybe he was only her driver. Oh, God, please let him be the driver. She'd never felt so self-conscious or tongue-tied as she did with this guy, evidence that she'd gone too long without male contact. Or at least, gorgeous male contact.

"You understood wrong, ma'am," he said smoothly, never breaking stride.

Abandoning the search for her papers, Kate concentrated instead on keeping up with him. Arriving at the front of the long line, she saw several military police scanning everyone's identification cards. Flashing his own ID, Major Rawlins stepped into the front of the line and looked expectantly at Kate.

"You should have been assigned a temporary identification card when you arrived at the processing center in Kuwait," he explained carefully. "Do you have it with you?"

"What? Oh, yes!" Setting her bag down on the table, Kate began rummaging through it. She'd purchased a bright orange lanyard for the card, specifically so she could locate it in a hurry, but with everything else she'd managed to stuff into the large tote, she couldn't locate the identification.

"Sorry," she mumbled, uncomfortably aware of Major Rawlins's growing irritation. "I know it's in here somewhere."

Pulling out two paperback novels, an MP3 player and a bag of trail mix, she set them on the table and continued digging through the contents of the bag. Behind her, she heard several soldiers mutter something under their breath and knew she was holding up the line. She glanced at the military police officer who watched her impassively with his arms crossed over his chest.

"Sorry," she muttered again.

"Here, let me help you," Major Rawlins offered.

Kate thought she saw the hint of a dimple in one lean cheek, and before she could protest, he took her bag and upended it, spilling the contents onto the table. Ignoring Kate's gasp, he swept one finger through the assorted flotsam and came up with the ID card attached to the orange lanyard. Yanking the card from the holder, he handed it to the military police officer.

"You see? That wasn't so difficult," he said, amusement lacing his voice. Accepting the ID card back from the officer, he returned it to Kate. "Wear this where it's visible. Follow me, please."

Dropping the lanyard over her head, Kate watched with rising annoyance as he made his way back toward the flight line. With one hand, she swept her personal items back into her shoulder bag and determinedly followed Major Rawlins.

"Find your gear and let's go," he said, nodding toward the three enormous piles of duffel bags sitting on the tarmac.

Kate glanced at his face to see if he was joking. With his sunglasses shielding his eyes, she couldn't decipher his expression, but it seemed he had no intention of helping her. Glancing at the daunting piles, she drew in a deep breath.

"Here, hold this," she said, and pushed her shoulder bag into his hands. She sensed his surprise, but he made no objection, tucking the bag under his arm as he watched her.

Kate had packed her belongings in a neon-pink duffel bag that had once belonged to Tenley, thinking it would be easy to spot. But she'd been wrong. Circling each of the piles, she couldn't see any sign of pink peeking through the dozens of army-green duffel bags, which meant her own was probably buried somewhere near the bottom. She prepared to grab the handles of the nearest duffel when a masculine voice interrupted her.

"Ma'am, are you looking for a particular bag?"

Turning, she saw two young soldiers walking toward her. Just moments earlier, they had been lounging against their own piles of gear, chatting idly.

Kate nodded. "Yes. I have a bright pink duffel bag, but I can't see it anywhere."

The second soldier, who looked to be no older than Tenley, grinned. "No problem, ma'am, we can find it for you." Turning, he whistled through his teeth to a group of soldiers gathered near the entrance to the hangar and motioned them over. "Hey, guys, give us a hand over here!"

Within minutes, there were a dozen young men enthusiastically digging their way through the piles of luggage, calling out names as they identified a tag or lettering painted on the outside of the bag. Kate stepped back to watch, amazed by their enthusiasm and efficiency. In less than five minutes, the first soldier held Kate's bag up in triumph.

"Is this it?" he asked.

Kate came forward and took the duffel from him. "That's the one," she said with a grateful smile. "Thank you so much!"

"My pleasure, ma'am."

Clutching the heavy bag, Kate turned back to Major Rawlins, who stood to one side with his arms crossed over his impressive chest, her tote dangling from one hand. She wasn't certain, but Kate thought she detected amusement on his face.

"Well, that wasn't so bad," she remarked cheerfully.

He raised an eyebrow and gave a noncommittal grunt. "Here, let's trade," he said, handing her the shoulder bag and taking the pink duffel from her. "I have a vehicle waiting out front."

Kate watched as he walked back toward the hangar, a tough-as-nails warrior carrying a pink duffel bag in his hand. She wanted to laugh at the incongruous sight, but seeing that none of the surrounding soldiers so much as cracked a smile in his direction, she suppressed her own amusement. Drawing herself up, she followed him once more. She was getting tired of seeing nothing but this man's backside, no matter how delectable it might be. And she had to admit, he did have a fine ass. Frowning at her thoughts, she hefted her tote bag over her shoulder and followed him.

"Major Rawlins, I'd like to get started right away," she said, trying to match his long strides. "I understand that with the sheer number of entertainers who are coming over, the USO ran out of room to accommodate my client and her band. I'd like to see where Tenley will stay while she's here. And do you know who will accompany me to the other bases?"

He did stop then, so abruptly that Kate nearly plowed into him. Slowly, he removed his sunglasses and turned to face her. His gaze drifted over her and that muscle worked in his lean cheek. Kate felt herself go hot beneath his regard, and she wondered what was going through his head.

"Just so that we're clear," he said carefully, "I am your single point of contact for whatever you require while you are here. We will travel together, eat together, view the venues together and basically be attached at the hip until you depart. This is a combat environment, Miss Fitzgerald, and I'm responsible for your well-being. You don't do anything without me, or without my permission. Understood?"

Kate stared at him, and for the first time since she'd made the decision to come to Afghanistan, realized the personal impact. The knowledge that she would spend the next three days in this man's exclusive company caused a shiver to go through her, but whether it was one of dread or anticipation, she couldn't tell.

Major Rawlins was unlike any man she'd ever met before. He was testosterone personified, and the way he looked at her made her go a little boneless. For the first time she could recall, she wasn't the one in control, the one calling the shots. That fact should have annoyed her. Instead, she found herself agreeing wholeheartedly to his conditions.

"Yes." She nodded. "I understand."

She thought he would turn and walk away again, but he stood watching for a moment longer, as if there was something about her that puzzled him. His eyes were a gorgeous shade of green, reminding her of the clear, warm waters of the Caribbean.

"I'm curious. Why are you here, Miss Fitzgerald?"

She frowned, taken aback by the question. "I beg your pardon? It's my job to ensure everything is ready for my client's visit."

"But why are you *here?* In Afghanistan? Why not some military base on American soil? Why come all the way over here when your client wasn't originally scheduled to perform as part of the Independence Day concert?" He rubbed the back of his neck. "No offense, but Tenley Miles is little more than a child, and you—" He broke abruptly off.

"What?" Kate asked. "I'm what?"

He gave a soft laugh. "Well, I just can't figure out why a woman like you would come over here, unaccompanied."

Kate hesitated. She had to assume that he knew the truth; that he'd seen the news reports and was aware that Tenley had directed her vitriol toward the military's policy of sending troops to Iraq and Afghanistan. She couldn't blame him for his attitude, but neither could she explain to him the reasons behind Tenley's meltdown. Her sister's precipitous marriage and subsequent annulment had to remain a secret.

She hesitated, wondering how direct she could be without giving him too much information. "Tenley has been going through a difficult time," she began cautiously. "She said some things about the military that were pretty horrible and, well…" She gave a soft laugh. "Let's just say that I'm hoping this tour will be a humbling experience for her."

"Oh, I'm certain it will be," he said, and one corner of his mouth lifted in a ghost of a smile. He glanced at his watch. "We should get going."

Outside, the unrelenting heat, combined with the weight of her overloaded tote bag, quickly sapped her strength. She felt tired and achy and unprepared for whatever lay ahead. A military Humvee waited by the curb, and Kate watched as Major Rawlins put her gear in the back.

"Thank you," she murmured as he held the door open for her. Climbing into the vehicle, she saw there was already another soldier behind the wheel. She expected Major Rawlins to get in the front passenger seat, and was unprepared when he slid in beside her, instead.

Sensing her surprise, he gave her a wry smile. "Attached at the hip, remember?"

Kate found herself staring at him. That small smile was enough to transform his features. How would he look if that smile were to expand to his eyes? She had a feeling that he might be irresistible.

"Where to, sir?" asked the driver.

"Take us to my housing unit."

"Yes sir." The driver grinned. "I know one female who is going to be very excited to see you again."

Kate slanted Major Rawlins a questioning look, but if he felt her silent query, he ignored it. She felt a tug of curiosity. What would it be like to be romantically involved with this man? To have his whole and undivided attention? To see his eyes go hot with desire? The thought sent a small shiver through her, further proof that she'd been way too long without sex. Men didn't usually have this effect on her, but having gone more than a year without intimacy of any kind, she suspected her hormones were on full alert and ready to revolt if she didn't do something soon to appease them. But this wasn't quite what she had in mind.

"Why are we going to your housing unit?" she asked. "Don't you think you're taking this attached-at-the-hip thing a little too seriously? I am not staying in your unit with you."

She watched, entranced, as a smile spread across his face. She'd been wrong. He wasn't just irresistible, he was downright devastating. His smile caused something to loosen inside her, and she found she couldn't look away.

"Miss Fitzgerald," he drawled, letting his gaze drift deliberately over her, "as attractive as you might be, I have no intention of sleeping with you."

3

CHASE REGRETTED THE WORDS the instant they left his mouth. Their driver gave a snort of laughter which he quickly hid behind a sudden coughing fit after Chase sent him a quelling look. But it was the stricken expression on Kate Fitzgerald's face that made him wish he'd kept his mouth shut. That, and the fact that a part of him recognized that given a different set of circumstances, she was the kind of woman he'd give his left nut to sleep with.

He wished like hell that she wasn't so damned pretty. The instant he'd spotted her standing in the long line of uniformed soldiers, he'd felt as if someone had kicked him in the solar plexus.

He'd been in Afghanistan for six months, and he'd spent most of that time in the stark, forbidding mountains of the Kala Gush region, living and sleeping outside and enduring the harshest of conditions. Seeing Kate Fitzgerald had been an unexpected and potent reminder of everything he'd left behind, and for just an instant, his heart had ached with longing.

He'd had a tough time catching his breath and had to mentally shake himself in order to stop staring at her. She stuck out like an exotic bloom among a bed of weeds in her jewel-colored shirt, and the bright sun picked out the deep red lights in her silky dark hair. Without the heavy cardigan she'd worn in the photo, he could see she definitely had curves. Nice curves. Curves that begged to be touched. And he wasn't the only one who had noticed. Every guy within fifty yards had been eyeballing her and he couldn't blame them. She looked good enough to eat.

Then she'd turned and looked at him.

He'd expected her to have blue or even green eyes, but hers were coffee-brown fringed with dark lashes. As he'd drawn closer, he saw the splattering of freckles across her face, as if someone had flung flecks of gold paint at her. And her mouth…Christ, he found himself conjuring up decadent images of just what she could do with that mouth. Her lips were pillowy plump and pink and had opened on a soft "oh" of surprise when he'd called her name. She'd looked achingly feminine and completely out of place among the soldiers who surrounded her.

Now, as he saw her reaction to his words, he felt like a complete dick. He'd hurt her feelings. Her mouth opened, and for a moment she looked at him, appalled, before she snapped her jaw shut. Chase watched as a slow flush crept up her neck.

Why had he said that he had no intention of sleeping with her? Had it been to remind himself that she was off-limits? Or to ensure she disliked him enough that she'd want nothing to do with him? Because he knew that if she gave any indication that she found him attractive, he'd be toast. Everything about her appealed to him. He'd almost forgotten how good a woman could smell, or how smooth her skin could be. Looking at Kate, he wondered how her skin would feel under his fingertips. She had turned her face toward the window and the sunlight picked out the golden freck-

les on her cheeks and forehead. He wanted to trace them
with a fingertip.

"Look," he finally said, "I'm sorry. That was a poor attempt at humor. I mean, obviously I have no intention of
sleeping with you—" He broke off at her expression of disbelief, as if she was amazed he was still talking. Lord, he
was making a mess of it. Biting back a curse, he scrubbed
a hand across his face and turned to the driver. "Step on it,
Cochran."

"Just so that we're clear, Major Rawlins," Kate said in a
low voice as she sat stiffly beside him, "I'm here strictly to
represent my client and ensure that everything is in order
for her visit."

Chase nodded, feeling like an idiot. "I understand, Miss
Fitzgerald."

She rolled her eyes. "And please stop calling me that.
My name is Kate."

He nodded. He could have told her his first name, but
that would have encouraged a familiarity he wasn't sure he
was willing to move toward. This woman lived in a world
so far removed from his that it might as well be in a different galaxy. She was the personal assistant to a superstar,
and even if that star was on the verge of imploding, this
woman—Kate—was accustomed to a world of bright lights
and privilege, where her associations ensured a luxurious
and pampered lifestyle. He, on the other hand, spent weeks
at a time crawling through the desert and mountains, without so much as a change of clothing or a shave, in the company of men whose specialties were the stuff of nightmares.
What could they possibly have in common?

The Humvee drew to a stop in front of a row of contain-
erized housing units, or CHUs, which were nothing more
than metal shipping containers outfitted for habitation. Since
arriving at Bagram, Chase had barely had time to meet with

Colonel Decker and then drop his gear off at the command headquarters before he'd had to meet Kate's flight. He was in desperate need of a shower and a clean uniform.

"Wait here," he said brusquely. "I just need to grab a few things."

Inside the housing unit, the furnishings were Spartan. A small office took up the front part of the unit, with a desk, a chair and his computer equipment. The back part was where he slept on a narrow bed, with only a small wardrobe and a bedside table for furnishings. He didn't even have a private latrine, but instead showered in the communal bathrooms with the rest of the troops. Since there were no other empty CHUs near his own, he'd had to improvise in finding Miss Fitzgerald a place to sleep where he could be nearby in case she needed anything. She wasn't going to like the arrangements.

Grabbing a clean uniform and underclothes from a shelf, he shoved them into a backpack, intending to snatch a quick shower at the first opportunity. As he straightened, he caught sight of himself in the small mirror over the dresser and nearly groaned aloud. His beard was longer than he normally allowed it to grow, and his skin was burnt to a mahogany hue. He'd lost some weight while he'd been on assignment and his face was leaner and harder than usual. He looked every inch a mercenary, and it was a wonder to him that Kate Fitzgerald felt comfortable enough to follow him anywhere.

Returning to the Humvee, he saw she was holding a cell phone out the window, fruitlessly searching for a signal. Throwing his backpack alongside her duffel bag, he opened the door and prepared to climb in beside her.

"Give it up," he advised drily. "There's no service over here."

Drawing her arm back into the vehicle, she turned to him

in dismay. "But how am I supposed to communicate with my people? With Tenley?"

Before he could answer, two soldiers rounded the corner. One of them, Sergeant Mike Donahue, called out to Chase.

"Hey, welcome back." He shook Chase's hand. "Tough break about the stand-down order. Have you been over to see Charity yet?"

Chase glanced at Kate, seeing the open curiosity in her eyes. "Uh, no. We just got back a few hours ago and I haven't had time. But as soon as I finish up here, I'll go see her. How is she?"

Donahue shrugged. "She hasn't been the same since you left. She just mopes around waiting for you to come back. Man, she is going to flip when she sees you."

"Uh-huh. Well, thanks for keeping an eye on her. I'll be over as soon as I can."

"You bet."

Chase climbed in beside Kate, but didn't offer an explanation. He could see the speculation in her eyes and knew she thought he had a girlfriend. How would she react if he told her that Charity was a homeless dog he'd rescued from the streets? He and his men had been performing a house-to-house search in a small village when they'd come across a group of boys abusing the dog. Chase had intervened, but he knew that as soon as he and his men left, the boys would continue to torture the poor animal. She'd looked at him with such soulful eyes that he hadn't had the heart to leave her. That had been six months ago, and she'd been with him ever since. The K-9 unit kept an eye on her when he was gone and had been teaching her how to track, which she picked up quickly.

He turned toward Kate, who was still trying to find a signal on her cell phone. "Look, I have a satellite phone in my housing unit. You're welcome to use that."

"That's fine for right now, but what about when we leave here and go to the next base?"

Amusement curved his mouth. "You think we have no way to communicate with the States? I promise you that 'your people' are only a phone call away, and a phone will be made available to you whenever you wish."

She continued to look at him, expectation written all over her face. Chase gave an exaggerated sigh. "Fine. C'mon, you can make your call now."

Climbing out of the Humvee, he opened the door to his CHU and indicated she should precede him inside. As he dialed the code for outgoing calls, he watched her out of the corner of his eye. She was staring with interest and undisguised dismay at his tiny rooms, even going so far as to peek into the bedroom at the rear. In the close quarters of the CHU, he could actually smell her fragrance, and his mind was immediately swamped with images of her spread across his narrow bed.

"Here," he said, holding out the receiver for her. "You can make your call."

She turned away from his bedroom and accepted the phone. He stood by her shoulder as she dialed the number, so close that he could see the tiny throb of her pulse along the side of her neck, and he had an almost overwhelming urge to bend his head and drag his mouth over the smooth skin.

Spinning away, he scrubbed a hand over his face. He was losing it. His only excuse was that he'd spent way too much time in the field, away from civilization. What other reason could there be for his unexpected reaction to her nearness?

"Tenley, it's me, Katie," he listened to her say. "If you're there, pick up please." She paused. "Okay, listen, there's no cell phone reception over here in Afghanistan, so you're not going to be able to call me." Putting her hand over the receiver, she looked at Chase. "What time can I call her back?"

Chase glanced at his watch. "It's four o'clock now, which means it's seven-thirty in the morning on the East Coast. What time would you like to call her back?"

"She's probably at the gym with her phone turned off. How does she expect anyone to reach her if she turns her phone off?" She blew out a hard breath and he watched as she pulled a small planner out of her shoulder bag and quickly flipped it open. As she scanned the appointments on her calendar, Chase watched the expressions flit across her face. Frustration, annoyance and then finally resignation. Removing her hand, she spoke into the phone. "Tenley, I see you have a crazy schedule today, so I'm going to call you back at six o'clock tonight. Please be there."

Chase wondered if she realized she would need to wake up at two-thirty in the morning in order to place the call. He didn't mind getting up at that hour, but he was trained to get by on very little sleep. Kate, on the other hand, had shadows beneath her eyes and he knew the extreme heat was sapping whatever energy she had left. With jet lag already kicking in, he suspected it would take more than an alarm clock to rouse her from a sound sleep at that hour. He found he was looking forward to the task.

She hung up the phone and looked at him. "Well, hopefully she'll listen to her voicemail messages."

"I'm sure she will," he said smoothly. "We'll come back in time to make the call."

She nodded, looking around, her gaze lingering on a plastic container on his desk filled with red and black licorice drops. They were his one weakness.

"May I?" she asked, indicating the candy.

"Sure, help yourself."

He watched as she unscrewed the top and reached in to take just two of the small drops. A stack of his mail lay next to the candy, and he didn't miss how she furtively scanned the top envelope as she replaced the cover on the canister.

"Thanks," she murmured, delicately popping a candy into her mouth. "Is this really where you live?"

"More like where I sleep, at least when I'm here, which isn't often. I don't spend that much time on the base." He frowned, having told her way more than he'd intended. "C'mon, I'll show you where you'll be staying."

He opened the door of his CHU, and after she'd stepped outside, turned back and grabbed the jar of licorice drops and shoved them into his backpack. Chase followed her to the Humvee, glad to be out of the confines of the CHU. As they drove across the base, he wondered how she would react when she saw the accommodations the USO had arranged for her. When they pulled up in front of a cluster of khaki-brown army tents, he sensed her confusion.

"Here we are," he said briskly, getting out of the vehicle and retrieving her duffel bag and his backpack. He waved the driver on, and Kate watched in dismay as the Humvee rumbled out of sight along the dusty road.

"What do you mean, 'here we are'?" she asked, coming to stand beside him.

She stared at the nearest tent, which Chase silently acknowledged looked as if it had seen both world wars. The canvas was faded in spots and sported patches and duct tape where the fabric had ripped or the tent had sprung a leak. The outside had been stacked with sandbags for protection and for insulation, as the temperatures could drop below freezing at night. Several female soldiers came out of the tent, their weapons over their shoulders. They gave Chase and Kate curious looks as they passed. Chase could hear feminine voices from inside.

"This is the best the USO could provide for sleeping quarters," he explained. "I hope you don't mind bunking with the troops for one night."

He watched as Kate pushed back the flap that covered the entry. Two dozen or more army cots were lined on either side of the interior. Several female soldiers were stowing their gear in foot lockers, and the floor was covered with duffel bags and military gear. The women gave Kate a nod, but otherwise ignored both her and Chase. One cot was conspicuously free of gear, with only a pillow and a tightly rolled sleeping bag placed at the foot.

"I'm assuming that's where I'm sleeping?" Kate asked Chase, eyeballing the empty bunk.

"You would assume correctly."

Kate gave him a helpless look that went straight to Chase's protective instincts. He silently cursed Colonel Decker for giving him this assignment, because he was within two seconds of telling her she could bunk with him in his CHU. Or without him in his CHU. He'd pretty much give her whatever she wanted if she would just stop looking at him like that. He reminded himself that he was an Army Ranger, a member of an elite force able to operate in any environment. Unless it was within fifty feet of a woman like Kate Fitzgerald.

Kate put her hands together and drew in a deep breath. "Okay. This is okay. I can definitely sleep here. Can you tell me where my client and her band will sleep when they arrive?"

"The concert will be held over at the parade field. There's an administrative building nearby that the USO will use to house the bands while they're here, but it hasn't been converted yet."

"Would it be possible to see it?"

"Absolutely," he assured her. "Why don't you stow your gear, and then we'll grab something to eat at the dining facility before we head over there? I don't know about you, but I could use a good meal."

Hefting her pink duffel over her shoulder, Kate walked into the tent, and Chase could almost read her thoughts as she stared around her. The walls were reinforced with plywood, and army blankets hung from the roof supports between several of the cots, providing a minimal amount of privacy. As she stepped inside, Kate's footsteps echoed on the plywood floor.

Seeing it through her eyes, Chase had to admit that it looked pretty bleak. Overhead, a large, flexible tube ran the length of the tent and pumped in cool air, but it couldn't compete with the blistering temperatures outside and the interior was stifling hot and smelled like musty canvas.

Dropping her duffel bag onto the empty cot, she turned to him with an overly bright smile. "This will be great," she assured him. "After all, it's not like I'll be doing anything except sleeping, right?"

He had another decadent vision of her, this time straddling his hips as he lay on one of the narrow cots. Oh, yeah. He'd been outside the wire for way too long. He'd told Kate point-blank that he had no intention of sleeping with her.

He'd lied.

4

KATE TRIED NOT TO LET Chase Rawlins see how completely horrified she was by the sleeping quarters he'd secured for her. Clearly, he belonged in this kind of Spartan, militaristic environment. He probably thrived on danger. He certainly looked as if he did.

Casting a dubious eye around the tent, she wondered how many spiders or other multilegged critters waited in the shadows.

Two soldiers lounged on their cots, chatting idly. Neither of them seemed concerned about eight-legged bunkmates, and Kate decided that if they could sleep in this tent, so could she. Pulling her small handbag out of her tote, she determinedly joined her chaperone outside the tent.

"So, can I call you Chase, or is there some kind of military protocol that demands you be addressed by your title?" she asked as they began walking across the base to the dining facility. "I'm sorry. I peeked at the mail on your desk. That *is* your name, isn't it?"

He slanted her an amused look. "It is. I have no objection to you calling me Chase, unless there are uniforms nearby, and then I would prefer you address me as Major Rawlins."

"Well, you can call me Kate even if there are other people around," she said, unable to resist the urge to tease him just a little. He was much too serious. "I prefer it, actually. I feel old when you call me Miss Fitzgerald."

Chase swept her with an all-encompassing look that missed nothing and caused heat to bloom low in her abdomen.

"I find that hard to believe," he finally said, "considering you're like…what, twenty-five?"

"Ha!" Kate gave a bark of laughter. "Thank you, but now I know you're trying to flatter me. I just turned thirty-one."

She could see by his expression that she'd surprised him.

"Really? I didn't think you were much older than your client. Maybe it's the freckles."

Kate couldn't suppress the pleasure she felt at knowing he had thought she was younger than she actually was. Unless he figured she was immature? He'd already implied she was nuts for having come over here by herself, when clearly no other celebrity representatives had felt the need to do so. But what he didn't know was that her relationship with Tenley went beyond business. Tenley was more than just a client, more than just a sister. Tenley was like her own child, and she'd do whatever she needed to do to ensure her comfort and safety.

"I used to hate my freckles for that exact reason," she said ruefully. "People always thought I was younger than I am."

"I don't know," he said, studying her face. "I like them."

To her dismay, Kate felt herself blushing. "That's because you've never had them or been teased about them. Just how old are you?"

He grinned. "I'll turn thirty-one next month."

So they were essentially the same age. Kate felt a wave of relief, which was ridiculous. It wasn't as if she had any interest in Chase Rawlins, regardless of his age. But a little voice whispered that she was a liar.

"When do the dining facilities open in the morning?" Kate asked, in an effort to move the subject to safer ground. She so did not need to be thinking about him in a romantic way. "Please don't tell me I have to be up at some ungodly hour or risk going without breakfast."

"For the most part, the peak hours are during the traditional meal times. But we also have a midnight chow, and then the dining facilities open for the day at 4:00 a.m." He slanted her a quick grin. "Don't worry. I'll make sure you don't go hungry."

Kate felt her pulse leap at his smile, and wondered how he would react if she told him she wasn't hungry for food, but for him. Shocked by her own thoughts, she focused her attention on her surroundings. As they walked between the rows of tents and housing units, Kate's feet kicked up dust and despite the fact the sun was dropping lower on the horizon, the intense heat hadn't yet begun to abate.

"How do you tolerate the climate?" she murmured, passing a hand over her eyes. "I've never felt so hot."

"Believe it or not, you do get used to it. In fact, it gets surprisingly cold at night."

Kate cast an appraising eye toward the mountains, where the sun was just touching the peaks. She'd heard that the desert grew cold at night, but right now she had a hard time believing it. "I'll take your word for it."

Chase stopped in front of a long building constructed of corrugated metal. "These are the female facilities. The men's showers are just on the other side. If you'd like, I'll wait for you here."

Kate stepped inside the women's bathroom, relieved to see there were plenty of shower stalls. Traveling for forty-eight hours had left her feeling sticky and uncomfortable, and she couldn't wait to get back here with a bar of soap and a change of clothes.

She washed her hands and then splashed cool water on her face, studying her reflection in the mirror over the sink. She looked pale. Her freckles stood out starkly against her skin, and her hair was coming loose from the ponytail holder. Pulling it free, she combed her fingers through it and then secured it in a loose knot at the back of her head. Pinching some color into her cheeks, she rejoined Chase outside. Reaching into his pocket, he withdrew a small, plastic device and handed it to her. Kate realized it was a beeper.

"If you need to use the bathroom during the middle of the night," he said carefully, "I want you to ask one of the female soldiers to walk here with you, or I want you to contact me. This is a beeper that goes directly to my phone. Just press this button, and I'll be at your tent in under five minutes. I'll walk here with you."

"I'm sure I can walk to the bathroom by myself," she said, studying the small device. Raising her gaze, she gave him a leering smile in an effort to lighten him up a little. "Unless, of course, you want to scrub my back."

To her astonishment, two ruddy spots appeared high on his cheeks and he stared at her for a moment as if he thought she might actually be serious. Kate waited breathlessly for his response.

"This is a combat environment, Miss Fitzgerald," he finally said, dragging his gaze from hers. "There are more than twenty thousand troops stationed here, and while I can personally vouch for my own men, I can't say with one-hundred-percent certainty that you would be safe walking across the base at night. So I need you to promise me that you'll ask one of the female soldiers to accompany you, or you'll contact me, understood?"

Kate swallowed. There was no way she'd call this guy in the middle of the night for any purpose, especially not one so personal. Just the thought of being alone with him after dark caused her imagination to surge. "I'm sure the last thing you want to do is escort me to the ladies' room."

"My job is to keep you safe. If you decide to go somewhere without me, I can't guarantee that safety. So you *will* call me."

His tone said clearly that it wasn't a request, and Kate nodded as she dropped the beeper into her pocketbook. "Okay," she promised. "I'll call you. But only if you stop calling me Miss Fitzgerald and start calling me Kate. Jeez."

They walked in silence after that, until they reached a large complex of buildings. Dozens of soldiers milled around outside, smoking cigarettes or talking, while other groups walked past them with purposeful steps.

"Here we are," Chase said, pulling open a door to a large building as Kate breathed in the enticing aromas of roast chicken and grilled hamburgers.

The dining facility was essentially an enormous cafeteria, complete with soup and salad bars, a drink fountain, separate lines for hot entrees or sandwiches, and one section for desserts. There must have been at least five hundred soldiers either eating at the long tables, or waiting in line, and the noise level was so cheerful and normal that Kate had a difficult time remembering that they were in Afghanistan. The air-conditioning was a welcome relief from the dry, dusty heat outside, and she wanted to slither to the ground and press her overheated skin against the cool tiles.

"C'mon," Chase said, accurately reading her thoughts. "Let's start you with a salad and plenty of fluids. Traveling can dehydrate you, and I don't need you to become sick."

He steered her toward the salad bar and, without asking her what she preferred, took a plate and began heaping it with salad greens and toppings.

"Is that for me?" she asked doubtfully.

"What?" he demanded. "You don't like salad?" He ran a critical eye over her. "Looks to me like that's all you eat."

Kate grimaced and took the plate from him. "Trust me," she said drily, "I can wipe out an entire container of Cherry Garcia ice cream in one sitting and still not feel satisfied."

To her surprise, he laughed. "I'd like to see that."

She stared at him, transfixed by the way his smile changed his face. His teeth gleamed white in the sunburned bronze of his skin, and she felt a nearly irresistible urge to press her fingertips into the deep indents of his dimples. His grin was so captivating that Kate had a ridiculous sense of pleasure that she had been the one to cause it.

"Well, maybe one day you will," she found herself saying as she returned his smile. In the next instant, she realized he would never see her gorge herself on ice cream. She would only be in his company for the next few days, until Tenley arrived, and then she would likely have no more opportunity—or reason—to share meals with him. Or anything else, for that matter. She found the thought oddly depressing.

"When you've finished building your salad," Chase said, "grab a seat at one of the tables over there. I'll go get us something a little more substantial to eat. What do you like… chicken, beef, pasta?"

Turning, Kate studied the menu board at the front of the food line. "I'll try some of the fried chicken. And mashed potatoes."

Chase nodded. "Good choice. It's kinda hard to screw up chicken and potatoes."

Kate watched as he turned and walked away, telling herself that she was *not* admiring his ass. But it was an effort to drag her attention back to putting toppings on her salad. She was vaguely aware of the interested glances she drew from several nearby soldiers, dressed as she was in a turquoise blouse and white jeans. Finally, she pulled a bottle of water from a cooler and selected a seat in the far corner of the cafeteria, where it was less crowded.

She picked at her salad, keeping one eye on Chase as he moved through the line, piling a tray with plates of food. When he finally made his way through the cafeteria toward her, she noticed how several female soldiers turned to watch his progress. She couldn't blame them. Major Chase Rawlins had a combination of good looks and an easy confidence that captured your attention and then held it.

He placed the tray on the table and began unloading the plates. Kate stared in astonishment at the heaping servings of fried chicken and mashed potatoes that he had chosen for her. But that couldn't compare with the double helpings of two different entrees that he had taken for himself. And he had no less than three bottles of chilled water.

"Are you going to eat all that?" she asked, before she could prevent herself.

But instead of looking insulted, he merely grinned. "Oh, yeah. I've been surviving on MREs for the past two weeks. This is going to be sheer ambrosia."

"MREs?" she asked, taking a mouthful of potatoes. "What is that?"

"Meals Ready to Eat, although some of the troops like to call them Meals Rejected by Everybody, or Meals Rarely Edible. They're prepackaged meals in a pouch, designed to provide the soldier with all the basic caloric and nutritional requirements for one day. They're basically field rations."

"Not so appetizing?"

Chase shrugged as he dug into a plate heaped with baked ziti. "They do the job. I don't pay much attention to what I eat when I'm in the field."

Kate could well believe that. He struck her as the kind of man capable of intense focus. If he was on a mission, one hundred percent of his attention would be on his work, not on food. She could easily envision him skipping meals simply because he was too busy to eat. But right now, he made short work of his dinner, devouring it with gusto.

"So what is it that you do, exactly?" she asked.

He glanced up, and quickly wiped his mouth with a napkin. "The usual."

Kate gave him a half smile. "Which is…what, exactly? You said you've been in the field for the past two weeks. What do you do when you're 'in the field'?"

Chase shrugged and took a long swallow of water, nearly draining the bottle. "A lot of nothing, actually." He gave her a quick smile. "At least, nothing very exciting."

He wasn't going to give her any information, she realized, studying his bland expression.

"Is it normal for soldiers to grow beards? I thought there was some strict protocol about being clean-shaven."

He smoothed his hand over his jaw, and Kate found herself wondering how his beard would feel against her skin. Would it be soft or bristly? If he nuzzled her neck, would he leave a rash? Disconcerted by the direction of her thoughts, she fixed her attention on her food, pushing it around the plate.

"Well, there wasn't much opportunity for a close shave while I was out there," he said offhandedly. "I got back to base just before you arrived, so not much chance to clean up, either. Sorry."

"So how did you end up becoming my escort?" she asked, her curiosity getting the better of her. "I don't know much about the military, but if I had to guess I'd say you were special forces. They're the only ones who get to grow facial hair, right? So why would they assign someone like you to bring me to the different concert sites? I promise you I'm not dangerous."

Chase stopped eating the second she suggested he was

special forces, and listened to her with a combination of amusement and surprise. But when she said she wasn't dangerous, he gave a soft laugh and muttered something under his breath that sounded suspiciously like, "you have no idea."

Now he sat back in his chair and considered her. "Okay," he said, a smile still tilting his lips. "You're right. I'm an Army Ranger, part of a special-operations unit. But my team screwed up on a recent operation and so here I am—" he gestured expansively with his hands "—anxious to prove to my commanding officer that I can complete this assignment without incident."

"Ah," she said, meaningfully. "So this is sort of like a punishment for you." Leaning forward, she lowered her voice to a conspiratorial whisper. "I promise to be on my best behavior."

"Uh-huh." His voice said he didn't believe her, but he couldn't hide the dimples that dented his cheeks, evidence of his amusement. "If I can't handle one woman, then I have no business being an Army Ranger."

Kate laughed in astonishment. "Oh, wow. Be careful what you say. That just sounded like a challenge."

Chase grinned. "Going to give me a run for my money?"

"I just might." Kate let her gaze drift over him. She watched his hands as he toyed with the saltshaker. They were a lot like him, lean and strong. She wondered how they would feel on her body. "I'd be doing you a favor. After all, I wouldn't want you to get soft, considering your current assignment is so easy."

He snapped his eyes to hers. "Trust me," he said drily. "There's no chance of that happening around you." Before she could register what he'd said, he stood up. "Are you going to finish your meal?"

Kate pushed the plate away. "No, I don't think so. I'm

actually not that hungry. What I'd really like is to head over to where the first concert event will be held."

Chase nodded and began stacking their plates on his tray. "No problem."

She watched as he disposed of their dishes, her heart still thumping unevenly. Had he meant his words the way she had interpreted them? That she aroused him physically? The very thought sent hot blood surging through her veins. She wondered what had happened to get him pulled off his last assignment. He had made light of it, but Kate could see it bothered him. She didn't know him at all, but guessed he would much rather be back in the field with his men than here with her. Especially if he found himself attracted to her. She didn't know him well, but guessed that he was the kind of guy who would keep his professional and private lives completely separate. And right now, she was definitely part of his professional life.

When he returned to the table, she drew in a deep breath. "Listen, Chase, if you'd rather not take me over to the concert site, I'm sure I can get someone else to go with me. I understand that this probably isn't your favorite thing to do."

"No chance," he said smoothly. "You've been assigned to me, and I'll be the only one to take you over there."

She'd been assigned to him. As if she were nothing more than a number, or an unpleasant project that he just needed to get done. Realistically, she knew that wasn't true, but in that instant she realized she wanted him to see her as more than a task or an assignment. She wanted him to see her as a woman.

"Okay." She stood up and pushed her chair in. "Then let's do this."

Outside, the sun had finally dipped behind the mountains and the base was quickly growing dark. Kate welcomed the change, both because the temperature had dropped and because the indistinct light made it more difficult for Major Rawlins to read her expression. They walked in silence, and she didn't miss how he adjusted his stride so that she could keep up with him. She was fading quickly from sheer exhaustion. Part of her wanted to suggest that they wait until morning to view the concert site, but the stubborn part of her—the part that wanted to impress this tough man—refused to capitulate.

Thankfully, the parade field wasn't far from the dining facility. A large stage had been constructed at one end of the field, and an enormous American flag had been hung behind it as a patriotic backdrop. Dozens of heavy-duty extension cords snaked across the ground near the stage, and two tall light poles provided illumination.

"This is where the bands will perform," Chase said, kicking several of the cords out of her way. "Of course, it will look much different once all the equipment is set up."

Kate walked around the stage, silently acknowledging that it would more than suffice for Tenley's band. She had brought her planner with her, and she jotted down notes as they surveyed the site.

"How far back will the audience be from the performers?" She measured off several paces from the front of the stage. "I don't want them too close, and I'm going to insist on security personnel to keep the crowds back."

Chase laughed softly and scratched the bridge of his nose. "I don't know what kind of audiences your client performs for, but this isn't a Texas roadhouse. This is the U.S. military, and they will be respectful."

Kate frowned, wanting to believe him, but recalling at least one instance when Tenley had been accosted by a fan who had breached the security and climbed onto the stage.

"Look at me," Chase said, and put his hands on her shoulders, dipping his head to stare directly into her eyes. "I will keep Tenley Miles safe, okay? You can trust me."

Kate searched his eyes and realized that she did trust him. He was bigger than life, a guy who obviously took his job seriously. Knowing that she could rely on him was an amazing feeling. She'd always had to be the strong one; the person who made all the decisions and ensured everything went smoothly. That this man was willing to take that burden from her meant more to her than she could express.

"Thank you," she said. "Tenley has already had one bad experience with a fan."

"You have my word that nothing like that will happen here," he said firmly. "But I'll arrange to have military police positioned around the stage and throughout the audience."

"Thank you. May I see the administrative building where the performers will stay?"

Chase preceded her through the large building directly behind the stage. Immediately inside the doors was a spacious auditorium where the band members could relax while waiting to perform.

"I'm not familiar with the exact details," Chase said as they walked through the room, "but I understand the USO will set up food and drink stations for the performers, and they'll have access to pretty much whatever they need."

The space was more than generous, and Kate could easily envision Tenley relaxing here as she prepared to perform. Even with other entertainers using the room, there was little likelihood that Tenley would feel crowded. Kate nodded her approval and took some more notes. Once she left here, it would be easy to get the sites confused, and she wanted to go over everything in advance with Tenley, so that her sister would know what to expect.

Leaving the auditorium, Chase led her down a main corridor and showed her several rooms that were in the process of being converted to bunk rooms for the entertainers. Try as she might, Kate couldn't find anything to criticize. Granted, the accommodations weren't luxurious, but they were adequate for Tenley's needs, especially considering they were on a military base in Afghanistan.

After snapping the lights off in the last room and closing the door, Kate fell into step beside Chase as they made their way back through the building to the parade field.

"Well, it certainly appears that the USO has thought of everything," Kate remarked as they stepped outside. "Will I have an opportunity to meet with the USO coordinators tomorrow? Tenley has some, um, unique requirements that I'd like to address with them."

Chase cast her one swift, questioning look. "Like what?"

"Well, she's deathly afraid of buses, so I want to be sure that she won't have to travel in one, not even from the flight line to where she'll be staying."

"Okay," he said quietly. "Can I ask why?"

"Her parents were killed in a bus crash when she was just six years old. Tenley was trapped in the wreckage with them for several hours before rescue crews could free her."

"Jesus," he breathed. "Poor kid."

Kate gave him a grateful look. "She claims not to remember anything about the crash, but some nights she has terrible nightmares."

Chase nodded. "The USO would normally transport all the entertainers in a troop bus, but I can arrange for a private vehicle to pick her up at the terminal. Anything else?"

"Just that I need to stay with her, in her sleeping quarters."

"Because of the nightmares?"

Kate nodded. "Something like that."

"Shouldn't be a problem."

Kate glanced at him, surprised at how easily he accepted Tenley's needs and agreed to accommodate them. In another place and time, Chase Rawlins was exactly the kind of man that she would have given anything to be with, even for just one night.

They walked in silence toward the tent where Kate would sleep, but she could almost hear the gears turning in his head.

"You've been great," she finally said, breaking the silence. "About everything. And I can't tell you how much it means to me. I had a lot of anxiety, not knowing what to expect, but so far you've managed to alleviate all my fears."

They reached her tent and he turned to face her. "I hope so," he said quietly. "I don't want you to be afraid of anything while you're here. That's why you have me."

His words caused her imagination to surge, and suddenly she wanted to know what it would be like to have him—to really have him. For one night, or for as many nights as she might be here. But she also knew she lacked the courage required to make any kind of move on him. He didn't wear a wedding band, but that didn't mean he wasn't already committed to someone else. So she just nodded, acknowledging the small promise he *was* able to give her.

"I do have a question, though," he said, watching her closely. "I'm pretty good at reading people, and there's something I just can't figure out."

"What's that?"

"I don't know anything about Tenley Miles, but I do know that your devotion to her seems to go beyond that of other entertainers and their publicists." He paused. "Am I wrong?"

Few people knew that Kate and Tenley were even related, never mind sisters. They didn't share the same last name, nor did they look at all alike, so no one made the connection and it wasn't something they publicized. Kate had no problem with anyone knowing about their relationship, but much of Tenley's popularity stemmed from the fact that she was the orphaned child of two famous entertainers. The fact that she'd been left alone in the world yet still managed to overcome her personal tragedy to fulfill her musical destiny was like a fairytale. If people knew that she'd actually had an adult sister who had dropped everything in order to be at her side and raise her, that fairytale would lose some of its luster. So when Tenley had first shown signs of being musically gifted, Kate had decided to present herself as Tenley's publicist, rather than her sister.

"No," she said, looking at Chase. "You're not wrong. Tenley is my sister. Well, my half sister, actually. If I'm a little overprotective, it's because she's been through so much."

His face registered his surprise, but he quickly schooled his features. "That makes sense. So did you also lose a parent in that bus crash?"

Kate nodded. "My mother. But I was eighteen at that point, and accustomed to being on my own. Her death hit Tenley a lot harder."

Chase looked at her for a long moment, and Kate wondered what he was thinking. Finally, he stepped back.

"Well, she's lucky to have you," he said. "You look beat, so I'm going to let you turn in."

"Okay," she said, nodding. "Thanks again. For everything." Kate turned toward the tent and then looked back at him. "So I'll see you in the morning?"

"If not sooner," he said, and closed one eye in a conspiratorial wink.

Kate knew her mouth opened, but before she could ask what he meant, he turned and walked away. Slowly, she entered the tent and got ready for bed. His words echoed in her head, and she knew she'd never sleep.

KATE WAS AWAKENED BY someone shaking her shoulder. She tried to bury herself deeper in her covers, but there was no escaping.

"Time to wake up, Kate."

The masculine voice shocked her into action and she sat up, heart pounding. Disoriented, Kate blinked at the hard-eyed soldier who stood over her, holding a flashlight directed at the ground. The indirect light was sufficient for her to make out Chase Rawlins's features. For a moment, she had no idea where she was, or why she was sleeping in a tent. Then everything came rushing back, and her gaze snapped to the entrance.

"What time is it?"

"Oh-dot-dark." His low voice was laced with amusement.

Kate could see it was still pitch black outside. "Why are you here?"

"Didn't you promise to call your sister?"

Kate stared up at Chase, bewildered. Looking around her, she could just make out the shapeless lumps of the other women asleep on their cots. "Yes," she whispered fiercely. "At six o'clock, not the middle of the night."

"I'm sorry to tell you that on the East Coast of the United

States, it's almost six o'clock in the evening. They're eight and a half hours behind us. If you still want to make that call, you'd better hustle."

With a groan, Kate realized she hadn't considered the extreme time difference. She was half tempted to change her mind about calling Tenley, but in her mind's eye she saw her sister waiting to hear from her. If she didn't place the call, Tenley would be frantic. She'd think the worst and put herself through hell. Kate couldn't do that to her.

She scrubbed her hands over her face. "Okay, fine. Give me ten minutes."

"You've got five. I'll wait for you outside."

She watched the bobbing light of his flashlight as he crossed the tent and disappeared through the flap, and decided she would need to speak to someone about tightening up the security on the sleeping quarters.

Pushing back the sleeping bag, she swung her legs to the floor, shivering in the predawn chill. Her eyes felt gritty and every muscle in her body ached with exhaustion. Fumbling on the floor beneath her cot, she found her shoes and pulled them on, not bothering to change into street clothes. Her flannel lounge pants and long-sleeve top were adequate, and would enable her to jump right back into bed after she'd talked with Tenley.

Despite her exhaustion, she'd been right about not being able to fall asleep after Chase had left her. Her biggest surprise had come when she'd unzipped her duffel bag and discovered a jar of licorice inside. It was the same jar from Chase's housing unit, and she realized he must have stashed it in her bag after she'd made that first failed telephone call to Tenley. She found the gesture oddly touching.

She'd lain awake thinking about him. Now she understood what he'd meant when he'd said he would see her sooner than the morning, but at the time her imagination had conjured up all kinds of erotic fantasies about him. On top of that, the cot was uncomfortable, and she was unaccustomed to sleeping in such close quarters with other people. The unfamiliar sounds of the base had kept her awake until finally she'd fallen into a fitful sleep, only to be wakened by Chase.

Yawning hugely, she pulled back the flap of the tent and found Chase standing just outside. His eyes swept over her, taking in every detail of her lounge pants and thin top, lingering just a little too long on her breasts. Glancing down, Kate saw her nipples were stiff from the cold and poked against the fabric of her shirt. She crossed her arms over her chest.

"You realize that I only fell asleep like fifteen minutes ago," she said crossly. "Why didn't you tell me I'd need to wake up at two-thirty in the morning if I wanted to talk to Tenley? I could have chosen a different time."

"Do you want to make the call or not?"

Kate frowned at his impatient tone, and guessed that he was no happier about being awake at this hour than she was. Her bones ached and she actually felt a little sick. More than anything, she wanted to crawl back into her cot and sleep, but she'd told Tenley she would call her, and she intended to make good on her word.

"Yes."

"Then let's go."

Without waiting for her response, he turned and walked away while Kate watched in dismay. He gave a low whistle and a dark shape materialized from the shadows. A dog trotted toward him, its tail wagging enthusiastically as Chase reached down and gave it a friendly rub behind the ears. The animal wore a harness and stayed close to Chase's side.

The night air was chilly, and for a brief second Kate debated on going back for a sweater, but Chase wasn't waiting for her. With a sound of frustration, she followed him. The roads were covered with small rocks, which made walking treacherous when you couldn't see where you were going. After she'd stumbled twice, Chase finally stopped and waited for her to catch up, using his flashlight to illuminate her path.

"So, did you wake up just so I could make my phone call, or do you not sleep?" Kate asked, hugging herself around the middle and trying to keep her teeth from chattering. She wouldn't have been at all surprised if Chase responded that he didn't require sleep; he was a machine.

"I caught some sleep, but I don't need much to get by."

"Will you go back to bed after this?" she asked, partly because she was interested, and partly because she was just trying to make conversation.

"Well, I guess that depends," he mused.

Kate shot him a startled look. Had she only imagined the sexual suggestion in his voice? She tried to read his expression, but the darkness made it nearly impossible.

"Actually," he continued smoothly, "I'm up for the day."

Kate should have felt relieved, but found his words left her oddly deflated. She remembered what he had said earlier that day: *I have no intention of sleeping with you.* Either the change in time zones had seriously messed with her biorhythms, or she had definitely gone too long without sex, because she spent way too much time imagining him naked. "Who's your friend?" she asked, in an effort to change the subject. Kate tried to pat the dog, but the animal shied away from her hand.

"This is Charity."

"Ah," she said meaningfully.

Chase looked at her. "What does that mean?"

Kate shrugged. "When you and the other guys were talking about Charity, I thought you had a girlfriend on the base. I never would have guessed you were talking about a dog."

"Well, I think Charity would disagree. I'm pretty sure she thinks she's human."

"So, do you?"

"What?"

"Have a girlfriend?"

He gave a surprised laugh. "No, I do not. Right now, Charity is the only female in my life." He glanced at her. "Aside from you, of course."

Kate had already noticed that he wore no rings, but felt a surge of satisfaction in knowing he was single.

"Where did you get her?" she asked, moving to safer territory.

"She was a stray that I rescued from a village in the mountains. I guess you could say we adopted each other."

"Do you keep her in your housing unit?"

"She won't come inside, but when I'm on base she'll sleep outside my door. When I'm in the field, I leave her with the K-9 unit. She gets along with the other dogs, and the handlers have been teaching her how to track."

The mention of his housing unit reminded her of the small gift he had left in her duffel bag. "By the way, thank you for the licorice. I feel guilty that you gave it to me."

"Don't." He rubbed a hand over his flat stomach. "I try to avoid sweets, but I can't resist licorice drops. It's better if you take them. Besides, my mother will send another jar in her next care package."

They had reached his housing unit, and Kate welcomed the warmth of the interior after the chill of the night air. As Chase dialed an outside line, she stood in the middle of the room and looked around. Although she had already been inside his unit once, everything looked different at night.

A desk lamp cast a warm glow, making the room seem al-most cozy.

While Chase was concentrating on the phone, she took a covert peek into his bedroom. Disappointingly, his bed was neatly made and there was nothing to indicate that he had slept there at all. She would have enjoyed seeing rumpled blankets or clothes on the floor—anything to indicate the guy wasn't completely perfect.

"Something interesting in there?" Chase asked, catch-ing her.

Kate flushed. "I was, uh, just checking out your bed."

His eyes grew hot, and Kate's body responded instantly. Her breathing quickened and her imagination surged with images of the two of them, naked and entwined in his sheets. She would have sworn those same images were swirling through his head, too, but then he thrust the phone receiver at her, breaking whatever spell she had been under.

"Make your call," he growled, and spun away.

Keeping a wary eye on him, Kate quickly dialed Tenley's number, frustrated when the call went to voicemail.

"Tenley, it's Katie. I told you that I'd be calling. Why aren't you there?" She lowered her voice. "I don't want you to worry about anything, okay? Russell will drive you to the airport tonight, and I'll be right here waiting for you when you arrive. Okay, I'll try to call you later."

She hung up the phone and stood for a moment, chewing the edge of her finger. Where was Tenley and why wasn't she answering the phone? She briefly considered calling Russell to ask him to check on her sister, and just as quickly discarded the idea. She'd asked both the housekeeper and Russell to keep an eye on Tenley and she trusted they would. There was a reasonable explanation for why her sister wasn't answering the phone. She was not going to freak out, espe-cially not when there wasn't anything she could do about it.

She blew out a hard breath. "She's not home."

"Jeez, what a surprise," Chase said drily. Seeing Kate's annoyed expression, he spread his hands. "What? She's not exactly Miss Responsible. If she was, you wouldn't be here."

"What is that supposed to mean?"

Chase gave her a tolerant look. "C'mon, Kate, don't play coy with me. We both know that the only reason you're here is to try and save your sister's career."

Kate desperately wanted to tell him he was wrong and that Tenley was coming over for all the right reasons. But seeing the truth in Chase's eyes took the fight out of her. Plunking herself down on the nearby chair, she dropped her head into her hands.

"You're right," she admitted in a weary voice. "I'm not even sure she'll come. I should have stayed behind and flown here with her, but she actually seemed excited about the prospect of coming." Raising her head, she looked helplessly at Chase. "What if she doesn't get on that plane? I mean, I can't make her. I just thought if I came first and assured her that it wasn't nearly as scary as everyone made her believe, then she wouldn't be so reluctant."

To her surprise, Chase dropped to his haunches in front of her, putting him at eye-level with her. He placed a hand on either side of her seat, effectively trapping her.

"I think what you're doing is completely harebrained," he said, but his sympathetic smile took most of the sting out of his words. "But I also think Tenley Miles is very lucky to have you on her side. I don't see any other publicists over here doing this for their clients."

Kate gave him a rueful smile. "That's just because they're not related."

"The bottom line is, if she isn't willing to do what it takes to fix the mess she made, then that's her problem, not yours.

At some point, Kate, you need to let her take responsibility for her own life."

Kate stared at him, knowing he was right. "That sounds easy in theory, but you don't know Tenley. She's just a kid. She couldn't find her own way across the street without someone to help her. The music industry would eat her alive. She *needs* me."

Chase pushed to his feet and stood looking down at her, and Kate could almost read his mind. He thought she was nuts.

"Look," she reasoned, "maybe I am a little overprotective, but trust me when I say you would feel the same way if you met her. She brings out the protective instinct in everyone." Kate gave a soft laugh. "Even you wouldn't be immune."

"It is hard for me to imagine that someone who's been in the public spotlight since she was young could have any vulnerability left," Chase said wryly.

Kate looked down at her hands. "Maybe that's what makes her so vulnerable."

"You were pretty young when your mother died," he said quietly. "It couldn't have been easy for you, either. What I don't get is why I didn't know that the famous country singer, Willa Dean, had another daughter. Hell, I'm not sure anybody knows."

Kate shrugged. "My mother was still in high school when she became pregnant with me. She and my dad tried to make a go of it, but she had her heart set on becoming a superstar, and he just wanted to be a car mechanic. They were only kids."

"So what happened?"

"They split up before I was a year old. I traveled with my mother and her band for the first six years of my life, until I started elementary school. Then I went to live with my dad and his new wife."

"That's rough," Chase said. "Were you happy with your father?"

Kate sighed, remembering. "I wasn't unhappy. But he and his wife had a new baby and hardly any money. Things were tough for a couple of years and I always had the sense that I was a burden. But then my mother started selling albums and she began to send some money to my father for my upkeep. That helped."

"Did you ever go back and live with her?"

Kate didn't look at him. "No," she said quietly. "My mother rose to the top of the billboard charts very quickly, and she didn't have time for a kid." She gave a rueful laugh. "Even after she had Tenley, she didn't have time for a kid. Sometimes, I think the only reason she brought Tenley on tour with her was because it helped her public image. She dragged that poor baby everywhere, and what the public didn't see was that when the cameras weren't around, Tenley rarely saw her mother. She spent most of her time with a nanny. But when people thought of Willa Dean, they automatically thought of her angelic little daughter. So when she died…" Her voice trailed off.

"You became Tenley's mother."

Kate laughed, refusing to dwell on those days. "Well, more like a doting aunt." She slanted him an amused look. "Were you a Willa Dean fan?"

Chase chuckled. "Still am. I'm from Texas, and there's nothing a Texas boy loves more than a good old country song. Man, I grew up listening to Willa Dean, and it didn't hurt that she was so damned gorgeous. In fact, my brother had a poster of her hung over his desk all through high school."

Kate couldn't suppress her smile, not at all surprised to hear that Chase's brother had kept a poster of her mother in his bedroom. She'd been a beautiful woman, and an amazing singer. Everyone had loved Willa Dean, the same way that they now loved her daughter, Tenley.

"Yes, my mother was an incredible woman," she agreed. She yawned hugely. "Oh, my God, I've never been so tired in my life."

Chase pulled her up, his hands strong and warm under her elbows. "C'mon, let's get you into bed. You're asleep on your feet."

"I'll be fine," she assured him. She thought of the long, chilly walk back to the tent and couldn't suppress the shiver that ran through her. "Maybe you have a coat or sweater that I could borrow?"

"I have something even better," he murmured, and turned her toward the rear of the small housing unit. She went, unresisting, until she realized they were in his bedroom. He bent down to pull back the blankets of the bed.

"What are you doing?" Her heart began an unsteady rhythm in her chest as she watched him peel back the sheets. "I'm not sure—"

"Shh," he said soothingly. "Your virtue is safe with me. Lie down and get some sleep."

He pushed her, unresisting, into a sitting position on the edge of the bed, and then crouched down to pull off her shoes. Kate studied his bent head and barely resisted the urge to run her fingers over his velvety short hair.

"Why are you doing this?" she asked. "Aren't there some kind of rules against having members of the opposite sex in your quarters?"

Setting her shoes aside, he looked at her. In the dim light of the bedroom, his eyes seemed to glow in his face. "Yeah," he acknowledged. "There are. But I'm not going to be here. I'm going to head over to command headquarters and catch up on some stuff."

"When will you be back?"

He glanced at his watch. "We'll leave for Camp Leather-neck at 0700 hours, but I'll wake you up well before that."

The temptation he offered was too great to resist. "Okay," she acquiesced. "You win. But I really, really want a hot shower, so if we could work that into the morning routine, I'd appreciate it."

He gave her a brief smile, but there was a tension in his expression that set her pulse tripping. He made a movement to stand up, and Kate impulsively caught his hand in hers. His skin was warm and dry, and she could feel the rough calluses of his palm. He glanced in surprise at their joined hands, and then looked at her face, and for an instant, Kate saw hunger in his eyes.

"Thank you," she murmured, and she leaned forward to press a kiss against his cheek. She meant for the gesture to be quick and impersonal, but he turned his face at the last instant, and her kiss landed on his lips. For a microsecond they both froze, and then Chase made a small sound of defeat and his mouth began moving against hers.

Kate stopped breathing. The guy knew how to kiss. His lips were warm and firm and she found herself tentatively responding. His beard was rough against her sensitive skin, but she didn't care. He didn't touch her except for where his mouth was fused to hers. Kate pressed closer, wanting more of the sensual contact. Chase complied, leisurely slanting his mouth across hers until her lips parted, and he tasted her. The slick contact of his tongue against hers caused heat to explode beneath her skin, and she felt a rush of liquid warmth to her center.

She shifted restlessly, curling her hands around Chase's neck to pull him closer. He made a small groaning sound, and for an instant, Kate thought he would resist. Then he pushed her back against the mattress and covered her body with his.

The sheets were cool through the thin material of her shirt, but Chase's body was warm and Kate dragged him closer, sliding her arms over the sleek muscles of his back. He deepened the kiss, exploring her mouth with his tongue and catching her small moans of pleasure. Kate speared her fingers through the velvet roughness of his short hair, reveling in the feel of it beneath her fingertips.

How long had it been since she'd felt a man's arms around her, or luxuriated in the hardness of a masculine body pressed against her own? Too long, apparently, because she was igniting beneath his touch. She no longer felt tired; every cell in her had come alive. Desire coiled tightly in her womb and then unfurled to radiate through her limbs and finally center at her core, where she pulsed hotly. She wanted to rub herself against him and relieve the ache that was building with every sensuous sweep of his tongue against hers.

Chase dragged his mouth away and Kate had a moment of panic when she thought he was leaving. But he moved his lips to her jaw and pressed hot kisses against her skin until he reached her ear, and then lightly licked along its contours. Kate shuddered and arched her neck to give him better access. He complied, following the path of her throat until he reached the neckline of her shirt. He glanced at her face, and Kate's breath caught at the heat she saw in his eyes.

She didn't object when he slid a hand over one breast and cupped it in his palm. But she was unprepared when he moved his fingers to the hem of her shirt and dragged it upward, exposing her to his hot gaze.

"Christ, you're pretty," he rasped, and slid a callused hand over the smooth skin of her stomach, until he covered one breast.

Kate made a small mewling sound of need and arched upward, wanting more of the sensuous contact. He complied, rubbing his thumb over her nipple and watching as it contracted. Then, as if entranced, he bent his head and kissed the underside of one breast, before drawing her nipple into his mouth, sucking gently on it and laving it with his tongue. She felt an answering tug of need between her legs and instinctively spread her thighs to cradle Chase's hips against her own.

He made an incoherent sound of approval and covered her other breast with his hand as he continued to suckle her. Kate couldn't get enough of him. Boldly, she slid her hands down the length of his back and over the firm rise of his buttocks, pressing him to where she ached for fulfillment. Nothing mattered except the man whose delicious weight pinned her to the mattress.

"You feel so good," she whispered against the top of his head. "I want to feel you inside me."

He groaned loudly, and his mouth stilled. He raised his head and then, almost regretfully, pulled her shirt down, covering her breasts.

Kate frowned, grasping for his hands as she tried to stop him. "What? Why are you stopping? Please don't stop."

But Chase carefully disentangled himself from her limbs and sat up, scrubbing his hands over his face. His breathing sounded uneven, and Kate cautiously sat up, feeling chilled without his warmth.

"That was a mistake," he said in a low voice, not looking at her. "I'm sorry."

"Please don't apologize," she murmured. "This was my fault, not yours."

He angled his head to look at her, and she could see remnants of the earlier heat lingering in his eyes. "My job is to keep you safe, not to take advantage of you."

Kate gave him a wry look. "I'm thirty-one years old, not sixteen. I know what I want."

"Do you? Because I think if you thought this through, you'd realize the last thing you want is a short-lived fling with a guy you'll never see again after this trip."

The thought of never seeing Chase Rawlins again caused a tightening sensation in her chest. She knew he was right, but at that moment, the only thing she wanted was to finish what they had begun and to hell with the consequences. Her job as Tenley's publicist kept her too busy to see anyone seriously, but Chase's touch had reminded her just how much she missed having intimacy in her life, even superficial intimacy with a near stranger. She was pathetic.

Gathering her dignity, she laid a hand on his arm and gave him a forced smile. "You're right. I'm sorry to put you in such an awkward position. I didn't mean to make this any more unpleasant for you than it already is."

"Jesus." Chase gave a disbelieving laugh. "You think that was *unpleasant* for me?" His eyes grew hot. "Do you know how badly I want you?"

Abruptly he stood up, adjusting himself quickly, but not before Kate saw the evidence of his arousal. Her hand fell away from his sleeve, and she pressed her fingers against her mouth, still feeling him there. He stood looking down at her for a long moment, before he dragged a hand over his hair, frustrated.

"I've gotta get out of here." His voice was no more than a husky rasp. "Get some sleep, Kate."

She watched as he left the bedroom, and then she heard the door open and close, followed by the click of a key in the lock. It was the first time he had called her Kate, and she wished she didn't like how it sounded coming from his lips. She lay down and dragged the blankets over her shoulder, staring into the darkness as she replayed the encounter over and over in her mind.

Turning on her side, she bunched the pillow beneath her

cheek. His scent clung to the fabric and she found herself turning her face into the cloth and breathing deeply. Only then did she drift into sleep.

6

"HOW LONG WILL IT TAKE us to reach Camp Leatherneck?"
Kate asked the following morning, as she rode in the passenger seat of a Humvee, watching Chase drive.

"A couple of hours," he said shortly.

As if by tacit agreement, neither had mentioned the incident from the previous night. But Kate couldn't help but
notice that Chase seemed a little short on patience and temper, and she wondered if he regretted what had happened.
She hoped he would lighten up a bit, because she wasn't
sure she could spend an entire day with him if he was going
to be surly.

She studied him furtively as he drove. He wore a clean
uniform and a camouflage-patterned baseball cap that was
frayed along the brim. He hadn't shaved his beard and he
still looked as if he kicked ass for a living. Charity lay obedi-
ently on the back seat, and Kate had been surprised to learn
the dog would travel with them to each base.

Chase had woken her up before seven o'clock by pounding with his fist on the door of his housing unit until she
opened it, bleary-eyed but feeling rested. He, on the other
hand, had looked tired and irritable. He'd retrieved her duf-

fel bag and belongings from the women's tent and had given her just ten minutes to dress and meet him outside.

Now they drove across the base, past the housing units and the dining facility. The smell of bacon wafted from the kitchens and her stomach growled loudly, reminding her that she hadn't yet had breakfast.

"Will we have a chance to grab a bite to eat before we leave?" she asked hopefully. "I could really use a cup of coffee."

"Later," he said brusquely. "I have some grub in my bag and we can eat on the way to Camp Leatherneck. But our flight departs in ten minutes and if we're not on board, it leaves without us."

Kate was silent after that. They continued to drive past the parade field, until the only buildings in sight were enormous hangars and storage facilities. But it wasn't until Kate caught sight of a helicopter landing pad, complete with military attack helicopters, that she began to understand just how they would travel to Camp Leatherneck.

"You're kidding," she breathed, and looked over at Chase for confirmation that he was, indeed, just pulling her leg. But he kept his attention fixed on the road, and the only indication that he'd heard her was a small smile that played at the edges of his mouth. "We're flying in a helicopter?"

"Not just a helicopter. A Black Hawk."

He drew the Humvee to a stop at the edge of the helo pad and climbed out of the vehicle, while Kate sat in the passenger seat and peered through the window at the helicopter. Were those rockets strapped to the underside of the small stub wings? Her heart began to thud hard in her chest.

Chase opened the door and waited for her to climb out before he reached in and grabbed their duffel bags and a rucksack. Charity hopped down, her tail wagging in anticipation of this new adventure.

"I brought you something," Chase said, opening the rear of the vehicle.

"A thermos of coffee?" she asked hopefully.

To her surprise, he pulled out a combat helmet and a flak vest. "Try these on for size."

Kate took the helmet from him and put it on, then waited while he fastened it beneath her chin. His fingers brushed the skin of her neck and she tried not to stare at his mouth. He was so close that she could see the tiny scar that bisected his upper lip. She wanted to rub her fingertip over it. When she raised her gaze to his, she found his light green eyes were fastened on her mouth. She had to resist the urge to nervously moisten her lips.

He helped her into the body armor, lifting her arms to tighten the Velcro fastenings on either side. The weight of the metal plates inside the vest were enough to make Kate's shoulders sag.

"Is this really necessary?" she asked, noticing that he wore neither a helmet nor a vest. "We're in a helicopter, after all."

Even without body armor, his uniform, combined with his expression, gave him a distinctly dangerous appearance. He nodded toward her vest. "Those metal plates are the only thing standing between you and a bullet. If we come under attack en route to Camp Leatherneck, you're going to be glad you're wearing them."

Kate knew her face went a little pale. "Is that a possibility?"

"That's always a possibility, Miss Fitzgerald."

"Where is your equipment?" He didn't respond, and Kate suddenly knew why. "Wait. Am I wearing your helmet and flak vest?" She couldn't keep the astonishment out of her voice. "Is that why you're not wearing anything?"

"Don't worry about me." Hefting his rucksack over one

shoulder, he lifted their duffel bags as if they weighed nothing, and handed her shoulder bag to her. "Are you ready?"

She wasn't, but she nodded mutely and followed him and the dog across the tarmac to the waiting helicopter. She felt humbled by the knowledge that he'd given her his protective gear, and his speech about the possibility of coming under attack had dampened her mood.

The sliding door on the side of the aircraft was open, and he threw their gear inside before climbing in. He snapped his fingers and Charity jumped nimbly in, enthusiastically sniffing at the interior before he gave her a command to lie down. Turning, he extended a hand to Kate and helped her up and into the main cabin. There were five soldiers inside, and two more in the cockpit. Kate saw with a sense of surprise that both pilots were women, as were two of the soldiers in the main cabin. They were occupied cleaning what looked like machine guns mounted inside two windows directly behind the pilot and copilot.

The pilot turned in her seat and gave Kate an appraising look before shifting her attention to Chase and the dog. A broad smile spread across her face. She extended her hand and offered the dog a treat, before shifting her attention back to Chase. "Hey, great to see you."

"Great to see you, too," he replied. "What have you been up to?"

"Keeping busy, doing the Afghan shuffle," she said with a grin. "When did you get back?"

"Yesterday."

Kate didn't miss how the other woman practically devoured Chase with her eyes, and she experienced an unfamiliar tightening in her chest at their obvious friendship.

"Let's catch up when we reach Camp Leatherneck," the pilot said, still smiling. "I have a lot to tell you."

"Yeah, I'd like that." Turning toward Kate, he indicated

one of the empty canvas jump seats. "Why don't you sit there and strap yourself in? We should be airborne in just a few minutes."

Kate did as he asked, fumbling briefly with the harness until Chase swept her hands aside and buckled her in himself. Kate told herself that her accelerated heart rate had to do with anticipation of the flight, and not with the way his hands brushed against her breasts. He took the seat next to her, and his hip pressed against hers in the narrow confines.

Kate watched as the two female soldiers slid the cabin doors closed and then took up positions at the open windows on either side of the cabin, their hands maneuvering the mounted machine guns with ease and confidence. Kate's stomach did an uneasy roll, and she was suddenly glad that she hadn't eaten breakfast. Glancing at the three male soldiers who sat in the other jump seats, Kate was relieved to see that none of them looked alarmed. In fact, one of them had tipped his head back against the seat and closed his eyes, apparently happy to sleep through the flight. Even Charity had settled down, curling up near Chase's seat with a small whine.

The pilot twisted in her seat and gave both Chase and Kate a smile. "Welcome aboard. I'm Captain Larson and your copilot today is Chief Warrant Officer Costanza. We'll be departing shortly. Our ETA at Camp Leatherneck is approximately 0900 hours. There's some adverse weather moving into the region, so the ride could get a little bumpy, but nothing to worry about." Her gaze touched briefly on Kate and then lingered on Chase. "Sit back and enjoy the flight."

The rotors whirred into life, and Kate forced herself to relax as she listened to the pilots go through their checklists for departure. Chase pulled a mobile device out of his pocket and began scrolling through his messages, as if he had no concerns at all. The action was so normal that Kate found herself relaxing in spite of herself.

"You okay?" he asked without looking at her.

"I think so. So the flight will take about two hours?"

"Give or take."

Even as he spoke, the enormous helicopter lifted from the ground. Through the window, Kate watched Bagram Airfield slide away beneath them. She found herself studying the two pilots and wondering what kind of woman would choose a career that endangered her life on a daily basis. Did Chase and Captain Larson have a romantic relationship? There was no question that the other woman was attractive, and Kate hadn't missed the way she looked at Chase, or how pleased he had been to see her.

"Will Tenley and her band also travel from Bagram to Camp Leatherneck in a helicopter?" she asked.

He glanced up briefly from his mobile device. "All of the singers and their band members will be transported in a Chinook. They're heavy-lift helicopters capable of transporting up to fifty-five people, so we should be able to get all of the performers in one trip, which means we have fewer helicopters tied up."

Kate tried to envision Tenley in a military helicopter but failed. She'd be scared to death. She couldn't picture her gentle sister over here, roughing it. How would she react to the sight of so many uniformed soldiers?

"Here, why don't you eat something?" Chase said, interrupting her thoughts.

Kate watched as he opened his rucksack and withdrew a large thermos and two cups. He poured them each a mug of steaming coffee and then passed the thermos to the other soldiers. Kate curled her fingers around the cup and inhaled the fragrance of the coffee.

"You had this in your backpack all this time and didn't tell me? Even though you knew I was dying for caffeine?"

Chase laughed softly and handed her a foil-wrapped Pop-Tart. "I can't have you thinking I'm a complete dick," he said, slanting her an amused look. "It's not a gourmet breakfast, but at least it's not an MRE." Reaching into the backpack, he withdrew a treat for Charity and let her eat it from his fingers, rubbing her head in approval when she took it gently.

Kate unwrapped the pastry and took a bite. "I haven't had a Pop-Tart since I was a kid."

They ate in silence, and Chase took her empty mug and wiped it clean before stowing it back in his rucksack. At that moment, the helicopter dipped sharply, and Kate would have come out of her seat if not for the harness. She gasped and reflexively clutched Chase's forearm.

"Relax," he soothed. "Just a little turbulence."

But when the helicopter suddenly dropped in altitude and shuddered violently, Kate saw that even the soldiers looked troubled. Charity lifted her head and gave a small whine, but Chase spoke to her gently and she dropped her muzzle back onto her paws. Instinctively, Kate clutched at Chase's hand, gratified when he didn't pull away.

"Are we crashing?" she asked, her heart slamming in her chest. "Maybe we should be wearing parachutes or something."

"Folks, we're encountering a storm front that's moving over the area," the copilot said over the intercom. "We're going to try and fly around it, but expect some turbulence."

"You see? Everything is fine," Chase said, and stretched his legs out and crossed his boots as if there was nothing to worry about.

Kate sat rigidly at his side, her fingers still curled in his, certain that he was wrong, that the pilots were only trying to avoid a panic in the cabin before they plummeted to the earth. Outside the windows, she could see the distant mountains and the dark storm clouds that had gathered on the horizon. She was only mildly comforted by the fact they were flying away from those mountains, and not directly into the storm.

"Try and get some sleep," Chase grunted. Pulling his hand free, he crossed his arms over his chest and dragged his baseball cap low over his eyes, effectively shutting her out.

Kate stared at him in disbelief. Even if she could relax enough to take a nap, the helmet and flak vest she wore made it nearly impossible to find a comfortable position. Her bottom ached from the angle of the jump seat, and the coffee and Pop-Tart sat heavily in her stomach. Looking around, she saw the other three soldiers had also closed their eyes, seemingly oblivious to the peril surrounding them.

With a deep breath, she sat back and tried to control her breathing, repeating her age-old mantra that when she had no control over the situation, she could at least control herself. But the flight took another nerve-racking two hours, where the helicopter occasionally bucked and dipped, and Kate only barely restrained herself from grabbing onto Chase again. It wasn't until they began to descend that he finally stirred and opened his eyes, looking rested and relaxed.

"Did you manage to get any sleep?" he asked innocently.

Kate gave him a baleful look, and then saw the telltale dimple in his cheek.

"You know I didn't," she said through gritted teeth.

"We'll be on the ground in just a few minutes," he said, glancing out the window.

Following his gaze, Kate saw another military base that looked remarkably like the one they had just left. "Are you sure we didn't just fly around in circles for two hours and land back at Bagram?" she asked doubtfully. Even the mountains on the horizon seemed exactly the same.

Chase chuckled. "I'm sure. Camp Leatherneck isn't nearly as big as Bagram, but the conditions are actually better. I may have to leave you for a bit while I secure accommodations for you."

Kate covered her mouth and yawned hugely. "As long as I can have another cup of coffee, I'll be fine." Reaching down, she patted her shoulder bag. "I have my book and my iPod."

They were met on the helipad by two soldiers in a Humvee. As they crossed the tarmac to the waiting vehicle, the wind tore at Kate's hair, dragging it loose from her ponytail and spraying sand against her exposed skin. Chase tried to shield her with his body, but the stinging wind was relentless.

"Oh, my God," she gasped when she was safely inside the Humvee. "Are we in a sandstorm?"

Chase tossed their luggage into the back of the vehicle and climbed in beside her. "No. If that was a sandstorm, you wouldn't be able to walk outside without face protection. This is just a storm front moving in. You can take off the helmet. Here, let me help you with the vest."

Chase deftly unfastened Kate's flak vest and helped her remove it. At the same time, the soldier driving the Humvee glanced at them in the rearview mirror. "We're due for some pretty nasty weather later this afternoon and through the night," he commented. "And you know what that means."

Kate looked at Chase in time to see him send the driver a silent warning with his eyes. "What does that mean?" she asked, a frisson of alarm feathering its way along her spine.

"There's a higher incidence of mortar attacks during bad weather," he said. "But I don't want you to worry. Even if we come under attack, the insurgents don't have the technology to direct their mortars with any accuracy."

Kate stared at him, appalled. "So a bomb could literally land anywhere on the base?"

"We have a good tracking system. The warning sirens will go off and we'll have time to get to a bunker." He tapped the helmet that lay on the seat between them. "But if you hear the sirens, make sure you don't go out without this."

Warning sirens? Kate knew her eyes had widened, but she hadn't really considered the possibility that they could come under attack. "What about you?" she asked. "If I have your protective gear, what are you going to wear?"

"We'll make a stop at the military supply office. They'll have a helmet and a flak vest that you can borrow while you're here, and we'll review the protocol for how to respond if the warning sirens should go off."

To hide her dismay, she stared out the window as they drove, pretending an interest in the buildings and military vehicles they passed. "Does that happen very often?" she finally managed, relieved that her voice didn't betray her inner fear.

"Not too often. As I said, we have a pretty good surveillance system set up on the perimeter, but a strike could occur at any time, so it's best to be prepared."

"Of course." She wondered what she would do if a strike happened during the night, when he wasn't with her? "So just where are these bunkers?"

"They're situated about every one hundred yards throughout the base," he assured her. "Don't look so worried. You'll be fine. I'm not going to leave you, so if anything should happen, I'll be right there with you."

That's what Kate was afraid of. She was more or less accustomed to being in the company of good-looking men, most of them associated with the music industry. But she wasn't used to having male attention focused on *her*. Most of the men she knew were only interested in how her association with Tenley could benefit them. Kate had simply been a means to an end, or completely invisible. Having Chase's full and undivided attention made her feel funny inside, as if she was either very fragile or very important. No man had ever acted as her protector before, or even indicated that he cared one way or the other about her well-being.

As the Humvee drove across the base, Chase pointed out various buildings along the way, including the base exchange store, a small post office, a recreation center and a fitness center.

"You seem pretty familiar with this place," Kate observed. "Do you spend a lot of time here?"

He shrugged. "This is my fourth tour. I've spent time on just about every U.S. base in the country at one time or another."

They pulled to a stop outside a large building constructed of corrugated metal, which Chase explained was the supply center. Inside, Kate saw it was really a warehouse filled with floor-to-ceiling shelves loaded with bins and bags. She followed Chase up and down the aisles as he selected items seemingly at random. Finally, when his arms were full, he made his way to a small window where a uniformed soldier dumped everything into a duffel bag and had him sign a hand-receipt.

"Think you can carry this?" Chase asked, handing her the duffel bag.

Kate took it from him, and nearly buckled under the weight. "What do you have in here?" she asked, grimacing. "Rocks?"

Reaching out, Chase took the bag from her as if it weighed nothing. "Your new protective gear." He grinned. "You won't be required to use it here unless we come under attack, but when we head to some of the FOBs, you'll need to wear it whenever you go outside."

They returned to the Humvee, and Kate watched as Chase stowed the duffel bag in the back of the vehicle. "What's an FOB?"

"A forward operating base. Those are the smaller bases that are essentially on the front lines, away from the central command centers. They don't have much in the way of amenities, which is why they really appreciate it when entertainers come out to visit them."

"Are FOBs dangerous?"

"They can be," he acknowledged. "Some more than others."

She digested his words silently, envisioning a primitive, fortresslike base surrounded by a perimeter of thick mud walls, sandbags and concertina wire, while terrorists lurked behind rocks and bushes, just waiting for the right moment to launch an attack.

"Having second thoughts?" he asked perceptively.

She tipped her chin up and met his eyes determinedly. "Of course not."

He studied her face for a long moment, and then raised a hand to briefly cup her cheek and rub his thumb over her jaw. "Good," he said.

As he climbed back into the Humvee, Kate put her fingers where his hand had been. In that instant, she understood that Chase Rawlins posed a greater danger to her than any mortars or insurgent attacks.

7

CHASE WANTED NOTHING MORE than to get Kate Fitzgerald settled in her own quarters so that he could get away from her, even for a few hours. No matter how he tried, he couldn't stop his imagination from retreating back to his housing unit at Bagram, and his bedroom, where he could once again envision her spread out beneath him. He hadn't meant to kiss her, but when she'd pressed her lips against his own, he'd been unable to resist her softness.

She'd smelled like sugar and vanilla and he'd wanted to consume her. He still couldn't believe he'd lost control the way he had. His only excuse was that he'd been in Afghanistan for way too long, away from everything soft and feminine and sexy. But goddamn, when he recalled how gorgeous she'd looked on his bed, with her luscious breasts in his hands, he grew aroused all over again. He could have taken her right then; could have used her welcoming body to satisfy his own raging desire.

But he didn't want her like that. He had nothing to offer any woman right now, not when he was committed to the Army and still had six months left of his current deployment. Kate didn't deserve to be used, and he wouldn't let himself take advantage of her, even if she thought it was what she wanted.

After he'd left her, he'd gone over to his command head-quarters building, intending to catch up on the reports he was required to submit regarding the hunt for Al-Azir. But he'd been so distracted and aroused that he'd finally headed across to the fitness center and worked out his frustration on the treadmill and weight machines. Then he'd found himself in front of his housing unit just before dawn, imagining Kate inside, sleeping in his bed. He'd been tempted to go in and wake her up and finish what they'd started, but common sense had overcome his libido.

For the first time, he wished he could be more like his twin brother, Chance, who never passed up an opportunity to get busy with an attractive woman. At least, he used to be like that. Now Chance was fully committed to the pretty Black Hawk pilot, Jenna Larson, who had flown them from Bagram to Camp Leatherneck. They weren't talking marriage—at least not yet—but Chase knew there was no way his brother was going to let Jenna get away. He was happy for both of them, but he wasn't looking for something similar. He didn't need to complicate his life with a relationship that had zero chance of going anywhere, no matter how appealing he might find Kate.

When he'd first learned that he would escort her to each of the bases, he'd contacted the USO at Camp Leatherneck and had learned that Kate could stay in the tent designated for the other performers. Chase suspected it would be very much like the one at Bagram Air Base, only this time there would be no other women bunking with her; she would be completely alone. Since he didn't have his own housing unit on Camp Leatherneck, Chase wouldn't have the option of letting her sleep in his quarters.

As he suspected, the Humvee drew to a stop in front of a

large tent, nearly identical to the one at Bagram. The wind had picked up and buffeted the canvas sides, causing them to billow out and suck back in. Kate stared out the window and Chase was unable to read her expression.

Climbing out of the Humvee, he opened the back and whistled to Charity, who bounded down and began exploring the area around the tent. He grabbed Kate's duffel bag and waited for her to join him.

"Why do I have a bad feeling about this?" she asked. The wind picked up tendrils of her hair and blew them across her mouth, and Chase had to resist the urge to brush them away with his finger.

"I doubt there's much difference between these accommodations and where you stayed at Bagram," he said reasonably. "I spoke to the woman over at the USO, who said this is where all the entertainers will stay while they're here."

He pushed through the entrance of the tent, sensing Kate directly behind him. The tent was larger than the one at Bagram, with at least three dozen bunk beds lined up along the walls. The USO staff had hung curtains between the bunks in an effort to provide some privacy. But where the other tent had been sparsely outfitted, this tent was equipped with metal lockers and several small refrigerators. Chase set the duffel bag down inside the door and turned to look at Kate.

"Please tell me you're joking," she finally said, turning to him. "There is absolutely no way that Tenley can stay here." She gave a disbelieving laugh and gestured toward the cots. "She's the only female in her band! Are you actually suggesting she sleep here with a bunch of guys, with only a scrap of material separating her from them?"

Chase crossed his arms. "Well, she'll have you to protect her."

"No way. There must be somewhere else. What about

the time Carrie Underwood visited? Are you telling me that she stayed here?"

"No. She stayed in a private housing unit, but unfortunately we don't have any available at the present time." He gestured around him. "This is the alternative, and if it's adequate for the other performers, I have to believe it's adequate for you and your sister."

Kate blew out a hard breath. "I knew the conditions over here would be harsh, but to have her sleep in the same tent with a dozen guys?" She gave Chase a helpless look. "Really, Chase? There's nothing else available?"

"Is she in any danger from her own band?"

He could see Kate considering this before she shook her head. "No, but it's not…appropriate. The point is, she shouldn't *have* to bunk with her band. She's an impressionable young girl, and she should have her own private accommodations. Wait…" She turned and stared at him. "Did you say I'm also staying here?"

"I did."

Chase watched her expression turn from dismay to horror.

"Am I supposed to sleep here tonight? Alone?"

Oh, man. He knew her words weren't an invitation, but he couldn't prevent his imagination from surging.

"Unfortunately, I don't have my own private housing unit for you to crash in," he said.

Kate's gaze locked with his and awareness flared in her eyes. Chase knew she was remembering what had happened between them, and when her lips parted on a soft "oh," he realized he had to leave. He couldn't stop thinking about the previous night, and now it seemed he couldn't stop talking about it, either.

"You'll be fine," he assured her. "Let's go over and check out the concert venue, and then grab some lunch."

He glanced outside. "This storm is going to be here before dark, so we should go soon."

"Before we do that, is there someone at the USO that I can talk to?" She gave him a pleading look. "You don't know Tenley. She'll be miserable if she has to stay here."

"Kate, trust me when I say I do understand. But this isn't Bagram Air Base, and they just don't have the resources here that Bagram has." He gestured toward the metal bunk beds with one hand. "This is what's available, and I'm sorry if it's not up to your usual standards, but it's what you get."

Blowing out a breath, she picked up her pink duffel bag and dropped it onto the nearest bunk. "For myself, I don't really care where I sleep. But Tenley deserves better."

Chase found his resolve crumbling beneath her obvious distress. At the same time, he couldn't help but admire how doggedly she looked out for her sister.

"Okay, look," he said, scrubbing a hand across the back of his neck. "Let's go over and talk to the USO folks. Maybe they can figure out alternate arrangements for the two of you." She gave him a grateful smile, and he raised a hand to forestall the words of gratitude that he knew hovered on her lips. "Just don't get your hopes up. They may not have anything else to offer you. When I talked with them, it sounded like they were stretched pretty thin."

Kate made a sound of frustration and sat down heavily on the bunk. "I don't know why I came over here," she lamented softly. "What was I thinking? Russell tried to talk me out of this, but I thought it was our only chance to save Tenley's career."

Chase had no idea who Russell was, but he felt a surge of jealousy that Kate somehow relied on this man. Worse, it sounded as if she was on the verge of tears. He could handle her anger and her indignation, but he wasn't sure how he would deal with her tears.

"Okay, c'mon," he relented. "Let's go over to the USO and then we'll take a quick look at the concert venue, okay?"

Kate didn't meet his eyes, but she nodded. "Okay." Her voice was subdued.

Chase frowned. Was she crying? He was torn between wanting to go to her, and wanting to run as fast as he could in the opposite direction. In the end, cowardice won out and he retreated toward the exit.

"I'll wait for you outside," he said.

The Humvee had departed. Chase would spend the night bunking with a Marine Corps battalion, and had given the Humvee driver instructions to drop his protective gear and duffel bag off at their tent. Now he wondered if he hadn't been a little hasty in sending the guys off. The wind was still blowing, and the small rocks and dust that it kicked up made it unpleasant to be outside for any length of time. When Kate finally emerged from the tent, she looked composed, but resolute.

"All set?" he asked.

She nodded. "Yes."

She didn't say anything else, and Chase didn't ask. He was just relieved that she wasn't crying. He could pretty much deal with anything, but not tears.

"The USO office is about a ten-minute walk from here," he said as she fell into step beside him. The wind was at their back, so they avoided the worst of the debris that was flying around. But when they finally reached the office, they were both covered in a fine coating of dust. The USO was housed in a large, one-floor building and consisted of a lounge equipped with oversize leather chairs, flat-screened televisions and a bank of computers and telephones. At least a dozen soldiers were sprawled in the chairs watching television, or sat at the computers, connecting with family members and friends back home. Chase could see two civilians inside the office, and pointed them out to Kate.

"Do you want me to come with you when you talk with them?"

"No, I can take it from here. This is what I do."

Chase sat down in a chair where he had a clear view of the office, and watched as Kate went in and closed the door behind her. Through the glass windows that separated the office from the public lounge, he could see her negotiating with the two USO representatives. She had her little planner with her, and was busy taking notes as she talked with the women. They were smiling and nodding, and she reached into her oversize shoulder bag and withdrew what looked like a handful of oversize glossy photos of Tenley Miles. She handed one to each woman. They spoke for several more minutes, and then Kate came out, looking extremely pleased with herself.

Chase rose to his feet. "All set?"

She smiled at him and tucked her planner into her bag. "They're going to provide a semi-private housing unit for Tenley when she arrives. She'll stay in a unit with me and two other women, but at least she won't have to sleep in the tent with the band members."

Chase had to give her credit. He had talked with the USO representatives in the hours before Kate had arrived and had been told in no uncertain terms that the only option was for her to stay in the tent.

"I'm impressed," he said to her as they left the building.

She gave him an arch smile. "It's amazing what a little bit of charm can get you. You should try it some time."

He grinned. "Didn't you notice? This is me at my most charming."

To his relief, she laughed. "Yeah, right."

"So where are you staying tonight?" he asked. "I'll make sure your gear gets moved to the new location."

"Unfortunately, it looks like I'll be in that tent by myself until the performers arrive. Then the two women at the USO are giving up their own beds for Tenley and me."

"Really? And where will they stay?"

Kate shrugged. "They said they can put some cots in the USO office and sleep there for a couple of nights."

"And you're okay with that? You don't mind displacing other people for your own convenience?"

Kate gave him a level look. "Not for my own convenience, for Tenley's. And it's not as if they'll be sleeping outside. They offered to do this. I didn't ask them to."

Chase didn't know why he should feel so disappointed, but he did. He admired the fact that she would go to any length to ensure her sister's safety and comfort, but he didn't like how easily she could disrupt other people's lives to do so.

"Does she have any idea that people bend over backwards to accommodate her, or does she just expect it?"

He watched as Kate drew in a deep breath, and then stopped to face him. "If you have a problem with this, Major Rawlins, maybe you should assign somebody else to escort me around. This is why I came over here—to make sure Tenley has everything she needs. She has no idea how much work goes into preparing for a concert. Like I said before, she's just a kid. She has enough to contend with, without having to worry about the logistics of where she is going to eat, sleep, etc. That's my job."

Charity gave a soulful whimper, as if sensing the tension between them.

"Okay, then," Chase said. "Let's go over and make sure the concert site meets with your approval."

They walked in silence after that. As much as Chase was

attracted to Kate, he couldn't help but think this assignment was a waste of his time. She could clearly take care of herself. Meanwhile, part of his team was up in the mountains doing his job for him. He wondered how they were doing, and how soon he could rejoin them.

Beside him, Kate's shoulders were rigidly set and she stared straight ahead. Even as they toured the staging area where the bands would perform, she pointedly ignored him. She made some notes in her planner, and examined where the bands would wait backstage, but didn't give him any indication of whether she approved of the site or not. But he'd seen Kate's face when she'd thought Tenley would have to stay with the other band members, and he knew that her misgivings stemmed from a true concern for her sister.

After viewing the concert venue, they walked over to the dining facility and had lunch. But unlike the day before, there was no small talk. They might have been complete strangers for all the attention Kate paid him. Chase tried several times to make conversation with her, but after receiving short, polite responses, he gave up. He told himself that if she wanted to keep him at arm's length, then he was fine with that. In another week she would be gone. He had no desire to get to know Kate Fitzgerald. He told himself for the hundredth time that she was simply an assignment, and once that assignment was over, he could get back to what he should have been doing all along: hunting and capturing Al-Azir.

This was exactly why he avoided women and tried not to encourage those who did show an interest in him; they were a distraction. Even now, when he should be spending his spare time coordinating with his team members and laying out a plan for their continued pursuit of Al-Azir, he found his thoughts consumed by Kate. He needed to get away from her, even if it was just for a couple of hours. He wondered if his brother was at Camp Leatherneck.

Chance was an Apache helicopter pilot, and his missions took him to many of the U.S. bases, although he was stationed at Bagram. But it hadn't escaped Chase's notice that his brother somehow managed to fly into Camp Leatherneck about once every two weeks, and it was no coincidence that the trips just happened to coincide with those times that Captain Jenna Larson was also at Camp Leatherneck. On second thought, he decided that even if his brother was on the base, Chase was unlikely to get any quality time with him. Chance would be fully occupied with Jenna.

He watched Kate eat her lunch. Although she deliberately ignored him, Chase could see that she was acutely aware of him. She watched him when she thought he didn't notice, and she was attuned to every movement he made. He hadn't been in his line of business for nearly eight years without being able to read body language, and everything about Kate screamed awareness of him.

He couldn't believe the difference a day made. Just yesterday, he'd been chomping at the bit to return to the field and resume his hunt for Al-Azir. Now, for the first time in years, he wasn't thinking about duty and country. With a sense of dismay, he realized he wanted more.

He wanted Kate Fitzgerald.

8

On a pretext of having business to attend to, Chase left Kate at the USO for the afternoon. He needed some time to get his head together and put things in perspective. Colonel Decker had made it clear that his only mission for the next week was to take care of Kate and her sister, but he also needed to touch base with the rest of his team. Even if the stand-down order was lifted in the next day or so, he was committed to remaining with Kate until the tour had ended.

Kate seemed happy at the prospect of spending time at the USO. She would have internet and phone access, and had insisted she needed to reach both Tenley and Russell. He'd desperately wanted to know if Russell was a boyfriend, but pride prevented him from asking. They had agreed that he would return to collect her after dinner. The dining facility was located directly next door to the USO, so she didn't need an escort. He felt a little disgruntled by the fact that she seemed happy at the prospect of eating a meal alone. She hadn't talked about staying in the large tent by herself, but the more Chase thought about it, the less he liked the idea, especially with a storm moving into the region. He'd already made up his mind to hunker down outside the entrance for the night, just in case she needed him. He'd slept in worse places, in worse conditions, so the idea didn't faze him.

By the time Chase jogged over to the USO to get Kate, the temperatures had dropped significantly, and the wind had kicked up a notch. Dust whipped across the ground in swirling clouds, and he could hear the patter of tiny stones as they clattered against the metal buildings. In the distance, flashes of lightning briefly illuminated the mountain peaks.

The storm was rolling in quickly, and it promised to be a good one. Kate was waiting for him by the entrance, her enormous shoulder bag over one arm. Even in the dim light he could see the apprehension on her face as she looked toward the northwest.

"C'mon," he said briskly, "let's get you back to your tent before the rain starts." He indicated the road, which was packed dirt and rocks. "You don't want to be out here once the ground gets wet."

"Is there any chance I can take a shower before I turn in?" she asked hopefully.

Chance had already planned on hitting the showers after he dropped her off at her tent, so it would be no big deal to walk her over to the bathrooms. "Absolutely," he assured her. "I'll leave you at your tent while I go and grab my own gear, and then come back for you."

The wind kept her from responding, so she just nodded and then put her head down. She kept pace with him as they walked quickly across the base. On the left, he pointed out the nearest bunker, illuminated by an orange safety light. The exterior of the concrete bunker was packed high with sandbags.

"There's another shelter just beyond the bathrooms," he said, drawing her close and raising his voice to be heard over the wind. "If the sirens go off while you're in the shower, use that bunker instead."

He left her at her own tent and then quickly jogged to the Marine battalion quarters, and stuffed a clean uniform and his shower gear into his backpack. Other soldiers were running to reach their destinations before the storm hit, and Chase looked to the sky, trying to estimate how much time they might have before the heavens opened up. They didn't often get storm fronts of this magnitude in southern Afghanistan, and when they did, they usually took the form of sandstorms. But he already knew that this particular storm was packing a lot of moisture, and the troops were battening down the hatches in preparation for a significant amount of rain. He knew that Kate would be okay; her tent had been erected on top of a wooden platform, so she would be safe from flooding. But the tents were prone to seepage, and there was a good chance that she would have several leaks during the course of the night.

It was almost completely dark by the time he returned to Kate's tent and found her waiting for him just inside the entrance. They jogged the short distance to the bathroom, not wanting to get caught in the threatening downpour.

Chase stepped into the entry with Kate. "I'll be right next door," he assured her. "Wait for me here. I'll give you a shout when I'm ready to walk you back to the tent, got it?"

Kate nodded. "I'll be quick."

"Okay, fine. I'll be back in ten minutes to get you."

Ducking into the men's showers, on the opposite side of the same building, Chase quickly stripped down and stepped under the steaming water, grateful to scrub away the dust and grit from the base. Since it was still the dinner hour, he had the entire facility to himself. He could easily have stayed under the hot water for hours, but sensitive to the fact that Kate would be waiting for him, he rinsed the soap from his skin and turned off the tap. Then, wrapping a towel around his hips, he stood over a sink and used a razor to scrape the beard growth from his jaw and neck. Scrutinizing his reflection, he decided he still looked rough around the edges, but at least he no longer resembled a mercenary.

He was wiping the last traces of shaving cream from his jaw when the lights in the bathroom flickered. Outside, he could hear the wind whistling across the base. The doors rattled on their hinges. Chase turned swiftly toward the stall where he had left his gear and a clean change of clothing, but he was too late. The lights flickered once more, ominously, before they went out, plunging the bathroom into utter darkness.

Abandoning his clothing, Chase made a beeline for the door, bolting through it and into the windy darkness outside. He knew it would only be a minute or two before the lights came back on or the backup generators kicked in, but he didn't want Kate to panic.

He burst through the doors of the women's bathrooms, calling her name. "Kate? Are you okay? It's me, Chase."

He heard her footsteps stumble toward him, and then she was in his arms, her hands groping blindly at him.

"Chase?" He could hear the surprise in her voice. "What are you doing in here? Isn't there some rule against— Are you *naked?*"

Her fingers encountered his bare torso, and before he could stop them, they skittered over his shoulders and arms, drawing heat to the surface of his skin wherever they touched. Grasping her wrists, he dragged her hands away.

"No," he snapped in irritation at himself and his body's reaction to her. "I am *not* naked. I was just getting dressed when the power went out. I didn't want you to be frightened, so I ran over. The backup generators should—" There was an audible click, then a buzz of electricity, and the emergency lights over the doors snapped on, illuminating the bathroom in an eerie red glow. "Kick in any second," Chase finished, his voice trailing off as he got a good look at Kate.

As lights went, they weren't much, but they were more than sufficient for him to see that she wore nothing but a pair of underpants and a bra, and his mouth went dry at the sight. He'd been right about one thing—she had curves in all the right places. Her hips flared out from a narrow waist, and her legs were slim and supple.

"Oh, my God," she breathed, her eyes widening as they traveled over him. For just an instant, Chase saw female appreciation and raw hunger in her expression, and in the next instant she spun away to snatch a towel from the nearby sink and hold it against her. "I'm fine, really," she said over her shoulder. "You can go now and—and put some clothes on."

Chase stood there for a moment, dumbstruck. Despite the fact that he'd already seen her partially nude and knew she had a gorgeous shape, he was blown away by the entire package. Even her back was lovely, and he took a second to admire the elegant line of her spine and the deep curves of her waist. Her rear was luscious and rounded, and he had an instant image of himself cupping her cheeks in his hands and driving himself into her warmth as she straddled his hips. Then he gave himself a mental shake. He was losing it, big-time.

"I'll see you in a few minutes," he muttered, and returned to the men's side of the shower facilities, his head still reeling.

For as long as Chase could recall, women had been attracted to him and his identical twin, Chance. But where Chance had welcomed every feminine advance and had been considered something of a player, Chase had been completely focused on his future as a Special Ops commando. He'd known from an early age that he wanted to join the elite unit, and nothing—not even a pretty face and a curvy body—could deter him from that path. He'd had girlfriends, but none of them had been more important to him than achieving his goal.

In fact, looking back, he realized he'd deliberately kept women at a distance because he'd known his dedication to the Army would prevent him from committing himself fully to a relationship. But right now, with his body aroused from just seeing her, he thought he would gladly trade his entire freaking career for just one night with Kate Fitzgerald.

Yeah, he'd definitely lost it.

Pulling on a clean uniform, Chase stuffed his dirty gear into his backpack, telling himself that he'd have no problem facing Kate. He'd seen plenty of women with less clothing on than the scraps of fabric she'd been wearing, and he'd never been so overcome by lust that he'd lost his self-control. He'd just keep it professional and act like he hadn't seen anything. Like he hadn't cupped and caressed her breasts less than twenty-four hours earlier. Like he had no idea how her nipple felt in his mouth, against his tongue, or how her small sounds of pleasure drove him crazy.

Yeah, right.

Bracing himself, he stepped outside. Rain was just beginning to fall in big, fat drops, and the sky flashed with lightning mere seconds before a roll of thunder caused the ground to tremble beneath his boots. He pulled a small flashlight out of his backpack and flicked it on, not because he couldn't find his way back, or because he couldn't see in the dark, but because he knew it would give Kate a sense of security. Standing just outside the door to the women's showers, he called her name.

She came out immediately, although Chase didn't miss how she avoided his eyes, concentrating instead on adjusting her bag over her shoulder. But when the first raindrops hit her face, she blinked in surprise and lifted a hand to catch several.

"Wow, this storm is moving in fast," she observed.

"They usually do out here," Chase replied. "We'd better hurry, or we'll find ourselves soaked to the skin before we reach your tent. Here, let me take your bag."

Ignoring her protests, he took the shoulder bag from her and slid a hand beneath her elbow. He sensed her surprise, but she didn't try to pull away. The rain was coming down in sheeting torrents now, mixing with the dusty road and creating mud that had the consistency of peanut butter. It sucked at his feet with every step, and if it weren't for the fact that his boots were laced up over his ankles, they might have been pulled free.

Kate wasn't so lucky.

She gave a small cry of distress and stumbled heavily, pulling Chase to an abrupt halt. He steadied her as she leaned her weight against him and balanced herself on one foot. Swiping the water from his face, Chase looked down to see one of her slip-on shoes buried in the muck. He pulled it free, and she grimaced as she pushed her foot back into it.

"So much for that shower," she shouted.

Chase peered up at the sky. "Yeah, well, you don't know the meaning of the word *shower* until you've experienced a desert storm. This is just going to get worse. C'mon."

But no sooner did they take another step, than Kate's other shoe became stuck in the mud. Chase flicked his light over the ground, seeing the water pooling quickly around Kate's foot. She could put the shoe back on, but he already knew they'd be retrieving her footwear from the mud with every step she took. The way he saw it, they had two choices: she could go barefoot all the way back to her sleeping quarters, or he could carry her. He told himself firmly that the thought of holding her in his arms for the five-minute trek did not send his pulse into overdrive.

"Okay, listen," he said, using his best authoritative voice, "I'm going to carry you back to the tent, otherwise we'll be playing hop-along the whole way."

She stared up at him, and in the beam from the flashlight, her lashes were spiky with moisture, and rivulets of water streamed down her face and slicked her hair to her scalp. She blinked furiously.

"You can't carry me," she protested. "First of all, I weigh a ton, and second of all, it's not necessary. I'll just go barefoot."

"No, that's not an option," he said briskly. "The road is loaded with stones and potholes. If you don't end up with a serious laceration, you could twist an ankle. Just let me carry you. You don't weigh a ton, trust me. I carry seventy pounds of equipment on my back whenever I'm in the field."

She gave him a tolerant look. "I weigh a little more than seventy pounds."

Chase handed her the shoulder bag. "Here, carry this. Now put your arms around my neck."

A brilliant flash of lightning, followed by a low boom of thunder, caused her to clutch his arm, and Chase took advantage of her startled reaction, bending down to slide an arm behind her knees. He lifted her effortlessly, and the thought flashed through his head that she really didn't weigh much more than seventy pounds. She turned her face into his neck as he strode along the muddy road, and even with the rain lashing against his face, he could smell her soap and shampoo. Her breath came in warm pants against his skin, and he arrived at her tent much too quickly. He set her down just inside the entrance.

"I lost my shoe back there," she said.

Chase looked down at her bare, mud-covered foot. "I'll

go back and get it," he offered. "Here, take my flashlight. The power's out, so the lights won't work in here. There's bottled water and some towels at the back of the tent that you can use to clean up."

"What about you?" she asked. "How will you see anything?"

He pulled out a second, smaller flashlight from a pocket on his camo pants. "Always ready," he said with a quick grin. "I'll be right back."

She nodded, swiping moisture from her face. "Okay, thanks."

Chase sprinted back the way they had come until he found her shoe. It was a flat-soled, cloth shoe that might have been blue or purple, but right now it was coated in a thick, yellowish mud. Wiping the worst of it off, he jogged back to the tent. Kate had put the flashlight on the small side table next to her bunk bed and stood toweling her hair dry. In the instant before she knew he was there, he saw the weariness on her face and in the droop of her slender shoulders. Her clothes were soaking wet and plastered to her skin. He cleared his throat and she turned toward him, smoothing her features into an expression of pleasant expectation. She grimaced when she saw the sopping shoe in his hand.

"Maybe I should just consider these shoes as collateral damage and throw them away."

"Leave them outside the tent and let the rain wash them clean," Chase suggested. "Once the sun comes out, they'll be dry within minutes."

Another bolt of lightning flashed brilliance behind him, followed by a sharp crack of thunder. Kate didn't jump, but Chase saw how she clutched the towel convulsively in her hands. He intended to spend the night just outside her tent, in case she needed him, but if Kate found out she would protest.

"Okay, listen, I'm going back to my tent to change into

dry clothes and grab my rain gear, and then I'll come check on you," he said. "If you want, we can play cards or something. I can hang out here until the worst of the storm passes."

She looked relieved. "I'd like that, thanks."

He turned to go, but her voice halted him.

"You're coming right back?" He could hear the anxiety in her voice.

"I'll be gone for less than ten minutes," he assured her. "Why don't you get out of those wet clothes and get warm?"

He knew she felt apprehensive about being alone in the big tent, and now he wished that he had tried to find her other accommodations until her client arrived. He told himself it was only for one night. Tomorrow, they would view the first concert venue in the morning and then drive to Kandahar, where the USO had arranged for the third and final concert. By the time they returned to Bagram two days later, Tenley Miles would have arrived. The performers would spend five days giving concerts and meeting the troops, then they would fly back to the States and Kate Fitzgerald would go with them. Two days ago he'd been resentful at the prospect of babysitting the publicist. Now he realized that he didn't want her to leave.

KATE WAITED UNTIL Chase left, then secured the entrance to the tent as best she could. The wind still whistled outside and the rain drummed against the roof. Chase had made the interior seem almost cozy with his height and broad shoulders, but now it seemed big and empty. The flashlight illuminated the area directly around her bunk, but the rest of the large tent was cast in dark shadows that undulated with the wind and rain and made her think that someone was on the other side of the canvas, trying to get in.

Shivering, she opening her duffel bag and pulled out a

pair of flannel lounge pants and a loose top. The walls of
the tent sucked noisily in and out with the force of the wind,
and Kate wished Chase would hurry. Fishing in her pocket,
she pulled out the beeper that he had given to her earlier,
and closed her fingers over it. Just holding it made her feel
marginally better. She wanted to push it, but then he would
know what a complete fraud she was, and that everything
about this trip totally freaked her out. Besides, he'd promised that he would be right back; what would she say to him
when he arrived? That she was afraid of the dark? That she
was afraid of being alone? That he made her feel safe?

Yeah, right. If only that was all he made her feel. She
recalled how he had looked in the bathroom, with nothing
but a towel wrapped around his hips. His body was layered
with lean muscle and sculpted to masculine perfection. He
was hot enough to bake cookies on. She could still picture
the thrust of his broad shoulders and the bulging biceps in
his powerful arms. She remembered again the feel of his
mouth on her breast, and how perfectly he'd fitted in the
cradle of her hips.

Just the memory of his body caused something to fist low
in her stomach. Most of the time, he looked at her as if she
was an annoyance, or just another mission that he needed
to complete successfully. He'd said the incident in his bedroom had been a mistake, but for those few moments in the
bathroom, she had seen something else in his eyes. Something hot and needy. Something that had caused a rush of
heat beneath her skin.

Shivering, she realized the temperature had dropped dramatically from what it had been earlier in the day. Chase
hadn't exaggerated when he'd said the nights could get cold.
Quickly, she stripped out of her wet clothing and changed
into the flannel lounge pants and top, and pulled on a pair
of socks. Still, she couldn't get warm. She shook out the

sleeping bag that had been left at the foot of the cot and un-zipped it, dragging it around her shoulders like a shawl. But even cocooned in its warmth, she couldn't stop shivering.

The flap of the tent billowed and then Chase was there, bringing the wind and rain with him, until he secured the entrance. Shrugging out of his rain poncho, he hung it from a support beam and turned toward Kate just as a crack of thunder sounded overhead.

Chase grinned. "I can't remember the last time I saw a storm like this over here. Are you okay?"

Kate nodded, relieved to have him there. "Are you sure it's safe to be in a tent? What if it gets struck by lightning?"

Chase sat down on the bed directly beside hers, leaning forward to link his hands between his knees. For the first time, Kate noticed that he had shaved his beard, revealing the strong, square line of his jaw. She wanted to stroke her fingers over the smooth skin.

"The tents are grounded," he said, "so you have nothing to worry about. More than half of the troops on this base live in tents, and we haven't lost one in a storm yet."

The rain thundered on the canvas roof, and Kate pulled the sleeping bag a little closer around her shoulders. "I guess I'll just have to trust you."

An odd expression crossed his face, and Kate was surprised when he stood up. "Right. Which is why I should leave. Try to get some sleep."

"What?" Pushing the sleeping bag off, Kate stood up and followed him across the tent. "Why are you leaving? I thought you were going to stay, at least until the storm passes."

Chase paused in the act of retrieving his rain gear and gave her a disbelieving look. "Kate, if I stay here with you, do you really believe we'll play cards?"

Kate's breath caught at the expression on his face, and her heart leaped in her chest. "Look, if it's about last night—"

"Yes, damn it, it is about last night." His voice was a low growl. He leaned forward until his face was just inches from hers and raked her with a heated look. "I'm trying very hard to keep this professional, but every time I look at you, I see you lying across my bed, making little gasping sounds as I touch you. Christ…" He spun halfway around and scrubbed a hand over his hair before turning back to her. "So just—give me a break, okay? Understand that this has nothing with my not wanting to stay with you. I *can't* stay with you. Not unless you want to be flat on your back in that bunk with me inside you."

His words caused Kate's heart to stop beating and then explode into overdrive. Part of her realized she should be at least a little bit frightened by this man, but the images he conjured up filled her with a buzz of awareness and a sense of her own feminine power. She knew that her eyes grew wide and her mouth fell open, but nobody had ever spoken to her so bluntly, or admitted that he wanted her enough that he couldn't trust himself to be with her.

Misreading her expression, Chase gave a rueful laugh.

"Pretty pathetic, huh? I guess I really have been deployed for too long."

Kate didn't know how to respond to that. Was it pathetic that he should find her attractive? And did he only find her attractive because he'd been deployed for so many months? How would he react if she told him that she hadn't been with a guy in almost two years? Now *that* was pathetic.

Outside, another flash of lightning illuminated the sky, and wind gusted through the entrance, bringing a spray of cold rain with it. Chase grabbed his poncho from the hook and dropped it over his head.

"You have my beeper," he said curtly. "Use it if you need me."

Kate stared at him in dismay, unable to comprehend that he was really going to leave her alone in the enormous tent while a storm raged outside. It was wrong to expect him to stay with her. She was a grown woman, after all, but she couldn't deny that she wanted him with her. "I don't need your damned beeper, Chase. I want *you*."

Chase held up a finger and gave her a warning look. "Don't. I'm barely holding it together here, Kate."

Before she could argue further, he pushed aside the flap and vanished into the night. Kate stood staring after him in disbelief for a full minute, expecting that he would reappear. But when an ear-splitting crack of thunder reverberated through the tent, Kate dashed back to her bunk and dragged the sleeping bag over her.

With her back pressed against the headboard, she sat with the flashlight in her hands, directing the beam at the entrance, certain that someone—or something—was going to get her before the night was over. The shadows seemed to grow and move in the corners, and the combined cacophony of rocks and sand being flung against the sides of the tent, as well as the hard rain drumming against the roof, guaranteed that she wouldn't get any sleep that night.

She realized she still clutched Chase's beeper in her hand, but nothing would induce her to press that button now. Not when he'd made it clear that he couldn't be alone with her. He obviously was a man of honor, and there was no way she would ask him to compromise his principles for her.

An ear-splitting crack of thunder directly overhead, followed by what sounded like an explosion very close by, made her jump with alarm. Drawing a deep breath, she pressed the beeper.

9

CHASE SAT JUST OUTSIDE the entrance of Kate's tent, hugging his poncho around his body, not that it did any good. The sheeting rain found its way inside the protective gear, and his clothing was soaked. Charity had refused to leave him, so he'd let her curl up beneath his poncho, but even she was dripping wet.

Beneath his feet, the ground was a swirling soup of red mud and rocks, and the wind caused the fabric of the tent to snap loudly. Reluctant to leave Kate alone, he had taken up watch for the night, just in case she needed him. The conditions were so bad that only the security vehicles were out, driving slowly through the flooded roads, their emergency lights cutting orange swaths through the wind and rain. Chase doubted there would be any chance of a mortar attack tonight, since the weather would drive even the insurgents for cover.

His tent was only a five-minute jog away, but he didn't want to risk anything happening to Kate in these conditions. The main power was still out, although the emergency lights were working. As he crouched by the entrance, a bolt of lightning lit up the sky, so close that he could feel the electricity in the air. The streak was followed immediately by a deafening crack of thunder, and a loud popping sound as the lightning struck a nearby transformer and caused it to explode, plunging the area into total darkness.

Chase pushed himself to his feet just as the beeper in his pocket began to vibrate. *Kate.* Making his way through the entrance of the tent, he stood just inside and swept the interior with his flashlight, looking for her. He found her huddled on the nearest bunk, wrapped in her sleeping bag and clutching the flashlight that he had given to her earlier.

"Are you okay?" he asked. He didn't come any closer. Water streamed down the rubber coating of his rain gear in heavy rivulets and pooled on the floor.

"How did you get here so quickly?" she asked. "I heard a noise, like an explosion, and it sounded pretty close."

"Yeah, the lightning took out a transformer just down the road."

In the indistinct light, he could see the speculation on her face as she considered him. "Were you standing outside my tent this whole time?"

"Just doing my job," he said evenly. "I meant what I said earlier—*attached at the hip.*"

Oh, man, if only. His words conjured up images that he had no business thinking about. Shaking off the disturbing thoughts, he strove for a professional tone.

"If you're okay, then I'll let you get some sleep. I'll be right outside if you need me." He turned to go.

"Wait!"

Chase stopped and looked at her expectantly. Another bolt of lightning flashed outside the tent, followed by a loud boom. To his surprise, Kate stood up, letting the sleeping bag fall onto the mattress. Her flannel pajama bottoms rode low on her hips, exposing a pale strip of skin along her abdomen. He swallowed hard and watched her approach, half hopeful, half filled with dread.

"As much as I appreciate you standing watch," she said, stopping just beyond the puddle of water he was creating, "I wouldn't put a dog out in these conditions." She looked pointedly at Charity, who stood in the doorway with her head down, shivering. "Not even a guard dog."

Chase hoped the hood of his poncho, combined with the darkness, hid his expression, because he knew he was eating her alive with his eyes. She looked warm and feminine and he ached to slide his hands into the back of her loose pajama bottoms and cup her luscious rear. He wanted to bend her over his arm and shove her shirt up so that he could lick her breasts. He couldn't remember when he'd had such a strong reaction to a woman, and he took a step back.

Kate hugged her arms around her middle, her expression one of concern. "Why don't you come in and dry off?"

"No, thanks. I'll just get wet again when I go back out."

"Look," she said, and Chase knew she tried to sound casual, but the way she rubbed her palms over her thighs told him she was nervous. "I'm not asking you to sleep with me, okay? But I'd feel safer if you were inside the tent with me. And since you're going to stand watch anyway, doesn't it make more sense to come in out of the rain?" She indicated a folding chair in the corner. "You can just as easily sit inside the entrance as you can outside, right?"

Chase rubbed a hand over his face. She'd never know how tempting her words were, but he had to admit that everything she said made sense. But he hadn't completely lost it. He still had a small vestige of brain cells left that functioned, warning him to retreat.

"General order number one prohibits any service member from entering the sleeping quarters of the opposite sex," he finally responded. "I shouldn't come inside."

"Well, I'm not a service member," she pointed out, "and surely allowances can be made for the fact that the weather is so terrible and all the power is out. You'd be able to do your job better if you were inside the tent. Besides, it's not like anyone is going to come out here in this weather to check on me—or you."

Still, he hesitated.

"Didn't you tell me that your job is to ensure my safety while I'm here?" she pressed. "That you are my single point of contact for everything, and that I don't do anything without you? If you refuse to do this, I will go to your commanding officer and tell him—"

"Okay, okay," Chase relented, interrupting her tirade. As threats went, hers was pretty ineffectual. As long as he kept Kate safe, his commanding officer had no interest in what he did or didn't do with her. He just hoped he wasn't making a huge mistake. "I'll bunk down inside the entrance, if you don't mind."

KATE FELT SOMETHING uncurl inside her at his words. No, she didn't mind in the least, and she stepped back to allow him to pass. Immediately, the space felt smaller, and she watched as he pulled the dripping poncho off. Beneath the rain gear, he wore a pair of camo pants and a T-shirt, and while she pretended to be absorbed in rearranging the sleeping bag on her cot, she observed him. He had set his flashlight down on the floor, and by the beam of light, she could see how his T-shirt molded itself to his contours. Charity shook herself briskly, and Chase laughed ruefully as she sprayed him with water.

"Oh, the poor thing," Kate said, and grabbed a towel from the nearby stack. Walking back toward Chase, she handed it to him. He blotted his face and then scrubbed it over his hair, before crouching down to briskly rub the dog's wet fur. Only then did she see that both his T-shirt and his pants were soaking wet.

"You're drenched," she exclaimed, returning with another towel.

"I'll dry," he said off-handedly, accepting the towel. He glanced briefly at her. "You should go back to bed."

"You won't leave?"

"I'll be right here."

Kate walked back to the bunk and climbed under the sleeping bag, curling on her side with the flashlight on the floor beside her. He stood up and was silhouetted in the beam from his own flashlight. She held her breath when he grabbed a fistful of his shirt and dragged it over his head, dropping the sodden garment onto the back of the chair.

He was breathtaking.

She released her pent-up breath on a shaky exhale. She'd realized after seeing him in the bathroom that he was fit, but the flashlight cast intriguing shadows over his body, emphasizing every dip and contour. As he toweled himself dry, she could clearly see the thrust of his shoulders and pecs. When he bent forward to blot the excess moisture from his pants, his abdomen resembled corrugated metal.

Kate felt herself growing warm. Recalling the intensity of his lovemaking the previous night, she knew he would be a good lover. Despite his size and obvious strength, his hands had been gentle on her body, coaxing a response from her until she'd been so aroused that if he hadn't pulled away when he did, she would have come just from rubbing herself against him. Even now, desire coiled tightly inside her and then unfurled, blossoming outward until her breasts ached and she shifted restlessly beneath the covers.

"You'll sleep better if you turn that light out," he offered, sitting down on the chair.

"Are you going to sit there all night?"

"That's the plan."

Kate's heart was beating fast. She reminded herself that

she didn't even know this guy, and that he'd all but told her that he had no intention of sleeping with her.

But she knew he'd lied.

There was no denying that they had chemistry. Sizzling chemistry. Maybe it was the storm that raged outside their tent, or the inherent danger that surrounded them from insurgents, but Kate had never been more desperate for human contact than she was at that moment.

Did she have the courage to proposition him? More importantly, would she have the guts to face him in the morning, regardless of whether he accepted or rejected her offer? If she did sleep with him, it would be with the knowledge that they wouldn't have any kind of relationship outside of a physical one, and even that would be short-lived. In a week, she would return home and he would resume his Ranger duties. But she also knew that she wanted this man more than she'd ever wanted any other. She'd made a lot of difficult choices in her life, some she'd regretted. This wasn't going to be one of them.

She watched as he tilted his head from side to side in an attempt to ease the tension in his neck. Charity lay on her belly beside him with her nose on her paws, and now she whined softly as Kate pushed back the covers and slid her feet to the floor. She didn't have to see Chase's face to know that his attention was riveted on her, although he never moved a muscle. His flashlight lay on the floor nearby, the beam of light angled slightly away from her, but she knew it provided sufficient light for him to see her. Outside, the wind howled and the canvas at the entrance flapped noisily.

"Kate," he warned softly.

"Shh," she whispered, standing directly in front of him. "Don't talk. I know what you're going to say, and you're wrong."

His voice was a husky rasp. "You're about to do something that you'll regret."

"Wrong again," she said, and with her heart in her throat, she slowly pulled her shirt over her head until she stood in front of him wearing only her loose flannel lounge pants and socks. She didn't try to cover herself. She wanted him to see her, to be tempted by her.

He made a sound that was half growl, half groan, and his hands formed fists on his thighs. "I'm giving you one last chance, Kate, but if you don't turn around right now and go back to bed, I won't be responsible for what happens."

But instead of retreating, Kate took a step forward, until her knees almost bumped against his. Chase's eyes glittered in the dim light as they slid over her, and his chest rose and fell swiftly, evidence that he wasn't nearly as composed as he seemed.

She didn't say anything, simply straddled his legs, forcing him to make room for her. She sat down, looping her arms around his neck. He sucked in his breath and the expression in his eyes was so heated that Kate wouldn't have been at all surprised if steam started rising from his damp skin. Her breasts brushed his chest as she leaned forward and feathered her lips over his in the barest whisper of a kiss. He groaned and turned his head, following her mouth with his own.

"Tell me that you want me," she demanded softly, and punctuated her words by taking his hand and placing it over one breast.

"Kate…" His voice was ragged.

"Tell me."

"Ah, Christ," he breathed in capitulation. He hauled her against his chest, sliding one hand over her bare back and thrusting his other hand through her hair to cup her scalp and angle her face for his kiss.

There was nothing sweet or romantic about the contact. His kiss was greedy and desperate, as if he'd hungered for her and now feared she might vanish before he could get his fill. His tongue swept past her lips and teeth to ravage the inside of her mouth. One hand slid down her back to press her closer as he ground his hips upward. He consumed her, sucking and licking at her mouth, fisting his hand in her hair to hold her still.

Kate had never experienced such complete and total possession before, and she welcomed it, sliding her arms around his shoulders and spearing her fingers through his damp hair to return his kiss eagerly. He tasted hot and sweet and his tongue slid sensuously against her own, driving her need higher. She heard a small moaning sound as she shifted closer, and realized with a sense of shock that it came from her.

"More," she managed to pant against his mouth, and cradled his head in her hands, deepening the kiss. She hardly recognized herself; she'd never been so consumed by lust, and all she could think about was the aching spot between her legs. She knew if Chase touched her there, he would find her drenched with moisture.

She gave a surprised gasp when he gripped her bottom in his hands and stood up, supporting her as if she weighed nothing. Kate locked her legs around his hips and hung on as he walked them over to the bunk and then bent forward, letting her fall back onto the mattress. As he straightened, she saw the hard thrust of his arousal beneath his camo pants, and the realization of what they were about to do hit her.

"I don't want you to stop, but what if someone comes?" she asked breathlessly, her gaze shooting toward the entrance where Charity lay and watched them curiously.

"I'm hoping that will be you," he said, his eyes glittering hotly as he looked down at her. His voice was a husky rasp. "Don't worry. You were right when you said that no-body will be out in this weather. Even if they were, they wouldn't come in."

"Are you sure?"

His hands paused in the process of unfastening his belt. "Having second thoughts?"

"No!" If he stopped now, she would die. She was sure of that. Sitting up, she brushed his hands aside and her fingers trembled as she eagerly unfastened his belt. "Definitely no second thoughts."

The buckle fell away and Kate tugged on the button of his pants until that too popped open beneath her fingers. Before she could unzip them, however, Chase sat down beside her on the narrow mattress, the metal bunk squeaking beneath their combined weight. Bending over, he unlaced his boots and pulled them off, dropping them onto the floor by the bed. Then he turned to Kate, and she felt herself tremble at the intensity of his gaze.

Chase slid a hand beneath her hair and cupped her jaw, searching her eyes in the dim light. "There's still time for you to change your mind," he said in a husky voice. "Don't get me wrong. I want you more than I've wanted anything or anyone in a very long time, but I can't make any promises to you. You'll be returning to the States in another week or so, but I'll be here for another six months."

Kate covered his hand with hers. Turning her face, she pressed a kiss into his palm. "I don't need promises," she assured him, desperately hoping he didn't hear the tremor of uncertainty in her voice. "I just want you tonight. Now."

Everything about this guy appealed to her, and it frightened her a little just how easily she could imagine him in her life. But she knew he was right; she couldn't keep him. She'd already decided that if she could just have him for this short time, she could walk away afterwards.

Chase gave a soft groan at her words and pushed her down on the bed, following her with the length of his body until he lay half beside and half on top of her. He braced his weight on one elbow as he slid his free hand over the curve of her rib cage and cupped one breast with a tenderness that bordered on reverence.

"I've thought of this more times in the past twenty-four hours than I can count," he admitted with a rueful laugh as he rubbed his thumb over her nipple. "Damn, you are so pretty."

Kate arched upward into his palm, and curled her legs around his hips as he dipped his head and kissed her. He fondled and caressed her breast, and the combination of his rough hand on her skin and his hot tongue in her mouth was like a drug, making her go boneless with desire.

Sliding her hands over the strong muscles of his back, she pushed at the waistband of his camo pants. He helped her to drag them down until he could kick them free of his legs, and then suddenly there he was. When he was about to bend over her again, Kate stopped him with a hand on his chest.

"Wait," she demanded, her eyes drifting over his shoulders and chest, following the deep groove that bisected his pecs and abdomen, to where his erection jutted out strongly from his body. For a moment, she couldn't breathe. "I just want to look for a minute."

"Here," he grunted, and dragged her hand down his body until he closed her fingers around his thick length. He pulsed hotly against her palm, and her heart rate quickened at the thought of having that part of him inside her. She skated her thumb over the blunt head, and it came away slick with moisture, causing an answering surge of dampness at her core. He made a guttural sound of pleasure and dropped his head to her shoulder, and Kate realized she had been stroking the length of him. His ragged breathing was a total turn-on, and she caught his mouth with hers in a deep kiss as she continued to fondle him. Overhead, the rain drummed loudly on the top of the tent, and the wind sucked at the canvas walls. But on the narrow bunk, with the warmth of the sleeping bag beneath her and Chase above her, Kate thought they might be the only two people in the world.

"Darlin'," he gasped, "you need to stop or this is going to be over before it's even started."

Reluctantly, Kate released him, but couldn't resist sliding her palms over the hard planes of his chest and torso, admiring his thick muscles. When she reached his neck, she cupped his nape and drew him down for another deep kiss. He tasted like fresh mint and smelled like spicy soap and clean, male sweat. She wanted to devour him.

"Help me take these off," she said quickly, using her free hand to push her flannel lounge pants down over her hips. Chase scooted back between her legs and hooked his thumbs in her waistband, pulling the pants off in one smooth movement. Then, with his eyes glued to her body and glittering hotly, he grasped one ankle in his hand and tugged her sock off, before doing the same to her other foot.

Kate knew she should feel embarrassed by his riveted attention, but she couldn't bring herself to feel any shame. It had been so long since anyone had looked at her as he was looking at her now; as if she were the most beautiful thing he had ever seen. Had anyone ever looked at her like that? She could no longer remember.

"Oh, man, you are so freaking gorgeous," he breathed. "But we can't do this."

FOR THE SECOND TIME in as many days, Chase had Kate Fitzgerald spread out on a bed beneath him, and while he'd believed that nothing short of a direct rocket attack would prevent him from making love to her, he'd been wrong.

Kate stared at him with a mixture of dismay and frustration. "What do you mean we can't do this?" Her voice was edged with desperation.

"Kate," he groaned, "I've been over here for six months, and I've just returned from two weeks in the field. Until yesterday, my entire focus revolved around my mission. I didn't exactly come prepared."

"Oh." Understanding dawned on her face. "Well, that's disappointing, but we could always improvise."

Chase lowered himself down beside Kate and pulled her into the curve of his body, using his free hand to leisurely explore her curves. "We could," he agreed. "In fact, we might not have another choice. As unromantic as it sounds, my job is to protect you, even in bed. I won't risk getting you pregnant."

Kate pressed against him and traced her tongue along his jaw to his ear. She caught his earlobe in her teeth and bit gently. "Then you can relax, soldier," she whispered. "I'm on the pill, and I don't have anything contagious. And I'm willing to bet that you don't, either."

Chase felt his blood begin to churn through his veins. The sensation of Kate's silken limbs entwined with his own, combined with the things she was doing with her tongue, was enough to make him discard his common sense and agree with her.

"I'm clean," he assured her.

"Well, then…" Kate rolled completely toward him and hitched one leg over his, slowly gyrating her hips against his. Her lips trailed a path along his neck and over his collarbone, while her fingers played with the small nubs of his nipples.

Flipping her onto her back, Chase used his knees to spread her thighs wide, and then caught her wrists in his hands, dragging them up over her head and pinning them there.

"I want this to last," he said, dipping his head and kissing her slowly. "But if I let you set the pace, I won't make it another five minutes. Trust me?"

She nodded, her breathing coming in fast pants. "Yes."

"Good," he smiled, "because I've been wanting to do this since I first saw you."

He kissed her slowly, a soft, moist fusing of their lips, before he moved lower, over her neck and upper chest, until he reached her breasts. He took his time, laving each one with his tongue before drawing a nipple into his mouth and sucking hard on it. Kate moaned and writhed beneath him, but Chase didn't release her. He kissed and suckled her other breast until both stood up stiff and rosy and gleaming with moisture. Then, releasing her hands, he eased backwards, dragging his mouth over her rib cage and belly, feeling her muscles contract as he moved lower.

When he reached the apex of her thighs, he skated his tongue along the seam of her thigh, and used one hand to cup her intimately. She sucked in a sharp breath and her hands flew to his wrists, which held her by the hips. Chase stilled, certain she was going to stop him. But after a moment she relaxed her grip on him. Smiling against her skin, he began to gently massage her as he kissed the inside of one thigh, and then the other.

Slowly, he slid one finger through her damp curls to the seam of her sex and gently parted her. She was slippery with arousal, and as his finger swirled over her clitoris, she gave a soft cry of pleasure and her hips jerked.

"That's it," he said approvingly.

He smoothed her curls out of the way, opening her with his fingers so that he could see the small rise of flesh that begged for attention. He glanced up the length of Kate's body and saw that she had raised her head and was watching him with eyes that were hazy with desire. Her hair was messy and spilled over her shoulders in thick waves, and her breasts rose and fell quickly with her agitated breathing. She looked like every fantasy he'd ever had, and his cock was so hard for her that he wasn't sure he'd last long enough to get inside her.

"I want to taste you," he said, his voice rough with need.

"Oh, God."

Taking that as assent, Chase bent his head and flicked his tongue over her, lightly at first, and then with increasing pressure and frequency as she moaned loudly and began rotating her hips beneath his mouth. Her fingers speared his hair, stroking and rubbing his scalp as she writhed beneath him. But when he inserted a finger into her she gasped. He could feel her inner muscles tighten around him, and knew she was close to losing control. He softened his tongue, swirling it around her clitoris as he inserted a second finger and thrust gently. Her hands gripped his head, and when he sucked on her, she cried out sharply and ground her hips against his face. He could feel her contract around his fingers, but didn't stop, drawing her orgasm out until she collapsed back against the pillow and pushed weakly at his head.

"No more," she begged. "I can't take it."

Chase withdrew, coming over her to kiss her deeply and let her taste her own essence on his lips. "Oh, you can," he assured her softly.

Reaching between their bodies, he positioned himself at her entrance and slowly surged forward, filling her. She was incredibly tight, her body closing around him so that he had a moment's certainty that he wouldn't last. Kate made a soft mewling sound, and reached down and cupped his buttocks, urging him closer.

"You feel so good," she breathed.

Oh, man, she had no idea.

He dropped his forehead to hers and paused, struggling for control.

"I want you to come again," he rasped, withdrawing and then sinking back into her in a series of thrusts that caused pressure to build at the base of his spine.

Pulling her knees back, Kate locked her ankles around his hips and wound her arms around his neck, drawing his head down for a kiss that he felt all the way to his soul. He increased his rhythm, driving himself deeper into her slick heat and feeling her inner muscles pulling at him. Kate dragged her mouth from his, her breath coming in fitful pants as she met his thrusts.

"C'mon, darlin'," he coaxed, "come for me."

Sliding a hand between their bodies, he stroked a finger over her, satisfied when he heard her sharp intake of breath and felt a renewed flood of moisture around his cock. But even as she began to tighten around him, he lost his own tenuous grip on his self-control. Overhead, a deafening crack of thunder split the air. With a hoarse shout, Chase came in a blinding rush of pleasure, aware that Kate was right there with him.

They lay together, breathing heavily for several long moments, before Chase had enough awareness to roll to his side and pull Kate into the curve of his shoulder. He pressed a kiss against her hair as the rain beat down on the canvas above their heads.

She traced a lazy pattern over his chest with one finger. "Wow," she said with a half laugh. "That was pretty amazing."

Chase had to agree. He couldn't recall the last time he'd been so turned on by a woman. Now, holding Kate in his arms, he knew that once wouldn't be enough. His rampant imagination conjured up explicit images of all the ways he wanted her, and he felt a little hollow inside at the thought of her leaving Afghanistan and returning to the States. She'd told him that she didn't need promises from him, but a part of him rebelled against having a relationship based solely on sex. For him, at least, it wasn't enough.

Gently pulling himself free, he searched for his clothing in the darkness and got dressed.

"What are you doing?" Kate asked, but her voice was heavy with sleep.

He found her shirt and helped her pull it on, and then laid her flannel pants along the bottom of the cot. She curled on her side, tucking her hands beneath the pillow.

"Try and get some sleep," he advised. "We'll be getting up early to head over to Kandahar to see the last of the concert sites."

"Aren't you going to stay the night?" Reaching out, she caught him by the belt and pulled him closer. "We have hours until morning," she murmured, but her voice was groggy and he could see she was just seconds away from slipping into total oblivion. "You don't have to leave."

Bending down, he gave her a lingering kiss, but when he pulled away, she was already asleep. "That's where you're wrong," he said softly. "If I don't leave now, then I'm totally screwed."

He pulled the sleeping bag over her shoulders and watched as she murmured incoherently and snuggled deeper into its warmth. More than anything, he wanted to slide back into the narrow bed with her and warm her with his own body heat. Chase grabbed his rain poncho and pulled it on. He paused only briefly at the entrance to the tent before he ducked his head and ventured outside, acknowledging that he'd lied to Kate.

He was already screwed.

_10_

IF IT WEREN'T FOR the deliciously tender places on her body, Kate might have imagined Chase's heated lovemaking of the previous night. He had awakened her the following morning by calling her name through the entrance of the tent, but he hadn't come in, telling her she had thirty minutes to get dressed and meet him outside.

The storm had passed during the night, and the morning air was clear. Even at that hour, the sun beat relentlessly down, drying the muddy roads and promising a hot afternoon. Kate packed her bags and went outside to meet Chase. He stood leaning against a Humvee reading his handheld device, while Charity lay at his feet, her tongue lolling. She called his name, feeling inexplicably shy. He looked up and for just an instant she saw the same heat in his eyes that she had seen last night. His gaze raked over her once, before he schooled his expression into one of cool politeness.

"Good morning," he said, pushing away from the vehicle to walk toward her. "Did you sleep well?"

She gave him a meaningful smile. "Like a baby. But what about you? You didn't need to leave."

He paused beside her. "Yeah," he said quietly. "I did.

What happened last night was amazing, Kate, but it can't happen again."

Kate's smile faltered and something twisted painfully in her chest. "You're saying it was a mistake."

Chase's expression was so intense that for a moment Kate thought he was going to pull her into his arms. "No," he said fiercely. "Not a mistake. Just not very smart, considering our situation."

Realistically, she knew he was right. Last night, she'd been convinced that she could have sex with Chase and not have any regrets; that she could have a brief fling without getting emotionally involved. But recalling what it had been like…what *he* had been like, she knew she'd been kidding herself.

Now she forced herself to nod in agreement. "I understand."

A muscle ticked in his jaw and he took a step toward her. For an instant, she thought he might actually kiss her. Instead, he made a small sound of frustration and ducked into her tent, reappearing a moment later with one of her duffel bags in either hand.

"You can use this protective gear for the remainder of your visit," he said gruffly, indicating the bag that contained her flak vest and helmet.

Kate watched as he walked quickly to the Humvee and tossed the equipment into the backseat. She wanted to tell him that he could take the stuff. There wasn't enough protective gear in the world to keep her heart safe from him.

Drawing a deep breath, Kate walked slowly to the Humvee and climbed into the passenger seat, placing her shoulder bag on the floor at her feet. She reminded herself that she was thirty-one years old and she had wanted Chase in her bed. In fact, he'd given her several opportunities to back off, but she'd been determined to have him. He'd been upfront with her about not being able to make any commitments. It wasn't as though he'd misled her. She had no reason to expect that he would suddenly treat her as if they were soul mates.

So why did she feel so miserable?

She watched as he opened the back of the Humvee and let the dog jump in before he climbed into the driver's seat and thrust the vehicle into gear. The roads were thick with mud and washed-out in some places, but the Humvee bounced over the ruts without any problem.

"Here," he said, handing her a paper bag. "I brought you some breakfast. And a coffee."

Kate accepted the bag, expecting to find another Pop-Tart pastry. Instead, she found a hot breakfast sandwich and some fruit inside. The unexpected gesture both touched and confused her.

"Thank you. Did you already eat?"

"What? Oh, yeah. I didn't get any sleep last night after we—" He broke off abruptly. "I was at the dining facility around 4:00 a.m." He glanced at her as he spoke, and twin patches of color rode high on his cheekbones, the only indication that he was thinking about their interlude, and that he wasn't as unfeeling about it as he would have her believe. Suddenly, Kate felt much lighter.

"Oh, well, thanks." She took a bite of the sandwich, realizing for the first time how hungry she was. Then she recalled the helicopter flight from Bagram to Camp Leatherneck, and felt her stomach rebel. "How are we getting to Kandahar?"

A brief smile touched his mouth, but he didn't look at her. "Not by Black Hawk."

"Perfect."

They headed back to the flight line, and Kate looked

across the tarmac to one of the biggest aircraft she had ever seen. Stuffing her sandwich in the bag, she turned to Chase.

"That's a C-17 Globemaster," he said, nodding toward the plane. "One of the Marine expeditionary units is transferring to Kandahar and bringing three Humvees with them, but they have some extra seats, so we're hitching a ride with them."

Kate swallowed hard, reminding herself that at least it wasn't a Black Hawk, and at least they didn't have to drive overland.

Inside the makeshift terminal, Chase took her body armor out of her duffel bag and handed it to her, and then pulled on his own protective gear. Outside, he snapped a long lead to Charity's harness and handed the end to Kate, who watched as he threw their duffel bags on a pallet, alongside dozens of other bags and assorted gear. Several soldiers began rearranging the baggage and then strapped it all down with an enormous net.

A military bus drew to a stop by the pallets. "This is our ride to the plane," Chase said, taking the leash and indicating she should precede him.

"Sir, I'm sorry but the dog isn't allowed on the flight," said a military police officer, stepping forward to prevent Chase from boarding.

Kate thought Chase might try to argue with the man, but instead he pulled a small card out of his pocket and showed it to the officer, who saluted smartly and stepped back. "My mistake, sir. Enjoy your flight."

They managed to get two seats together near the front of the bus, and Charity scooted in under their feet. Kate turned to Chase.

"What was that you showed the soldier?" she asked.

Reaching into his pocket, Chase withdrew an official looking ID card, but this one had a photo of Charity, and beneath it the words *Military Working Dog,* and what Kate guessed was the number of Chase's unit.

"Is she really a working dog?" she asked in surprise. "I thought she was a stray that you rescued."

"She is a stray, but the K-9 unit has been working with her for the past six months." Chase reached down to rub the dog's ears. "Her test scores are higher than most of the other dogs, and her conditioning is exceptional. My guess is that she was a military working dog with the Afghan army and somehow got separated from her handler and ended up in that village. She's not actually part of the K-9 team, but the unit was good enough to give her an ID card so that I can bring her with me when I travel."

"What about when you return to the States?" Kate asked. "Will you be able to take her home with you?"

He shrugged, but Kate didn't miss the regret in his eyes. "Probably not. Officially, she's not on any military roster and there are strict prohibitions about adopting local dogs. I'm fortunate that nobody has objected to my rescuing her, but locally adopted pets aren't allowed to travel in crates owned by the military, nor are they permitted to fly on military flights back to the States."

Kate stared at him. "You're not going to leave her here?"

"I don't want to, but the logistics of transporting her to a commercial airport and getting her on board are complicated. I can't accompany her myself so I'll need to find a sponsor to travel with her and make the right connections. That's difficult and expensive."

They fell silent, and Kate considered what would happen to Charity if she were left in Afghanistan. The K-9 unit might continue to look out for her after Chase left, but eventually they would return to the States, too. What would happen to the dog then?

She watched as dozens of soldiers climbed on board and

shuffled past them, all wearing helmets and flak vests and carrying heavy backpacks. She drew curious glances from most of them, but one look at Chase's face and they moved quickly past. When the bus was filled, it rumbled away from the terminal and across the tarmac, and pulled up alongside the enormous plane. Chase stood up, blocking the aisle so that Kate could slip out in front of him and exit the bus. On the tarmac, she gaped. There was no set of stairs. Instead, the entire back of the aircraft was open and a wide ramp extended onto the runway.

Kate watched as soldiers climbed up the ramp and disappeared into the cavernous interior. She looked questioningly at Chase.

"This way," he said, and with the dog in the lead, he took her elbow to help her up the ramp. At the top, Kate couldn't suppress a gasp.

"Are those Humvees?" she asked in astonishment.

Three of the military vehicles were parked end to end down the center of the plane, secured to the floor with chains and enormous nets. Along the walls were dozens of jump seats, and Kate watched as the soldiers quickly sat down with their backpacks on their knees.

"Sit here," Chase said, and drew Kate down onto a canvas seat with nylon webbing for the back. Chase took the one next to her, and after ensuring that her seatbelt was fastened, tucked her shoulder bag beneath his feet and gave Charity a command to lie down. "Comfortable?"

Kate couldn't imagine anything more uncomfortable, but understood that this was a military flight, designed for efficiency, not comfort. "It's fine," she assured him.

Within fifteen minutes, the rear of the aircraft closed and it began taxiing down the runway. There were no windows in the plane, and the interior was simply an enormous cavern of wiring, buttons and electrical equipment. The three

Humvees were so close that if she stretched out her legs, her feet would touch the wheels, and it was impossible to see anything in the rest of the plane because their sheer size blocked her view. With a sigh, she put her head back and closed her eyes. But she was acutely conscious of the man who sat so close beside her that she could feel his pant leg brush against her own, hear his breathing, and smell the unique scent that she had come to associate with him.

"We'll be at Kandahar in about ninety minutes," Chase said, as the big plane lifted into the air.

She nodded. The roar of the engines effectively prevented any conversation, so she simply closed her eyes again. The throb of the engines lulled her into a state of relaxation, and she passed the time by recalling the events of the previous night in minute detail. It seemed no time had passed, when suddenly the big plane banked steeply and began to descend.

Kate glanced beside her, but Chase had his head tipped back against the seat and his eyes closed. Even in sleep, he was mouthwatering, and she allowed herself the luxury of studying his features. The soldiers closest to her were alert, but not alarmed, so she wasn't worried. The plane continued to bank and descend, though, as if it were riding an invisible roller-coaster track.

"Why is it doing that?" she asked Chase. "It feels like we're spiraling downward."

"We are actually," he said. "The pilot is making what's called a combat landing, descending in a tight spiral to make us less vulnerable to attack."

At the last minute, the plane leveled out and the wheels bounced against the runway. They had landed, and Kate watched as the soldiers began gathering their gear. Tenley and her band would arrive here in just two days, and Kate would be fully occupied with ensuring her sister had everything she needed. Suddenly, Kate wasn't ready for Tenley to intrude. She wasn't ready to slip back into her role of provider, counselor and surrogate parent to her sister. Most importantly, she wasn't ready to give up Chase. She wasn't naive enough to think that once Tenley arrived, she would have any time with him. She knew his focus would shift from escorting her to protecting the entire group of performers. She would have no more opportunity to be alone with him.

Less than a week ago, she never would have thought she'd meet someone in Afghanistan who aroused her enough to sleep with him, knowing that the likelihood of having any kind of meaningful relationship was next to nil. She'd had one-night stands and brief flings before, and they always left her feeling empty and lonely. She'd decided a long time ago that she wouldn't do that to herself again. She deserved better. She wanted the whole package, including the house, the white picket fence and the happy-ever-after. But she also knew that she'd never meet a man like Chase again, and even if she'd never have a repeat of their night together, she had no regrets.

The plane taxied to the terminal, and the rear ramp lowered. With Charity's lead in one hand, Chase carried Kate's bag over his shoulder and took her elbow as they disembarked and waited while the pallets of baggage were removed and placed along the flight line.

Fifteen minutes later, they were in the backseat of another Humvee, with two soldiers up front. Chase helped Kate remove her protective gear and stowed it away in the duffel bag, before removing his own.

"We won't need to wear this unless the sirens go off," he said. "Let's get you settled and go get something to eat, and then I'll bring you over to the concert site. This is an enormous base, and you'll have semi-private housing here."

"How many troops are here?" Kate asked, but just looking out the window of the Humvee told her that this was no forward operating base.

"There are more than twenty thousand coalition troops stationed here, and hundreds of civilian contractors." He slanted her an amused look. "There's even a boardwalk with some American fast-food restaurants and a bazaar of sorts where vendors sell local goods. We could walk over there and grab a bite."

Looking out the window, she noticed that the air was hazy and had a yellowish tinge to it.

"Is this smog of some kind?" she asked, having seen something similar in California.

"No, ma'am," replied the driver. "What you're seeing is dust. The air is always full of it, even indoors."

They drove in silence for several more minutes, and Kate was astonished at the sheer size of the base. "I expect the USO brings a lot of entertainers here, given how big the place is," she commented.

"I expect so," said Chase. "You're the first celebrity assignment I've had, and I spend so much time in the field or at the remote operating bases that I don't usually catch any performances. At any rate, the local USO is accustomed to providing accommodations for visiting celebrities and dignitaries, so I think you'll find the conditions here are much better than at Bagram or Camp Leatherneck."

In other words, there was no chance that she would end up alone in a tent where she would need to rely on Chase to watch over her. Even if she did, there was little likelihood that she would get a repeat performance of the previous night.

Leaning forward, Chase spoke quietly to the driver, directing him. Kate was amazed at the number of soldiers, military vehicles and buildings that they passed. They had been driving for fifteen minutes and still had not reached their destination. The Humvee pulled up in front of a long row of modified trailers, each reinforced with sandbags. They were housing units, Kate realized, nearly identical to Chase's CHU back on Bagram.

"Is this it?" she asked, as Chase pulled her luggage out of the back and commanded Charity to stay.

"This is where you'll be housed with Tenley," Chase confirmed. "This entire row is reserved by the USO. They don't have any empty units at the moment, but there are two female actors in one of the trailers, and they have an extra bunk bed that the USO said you and your sister can use."

"That's great," Kate said, meaning it. She had no desire to sleep in a tent by herself, especially now that Chase wouldn't be spending the night with her. "Do you know who the women are?"

Chase shrugged. "I don't, sorry."

Inside the unit, Chase dropped her bags on the floor by the nearest set of bunk beds. Kate looked around curiously. There was one large bedroom in the front, with a bunk bed against either wall and a sofa under the front window. The two bottom bunks were obviously occupied, with overnight bags sitting on top of the blankets, and a pair of shoes under each bed. The interior of the unit was unpainted plywood, and someone had tried to make the place more cheerful by hanging posters on the wall.

Kate turned to Chase. "How long will the other two women be here?"

Chase leaned against the open door frame. "They're leaving tomorrow on the return flight that your sister and the other performers are arriving on. Why? Would it be a problem if they were staying?"

"No," she assured him. "This will work out beautifully. Where will you be?"

He paused, halfway to the door. "In a barracks hut. You have my beeper. I'll be close by."

Kate chewed her bottom lip, understanding that there would be no opportunity for them to be together tonight. Still, she couldn't just let him walk away, at least not without trying to convince him that last night meant something to her, and that if he was willing, they could have some kind of relationship. She knew that Chase would be here in Afghanistan for another six months, but that didn't matter to her. She'd been alone for a long time. Waiting six months for someone like Chase would be no hardship—if he agreed.

"Chase," she called softly, before he could leave. "Wait."

He turned in the doorway, and for an instant she saw an expression in his eyes—a combination of agony and hope—that gave her courage. "What is it?" he asked, glancing toward the Humvee, where the two soldiers sat waiting for them.

"Chase…about last night…I know you think it was a mistake, but you're wrong."

Something twisted in his face as he looked back at her. "Kate. Last night was…well, it was incredible. Would I like a repeat performance? Damned straight." He muttered a curse beneath his breath and raked a hand over his hair. "But Jesus, Kate, there's no future in it, and I can't—I can't—" He broke off and turned to stare out the door toward the street, where vehicles drove past and several soldiers walked by.

Kate stared at his rigid back, and then took a step toward him, but didn't dare touch him. "What?" she asked softly. "What can't you do, Chase?"

He turned around and Kate took an involuntary step backwards at the expression on his face. "I can't be around you without wanting you. It took all my strength to leave you last night, but it can't happen again, Kate. It's not fair to you. Or to me."

"Chase, I know you didn't want to escort me around, and that you have more important issues on your mind—" He started to interrupt and she held up a hand to forestall him. "But last night meant something to me. And I think it meant something to you, too."

Chase made a growling sound of frustration. "It doesn't matter if it meant something to me or not. Tomorrow your focus will shift to your sister, which is great. That's your job. But five days later, you'll be gone."

Kate took a step toward him. "Then we shouldn't waste any time."

Reaching out, she put a hand along the side of his jaw and reached up to press a lingering kiss against his mouth. He resisted for several seconds, and then with a groan, his arms came around her, and he lowered his head, covering her mouth with his own. Kicking the door shut, he walked her backward until the backs of her knees bumped against the sofa and she sat down. He followed, pushing her against the cushions, his lips still fused to hers.

Kate welcomed him, winding her arms around his neck and pulling him down on top of her. He kissed her deeply, spearing his hands into her hair.

"God, you taste good," he muttered against her lips. "I still think this is a bad idea, but I have no willpower where you're concerned."

Kate smiled against his face. "And here I was beginning to think that you might not like me."

Chase groaned, and planting another kiss on her mouth, pulled her with him to a sitting position. "My problem has nothing to do with not liking you, and everything to do with liking you too much," he growled.

"Then find a way for us to be together tonight," she

breathed, searching his eyes. "If this is the last night we have alone before I go home, spend it with me. This base is huge. There must be somewhere we can go to be alone. You know you want to."

He gave her a tolerant look and stood up, rubbing a hand across the back of his neck. "Jesus, Kate, it has nothing to do with what I want or don't want to do. Last night was different. We were in the middle of a monsoon and there was no chance that anyone was going to catch us together in that tent. But things are different here. Neither of us has our own unit, and even if there was a place that we could go, you can be sure that someone else will already have found it."

Kate nodded. "Okay. I would never want to get you in trouble. I just want to spend time with you before I leave."

"I want that, too, believe me." He glanced out the window at the waiting Humvee. "But if we don't make an appearance within the next minute, those soldiers are going to start getting ideas about what we're doing in here. In fact, I'm pretty sure they saw you kiss me before I shut the door."

"Oh." Kate glanced toward the closed door. "Then we should definitely get outside before your reputation is completely ruined."

Chase gave a rueful laugh. "Too late, darlin'. I think my reputation was destroyed the moment I laid eyes on you. I haven't been able to focus on anything but you since I first saw you standing in the terminal at Bagram."

"Well, considering I'm your current assignment, you *should* be focused on me."

"Yeah, well, let's get back to the vehicle before I become so focused on you that I forget everything else." He opened the door and placed a hand at the small of her back, indicating she should precede him.

As she climbed into the backseat, Kate didn't miss the knowing look the two soldiers gave each other before they stoically fixed their attention straight ahead. But as Chase climbed in beside her, he covered her hand with his own and squeezed her fingers, letting her know that even though he might be on duty, he no longer considered her to be his duty.

11

AFTER A LONG day of visiting the concert sites, meeting with
the USO representatives, and exploring the small bazaar
at the center of the base, Kate returned to her housing unit
after dinner to find it occupied by her two roommates. Both
women were in their forties, and welcomed Kate with a mug
of hot tea brewed in an electric kettle that sat on the small
side table. The women played characters on a popular sitcom. Kate knew she should recognize them, but she rarely
watched television, preferring movies or books when she
had any spare time.

"So, what brings a pretty young thing like you out here
all by yourself?" asked Jessica Cochran.

"You have to ask?" Marion O'Connell gave a suggestive
wink. "Have you looked around here? There are literally
hundreds of good-looking, hard-bodied young men running
around. I'll tell you what. If I was as young and attractive
as Kate, I'd be looking for excuses to come over here on a
regular basis!"

Kate laughed. "Well, I agree that some of the guys are
pretty amazing, but I'm hoping this will be my first and
last visit."

"The USO said you're a singer?" asked Jessica, sipping her tea.

"Not me," Kate said quickly. "I'm Tenley Miles's publicist. I came over a few days early just to check things out and make sure everything's ready for her. She flies in tomorrow."

"Tenley Miles?" Marion's face lit up with recognition. "My niece adores her. But wasn't she involved in some recent scandal?"

Kate took a gulp of hot tea, hoping to avoid answering, but Marion was going through her mental Rolodex of celebrity scandals until finally her expression registered recognition.

"I know," Marion declared in triumph. "She made some disparaging remarks about the military. I'm surprised she wants to come over here and entertain the troops, considering some of the negative things she had to say."

"Yes, well that's why we decided to come," Kate admitted. "Tenley's only eighteen and she can be impulsive. She doesn't really mean what she said, and we're hoping that this tour will help to demonstrate that."

Jessica shook her head and made a tsking sound. "I don't know. You can do a lot of stupid stuff, but when you start maligning our men and women in uniform, that can be a tough one to recover from."

Kate set her cup down. "I think I'll head over into the shower before it gets too late."

"That's a great idea," Marion said, putting her own teacup aside. "I hate the thought of walking all that way by myself."

"How far is it?" Kate asked. She had been looking forward to calling Chase on his beeper so that he could walk with her.

"It's about a ten minute hike," Jessica replied, gathering her gear together.

Realizing she had no valid reason to call Chase, Kate

reluctantly pulled her toiletries out of her duffel bag, along with a clean change of clothes. It was still light outside as they set off. At the end of the road, they turned left and continued along another row of housing units, until Kate saw the shower facilities in the distance. They passed groups of soldiers, who nodded politely to them, and twice they had to stop so that Marion and Jessica could sign autographs.

While Kate waited for them, she noticed a female soldier walk past and found herself staring, mainly because she was so tall. Kate guessed the woman was close to six feet, but she walked with a feminine, athletic grace. Rather than the typical camouflage uniform, she wore a green flight suit, and something about her struck Kate as familiar. As the woman drew closer, she looked at Kate and smiled.

Kate raised a hand in greeting, recognizing the woman as the Black Hawk pilot who had flown both her and Chase from Bagram Air Base to Camp Leatherneck. She watched as Captain Larson stopped outside one of the housing units and fitted a key into the door, opening it and disappearing inside. Kate frowned, wondering if Chase knew that she was at Kandahar. She recalled the way the other woman had looked at Chase when they had boarded the helicopter, making her suspect they might be involved. She couldn't blame the other woman for ogling Chase; he was pretty hot. But she knew she wouldn't be the one telling him that Captain Larson was less than a stone's throw away.

"Are you okay, hon?"

Jessica was watching Kate with a mixture of concern and curiosity.

"I'm fine," she assured the older woman. "I thought I saw someone I knew, but I was wrong."

"Well let's get going. I want to be back in our own little house before it gets dark."

Jessica was right; daylight was disappearing, and the temperatures was dropping. But the showers were private and hot, and Kate took her time under the steaming spray until she could hear the other women in the outer changing area.

Kate quickly dried herself off and got dressed, wrapping a towel around her wet hair for the walk back. When they left the shower facilities, the sun had set and the sky was beginning to darken. Kate listened to Marion and Jessica's chatter, mostly gossip about the sitcom and who they thought would get the ax next.

As they turned the corner to the street where Captain Larson's housing unit was located, Kate saw a familiar figure walking toward them. *Chase.* Her pulse kicked into overdrive in anticipation and her hand flew self-consciously to the towel wrapped around her head. He was still more than fifty feet away, and hadn't yet seen her and her companions rounding the corner.

She couldn't prevent a smile, and was about to call his name when he suddenly stopped and knocked lightly on Captain Larson's door. Kate stopped, too, stunned when the pilot opened for him. Unaware that they had an audience, Captain Larson reached up and planted a lingering kiss on Chase's mouth, before she drew him inside and closed the door quickly behind him. Although the shade in the small window was pulled down, Kate saw a shadow pass in front of it, and then another. But when the two shadows merged, there was no doubt in her mind what was happening behind that closed door, and for a moment she thought she might actually be ill.

She continued walking, her eyes glued to the silhouette of the embracing couple. As she drew alongside the unit, Kate heard the distinct sound of a man's voice, followed by Captain Larson's low, throaty laugh.

Both Jessica and Marion gave each other knowing looks, and Kate hoped the fading light disguised her own stricken expression. It took all her strength not to race up to the door and wrench it open.

Instead, she tipped her chin up, aware that her breathing was coming in quick, shallow pants. Her throat felt tight and her chest ached. What had he said to her just hours earlier? That he had no willpower where she was concerned? It seemed he had no willpower where Captain Larson was concerned, either. She recalled his agonized words as he'd turned away from her in the housing unit. *There's no future in it, and I can't—I can't—*

It all made sense to Kate now.

The reason there was no future in it was because he was already committed—to Captain Larson. She nearly groaned aloud. He'd tried to tell her that they had no chance for a relationship, and she hadn't listened. But he hadn't put up much resistance, and he certainly hadn't seemed overly concerned about his pilot girlfriend when he'd spent the night with Kate in her tent.

She was such an idiot. When would she ever learn?

They reached their housing unit, and Kate made a pretense of being interested in the women's conversation until she thought she might scream.

"You know, I have a splitting headache," she fibbed. "Would you mind if I just climbed into my bunk and went to bed?"

"Oh, honey," Marion said in sympathy, "you go right ahead. In fact, we'll go to bed, too, and then the light won't disturb you."

"Oh, no," Kate protested. "Please don't do that on my account. Besides, I overheard you telling Jessica how much you were looking forward to another cup of tea, so you should have one. I promise you, I'm so tired that nothing will disturb me."

After convincing the two women to have their tea, Kate

climbed up into the top bunk and pulled the blankets over her shoulders, turning her face toward the wall. She replayed the scene over and over again in her mind. At one point, she'd nearly convinced herself that it wasn't Chase she'd seen; it had been another soldier who'd merely resembled him. But when Captain Larson had opened the door, the interior light had clearly revealed his face. There was no doubt in her mind that it had been Chase. She still couldn't believe how well he'd hidden his feelings for the pilot when they'd flown in her helicopter. Captain Larson hadn't hidden her interest in Chase, but he had been all business.

Kate lay curled on her side and determined that he would never know how much he'd hurt her. If he'd been honest with her and had just told her that he was already involved with someone else, she would have backed off. But he hadn't. He'd taken full advantage of everything she'd offered. She'd been foolish enough to sleep with him, but it wouldn't happen again. She deserved better. Tomorrow, she thought fiercely, things would change. She would be all business, and nothing Chase said or did would break through the protective barrier she was erecting around her heart.

CHASE SPENT THE NIGHT at the Special Ops headquarters office on base. He and the special-operations teams stationed at Kandahar performed many joint missions, and one of them was the hunt and capture of Al-Azir. The previously issued stand-down order was still in effect, but that didn't prevent him and his team of commandos from gathering intelligence and planning their next move. Chase and the other team members spent hours analyzing satellite photos and images taken from their drone aircraft, which indicated a large group of men had left the village where Al-Azir had been hiding, and had moved into the nearby mountains.

Chase knew the area was riddled with caves, and that

Al Azir and his men could successfully hide out there for months. But at least they had an idea where he had fled to, and once the stand-down order was lifted, his team would resume their hunt for him.

Having gotten less than four hours of sleep on a cot in the back room of the operations shack, Chase woke up at dawn and made his way to the showers. He passed the housing unit where Kate was staying, and his footsteps slowed. Had she been in there alone, nothing would have prevented him from going inside and climbing into her bunk with her. He desperately wanted to be with her again, and he'd known a keen sense of frustration when the USO personnel had told him that she would not have her own housing unit while at Kandahar. With her sister arriving that morning, there would be no opportunity for them to be alone again before she returned to the States. Reluctantly, he continued past Kate's unit toward the showers. He was lost in his own thoughts and didn't see the soldier who stepped quietly out of a housing unit on his left, until he heard his name called.

"Chase!"

He stopped and turned, surprised to see his brother walking swiftly toward him. "Hey, I was wondering if I might see you here," he said, grabbing his brother's hand and pulling him into a swift, hard hug. "I thought you might be up at Kabul."

They drew apart, and Chase stared at his brother's face, identical to his own except for the perpetual cocky grin.

"I was," Chance grinned, "but they sent us down here yesterday to provide cover for a VIP visit."

Major Chance Rawlins was an Apache helicopter pilot, permanently stationed at Bagram Air Base, although his missions frequently took him to the other bases in Afghanistan. He and Captain Jenna Larson had had a brief fling several months earlier, when they'd both been assigned to

Fort Bragg in North Carolina. But when she'd turned up in Afghanistan, Chance had been quick to turn their relationship into something a little more permanent. Now the two were committed to each other.

Chase glanced from his brother to the housing unit he had just left, and felt a smile tug at his mouth. "I take it you didn't stay alone last night?"

Chance's eyes gleamed. "Are you kidding? How often are Jenna and I ever on the same base? Just try keeping me away from her."

"Yeah, well, don't get caught."

His brother sobered. "She's returning to the States in just a few weeks, while I'll be over here for another six months. Man, that's going to suck."

Chase felt his brother's pain, he really did. Just the thought of Kate leaving made his chest feel tight. He hadn't really explored his feelings for Kate, but he knew he wasn't ready to say goodbye to her. Not by a long shot.

"How long are you going to be at Kandahar?" he asked.

Chance shrugged. "I'm scheduled to escort a VIP to Bagram tomorrow, but Jenna left around 4:00 a.m. this morning for the Kalagush region."

Captain Larson's primary mission was to transport troops and personnel from one base to another, and although she was assigned to Kandahar, her missions took her to every base in Afghanistan, including some of the remote operating bases. She usually flew in tandem with another Black Hawk, and sometimes with an Apache escort, as well.

"So I take it you're not flying escort with her?"

Chance shook his head. "No such luck, I'm afraid." Reaching out, he gave Chase's shoulder a friendly punch. "But what the hell are you doing here? Jenna said she gave you a lift from Bagram to Camp Leatherneck, but I didn't know you were going to be here at Kandahar." His grin widened. "Not that I would have changed my plans with her to come and see you, of course. So why are you here?"

"The Pentagon has temporarily halted all special-operations missions," Chase said grimly.

"Ah," Chance replied. "I heard an airstrike went wrong about thirty miles from here last week. Is that why you're here? Part of the investigation?"

Chase gave a snort. "Hardly. I was yanked out of the field and given a personal security assignment."

"Really?" His brother's face registered interest. "Anyone good?"

Oh, yeah.

Chase shrugged. "Some teenaged country singer and her publicist. Part of the big Independence Day concert tour that begins tonight."

"Oh, man. I'm sorry, bro. I know how you hate those assignments."

"Yeah." His voice was noncommittal. He hated the assignment so much that he couldn't wait to get showered and dressed and over to Kate's housing unit to see her. But he wouldn't tell his brother just how soft he'd become. Chance would have a field day if he knew his tough-as-nails, all-business brother had violated even one rule for the sake of a woman.

To his surprise, Chance burst out laughing.

"What?" he demanded.

"Man, you are so freaking transparent," Chance said, still laughing. "Jenna told me all about your *assignment*. A pretty, curvy brunette who looked like she wanted to kill Jenna for just talking with you." He gave Chase a knowing look. "You dog. You put the moves on her, didn't you? C'mon, you can fool some people with your badass attitude, but not me, bro. I can see the truth. It's written all over your face. You *like* this woman."

He said it as a statement of fact, and not a question. But he was right; Chase had never been able to keep a secret from his twin and there was no point in even trying.

He blew out a hard breath. "Jesus, Chance, I've been with her all of three days and she's so deep under my skin…" He scrubbed a hand over his hair. "But her client, the singer, flies in today, so it's not like we're going to have any chance to be alone again. And then in five more days, she leaves."

Chance considered him for a long moment. "Okay, I tell you what. Jenna already left. She'll be gone for at least a week. I was going to crash in her unit tonight, but I can always go bunk with the itinerant pilots. Why don't you and your lady friend use her place tonight? Hell, use it for as long as you're going to be here. I know Jenna won't mind."

The offer was so tempting that Chase was half inclined to retrieve Kate right then and drag her over to Captain Larson's housing unit just so he could be alone with her. He ached to feel her body pressed against his own, and needed to hear her small cries of pleasure as he made love to her. He couldn't remember the last time he'd been so eager to spend time with a woman.

Now he shook his brother's hand. "Thanks. I appreciate the offer."

"You bet. Look, I have to run, but it was great to see you."

"You, too," Chase said, and gave Chance the key to Captain Larson's unit. "You take care of yourself, okay?"

He watched as Chance jogged away, then continued walking to the showers feeling lighter and more hopeful. He would be with Kate again that night, even if it was just for a few hours. He'd find someone to keep an eye on Kate's sister for the time that they would be away from her.

Whistling softly under his breath, he thought the coming day might just be the best one he'd spent in Afghanistan so far.

12

PULLING ON HER SHOES, Kate decided this was going to be the worst day of her life. Even the prospect of seeing Tenley again didn't raise her spirits. If anything, she felt exhausted at the idea of looking after her sister for the next several days. She just wanted the tour to be over and to return to the States. She'd spent most of the night lying in her bed thinking about her own future. One that didn't include Major Chase Rawlins. Just the thought of him brought a painful lump to her chest.

Once the tour was over, she would return to Nashville with Tenley, but she'd decided that it was time to find her own place to live. She would continue to act as Tenley's publicist, since it was clear that her sister needed her, but there was no reason for them to continue to live together. And then perhaps, in a couple of years, she could persuade Tenley to find another publicist. As for Chase...she would chalk it up as a learning experience and not make the same mistake again.

She gave her laces a hard yank. Did Captain Larson have any idea that Chase wasn't faithful to her? Maybe they had an open relationship. Kate didn't know and didn't care; she only knew that she could never share Chase with another woman. She had a vivid image of him making love to the pilot, and her stomach twisted.

"You okay, hon?"

Kate jerked her head up to see Jessica standing in the open door of the housing unit, watching her closely. She nodded and finished tying her other shoe. "Never better. My client comes in today and we can finally get this show on the road. I'm just anxious to get this over with so I can go home."

"Amen," Jessica said, leaving the door open as she came in. "We missed you at breakfast this morning, but I brought you a nice pastry." She held out the offering, neatly folded in a white napkin. "Full of lemon custard. Looks delicious."

Kate forced a smile and sat up straight on the small sofa. "Thank you, that was very thoughtful."

"Oh, no bother at all," Jessica replied, sitting down on the lower bunk, across from Kate. "So how are you really doing? You look a little peaked to me."

Kate waved a dismissive hand. "No, I'm fine, really. Like I said, I'm just looking forward to going home." She turned to pick up her watch from the side table. "I've decided that as much as I respect and admire what the troops are doing over here, if I never see another uniform in my life, it will be too soon. *You* might think they're all hotties, but from what I can tell of the ones I've met, they're just walking testosterone in combat boots."

The masculine clearing of a throat had her turning guiltily toward the door, where Chase's broad shoulders nearly blocked the daylight. He looked so strong and commanding in his uniform and his sunglasses that for a moment Kate's heart leaped. Then the scene from the previous night came rushing back, and she determinedly looked away.

"Hmm," murmured Jessica with a knowing smile. "You were saying?"

Kate stood up, but didn't apologize, despite the fact she knew that Chase had overheard her disparaging remarks.

"Good morning," she said, picking up her shoulder bag.

The sunlight behind him cast his face in shadow, and with his sunglasses on, it was impossible to read his expression. "Good morning," he said carefully. "If you're ready, we can head over to the concert site and check it out. Your client's flight isn't due to arrive for another two hours, which leaves us plenty of time."

"Fine," she said coolly. She turned to Jessica and Marion. "It was really nice meeting both of you. Maybe I'll see you over at the flight line, but in case I don't, have a safe trip back to the States."

Marion gave her a hug. "Just remember that most guys are jerks," she whispered in Kate's ear. "Don't be too hard on him."

Kate gave her a stiff smile and pulled away.

"Now you listen to me," Jessica whispered, as she hugged Kate. "I don't know who this guy is, but I do know that he isn't deserving of a second look from you. I saw what he was up to last night, too, so don't you give him the time of day."

Pulling away, Kate smiled at both women and turned to Chase. He jerked his sunglasses off and frowned, his sharp gaze sweeping her from head to toe and missing nothing.

"Everything okay?" he asked as they walked toward the Humvee that waited for them. "You have shadows under your eyes. Didn't you sleep?"

"Not really," she said stiffly. "Looks like you didn't get much sleep, either."

"I managed to grab a couple of hours."

Kate barely suppressed a disdainful snort. She didn't want to think about what Chase had been doing that prevented him from sleeping, and she certainly didn't want him to know that she had witnessed him kissing Captain Larson.

He was the Special Ops guy; let him figure out why she was in a bitchy mood this morning.

They rode in silence for several long minutes. She could sense his puzzlement and his concern, but refused to look over at him, or speak.

"Are you sure everything is okay?" he finally asked. "Because if there's anything you need to talk about, I'm here for you." His voice was so warm and compassionate that Kate's resolve almost wavered.

Almost.

Instead, she turned and gave Chase a level look, despite the fact her heart was hammering inside her chest. "I'm fine. Really."

"You know," he mused, "I grew up on a ranch in Texas, and while it was just my parents and me and my brother, my uncle owned the neighboring ranch. He had five daughters. *Five.* Those girls spent as much time on our ranch as they did on their own, and I became pretty good at interpreting their moods."

Kate gave him a tolerant look. "So?"

"So I know that when a woman says things like 'I'm fine,' and 'Really,' what she's actually saying is 'Screw you, I'm pissed at you,' and 'Leave me alone.'"

Kate couldn't prevent her quick smile, but then she sobered. "Well then, if you've broken the code, you should heed the hidden message."

"What's going on, Kate? You can tell me anything."

Kate gave a disdainful laugh and turned her attention out the window. "Thanks, but I don't think so. Why don't we just go look at the site, okay?"

She sensed his frustration, but he was nothing if not intuitive, and thankfully he didn't pursue the topic. They drove in silence after that, until they arrived at an enormous parade field with a covered stage at the far end. Both the field and the stage swarmed with soldiers and technicians who were busy running electrical cables and wires, and setting up the amplifiers and speakers. A gigantic American flag provided the backdrop for the performers, and Kate watched as the lighting specialists flicked through all of the possible combinations.

"Wow," she said, climbing out of the Humvee.

She walked toward the stage, taking note of the work being performed all around her. Along the perimeter of the parade field, food tents had been set up and Kate watched as the soldiers dragged out long tables and prepared enormous grills for what would surely be thousands of burgers and hot dogs over the course of the next two days and nights.

"This is amazing," she said, turning to Chase. "You really get the sense that these guys have done this before."

"They have," Chase assured her. "This is the biggest base in Afghanistan, and hundreds of performers come through here. C'mon, I'll show you where your client will be able to relax when she's waiting to go onstage."

He took her elbow in a gesture that should have been impersonal, but Kate couldn't prevent herself from stiffening at the contact, and then pulling her arm away. She heard Chase mutter a curse and sensed that he wanted to confront her, but there was no way she could let him do that. She didn't feel strong enough to get into it with him about Captain Larson, and she absolutely did not want him to see how much it hurt her that he could go from her bed to another woman's bed.

Ignoring his frustration, she took her time examining the stage and the equipment preparations. She had been around concert performances for most of her life, first with her mother and then with Tenley. Watching the setup was as natural to her as breathing. When she had seen enough, she followed Chase into the building directly behind the stage. The USO had converted a dining facility into a large lounge area, with sofas and food stations, and just about everything the performers could want to either relax or practice before going onstage. There were several small rooms off to the side where they could even catch a quick nap.

Chase came to stand beside her. "The USO has arranged to have massage chairs set up for the performers, and there are some rooms in the back where they can warm up, if they choose to."

Kate nodded, satisfied with everything she saw. "What time is the first performance?"

Chase pulled a small notepad out of a pocket on his camo pants and quickly scanned through it. "The first performance is tonight, but it's more of a warm-up, with each group only doing one or two songs. Tomorrow, two groups will each perform three sets during the Independence Day barbecue while the other groups do photo signings and meet and greets. The real show begins early tomorrow evening, with all the groups performing well into the night."

"So when will Tenley go onstage?"

"I don't have the order of the performances. If you'd like, we can talk to the USO. They'll have that information."

"I know where they're located," Kate said quickly. "You don't need to come with me."

Chase looked swiftly around, then caught Kate by the wrist and all but dragged her to one of the anterooms. He pushed her up against a wall and trapped her there with a hand on either side of her head. She would have to duck beneath his arm in order to escape, but she could see by the grim expression on his face that even if she succeeded, she wouldn't get very far.

"What the hell is going on, Kate? When I left you last night, everything seemed fine, and then this morning you begin treating me as if I'm a goddamned leper." His eyes flashed. "Have I done something to offend you? Tell me what it is, so I can least try to fix it."

Kate swallowed hard. She'd known he wouldn't let her behavior go unnoticed, but she hesitated to tell him why she was angry. Too many times, her relationships had ended because the guy she'd been involved with had chosen to leave. She'd had no choice and hadn't been given an opportunity to try to correct the issue. She found she couldn't do the same thing to Chase without giving him the satisfaction of an explanation. She knew from experience what that was like, and it sucked.

Raising her chin, she met his eyes squarely. She could see the frustration and concern in their green depths, and something else, too. Heat. He wanted to kiss her, and the knowledge both thrilled and infuriated her, providing her with the courage to speak.

"I saw you last night," she blurted. "On my way back from the women's showers."

He cocked his head and looked expectantly at her. "So...? Why didn't you let me know? I thought we had an agreement that you wouldn't walk to the showers alone. You should have called me."

Kate compressed her lips and stared mutely at him, willing him to come clean with her, and not continue this farce of pretending he had no idea what she was talking about.

"I didn't call your name because it was clear to me that you were preoccupied with *kissing Captain Larson*." She shoved angrily at his chest, but he didn't budge. "I saw you, Chase! I know you spent the night with her. The least you could have done is told me you were already involved with someone. Do you know how that makes me feel? Do you?"

To her astonishment, he didn't look guilty or ashamed at having been caught. In fact, his green eyes were alight with what might have been amusement and relief.

"Tell me how it made you feel," he said softly, crowding her with his body. "I want to know."

Kate couldn't believe he could be that cruel. His demand was equivalent to emotional torture. Lifting her chin, she glared at him.

"You want to know how it made me feel? Fine, let me tell you. It made me feel angry. And hurt. And stupid for having believed that you wanted me. And so mad that it took all my strength not to go in after you and scratch that woman's eyes out!" She stared at Chase, her breathing coming in aggravated gasps. "There, are you happy now? I wasn't even going to tell you that I saw you. I was just going to leave—go back to the States and pretend I never met you. But you—you—"

She made a sound of extreme frustration and tried to break free, but he clamped his hands on her upper arms and hauled her up against his chest.

"Katie," he said softly, searching her eyes, "do you really think I could so much as look at another woman after being with you? Do you really have such a low opinion of me?"

"I. Saw. You." The words came out through gritted teeth.

He considered her for a brief moment, then caught her by the hand and dragged her out of the room. "I want to show you something," he said over his shoulder. "Then, if you still want to hate me, you can."

Kate hung back, not wanting to go anywhere with him, but resistance was futile. He hauled her effortlessly in his wake across the parade field and back to the waiting Humvee. "No, wait!" she protested. "Where you taking me?"

"You'll see," he said grimly, and thrust her into the back seat, before climbing in beside her. "Take us to the flight-operations shack," he said, leaning forward to speak to the driver.

Kate stared at him in horror. "Oh, no," she said, reaching

for the door handle. "There is no way I am going to have a face-off with Captain Larson."

But Chase leaned across her body and covered her hand with his own before she could open the door and jump out. He searched her eyes, and what she saw in their depths made her pause. "Trust me, Kate, okay?" His voice was low and compelling. "Just give me this, and I promise I won't ask anything more from you."

Slowly, she released the door handle and sat back, still staring at him. "Okay," she muttered.

Satisfied, he resumed his position beside her, and they drove in silence across the base to the flight line. But instead of pulling up to the terminal, the Humvee drove to a separate building with a sign over the door that read Flight Operations.

Kate's heart was pounding so hard, she thought for sure that Chase must hear it, but he seemed too intent on getting her into the building to notice. Inside, three soldiers sat in a reception area, fielding phone calls and monitoring computers. The first soldier looked up, his gaze flicking from Chase to Kate, and then back again. If he thought it unusual that Chase was dragging a civilian female into the flight-operations center, he was too well-trained to let it show.

"The pilots are in the conference room," he said without preamble.

"Thanks," Chase muttered, and pulled Kate along a corridor until they reached a closed door. Without knocking, Chase opened it just enough to poke his head inside. "Sorry for the interruption. Can I speak with you privately? Now?"

Kate couldn't see who he directed his question to, but knew it was Captain Larson. Drawing a deep breath, she mentally steeled herself to face the pilot, vowing that she would never speak to Chase again for putting her through this humiliation. But it wasn't a female pilot who came out of the conference room.

Kate stared in dismay at the tall, broad-shouldered man who stepped into the corridor and closed the door carefully behind him. He wore an army-green flight suit with the US flag on one shoulder and an insignia patch on the other. Kate gaped at him, and her eyes dropped to the name patch on the front of his uniform. *Rawlins*.

"Oh, my God," she breathed.

She stared at him, registering the translucent green eyes, alight with interest, the square jaw and sensuous, smiling mouth and the deep dimples in each cheek. Like Chase's, his brown hair was cropped close to his head, and Kate could see the bronze and gold glints in the short strands. He was identical, in every way, to Chase. Except that where Chase's expression was grim and unsmiling, this man seemed to have a perpetual glint of devilment in his eyes. Now he looked from Kate to Chase.

"Ah," he said meaningfully and with great relish. "This has a distinct déjà vu feel to it."

"Kate," Chase said, "I'd like you to meet my brother—my *twin* brother—Chance Rawlins. He arrived yesterday morning from Bagram Air Base. He's an Apache helicopter pilot."

Chance gave her a winning smile. "I suspect that the reason you're here is because you saw me with a certain female pilot and mistakenly believed I was Chase."

Feeling light-headed, Kate threw out a hand to steady herself, but Chase was already there, putting an arm around her back and supporting her. "Are you okay?"

"I'm just…astonished," she finally admitted, leaning against Chase. "I had no idea…you said you had a brother, but you didn't tell me you were *twins*." She passed a hand over her eyes. "I feel like such an idiot."

"Don't," Chance said, still grinning. "Not so long ago,

Jenna—Captain Larson—actually propositioned Chase, believing he was me. Don't worry, he turned her down. So this is all very cathartic for me. I don't often get to see my brother in this situation."

"Careful," Chase warned. He turned to Kate. "Are we okay? Are we good?"

Something loosened and then broke free in Kate's chest, and she felt her throat tighten with emotion. *Chase hadn't cheated on her.* Unable to speak, she just nodded.

"Okay, let's get out of here," he said. "Thanks for clearing things up, bro."

"My pleasure," Chance replied, his hand on the doorknob. "Oh, and don't forget my offer. Something tells me you're going to need it."

Chase steered her out of the building and over to the Humvee. "Are you sure you're okay?" he asked.

Kate looked up at him, not hiding anything. "I'm more than okay," she assured him, smiling. "I didn't get any sleep last night. I just kept replaying what I'd seen over and over again in my head until I thought I was going to lose my mind." She waved a hand dismissively. "I'm such an idiot, because it's not like I have any claim on you, right? You made it clear that you couldn't make any promises to me, and you're free to do what you want."

Chase frowned and blew out a hard breath. "Look, Kate, I said a lot of stupid things. When I said I couldn't do this, I only meant that it wouldn't be fair to ask you to wait for me. I hope you don't really believe that I'm capable of leaving your bed to climb in with another woman?"

It wouldn't be fair to ask you to wait for me.

The words reverberated through Kate's head. Had he really considered asking her to wait for him? Her heart lodged somewhere in her throat as she searched his eyes.

"No," she finally said. "I think you have more integrity and class than that."

He gave her a wry smile. "Thanks." He hesitated, and when he finally spoke, his words were carefully measured, but Kate didn't miss the intensity behind them. "Listen, I know this will probably seem crass, considering what you just went through, but Captain Larson is gone for the next few days and we've been offered a chance to use her housing unit. If you want to, that is. I could arrange for a security detail to watch over your sister, if that's a concern. But it's totally up to you, and I'll understand if you can't."

Just the thought of spending another night with Chase was enough to send her blood churning through her veins in anticipation. Did she want to be with him again? More than anything. Even the knowledge that they might not have any kind of relationship after she left Afghanistan wasn't enough to deter her. She didn't have the courage or the strength to refuse him. They only had these few remaining days together, and maybe she would never hear from Chase Rawlins again after that, but she was going to take whatever he had to offer and to hell with the consequences.

"Tenley will be jet-lagged and exhausted when she arrives," she finally said. "If I can get her to turn in early, then I'd like to take you up on that offer."

Chase grinned in relief, the dimples in his cheeks transforming his face so that Kate caught her breath, and she barely resisted reaching for him. "I'm glad," he said simply.

They both heard the roar of the jet at the same time, and turned to watch as an enormous plane approached the flight line, coming in on a steep spiral maneuver. Kate was certain the aircraft would slam into the ground. But at the last minute it leveled out and its wheels touched down on the runway, the engines throttling back as it screamed to a stop.

"Wow, that was pretty impressive," Kate said in admiration.

"You bet," Chase said. "Most flights make that combat landing. C'mon, let's get over to the flight line." He gave Kate a meaningful look. "Your sister is here."

13

KATE STOOD WITH Chase as the enormous aircraft taxied to a stop on the tarmac not far from them. Had it really been just three days ago that Kate had arrived at Bagram Air Base? She slid a sideways glance at the man standing beside her with his arms crossed over his chest, looking every inch the badass soldier that he was. She remembered how impressive he had seemed to her that first day, and how intimidated she had initially been by his don't-mess-with-me attitude. How would Tenley react to him? She was extremely sensitive and easily intimidated. Kate should have warned Chase.

"Listen," she said as an aside. "Tenley is very sweet and very friendly, but she might find you a little overwhelming. Be nice to her, okay?"

Chase slanted her an amused look. "Don't worry, I'll be on my best behavior. Relax, okay? Everything is going to be fine, you'll see."

Inwardly, Kate had her doubts, but she gave Chase a grateful smile, and then watched as the airplane stairs were rolled over to the side of the aircraft, and passengers began to disembark. At first, only uniformed soldiers made their way down the steps, but then several civilians appeared, wearing blue jeans and Western-style shirts. Kate recognized two of them as country music's biggest stars, and a cheer went up from the soldiers on the flight line. The musicians waved at the troops, and only the military police kept them from getting mobbed as they stepped off the stairs.

Kate stood straighter, hardly aware that she clutched Chase's sleeve. "Here they come," she said unnecessarily.

And then they saw her. Tenley's face appeared in the jetway, and she made her way carefully down the stairs. She wore her signature blue jeans and cowboy boots, and a white top with sparkling jewels around the neckline. Her blond hair hung in tousled waves around her face, and she carried her bubble-gum-pink guitar case in one hand. Hearing the cheers of the soldiers, she smiled brightly and raised a hand in greeting. The wind blew her hair around her face, and as she reached the bottom step, she tripped and fell, sprawling face-first on the tarmac with her hobo bag and guitar case in disarray around her.

Kate gasped and jumped forward, but Chase was already there, picking her up and crouching down to examine her knees and then her hands, before he scooped up her guitar and belongings. Tenley's face had turned a blotchy red, but she smiled and waved at the soldiers, and Kate could hear her telling Chase that she wasn't hurt. Seeing Kate, she smiled hugely and ran toward her.

"Oh, Tenley," cried Kate, reaching out and pulling the younger woman into an embrace. "Are you okay?"

"I'm fine," Tenley said, her voice muffled against Kate's shoulder. "Just embarrassed."

"Well, I'm so glad you made it here. I tried calling you to make sure you had the correct flight times, but you didn't answer." She pulled back and frowned at her sister. "Why didn't you answer?"

Tenley pulled free from Kate's arms, laughing. "I can't remember! Maybe I was over at the shelter. I've been trying to spend more time there, especially since they got a new shipment of dogs in."

Tenley loved animals, but believed her own hectic schedule didn't permit her to own a dog. Instead, she volunteered her spare time at a local rescue shelter. "Don't worry, Russell took good care of me."

"Well, you're here now," Kate said. She put an arm around the younger woman's shoulders and drew her toward Chase. "Tenley, you've already met Major Chase Rawlins. He's been my escort these past few days. He's going to look after us while we're here. We've been to three different bases, looking at the concert sites, and guess what?"

Tenley gave her an expectant look. "What?"

"I flew in a Black Hawk helicopter."

"Wow, that's amazing!" Tenley smiled, and then frowned. "What's a Black Hawk?"

"It's a military helicopter," Kate said, grinning at Chase over her sister's head. "Very cool."

Tenley turned to Chase. "Thank you for helping me back there. I'm sort of a klutz, so you'll have your work cut out for you in keeping me safe."

Chase inclined his head. "I'm up for the challenge, Ms. Miles."

"Oh, please call me Tenley." She turned to Kate. "Can we get out of here, please? I'm dying for a shower and a change of clothes." She made a face and put her hand over her nose. "What is that horrible smell?"

"That would be the Kandahar Riviera," Chase said, his dimples flashing.

Tenley turned to him in surprise. "They have a Riviera over here?"

"No, Tenley, they don't," Kate said patiently. "What you're smelling is the waste-treatment facility."

Her sister made a gagging noise. "It smells like rotten

onions. Do the poor soldiers who live here have to breathe that? I know this isn't the States, but surely we can provide them with clean air?"

"You get used to it," Chase said blandly. "Why don't I grab your luggage?"

"Okay, let's just go back to the housing unit so you can shower and eat and get some rest before tonight."

"What do you mean, tonight?" Tenley squeaked, a look of panic flitting across her face. "Please tell me I am not required to perform tonight. There's no way I can be ready to give a performance so soon!"

"Shh," Kate said soothingly, taking Tenley's guitar case from her and leading her toward the Humvee. "It's just one or two songs, not even a full set. Every group is performing tonight, just to get the troops in the mood."

"Are you sure they want me to?" Tenley asked, her voice anxious. "I think I heard a few soldiers booing me as I came off the plane. Why would they boo me?"

"Why do you think?" Kate asked calmly, putting her arm around Tenley's shoulders. "You insulted them. But that's why you're here—to show them that you didn't really mean what you said. Right?"

Tenley made a sound of distress. "I did mean what I said, just not toward all military. Just the ones who shipped Doug off."

Kate knew that if her sister ever discovered that she had been the one responsible for having Doug shipped overseas after their forced annulment, Tenley would never forgive her. She glanced over her shoulder to see Chase easily dismantling a pile of luggage in his search for Tenley's pink duffel bag. "So, listen…I told Major Rawlins that we're sisters…" She let her voice trail off.

Tenley pulled back to look at her. "You did?" Her voice registered her surprise. "I mean, that's great! If it were up to me, I'd tell everyone we're sisters, but I know you think it's better for my career if nobody knows we're related."

Kate nodded. "Right. But I'm not worried that Major Rawlins is going to alert the media."

Chase caught up with them, carrying an enormous pink duffel in one hand. He put it into the back of the Humvee and opened the door for Tenley and Kate.

"Wait," Tenley said, and glanced back toward the flight line. "What about the band members?"

"The USO is taking care of them," Kate assured her. "See? If you look over there, you'll see them getting on a USO bus. We'll have dinner with them later today."

Tenley looked in the direction Kate pointed, and a slight shudder ran through her slender frame. "Is that bus safe?"

"Don't worry," Kate said soothingly. "They're perfectly safe, and they only have a few miles to travel. In fact, we won't be too far from where they are. We have our own little trailer, just the two of us. Nice, right?"

"Absolutely," Tenley agreed, dragging her attention away from the bus and sliding into the Humvee. "I'm looking forward to it."

Chase held the door for Kate, and when their eyes met, he gave her a meaningful look. She wanted to kiss him for being so patient, but could only mouth the words thank you as she climbed in beside Tenley. He gave a philosophical shrug and a wink, and then closed the door firmly behind her before sliding into the front passenger seat.

"Oh, my God," Tenley moaned when they were underway. "I am so tired. How long before we're at our trailer?"

"We'll be there in less than fifteen minutes," Chase said over his shoulder.

But Tenley wasn't listening. She had pulled an iPhone out of her bag and was holding it at different angles, trying to get a signal.

"Don't even bother," Kate said drily. "There's no cell phone reception over here. Just put it away."

Tenley stared at Kate in disbelief. "Really?"

"Why don't you think of this as a little technology vacation?" Kate suggested, smiling. "You don't need to worry about any of that while you're here."

"Mmm, you're probably right. You always are. Ooh, my feet hurt." Tenley turned sideways on the seat, lifted her legs and plunked her feet in Kate's lap. "Take my boots off, Katie. I need a foot rub."

Giving Tenley foot massages was something that Kate had always done, but usually only after a performance, when her sister had been on her feet for several hours. She laughed. "Really? You want me to give you a foot rub right now?"

"Please?" Tenley stuck out her lower lip and gave Kate her sad-puppy face. "Pretty please?"

Kate sighed, acutely aware of Chase in the front seat, listening to everything. What must he think of Tenley, and of her for that matter?

"Fine," she relented. Grasping one boot by the toe and heel, she gave it a firm tug. "Pull, Tenley."

The boot came free, and Tenley wiggled her toes in bliss. "Oh, that feels so good. Now the other one."

Kate dropped the boots on the floor and waved a hand under her nose. "Oh, man, are you sure about this? Your feet are…" She lowered her voice. "…sweaty."

"Sorry," Tenley said, sounding anything but. She waggled her toes in anticipation.

Taking a deep breath, Kate grasped her sister's foot and began to massage it, digging her thumbs into the arch until Tenley moaned with pleasure. "Oh, that feels so good! Oh, yes, harder. Deeper!"

In the rearview mirror, Kate saw the driver watching them, his eyes alight with masculine interest.

"Tenley," Kate admonished with an embarrassed laugh. "Keep it down." Glancing at the two men in the front seat, she dropped her voice to a whisper. "You sound like you're having an orgasm!"

"Right now, I'll take this over any orgasm," Tenley moaned, making no effort to lower her voice. "Any man would be lucky to have you, Kate, just for your foot massages."

Chase twisted in his seat until he met Kate's eyes, and she could see the amusement lurking in the green depths.

"Okay," she said firmly, pushing Tenley's feet aside. "We're done."

"Kate," she wailed. "You didn't even do my other foot!"

"And I won't if you continue to embarrass me," Kate hissed. "Honestly, Tenley, you're behaving like a child."

"Sorry," Tenley said, and sat up, searching for her boots.

"Here we are," Chase said as the Humvee drew to a stop outside the housing unit where Kate had slept the previous night.

Tenley pushed the door open and got out, staring at the unit. For a long moment, she didn't move or say anything, but Kate knew she was thinking about Doug and wondering if his accommodations were as luxurious as this modified trailer.

"This is where we're staying," Kate said brightly and linked her arm through Tenley's. "It's actually very cozy inside. Just wait until you see the accommodations at Camp Leatherneck."

Behind her, she heard Chase start to laugh.

THE SUN WAS BEGINNING TO SET, taking the worst of the day's heat with it, as the entertainment got underway. Kate had stayed backstage with Tenley until it was time for her to perform, listening as she moved among the other performers, chatting and laughing with them. She had a vibrancy that drew people effortlessly to her, and she seemed to thrive on the attention. Whereas she had been exhausted when she first arrived, now she seemed upbeat and excited.

Kate watched as Tenley took her guitar and stepped onto the stage and waved to a mixed reception of cheers and clapping and a smattering of boos. Kate walked over to Chase, who stood in the entry, and shrugged.

"Well, this is it," she said. "This is the reason we're here. Let's see how it goes."

"Are you kidding me?" Chase asked. "That girl is going to be fine. Look…they love her."

Kate laughed and together they made their way outside to stand at the edge of the parade field to watch Tenley perform. She silently acknowledged that Chase was right; the audience was cheering her sister's performance, the sound deafening.

"She sounds great," Chase commented.

Kate had to agree. Tenley strutted across the stage, stroking the strings on her guitar and swinging her blond hair around. Her voice was strong and pure, and she belted out the lyrics to her top hit with confidence. She wore a pair of white jeans and boots, paired with a blue corset adorned with sparkling stars. Against the backdrop of the American flag, she looked like every soldier's fantasy of the gorgeous girl next door.

"She's just so beautiful," Kate said wistfully, watching her.

"I agree," Chase said, but when Kate turned to him, he was looking at her, not Tenley.

"At least she didn't get my freckles…I inherited those from my father," she said, self-conscious. "When I was young, I would have given anything to have skin like Tenley's."

"Really? I love your freckles."

Kate gave him a disbelieving look. "You're kidding."

Uncaring of who might be watching, Chase stepped closer and traced a fingertip over her cheek. "I'm not kidding. A face without freckles is like a night sky without stars."

He shifted his gaze to hers, and for a moment Kate couldn't breathe. Without conscious thought, she leaned toward him, her lips parting.

A sudden commotion snapped Chase's attention away from her, and Kate turned to see what was happening.

A young soldier had pushed his way to the front of the crowd, avoiding the security guards, and pulled himself onto the stage. Kate stiffened and then sprang forward, but Chase was already moving, sprinting backstage to gain quicker access to the stage and intercept the soldier. At first, Tenley didn't realize the young man was right behind her, but when she turned around and saw him, her fingers slipped on the guitar strings, and the amplifiers made an earsplitting screech.

She stared at him for a split second, and then he stepped forward and took her by the arms. His lips were moving urgently, but Kate couldn't hear what he was saying. She could only see the look of disbelief on Tenley's face. Then Chase was there, yanking the soldier away from Tenley even as the security detail leaped onto the stage.

As Kate watched, the soldier stopped struggling and allowed Chase to escort him backstage. Tenley stood there for a moment, clearly shaken, but when her band picked up the strains of her interrupted song, she rallied. Clearly it was an effort for her to continue with the performance, but she managed to get through the number without any more incidents.

As soon as she finished, the crowd erupted into applause and cheering, and Tenley waved before jogging backstage. Kate met her there, anxious to see for herself that she was okay. There was no sign of either Chase or the young soldier who had attacked Tenley.

"Are you okay?" Kate asked, framing Tenley's face in her hands and searching her eyes.

"Yes, I think so," Tenley replied, but she seemed shaken by the incident. "He just surprised me, is all."

"What did he say to you?"

Tenley looked distracted, and her eyes were unfocused. Kate repeated the question.

"What?" Tenley shifted her attention back to Kate. "I, um, can't remember what he said. Everything happened so fast, and it was so loud up there that I couldn't really hear him that well."

There was no more opportunity to ask questions as Tenley's band members surrounded her, wanting to know what had happened. Kate hadn't gotten a good look at the soldier, but something about him had seemed vaguely familiar. She made her way back to Tenley.

"Did you know that young man?" she asked.

Tenley turned to her with a look of surprise, and then quickly seemed to compose herself. "No, of course not," she said quickly.

"Okay," Kate said. "I just thought…well, never mind."

Tenley shrugged and spun away, but Kate didn't miss how she chewed her finger, a sure sign that she was distressed. It was the same thing that Kate did when she was upset. "These guys all look exactly the same," Tenley said. "Same haircut, same uniform, same conformist mentality. He looked familiar to you because he looks like every other soldier."

Chase returned at that moment and approached Tenley. "Are you all right?" he asked.

"Yes, I'm fine," Tenley said, clearly exasperated. "What's going to happen to that soldier?"

"He'll be reprimanded, and probably banned from attending the rest of the Independence Day festivities."

Tenley frowned. "Please don't ban him on my account. I don't want him to get in trouble. I mean, it's not like he did anything really wrong. He just surprised me, that's all."

"We should put more security personnel around the stage," Kate said to Chase. "This is exactly why I asked that the troops be kept at least fifteen feet back from the stage. I don't want Tenley to have to go through this again."

"I agree," Chase said smoothly. "Why don't I escort you both back to your housing unit? I'm sure you're tired and it's probably a good idea to call it a night."

"No!" Tenley said quickly, then seeing Kate's surprised expression, she lowered her voice. "I mean, I'm not tired, and I don't want to go back to the housing unit. I'd like to hear the other performers."

Kate studied her sister. "Okay, if you're sure. Why don't I get you something to drink. Maybe a lemonade?"

Tenley gave her a grateful smile and sank into a nearby chair. "Thanks, that sounds great."

Chase fell into step beside her as she made her way to the food table. "Well, I understand why you feel so protective toward her. She does seem rather fragile and young."

Kate laughed. "Oh, no. Another country conquered by the fair Tenley. Russell says she's dumb like a fox."

"Who the hell is Russell?"

"Russell Wilson is Tenley's agent. He's the one who arranged for her to participate in this tour. He handles her concert tours, and I handle the rest. We're a good team, but sometimes he just doesn't understand Tenley."

"And I suppose he understands you?" Chase's voice was a low rumble.

Kate ordered a glass of lemonade and looked at Chase in surprise. "If I didn't know better, I'd think you were jealous."

"Damn straight," he said. "I'm jealous of any man who gets to spend time with you."

"Trust me, he has no interest in me," Kate said drily. "He's all about Tenley and the money she brings in."

She turned to take the lemonade to Tenley, but Chase stopped her with a hand on her shoulder. Kate looked at him expectantly, but his eyes were on Tenley. She had removed her white boots and was lounging back in her chair, laughing with one of the other performers.

"She's a great kid," Chase commented. "But I think she has you fooled, too."

Kate frowned. "What do you mean?"

He gestured to Tenley, who was now belting out an impromptu tune to the accompaniment of a guitar. "I think Tenley Miles can take care of herself. She's what…eighteen? She doesn't seem to have any trouble putting herself out there."

"Age is just a number," Kate said archly. "Tenley is a very young eighteen, and I'm in no hurry to push her out of the nest."

He raised an eyebrow, but she didn't miss the dimple that appeared briefly in one cheek. "I don't know if you've noticed, Kate, but she's already out and flying on her own. She's not a child anymore."

Kate frowned. No matter how successful Tenley might be, she couldn't stop thinking of her younger sister as a child. Maybe it had something to do with the fact that she wouldn't fully come into her inheritance until she was twenty-one. Both of her parents had been successful stars in their own right, and had left Tenley the bulk of their impressive estates, but she could not claim control of her fortune until her twenty-first birthday.

Chase was right. Legally, at least, she was an adult. But Kate cringed to think of Tenley trying to negotiate her way through life. She wouldn't be able to find her own way home from the corner coffee shop if Kate weren't there to guide her, and her soft heart left her vulnerable to those who would take unfair advantage of her.

Tenley chose that moment to set her guitar aside and walk toward them. "Hey, I hate to be a wet blanket, but I'm pretty beat. Must be the time difference."

"Are you ready to call it a night?" Kate asked in surprise, handing the lemonade to her sister. "I thought you wanted to stay and hear the remaining groups play."

Tenley yawned hugely. "I do, but I don't think I can keep my eyes open for another minute. But I don't want to ruin your night. If you don't mind walking me to the trailer, I'll be fine on my own and you two can come back and enjoy the rest of the festivities."

Chase gave Kate a meaningful look and she knew he was thinking about Captain Larson's empty CHU.

"Okay," she said, too quickly. "I mean, if you're sure…"

"Oh, I am," Tenley said. "I am completely exhausted."

"I'll drive you back," Chase offered.

"Where is the rest of my band staying?" Tenley asked.

"They have a large tent not far from here," Kate told her.

"A tent?" Tenley squeaked as she followed them to the Humvee. "Are you serious?"

"Well, it's more like a big fest tent," Kate explained. "Don't worry, they'll be very comfortable."

"If you're sure," Tenley replied. "I hate to think of them roughing it."

"Once they're asleep, it won't matter where they are," Kate assured her. "C'mon."

Twenty minutes later, Kate slipped out of the housing unit and Chase materialized from the nearby shadows. "How is she?" he asked.

Kate smiled. "Exhausted, but too keyed up to relax. I

gave her a mild sleeping tablet, so she should be out until morning."

"Did you give her the beeper?"

"Yes. I showed her how to use it and left it on the bed-side table."

"We'll be less than five minutes away if she needs us. But she won't."

They walked along the street without touching, although Kate was acutely aware of every movement he made. She could hardly believe she was going to do this—sneak away in the night to be with Chase. She felt as young as Tenley.

"Having second thoughts?" he asked quietly.

"Absolutely not," she said, flashing him a quick smile. "Just a little nervous. How about you?"

He laughed softly. "Nervous? Not on your life. It's been the single thing on my mind all day."

"Well then," Kate said, grabbing his hand and break-ing into a light jog. "We should hurry. I'd hate to disap-point you."

14

"DARLIN," HE GROANED, "I don't know how you could think you could ever disappoint me. I mean, look at you."

They had reached Captain Larson's housing unit, and Chase had gotten them both inside without anyone seeing them. He turned on a small light next to the bed, and then took his bandana and laid it across the top of the lampshade to create a soft, muted glow.

As soon as he'd finished that, he'd turned to Kate and caught her hands in his, spreading her arms wide so that he could look his fill. Kate tried not to feel self-conscious, but couldn't help wishing that she had something more feminine and attractive to wear instead of her cargo pants and soft jersey top.

But Chase didn't seem to notice or care.

"Come here," he said roughly, and pulled her into his arms, hugging her tightly against his hard body. "You have no idea the hell I went through this morning when you gave me the frost treatment."

Kate tipped her head back and let her gaze drift over his features, committing them to memory. She traced the contours of his lean cheeks and square jaw, before she bracketed his face in both hands and drew his head down for a kiss.

"You don't know the hell I went through when I thought you had spent the night with Captain Larson," she murmured against his mouth. "I hope I never have to go through anything like that again."

With a groan, Chase deepened the kiss, sliding his tongue against hers and feasting on her mouth. Kate's blood began to hum through her veins, and she wove her fingers through his hair, loving the velvet-rough sensation against her palms. He smoothed his hand down over her hips and cupped her rear, pulling her up against his arousal.

When he released her and stepped back, Kate blinked. "What's wrong?" she asked.

"Absolutely nothing. But I want tonight to be special. And I've dreamed of undressing you, slowly, revealing you inch by inch." So saying, he reached out and unfastened the top button of her blouse, and then the next one, folding the fabric back and bending his head to press a kiss against the exposed skin. By the time he got to the last button, he was crouched in front of her, holding her hips in his big palms as he dragged his lips over her stomach. Kate ran her hands over his head, encouraging him.

"You're so soft," he muttered, and his fingers went to the fastening of her jeans. He drew the zipper down slowly, pushing the material aside and pressing his face into the open V, breathing deeply before kissing her through the silky fabric of her panties. "You smell good enough to eat."

True to his word, he undressed her slowly, pulling her pants free of her legs, and easing her blouse off until she stood in front of him wearing nothing more than her bra and panties. Standing up, he held her arms out and the heat and masculine appreciation in his eyes gave Kate a sense of feminine power.

Smoothing her hands over her stomach, she reached up and skated her fingers over her breasts before reaching behind her to unfasten her bra. Chase swallowed hard and she saw a muscle flex in his lean cheek.

"Do you want me to take this off, or would you rather do it?" she asked, tipping her head and giving him a sultry smile.

"No. I mean, I want to watch you take it off," he said, his voice husky.

Kate was amazed at how quickly and easily the tables had turned. She'd thought that he would pounce on her the second the door was shut; that he would consume her and possess her before she even knew what had happened. But he'd taken his time, and he'd made the mistake of letting her wield her power over him. She liked that feeling, and she wanted to keep it going.

Slowly, without taking her eyes from him, she slid the straps of her bra down her arms, letting the cups catch on the tips of her breasts until, finally, she let the garment drop to the floor. Chase released his breath on a soft groan, but when he would have reached for her, she held up a hand to forestall him.

"Not yet." She smiled. "You wanted to take this slow, so that's what we're going to do. Right now, all you get to do is watch."

Hooking her thumbs in the lacy waistband of her panties, she shimmied them over her hips and let them slide down the length of her legs until she was able to kick them free. She watched as Chase's eyes darkened with desire, and she could see the evidence of his arousal beneath his camo pants. Emboldened, she skimmed her fingertips over her breasts and stomach, and down to the apex of her thighs, wanting to tease him just a little.

"Kate," he warned in a soft growl. "You're killing me."

She felt no embarrassment at standing nude in front of Chase; the expression on his face told her clearly that he more than liked what he saw. But she wanted to do more than just arouse him; she wanted to completely rock his world and give him something to remember long after she was gone. Keeping that in mind, she walked slowly toward him.

"I don't want to do that," she assured him. "But I do want to kiss you."

Looping her arms around his neck, she allowed her breasts to brush against his chest, before she cupped his head in her hands and angled her mouth across his, licking along the seam of his lips until he gave an audible groan and opened beneath her onslaught. He tasted faintly of mint, and the sensation of his tongue sliding hotly against hers caused heat to slip beneath her skin until her entire body felt over-heated and achy with need.

As she kissed him, her fingers worked the buttons of his camo shirt, and she tugged the hem free from his waistband. She slid her hands under the fabric, over the smooth, hard ridges of his abdomen. His skin was like hot silk, and dragging her mouth from his, she forged a path of moist kisses down his neck and over his chest, flicking her tongue against the small, flat nubs of his nipples.

He groaned, and when her fingers dropped to his belt and fumbled with the buckle, he brushed her hands away and unfastened it for her. Kate popped the button of his pants and slowly drew the zipper down. Chase's breathing was uneven now, but when Kate would have dropped to her knees, he caught her by the elbows and pulled her back up.

"What?" she asked. "I want to touch you."

"Ah, darlin', I want the same thing, but I don't want you on your knees." So saying, he backed her up until her legs encountered the edge of the bed and she sat down.

"Hmm," she said approvingly, now that his hips were at eye-level, "I like the way you think."

He looked incredibly sexy, with his camo shirt unbuttoned, revealing the corrugated muscles of abdomen, and Kate's mouth began to water. Chase's expression was taut as he watched her through heated eyes. Swallowing hard, she put her hand against him, feeling his hard length thrusting against her palm beneath the fabric of his pants.

"You're so hard," she breathed, glancing up at him.

A dimple appeared in one cheek. "You bet."

Kate pushed his pants over his hips, and slid her hand inside the waistband of his underwear. His breathing hitched as her fingers curled around him. Pushing his briefs down over his hips, she released him. He was long and thick, and the blunted head of his penis reminded her of a ripe plum. She wanted badly to taste him.

His hands stroked her hair as she bent forward and ran her tongue over him. He gave a loud groan, and his fingers traced the curve of her ears, but he didn't apply any pressure. Emboldened by his response, Kate took him in her mouth and swirled her tongue over his length, while she curled her fingers around the base and gently squeezed.

He tasted delicious, and she wanted more. With her free hand, she stroked his hip and buttock, and then cupped his balls, teasing him as she slid her mouth over him. His breathing was ragged now, and looking up at him, she saw he had put his head back. His eyes were closed and he looked like every decadent fantasy she had ever had, and her body responded instantly.

She increased the pressure and tempo of her mouth, until he began to thrust helplessly against her, and then pulled completely free.

"I can't last if you do that," he admitted raggedly, and bent down to unlace his boots and kick them off, and then push his underwear and pants free. Kate sat back and just stared. The guy was in amazing condition, and her fingers itched to explore the deep grooves of muscle that ran diagonally from his waist to his groin. Even his thighs were hard and muscled.

Peeling his shirt off, he bent down and slanted his mouth against Kate's as he pushed her back on the bed, licking and sucking at her tongue. His fingers kneaded her breasts as he kissed her. Sliding a hand behind one leg, he dragged it up and around his waist, and settled himself against the entrance to her body.

"I've been dying to do this," he muttered against her mouth. Easing himself to her side, he smoothed a hand over her stomach and dipped his fingers between her legs. Bending his head, he took a nipple into his mouth, sucking on it as he stroked her inner thighs, and then slid his fingers along her cleft until he found her center.

"Oh, man, you are so wet," he said against her skin. Kate cried out as his fingers tormented her clitoris, before he thrust a finger into her. "I want to watch you come."

Desire spiraled sharply through her, and her sex pulsed strongly around his finger. She felt hot and swollen and ached for release. Reaching for him, she wrapped her fingers around him and stroked his hard length, loving his grunts of pleasure. The torment of his fingers, combined with his sexy words, was too much.

"Oh," she gasped, feeling an orgasm building, "I'm going to..."

"Look at me," Chase demanded, slicking his fingers over her swollen flesh.

Kate did. His breathing was ragged, but his fingers never stopped working their magic. His green eyes were slumberous and seemed to glow with his arousal. Dipping his head, he licked her breast and then flicked his tongue against her nipple.

"C'mon, darlin'," he said hoarsely. "Come for me."

Kate did, and Chase caught her frantic cries with his

mouth as her hips bucked against his hand, flooding his fingers with her moisture. He didn't stop until he'd wrung every last shudder from her body, and she pushed weakly at his hand.

"Stop, please," she gasped, "I can't take any more."

Chase did, withdrawing his hand and pulling her against his chest. "That was amazing," he rasped against her temple. "Your entire body flushes when you have an orgasm. I could feel you tightening around my fingers, and you were so slippery."

Kate smiled and turned her face into his neck, embarrassed by his graphic description of her orgasm. Her muscles still thrummed with pleasure, and she reveled in the feel of Chase's warm body against hers. Reaching down, she ran the back of her fingers along his erection. He jerked against her, and when she stroked her thumb across the small slit, it came away slick with moisture.

"I can't believe I'm saying this, but I'm still aroused," she admitted, pressing a soft, moist kiss against his mouth. "I want to feel you inside me."

"Ah, babe," he growled softly. "You are so freaking sexy. Here, turn onto your stomach."

Kate did as he asked, bending her arms over her head. He straddled her legs and for a moment he just stood looking at her.

"You have a gorgeous back," he said, stroking his hands down the length of her spine. "And this, right here, where your hips flare out, is amazing." He cupped her buttocks and squeezed them, pulling them up and apart until she felt a sharp tug of arousal in her sex. He smoothed his hands over her buttocks, and then slid a hand between them to stroke her intimately from behind. "Oh, yeah, so wet…here, bend your knees."

He raised her hips up until her knees were bent and

splayed, and Kate knew he could see everything. Instead of feeling embarrassed, she grew even more aroused, knowing that this incredible man wanted her, and would soon take her with his own body.

He slid his hand over her, using a finger to part her. "Oh, man, if you could see what I'm seeing," he groaned. "You look amazing."

"I want you inside me," she said, sliding her hands beneath the pillow and arching her back even more. Turning her head, she watched as he looked at her. He had his thick cock in his hand and he gave it two quick strokes before he fitted himself against her entrance. His face was dark and flushed with arousal, his attention sharply focused on the spot where he entered her. Grasping her hip with one hand, he eased himself into her.

"You're so snug," he muttered. "Don't move."

He pushed further, and Kate moaned softly at the sensation of being stretched and filled. When he was finally fully inside her, he began to move, and Kate gasped with pleasure. The position and angle made him feel huge, and she welcomed how he grasped her hips and thrust strongly into her. He was long and hot, and the friction of his movement caused an answering heat to build inside her. She began to move against him, rotating her hips as he ground against her.

He moved completely over her, bracing his weight on one hand as he slid the other hand over her breasts, kneading them and tugging at her sensitized nipples. But when he slid his hand over her stomach and between her legs, lust exploded inside her. He stroked her clitoris as he filled her, and Kate cried out softly, feeling another orgasm begin to build.

"Oh, my God," she gasped, "you feel so good."

He grunted and swept her hair aside, kissing her neck and then swirling his tongue over her ear. "I want you to come again," he growled, and punctuated his words with another bone-melting thrust.

Kate was so close, but when he rubbed her hard, she came apart, crying out as she convulsed around him. She heard him give a deep, guttural groan, and then he surged into her one last time. He pulsed hotly inside her for several long seconds, holding her tightly, until finally, they both collapsed against the mattress.

"Oh, man," he said, withdrawing from her body and pulling her with him as he eased himself onto his side. "I think you killed me."

Trying to control her uneven breathing, Kate put her head on his shoulder and curled herself around him. Her body gave one last, convulsive shiver and Chase slid his arms around her, hugging her tight.

"That was...unbelievable," she said softly, and tipped her face up for his kiss.

Chase cupped her face in his hand and explored her mouth in a long, slow kiss that Kate felt all the way to her toes. When he finally pulled away, she thought he looked more content than she had ever seen him before. A smile played around his mouth and the lines of stress and fatigue were gone from around his eyes.

"I wish we could stay like this forever," she said, before she could stop herself.

He looked at her, sobering. "Yeah, me, too."

"I guess the military is going to want you back to do real work sooner or later."

"I guess so."

Kate raised herself on her elbow, propping her head on her hand as she studied him. She traced a finger around one of his nipples, and down the groove that bisected his body. "So why would they send someone like you to escort me around?"

"I'm with Special Ops, and the Pentagon issued a stand-down order the same day that you flew in. I was on a mission in northern Afghanistan when we got the order to return to base immediately." He gave a huff of laughter. "I was pretty irritated when I found out I was going to have to babysit a couple of entitled celebrities." He slanted her an apologetic look. "At least that's what I thought I was getting. Little did I know."

"And what did you get?" she asked, smiling.

"I got the sexiest woman I've ever known, and I think you care very much about your sister."

"Hmm. So if I'm hearing you correctly, you're not all that irritated anymore?"

Chase rolled over and pinned her beneath him, easily capturing her hands and holding them over her head. "No," he said, his eyes gleaming. "I trust my team to do their job until I return. In fact, I'll take great pleasure in showing you just how happy I am to be assigned to you…day and night."

He lowered his head and covered her mouth with his own, and Kate sighed in happy submission.

WHEN CHASE FINALLY walked Kate back to her own housing unit, it was almost 3:00 a.m. The roads were dark, and Chase used a small flashlight to illuminate their way. They didn't pass anyone, and when they reached the door to her unit, Chase took her in his arms and kissed her. After a long moment, he raised his head and gave her a rueful smile.

"I don't want to let you go, but you need to get some sleep. I'll come get you both for breakfast in about five hours, okay?"

Kate nodded, pressing her fingers against her lips as if she could still feel him there. She let herself quietly into her room and undressed without turning on the light. On the lower bunk next to hers, she could just make out the shapeless lump of her sister, sleeping soundly. Easing herself into her own cot, she winced as the springs made a loud squeaking sound. But Tenley didn't move or make a noise, so Kate lay down and pulled the blankets over her shoulder.

She lay on her side for a long time, thinking about her time with Chase. She had no regrets. In fact, she couldn't remember when she'd last felt so happy. They hadn't talked about what would happen when she returned to the States, but Kate knew they could keep their relationship alive. Tennessee wasn't so far from North Carolina that they couldn't make it work.

Rolling onto her back, she looked over at Tenley's bed. She was brimming with so much inner excitement that she knew sleep would be an impossibility, and she wanted to share it with someone.

"Tenley!" she whispered. "Wake up." There was no sound from the other bunk, so she leaned over and shook the mattress. "Tenley!"

When there was still no response, Kate frowned and flipped on the small light. She stared in dismay at Tenley's empty bed. What she had thought was her sister was just the rumpled blankets and Tenley's backpack. Leaping out of her own bed, she quickly checked the top bunks, which were also empty. Her first panicked thought was that Tenley had been abducted. She recalled the young soldier who had jumped onto the stage. Had he somehow found out where Tenley slept? Checking the small side table, she found Chase's beeper exactly where she had left it earlier. Picking it up, she prepared to press the button when the doorknob of the housing unit opened, and Tenley entered.

"Oh, my God," she said, sagging in relief. "Where were you? I've been frantic!"

Tenley avoided her gaze. "Nowhere. I mean, I went to the bathroom."

"By yourself? I thought we talked about this. You aren't supposed to go anywhere without an escort."

Tenley gave Kate a helpless look. "Well, it wasn't like you were around to go with me. Where were you, anyway? And don't tell me the bathroom, because then I'd know you were lying."

"It doesn't matter where I was," Kate hedged. "You should have used the beeper like we agreed."

"I'm sorry," her sister said, sounding sincere. "I was tired and I really had to pee and I guess I forgot."

Kate drew in a deep breath and struggled for patience. "Okay. The important thing is that you're safe. Get some sleep."

She didn't miss how Tenley avoided her eyes as she sat on the edge of the bunk and kicked her shoes off. But as Kate waited for her sister to climb under the covers, Tenley flipped her hair back, inadvertently revealing a purplish bruise on her neck. Kate's fingers paused on the light switch.

"What the hell is that on your neck?"

Tenley at least had the grace to look embarrassed, and put a hand to the spot in an attempt to cover it. "It's nothing," she mumbled. "I've had it for a while."

"You have, my ass," Kate said, and reached over to pull Tenley's hair aside and inspect what was clearly a very large, very recent hickey. "How did you get this?"

"Stop it," Tenley said, pushing her hand away. "It's nothing."

"You didn't go to the bathroom," Kate accused. "You were with someone, and I want to know who it was."

"Yeah, right," Tenley retorted with uncharacteristic bitterness. "Like I'm going to tell you. Why don't we just share all our secrets? You can start by telling me who you were with tonight, as if I couldn't guess."

"What are you talking about?"

"I'm talking about your watchdog, Major Rawlins. The guy can't keep his eyes off you, and anyone can see he couldn't wait to get you alone. So I'm guessing that he succeeded, and that's where you've been all night. So leave me alone, okay?"

Kate felt herself go warm beneath Tenley's knowing regard. "The difference is that I'm an adult, Tenley, and I've at least had a chance to get to know Major Rawlins. You've been here for less than twenty-four hours and you've already hooked up with some stranger!"

Tenley climbed into her bunk and deliberately turned her back to Kate. "I don't want to talk to you about it," she said over her shoulder.

Kate tried one more time. "Tenley, you're a beautiful girl, but your status as a celebrity singer makes you a target. What do you really know about this guy?"

"I said," Tenley bit out, "that I don't want to talk about it."

Kate sighed, feeling more frustrated and confused than she had in a long time. She was losing Tenley, she could feel it. As she turned out the light and laid down, she recalled all the times Tenley had turned to her for advice. She'd been such a sweet, adorable little girl and Kate had loved looking after her. When had her baby sister become so grown up? When had she become capable of sneaking around behind her back?

Kate thought it had all started in Las Vegas, when Tenley had run off and gotten married to that soldier, Corporal Doug Armstrong. Believing him to be a gold-digger, Kate had moved quickly to have the marriage annulled. Then she'd made a few phone calls and had registered a complaint with his commanding officer. Within twenty-four hours, he had been shipped overseas.

Looking back, Kate knew she could have handled the entire situation differently, but she'd felt an enormous sense of responsibility toward Tenley. She couldn't let her sister ruin her life by getting married so young, and to a boy she barely knew. Thank goodness she'd been able to keep it a secret from the press, and even if Tenley's attitude had changed toward her, she had no regrets about what she'd done.

Curling on her side, she acknowledged that a chapter in her life was coming to an end. She would hang on to Tenley for as long as she could, but she knew, eventually, she would need to let her go. She only hoped she could.

15

THROUGHOUT THE NEXT DAY, Tenley made a point of avoiding Kate. She smiled and laughed at all the right times, and responded to her questions, but she made sure that Kate never had an opportunity to get her alone.

She and her band had performed two flawless sets, and the crowd had loved her. Afterwards, she posed, light-hearted and happy, for photos with the soldiers. She flirted with them and answered questions, and seemed genuinely interested in their comments. Over the course of the afternoon, she autographed dozens of glossy photos of herself without complaint. In fact, she smiled so brightly that Kate thought her face might split.

Music echoed across the base as each band took its turn entertaining the troops to thunderous applause and cheers. On the perimeter of the parade field, the food lines to the grills were hundreds of soldiers deep. Overhead, Kate noted several helicopters patrolling the skies, ensuring nothing happened to disrupt the festivities.

"She's doing a great job," Chase observed quietly as they watched Tenley pose with a group of young men. "How are you holding up?"

Kate hadn't had an opportunity to speak privately with

Chase until then. She wanted badly to touch him, and thrust her hands into her pockets. "When you walked me back last night, Tenley wasn't in her bed."

Chase gave her a questioning look. "Where was she?"

"That's just it, I don't know. She claimed to have walked to the bathroom, but she had a huge hickey on her neck."

His eyebrows rose. "Maybe she got it before she came over here."

Kate shook her head. "No, she was definitely hiding something and refused to talk to me about it. She hooked up with someone last night, but I have no idea who. What a disaster," she moaned. "I should have been there. I should never have left her alone."

Chase frowned. "Kate, she's not a child. You can't watch over her every minute of every day."

"But don't you see? I don't even have the right to criticize her about her behavior, because my own hasn't been much better."

She watched as twin patches of color rode high on Chase's cheekbones and realized she had angered him. "So what are you saying?" he asked. "That our being together last night was a mistake? A disaster?"

She gave him a pleading look. "No, that's not what I'm saying. But it was irresponsible. I had a duty to watch out for Tenley, and I failed. I left her alone to satisfy my own needs, and look what happened!"

"What? What happened that's so terrible?" Chase demanded. "Look at her, Kate. She's absolutely fine. You're her sister, not her mother. She's old enough to make her own decisions." He swept her with a hard look. "And so are you."

Without another word, he turned and walked toward Tenley, moving through the crowds with an easy authority that had soldiers clearing a path for him. He stood by Tenley's shoulder, an imposing bodyguard in case any of the young men surrounding her decided to get too friendly.

Kate blew out her breath in frustration. But there was a part of her that believed she *had* behaved recklessly last night, and no matter how wonderful her time with Chase had been, she'd left Tenley alone and vulnerable.

She spent the remainder of the afternoon on the perimeter of the festivities, keeping Tenley in sight but not speaking with her. Chase had apparently made it his mission to watch over her, and was never more than a couple of feet from her side, his muscular arms crossed over his chest and his face set in grim lines.

Kate chewed the side of her finger and watched them, certain that in addition to losing Tenley, she may have lost Chase as well.

FROM BEHIND HIS DARK SUNGLASSES, Chase watched Kate. She looked lost and uncertain as she stood near one of the drink stations, observing Tenley with a mixture of concern and pride. More than anything, he wanted to go and reassure her that everything would be fine, but her comments still rankled. He sympathized with her, he really did, but only because he sensed that Tenley meant more to her than she would ever admit, maybe even to herself.

But he'd meant what he said. Tenley was legally an adult. She had to take responsibility for her own actions. In the end, it was her life, not Kate's.

Now he watched Tenley as she smiled and laughed with the troops. She had a star-spangled bandana tied around her neck, effectively hiding whatever mark Kate had seen. He thought of the young man who had leaped onto the stage the night before, and wondered if he had anything to do with the love bites. The soldier had been silent and subdued when questioned, and he'd refused to reveal why he had interrupted Tenley's performance. All he would say was that he had something he needed to tell her and that it was for her ears only. The military police had decided the incident was nothing more than the exuberance of an overexcited fan, but Chase had his doubts. In the few seconds before he'd subdued the younger man, he had heard what he'd said to Tenley: *It meant something to me, too.*

Pulling out his BlackBerry, he sent an email to his team back at Bagram, requesting they send him an electronic version of Tenley's file. When he'd first received the dossier, he hadn't given it the same attention that he would have given the file of an enemy combatant or top Taliban leader. Now he kicked himself for his oversight. He'd been trained better than that. He knew better. He hoped the file might contain information that would give him some insight into both Tenley's and Kate's lives.

He smiled now as he watched Tenley pose for photos. He had to hand it to her; she had done a terrific job entertaining the troops. He glanced at his watch. The sun would be setting soon. One more group of performers was scheduled to play, and then the Independence Day celebration at Kandahar would be over. He would accompany Kate and Tenley to Camp Leatherneck in the morning, where they would do it all again before they flew to Bagram Air Base for the final performances.

Tenley caught his attention, waving him over with a smile.

"I'm so tired," she said when he bent his head to hear her over the crowd. "Can I go back to the trailer and take a nap?"

"Of course," he replied. "I'll walk you there myself." He waited while the USO representative made her excuses to the throngs of soldiers still hoping to get a photo or an autograph, and then walked with Tenley along the edge of the parade field, toward Kate.

"Have you talked with your sister today?" he asked.

Tenley shrugged, but Chase didn't miss the hot color that swept into her cheeks. "I've been busy."

Chase gave her a tolerant look. "She only has your best interests at heart. I think you know that. This is my fourth deployment to Afghanistan, and I've seen many, many performers come through here. But I have never seen a publicist care so much about her client's well-being that she would voluntarily come over in advance. By herself. Even if you are sisters."

But instead of showing gratitude, Tenley turned defensive. "That was her own decision," she said. "Nobody asked her to do it. That's just the way she is—a control freak."

"She obviously loves you a great deal. You might want to remember that."

"Just who are you supposed to be watching out for?" Tenley asked, slanting him an amused look. "Because if I didn't know better, I'd swear it was her."

They had reached Kate, who stood with her arms crossed, observing them. Now she smiled at Tenley. "That was a great performance."

"Thanks," Tenley said, not meeting her eyes. "I'm really tired so I asked Major Rawlins to walk me back to the trailer."

"I'll go with you," Kate said quickly, falling into step beside her. "I'm pretty tired, too."

"I'm not surprised," Tenley murmured, and looked meaningfully at Chase.

"Get some rest, Tenley," Chase said. "I'll come back in an hour or so, and if you're up for it, we can have someone drive us to the boardwalk to grab a bite to eat."

"The boardwalk?" asked Tenley. "That sounds almost civilized."

"We do our best," Chase said.

They reached the housing unit, and Chase stood aside as Tenley entered. Kate paused at the door and turned to look at him. He raised his chin and stared back at her, waiting.

"Chase," she began, "about last night—"

"Kate, I need you!" shrilled Tenley from inside the unit. "There's an enormous bug on the floor! You know how I hate bugs! Come and get rid of it!"

Kate frowned. "Be right there, Tenley." She looked at Chase and lowered her voice. "About last night...I don't regret any of it. I was where I should have been."

Chase felt something shift in his chest, and he didn't realize until that instant how much he had needed to hear those words. He didn't want her to regret anything about the previous night, not when it had been so perfect.

Not caring who might be watching, he stepped forward and hauled Kate into his arms. "If your light is on later, I'll knock," he murmured, and lowered his mouth to hers in a brief, hard kiss. "But first I'll get rid of your little pest so you can get some sleep."

"You mean Tenley?" she asked, smiling against his lips.

Chase chuckled and set her gently aside to step into the housing unit.

AFTER CHASE HAD CAPTURED and disposed of the harmless beetle, Kate changed into her pajamas and looked over at Tenley. "Do you want a cup of tea? That might help you sleep."

"Sure, but what I could really use are a couple of those sleeping tablets you wanted me to take last night. I feel too wound up after the concert to sleep."

"You mean the ones you didn't take?" Kate asked archly.

"I'll take them tonight," she promised, her eyes wide and innocent. "I really need to get some sleep."

Kate rummaged through her bag until she found the pills

and shook two into Tenley's palm. "Best take them with something to drink."

"How about having a cup of tea with me?"

"No, thanks. I'm not crazy about tea." Kate watched as Tenley turned on the kettle. In the next instant, she regretted her decision. She wasn't about to turn down what appeared to be a peace offering. "You know what? On second thought, I will have that cup of tea. Thanks."

She sat on the edge of her bunk and brushed out her hair, smiling her thanks as Tenley set her cup down on the bedside table.

"This is nice," Kate remarked. "It reminds me of the early days when I used to drive you all over the place to do auditions and gigs. Do you remember?"

Tenley smiled. "I remember. At least the hotels we stayed at were better than this place."

Kate blew on her hot tea and took a sip. "Well, just remember that most of the soldiers here don't have accommodations as good as these. Most of them are in tents."

They drank their tea in silence, until Kate yawned and put her cup down on the side table. "I guess I really do need that nap," she said. "I can barely keep my eyes open."

"Drink the rest of your tea," urged Tenley.

"No, I've had enough, but thanks." She grimaced. "I was never a big fan of tea and now I know why. It's too bitter." Sliding beneath the blankets, she bunched the pillow under her cheek and closed her eyes, sighing blissfully. "Turn out the light, Tens. I'm done."

A LOUD BANGING WOKE Kate from a deep sleep, and she pushed herself to a sitting position, groaning when she whacked her head on the underside of the top bunk. For a moment, she was disoriented, and scrabbled for the light, flicking it on and blinking in the sudden glare.

Someone was knocking on the door. Pushing back her blankets, she got to her feet and stumbled to answer it. Her head felt fuzzy and her mouth tasted terrible, like bitter tea.

"I'm coming," she called when the knocking persisted. Opening the door, she found Chase standing on her step. "What are you doing here?"

"I've been coming back every hour to check on you, but when your light never came on, I thought I should knock and make sure you're okay." His sharp gaze raked over her, missing nothing. "Are you? Okay?"

"Yes, of course," she said. "Just tired. What time is it?"

"Nearly 5:00 a.m. You've been sleeping for almost ten hours."

"What? That's impossible. I just lay down like ten minutes ago!" Whirling around, she checked Tenley's bunk, and let out a small wail of frustration. "I can't believe it! She's gone!"

Chase came into her quarters and closed the door behind him. Cupping her face in his hands, he searched her eyes. "Look at me," he commanded. "Your pupils are huge. Did you take a sleep aid?"

"No, I never take anything."

"Did Tenley take a sleep aid?"

"Yes, I gave her two…" Kate stopped speaking, as realization dawned. "Why, that little brat. She must have dumped those caplets into my tea! I wondered why she was being so nice, offering to make me a cup. And it tasted terrible."

"Well, my recommendation is to wait here until she comes back."

Kate stared at Chase in astonishment. "No, we have to find her. I want to know who she's with, Chase. We don't even know for sure that she's safe. We need to find her!"

Chase looked grim, and a muscle worked in one cheek. "Fine. But you may not like what you discover."

"As long as we find Tenley, I'll be happy."

Chase opened the door and gave a low whistle, and Charity trotted in, her tail wagging happily when she saw Kate. "Do you have something that Tenley wore recently? A shirt, maybe?"

Kate rummaged through Tenley's bag until she found the white jeans and top that her sister had worn to the concert earlier that day. "Will these do?"

"Perfect." Reaching into one of the deep pockets of his camo pants, he withdrew the dog's lead and snapped it onto her harness. Taking the clothing, he held it to Charity's nose. "Find."

Immediately, the dog began to sniff the room, and then turned to the door. Chase looked at Kate. "Put some shoes on and let's go."

"She can really smell Tenley?"

"You bet. She can scent a trail up to twenty-four hours after the subject has walked it."

Kate pulled on her shoes, still not convinced. "Even when her scent is mixed in with so many others?"

"A human loses up to forty thousand skin cells every minute," he said. "Those particles fall to the ground or get mixed in the air currents. A good tracking dog can distinguish the scent of your skin cells from those of another person."

Okay, maybe she was a little impressed. "I'm ready. Let's go."

Chase gave Charity a good thirty feet of lead, letting her set the pace. The dog moved quickly, her tail wagging happily. They passed the other housing units and turned down several small alleys, until they found themselves back on the parade field.

"Where is she taking us?" Kate asked.

"Looks like she wants to go to the building behind the stage," Chase replied.

They followed Charity through the door of the dark building, and into the large room that had served as a lounge for the performers. Chase flicked his flashlight around the room, but it was empty. The dog gave a whine and strained at the leash.

"She wants to go to that anteroom," Chase said, pulling the dog back toward him. "Wait here while I check it out."

"Not on your life," Kate muttered.

Chase wrapped the excess leash around his fist and allowed Charity to lead them to a closed door on the far side of the room. With a warning look at Kate, he put his hand on the doorknob and pushed it open, flashing his light into the dim interior.

Kate heard a startled shriek, and then Chase reached inside and flipped the overhead light on. "She's here," he said unnecessarily, stepping back so that Kate could push past him.

Kate stared in disbelief at the sight of her sister curled up on a cot with the young man who had jumped onto the stage the day before. Both of them scrambled to cover their nudity, and Kate looked quickly away.

"What are you doing?" she demanded.

"Kate!" wailed Tenley. "Why can't you ever leave me alone?"

Kate could hear both of them getting dressed. Chase stood just outside the door with his eyes straight ahead, and it wasn't until Tenley walked out of the room that he turned, his attention going to the young man who stood defiantly just inside the room.

"How many sleeping pills did you put in my tea?" Kate asked.

"I gave you four," Tenley admitted, keeping her eyes on the ground. "Just enough to make you sleep through the night."

"Don't blame Tenley," the young soldier said quickly. "None of this is her fault. I made her do it!"

"I hope for your own sake that's not true," Chase growled.

"Be quiet, Doug," Tenley snapped. "Let me handle this."

Doug. Kate refocused her attention on the young man, recognition flooding back. He was the same young soldier that Tenley had eloped with.

"You," she said, advancing slowly on him. "It was bad enough that you seduced my sister, but to have the nerve to—"

"Stop it!" Tenley shouted, and stepped between Kate and the young soldier. "I love him!"

"Love him?" Kate exclaimed in disbelief. "You hardly know him!" She directed her gaze to the man who stood behind Tenley. "It wasn't enough that you nearly ruined her life. Now you just can't leave her alone. How did you know she was going to be here?"

"I've never stopped loving her," he said fiercely. "I had no idea she was going to be here until I saw her up on that stage. You may have succeeded in having our marriage annulled, but you can't stop us from being together."

Kate turned to Chase. "I want this man arrested."

Chase was looking at Kate as though he had no idea who she was. "You had their marriage annulled?"

"We met during one of my concerts in Las Vegas," Tenley said. "Doug had scored a backstage pass, and as soon as I met him, something clicked. I knew he was the one."

Kate made a scoffing noise. "How could you possibly know that after thirty minutes with him?"

"It was an entire night, Kate!" Tenley shouted. "You were too busy talking on the phone and promoting my next tour to even know what I was doing. You didn't even know I was gone until the next morning." She turned to Chase. "Why don't you ask Kate what happened after she tracked us down and had our marriage annulled?"

"Tenley," Kate protested, her voice weak. "Don't."

Ignoring her, Tenley leaned forward until her face was mere inches from Kate's. "The military shipped him off to Afghanistan! We were in love, Kate, and you tore us apart without a second thought. You didn't even ask me how I felt! They shipped him off to the other side of the world, and because of your restraining order, I couldn't even find out where he was sent."

"You're little more than a child!" Kate argued. "You barely know him! And it's impossible to fall in love that quickly. This isn't some romantic remake of Romeo and Juliet, this is real life!"

"I'm not a child," Tenley asserted, drawing herself up. Stepping back, she put her arms around Doug. "I love him, and I'm going to marry him. Again."

Kate put a hand to her forehead. "I don't believe this. Tenley, think about what you're doing. Come back with me now and we can at least talk about it. I mean, what do you really know about him? You haven't been with him long enough to know if you love him."

Tenley's glance flicked between Kate and Chase. "Maybe *you* need more than a few days to decide if you love someone," she said, "but not me."

"Tenley—"

"I can't do this anymore, Kate." Tenley looked at her imploringly. "I need to make my own decisions, not have you make them for me."

"Please—"

"You're fired, Kate. I don't want you as my publicist or my personal assistant. In fact, as soon as we get home, I'm finding my own place to live."

Kate stared at her, unable to comprehend what was happening. "What? No! Don't do this, Tenley."

"Don't you see?" Tenley asked, her voice softening. "I have to. I can't let you make all my decisions for me. Not anymore. What's right for you isn't necessarily right for me. That's why I have to do this, Kate."

Kate took a step back, stunned. She would have stumbled if not for Chase's strong arm supporting her.

"C'mon," he said quietly. "I'll walk you back." He pinioned the young soldier with a hard look. "I want Tenley returned to her housing unit within thirty minutes, Corporal. If she's not there, you'll answer to me. Are we clear?"

Doug nodded. "Yes, sir. Thank you, sir."

"C'mon, Kate," Chase said, putting an arm around her shoulders and leading her out of the building. "I'll make sure she gets back safely. Let's get you some coffee and then we can figure this thing out."

She nodded and let him hug her as they walked, too stunned to argue. Surely she was still asleep and this was all just a bad dream. Right now, Chase was the only sure thing in her life, but if Tenley had really meant what she said, then he was also the next person she would need to say goodbye to. Because if Tenley didn't want to work with her, then she would not be traveling to the other bases; she would be on the next flight back to the States.

Her chest ached at the thought of leaving Chase, but she recalled what she had said to Tenley with such great authority: *You only knew him for a few days! It's impossible to fall in love that quickly.*

Did she love Chase? She didn't know. But she did know one thing; she wasn't going to make the same mistake her sister had.

16

CHASE COULDN'T EVER RECALL feeling such a strong protective instinct toward anyone as he did now with Kate. He'd seen the stricken expression on her face when Tenley had told her she was fired. Knowing how much Kate had sacrificed for her sister, he could only imagine what she was going through.

He took her back to Captain Larson's housing unit and made her a strong cup of coffee in an effort to combat the residual effects of the sleeping pills. She sat curled up on the small sofa, her hands cupped around the mug as she told him stories of how she had raised Tenley after she was orphaned. Kate had been little more than a child herself at the time, barely the same age as Tenley was now. His heart ached for her. It had to have been difficult, no matter how perfect she tried to make it sound. Knowing Kate, she'd tried to provide Tenley with the perfect childhood that she herself had been denied, even at the cost of her own dreams.

For the first time, Chase understood the enormity of what Kate had sacrificed for her sister, and also what she had just lost. He crouched in front of her and gently took the cup of coffee from her hands and set it down, curling his own hands around hers.

"Listen, Kate," he began, "I think if you give Tenley some time, she'll come around. She loves you, and I know she doesn't want to hurt you. But maybe some space between the two of you isn't such a bad thing."

Kate smiled ruefully. "I guess I didn't want to admit that she was all grown up. I wanted to hang on to her for as long as I could. But still, to *fire* me?"

"Maybe she'll reconsider."

To his surprise, Kate laughed. "That's not possible. You see, I didn't get paid for what I did. She never actually hired me. I just sort of assumed the role of personal assistant because we didn't want to publicize the fact that she was being raised by a sibling, and not some court-appointed guardian, like the media believed. So technically, I never actually worked for her."

Chase frowned. "You did all that for her without getting paid? How do you get by? Pay your bills?"

"I have a small trust fund that I use for expenses." She shrugged. "But I do a little web-design work on the side that provides me with pin money."

"You're a web designer?" He couldn't keep the astonishment out of his voice.

"Well, I *wanted* to be a web designer," she clarified. "I attended three years of night school to become a webmaster, but dropped out when Tenley was nine years old, because it was clear even then that she had talent. But I did design her website, and a few others, too. They've even won awards. I was hoping I'd be a lot closer to starting my own business by now, but Tenley's career has kept me too busy for much else."

"I'm impressed." He was. And happy to know that she had something she could focus on besides Tenley. "Maybe this is your chance to get your web-design business up and running."

She made a face. "I don't know. Maybe."

Chase looked down at their linked hands and gathered his courage. He'd never felt so uncertain, even when he'd been on a dangerous mission with no idea if it would end well, or badly.

"Here's the thing," he finally said. "I have to be here for another six months, but I want us to stay in touch. More than stay in touch, actually." He looked up at her. "I want you to wait for me, Kate."

Her lips parted on a soft *"oh"* of surprise. "Wait for you? As in *wait for you?* What are you saying?"

He gave a self-conscious laugh and peered up at her. "You really don't know? I'm saying that I want an exclusive relationship. We can video-chat with each other whenever I'm on a base. And when I get back, I'll return to Fort Bragg. That's about ten hours from Nashville, but we could make it work."

Kate stared at him in bemusement, until finally she pulled her hands away and stood up. "This is all moving too fast," she murmured.

Chase dipped his head to look into her eyes. "We can go as slow as you want, darlin'. I just need to know if you'll wait for me."

He'd surprised her. He could see it in her eyes. "You hardly know me," she said softly.

Chase struggled to keep his voice low and patient. "Then let's take the next six months and get to know each other the old-fashioned way. We'll talk and send letters, and when I get back, we'll go away somewhere, just the two of us. Did I tell you that I have a little place on the beach in Beaufort?"

Kate smiled. "Chase, you make it all sound so lovely, but I can't make any decisions right now. I've just lost the only job I've ever had—"

"Which is a good thing," Chase enthused. "You can do web design anywhere. Come to North Carolina. You'll love it, I promise."

He understood that her life had just been turned upside down, but there was no way he was going to let her run away to lick her wounds. He wanted to give her something to hope for, to look forward to. He wanted to give her a new start, with him at her side.

"What if you change your mind?" she asked, searching his eyes. "Six months is a long time. What if I come down to North Carolina and you realize you made a mistake? What if you no longer find me attractive?"

Chase laughed softly and cupped her face in his hands. "That is not going to happen. Don't you get it? I'm crazy about you." He lowered his head and covered her mouth in a slow, sweet kiss designed to show her just what she meant to him. When he finally pulled away, he was gratified to see her eyes had gone hazy with pleasure. "Have I convinced you yet?"

She leaned into him with a soft sigh, her hands curling around his shoulders. "Not quite. I may need a little more persuasion."

"With pleasure," he rumbled softly, taking her fully into his arms. "If it's okay with you, I'm going to spend the next few hours persuading you."

He heard her breath catch, and his own quickened at the sensual promise in her eyes. "Then I won't tell you how gullible I am, or that I have no willpower to resist you," she said breathlessly.

Chase chuckled. "I'll take that as a *yes*."

CHASE PICKED HER UP the following morning before dawn, having secured a seat for her on a flight to Kuwait. From there, she would fly to Atlanta, and make her way home to Nashville. He had walked her back to her housing unit before dawn, but she hadn't gone to bed, too consumed with thoughts of Chase to sleep. For the first time that she could recall, she was filled with a sense of hope and excitement.

She couldn't even feel remorse over the fact that Tenley had fired her, because in doing so she'd opened up endless opportunities for Kate. And while she hadn't verbally agreed to relocate to North Carolina, she'd let Chase do his best to persuade her.

Now she watched as he stowed her duffel bag in the back of the Humvee. Charity sat in the backseat and her tail thumped happily as Kate reached over to rub her head. "I am going to miss you," she said, stroking the dog's ears.

Chase grunted as he climbed into the front seat beside Kate. "I can't believe I'm jealous of that mutt."

"I'm going to miss you, too," she said, letting her gaze travel over his face, memorizing his features.

He turned toward her in his seat. "I'll call you as often as I can, but I don't want you to worry if several weeks go by without hearing from me."

She took a deep breath and laced her fingers with his. "I know you'll be careful."

"You bet."

Too soon, they arrived at the terminal. Kate's flight wasn't due to depart for another three hours, but passengers were required to arrive early. Even at this hour, the lobby was filled with soldiers waiting to catch a flight, and military duffel bags and gear littered the floor. As they made their way through the lobby to the check-in line, Kate grabbed his sleeve and pulled him to a stop.

"Look," she breathed, staring at one of the flat-screen televisions mounted on the wall.

Chase followed her gaze and felt his stomach drop. There, on national television, was a video of Tenley Miles locked in a passionate embrace with a uniformed soldier backstage at the Kandahar concert. The crawl line across the bottom of the screen read, Beyond the Call of Duty?

Kate turned to him. "Chase, I need to see Tenley. She's not going to know how to handle this. She needs me to do damage control!"

"Kate," he said warningly.

"I have to do this," she insisted. "Just last week she was ripping the military apart, and now she's caught kissing some soldier? You and I know the truth, but the media is going to have a field day, never mind the embarrassment this will cause for the Army!"

She knew the instant he realized she was right. "Fine," he bit out. "Let's go. But just for the record, I'm all for letting her handle this one on her own."

They drove over to the tent where the performers were sleeping, but Tenley was already awake and sitting outside at a picnic table, sharing a cup of coffee with Doug. Kate had to admit that the two made an attractive couple.

"I'll tell her," Kate said to Chase as she grabbed the door handle.

Chase put his hands in the air. "Absolutely. You'll get no argument from me on that."

Kate didn't miss the way Tenley stiffened when she saw her.

"Tenley, I need to talk to you," Kate said without preamble, sitting down next to her sister. "I just saw a video clip of you and—and Doug on television. You were caught on camera kissing backstage. The media is going to have a field day with this, but I think I have a way that we could explain it and make the public sympathize with you."

Tenley's face had gone pale, but now she reached over and covered Doug's hand with her own, smiling in a way that Kate had never seen before.

"Kate," she said gently, "you're not my publicist anymore. This isn't your problem to handle."

"But you're still my sister." Kate frowned. "And whatever you might think of me, I know how to work the media. I can fix this, Tenley."

"Nothing needs to be fixed," Tenley insisted. "I don't care if the whole world knows I was kissing Doug backstage. I love him. I'm going to be honest and tell the press that Doug and I met and fell in love in Las Vegas last month. There's a reason I came to Afghanistan, Kate. I didn't plan for this to happen, but now that we've found each other again, I'm not letting go." She gave Kate a sympathetic look. "Don't worry. I know what I'm doing. And even if this backfires on me, I'm a big girl. I can accept the consequences, Kate."

Kate stared at her sister, barely able to believe what she was hearing. "Are you serious?"

Tenley leaned forward and gave her a hug. "I'm completely serious." Reaching out, she took Kate's hand between her own. "I know you're upset that I fired you, but I can't let you put your life on hold for me any longer."

Kate shook her head. "I haven't put my life on hold, Tens."

"Yes, you have. You think I don't know what you've given up for me? *Everything.* You left college to take care of me. I know you had dreams of starting your own web-design business, and instead you've given that up to take care of me. I love you, but I want to make my own choices, even if they're not always the right ones. I'm giving you back your life, Kate." Her gaze flicked to Chase, standing by the Humvee. "Don't waste it."

Kate returned her hug, watching Chase over her sister's shoulder. He had his cell phone pressed to his ear, oblivious to the momentous event that was unfolding at the picnic table.

She dragged her gaze away. "I'm proud of you, Tens, I really am," she said.

Tenley pulled away and looked at Kate. "I want you to stop worrying about me. I'll be fine." Reaching over, she grasped Doug's fingers. "I have Doug now."

Kate drew in a deep breath, realizing this was a new beginning for both of them. "Okay," she said, forcing a smile. "But you know how to reach me if you need me. If you're sure…I have a plane to catch."

For just an instant, an expression of doubt and regret flashed across Tenley's features. Then she looked at Doug and seemed to draw strength from his smile.

"Have a safe flight," she said to Kate, and hugged her again.

Reluctantly, Kate rose and walked back toward the Humvee. Chase was still talking on his cell phone. As she watched, he snapped it shut and Kate couldn't help but notice a new determination in his stride as he returned to the vehicle.

He slid into the driver's seat and turned the key. "Everything go okay?"

"Surprisingly, yes. I mean, Tenley isn't at all concerned about the publicity, and she seems to actually have a plan."

"That's a good thing, right?"

"Yes, I think it is. Who was that on the phone? It seemed like a pretty intense conversation."

Chase thrust the vehicle into Drive and they bounced along the uneven roads of the base, back toward the flight line. "The stand-down order for Special Ops has been lifted. By this time tomorrow, my team and I will be back in the field."

Kate stared at him and her heart seemed to skip a beat at the thought of him in danger. "So if you're returning to duty, who will travel with Tenley and the rest of the performers?"

Chase glanced over at her. "You have nothing to worry about, Kate. She'll be well taken care of."

She nodded. "I know. I guess some things are just harder to let go of."

His hands tightened on the steering wheel. "Tell me about it."

The remainder of the trip was made in silence, and Kate couldn't help but think that she was going home a very different person than she'd been when she had first arrived, just five days ago. She was leaving Tenley behind. She was leaving Chase behind.

She was leaving her heart behind.

They reached the terminal, and Chase hooked the lead to Charity and let her join them as they made their way through the lounge to the flight line. He waited while Kate checked in, and then walked outside with her. A bus was already there to take them across the tarmac to the plane.

"So I guess this is it," she said, smiling brightly at him. She had told herself a hundred times that she would not cry.

Chase reached into his breast pocket and pulled out a small card. "I want you to keep this close," he said. "Here is my address and the phone number for my headquarters offices, both here and at Fort Bragg. This is my email address, and on the back, I've written my stateside address and phone number. And just in case you can't reach me, I've included my brother's address."

Kate took the card and turned it over in her hands. "Thanks. I guess I don't have to give you my information, right?"

"I have your personal information," he confirmed, his eyes gleaming. "Do me a favor and let me know when you get home safely, okay?"

Kate nodded. "Okay."

"Come here," he said roughly, and hauled her into his

arms, uncaring of who might be watching. "You look after yourself. And call me if you need anything, got it?"

Kate nodded, feeling as if something in her chest was about to break. "I'll call you," she promised. Not wanting him to see how close to tears she was, she pulled free of his embrace and bent down to hug Charity. "What will happen to her?" she asked, burying her face in the dog's rough fur.

"I don't know," Chase admitted. "I haven't found anyone willing to sponsor her yet. But I'm not giving up. I still have six months."

"I'm sure it will all work out," Kate said, standing up.

Chase looked beyond her to the flight line. "Looks like your bus is boarding," he said.

With a small sob, Kate flung her arms around him and pressed a hard kiss against his mouth. Then, afraid of what she might do or say, she turned and walked swiftly toward the bus. She felt his eyes watching her the entire way, but she refused to look back. Only when she was on the bus did she finally allow herself to glance back where she had left him.

He was gone.

17

Six months later

CHASE DIRECTED THE taxi driver along the sandy road that paralleled the beach, his eyes scanning the street until his little beach cottage came into view. Had it really been more than a year since he'd been home? He drew in a deep breath, willing his heart to slow down. He couldn't recall the last time he'd been this nervous and excited all at the same time. Even when they'd finally managed to capture Al-Azir, in a mission that had challenged him on every level, he hadn't felt the way he did now.

Uncertain.

Optimistic.

Scared as hell.

He had four weeks of leave ahead of him before he needed to report back to Fort Bragg. He could have gone to Texas to spend time with his folks. Instead, he'd come directly from the airport to Beaufort, North Carolina, because that's where Kate was waiting for him. He hadn't even changed out of his uniform.

"Pull up here," he instructed the driver, peeling some bills from his wallet and handing them over.

Grabbing his gear from the trunk, he set everything down at the end of the walkway and took a minute just to look. The cottage was exactly as he remembered, with the overhanging porch and weathered shingles. Only now, flowering pots hung between the pillared supports and someone had put a fresh coat of paint on the door and windows. A small table and two chairs had been placed on the far end of the porch, where the view of the water was unobstructed.

He'd hoped to see Kate waiting for him on the porch, but maybe she was inside. Drawing another deep breath, he picked up his duffel bags and made his way to the door. It opened beneath his fingers, and he stepped into the house, knowing instinctively that he was alone.

Kate wasn't there.

His spirits dipped in disappointment.

Setting his gear down in the corner, he walked slowly through the rooms, his boots heavy on the wood floors. Everything was the same, yet different. He noted the subtle changes, like the floral rug in the living room that brightened the small space and drew his attention to the fresh flowers on the coffee table and on the fireplace mantel. In the kitchen, a pale green sweater lay draped over the back of a chair. Chase picked it up and carried it to his face, breathing in Kate's scent.

Where the hell was she?

After she'd left Afghanistan, he'd spent hours on the phone and online, persuading her to move to North Carolina and into his beach cottage. It made no sense for the house to sit empty when she could use it, he'd argued. There was a spare bedroom if she didn't feel comfortable sleeping in his bed. She could use the time to get her web-design business up and running, and if she wanted to find her own place after he returned, he wouldn't argue. She'd be doing him a favor by looking after the place for him.

In the end, she'd relented and he'd known a fierce sense of satisfaction in picturing her there, in his house. Sitting on his porch. Using his shower. Maybe even sleeping in his bed.

Walking down the hallway, he pushed open the door to his bedroom, and gave a huff of disappointed laughter. Definitely not sleeping in his bed. Not yet, anyway. His room was as Spartan as it had been when he had left it more than a year ago. There were no traces of Kate here.

Closing the door, he continued down the hall to the next room. What had been a sparsely furnished storage and guest room was now a distinctly feminine bedroom. Gone were his Texas Rangers bedspread and the stash of spare army gear he'd kept piled in one corner. The bed now boasted a downy comforter in a floral pattern, and at least a half dozen pillows. More cut flowers stood on the nightstand and dresser, and feminine underclothes lay strewn across the bed and on a nearby chair. A dozen framed photos adorned the walls and he stepped closer to inspect them, seeing they were pictures of Kate and her sister, and even one of a very young Willa Dean holding an infant.

A work table had been set up against one wall as a makeshift desk. A pile of books and papers surrounded Kate's laptop, which sat open and blinking. Curious, he tapped the keyboard and the monitor flared into life. He could see she was in the middle of designing a website, and he bent down for a closer look, impressed when he saw her client was a top model.

Leaving her room, he went into the backyard. Flower beds had been planted near the house, and a new set of outdoor furniture sat beneath a bright patio umbrella. Kate had left a plate and a half-empty glass of lemonade on the table. Chase was getting ready to carry them into the house when he heard the crunch of gravel in the driveway.

He paused, listening. He heard one car door slam, and

then another, followed by the loud barking of an excited dog. Setting the dishes back on the table, he rounded the side of the house to the front yard. He didn't recognize the gray sedan parked in the driveway, and for a minute he didn't see anyone. But another excited bark drew his attention to the front porch. A woman stood with her arms around two bags of groceries, while a dog on a leash nearly pulled her off balance. Setting the bags down, she bent to try and quiet the animal, who leaped up and gave her face a happy lick.

Kate. And she had Charity with her.

His heart began to pound fast in his chest, and his first instinct was to bound up the stairs and grab her. Instead, he rubbed his palms against his thighs and walked to the bottom of the steps.

"Kate."

She whirled around, but before she could respond, Charity gave a yelp and lunged forward, leaping off the porch and yanking Kate with her. Chase reacted quickly, grabbing the dog and the leash, and extending an arm to catch Kate as she pitched down the steps, the bags of groceries falling out of her arms and spilling across the walkway. She clutched at his shoulders, laughing, as Charity squirmed with delight and tried to lick him anywhere she could reach.

Keeping an arm around Kate, he crouched down to greet the dog, rubbing her head and ears, and murmuring words of affection to her. When she rolled onto her back, he scratched her belly and then, with a final pat, stood up and pulled Kate into his arms. She gazed up at him, her coffee-dark eyes filled with welcome and an enticing shyness.

"You're even more beautiful than I remembered," he said, his voice husky.

She flushed and looked down, and then determinedly lifted her chin and met his gaze. "Thank you. I was hoping to have dinner ready for you before you arrived."

He trailed the backs of his fingers along her cheekbone. "You think I'm hungry for food?" he growled softly, teasing her. But it took all of his self-restraint not to pick her up and carry her bodily into his bedroom. For six months he'd fantasized about this moment, but he wasn't going to ruin it by moving too fast.

Crouching, he scooped pasta and bread and fresh vegetables back into the bags. "How did you manage to bring Charity back?" he asked, reaching out to rub the dog's ears. He felt an unfamiliar tightening in his throat as he patted the animal. He'd thought he'd never see her again. "I left her with the K-9 unit three months ago, when I had to leave for a mission. When I came back, she was just gone. I was told her owner had come back to claim her."

Kate smiled and bent down to retrieve a tomato that had rolled into the grass. "I'm so sorry. I asked them not to tell you. I wanted to surprise you when you came home. Actually, it was Tenley who arranged it all," she said, on eye level with him. "She heard through Doug that one of the women from the USO was coming back to the States on a commercial flight. Tenley asked if she would be willing to escort Charity, and she said she would. We weren't sure if we'd have another opportunity like that one, so we just grabbed it."

Chase gave a disbelieving laugh. "Wow. That's amazing. So Tenley and Doug are still together?"

"They're married, for keeps this time. He came home about a month ago. She's taking some time off from touring, and so far they seem to be doing great."

"And you and Tenley…?"

"Also doing great," Kate assured him, rising to her feet. "In fact, it's amazing how our relationship has changed, now that I'm not trying to run her life. I finally have the sister I always wanted."

"And you and me…?" Chase stood up and threaded his fingers through her silky hair, studying the strands. "How are we doing?"

Kate stepped closer to him, her hands going to the front of his uniform, where she rubbed her fingers over his embroidered name tag. "Much better, now that you're home."

Home.

He couldn't believe how much promise that single word held. Cupping her face in his hands, Chase bent down and kissed her, putting everything he had into it and letting Kate know how he felt. When he finally raised his head, her eyes were shining with unshed tears. "I've missed you so much, Chase. I still can't believe this is real."

Chase smiled and tipped his forehead to hers. "What can't you believe?"

"All of this. You…being here…finally doing all the things I want to do."

"Oh, it's real," he assured her. "Let me show you."

Without giving her a chance to protest, he swept her into his arms and took the steps to his house two at a time, with Charity following close on his heels. Kate threw her arms around his neck and hung on tight, but he could feel her smiling against his neck. He didn't pause until he reached his bedroom, where he stopped in the doorway and looked down at the dog. She stared at him with hopeful eyes, her tail wagging.

"Sorry, girl," he said, leaving her in the hallway, "but this mission is all mine."

Turning toward the bed, he kicked the door closed behind him.

* * * * *

NO HOLDS BARRED

BY
CARA SUMMERS

Was **Cara Summers** born with the dream of becoming a published romance novelist? No. But now that she is, she still feels her dream has come true. And she owes it all to her mother, who handed her a romance novel years ago and said, "Try it. You'll love it." Mum was right! Cara has written over forty stories for Blaze, and she has won numerous awards including a Lifetime Achievement Award for Series Story-teller of the year from *RT Book Review*s. When she isn't working on new books, she teaches in the writing program at Syracuse University.

To my grandchildren, Marian and Andrew.
All my love for the future.

Prologue

Glen Loch, New York, Summer, 1812

ELEANOR CAMPBELL MACPHERSON stood on the cliffs alone, except for her memories. And there were so many good ones. In a marriage that had lasted over fifty years, she and Angus had come here so often. The caves below in the cliff face had always been one of their secret places. They'd picnicked there often during the early years of their marriage, sometimes climbing up from the lake below and sometimes climbing down. And later, after the children and even the grandchildren had arrived, it had been one of their secret trysting places. Sneaking away to make love here with Angus had always made her feel wicked and wild and very like the young girl who had allowed him to sweep her away all those many years ago.

She missed him so much. How often had they walked together here on mornings just like this one?

The mists swirled over the lake, but the newly risen sun, a bright red ball, would burn them away quickly. To the west on a rocky promontory stood Castle MacPherson, the home that Angus had built for them.

There it rose, three stories high, strong and graceful and as enduring as the life they'd built together. Beyond it she saw the gardens that gave her so much pleasure. And at the far edge, nestled at the foot of a sharply rising hillside, she could make out the top of the stone arch that Angus had built for her.

It was a replica of an older arch that had stood in the gardens of her family's estate in Scotland and it had a legendary power from ancient times—the power to unite true lovers. The story had been passed down for years in the Campbell clan—the man or the woman you kissed beneath the stone arch would be your true love forever. Angus had even stolen some of the stones from the original arch so that this one would carry the same power.

With a smile, Eleanor let her mind drift back to that long ago night when she and Angus had met beneath those powerful stones on the Campbell estate for the last time. Her family had thrown a ball to celebrate her upcoming wedding, and she'd been wearing her future husband's gift to her—a sapphire necklace and earrings that had been bestowed on his family for service to the Scottish court. Mary Stuart had worn the jewels at her coronation, and Eleanor's husband-to-be had insisted that she wear them at their betrothal ball as proof of his love for her.

She'd snuck out of the ball to meet with Angus and to tell him that their secret meetings had to end. She'd practiced the speech for days. There was no future for them. Their families had been locked in a blood feud for years. She was promised to another man, a fine man from a prominent family. Then Angus had kissed her the moment she'd arrived—before she could say a word.

And that had been that.

Oh, she'd tried to talk some sense into him, but he wouldn't listen. Impetuous, impatient, irresistible, Angus hadn't taken no for an answer. He'd simply promised her everything and carried her away.

Thank God.

Eleanor let her gaze linger on the castle, with its lovely gardens and the stone arch. Angus had delivered on his promise. He'd given her everything. Going with him and settling here was the best decision she'd ever made. She only had one regret. And that was what had brought her to the cliffs this morning.

Slipping her hand into her pocket, she closed it over the leather pouches that held the Stuart Sapphires. Having them had always troubled her conscience. A man who'd loved her had given them to her. Not only had she betrayed that love, she'd also become a thief. Everything had happened so fast the night she'd fled with Angus, and any attempt at sending the jewels back later might have given her family some clue as to what she'd done, where she was. It was better that she just vanish.

But Angus had always known about her feelings. It was why he was visiting her now in her dreams, helping her to make things right. He'd always been so very good at making things right.

The latest dream had come this morning, and it had brought her here to the cliffs. She would tell no one what she was doing. Her sons and her daughters-in-law wouldn't be pleased. They'd always assumed that the sapphire necklace and earrings she'd worn in her wedding portrait had been her dowry, the gift that her family had given to her when she'd married Angus.

The stone arch had played a part in the first dreams that Angus had sent her. In them she'd seen a young girl with reddish-gold curls finding one of the Stuart earrings in the stones. Angus had said her name was Adair. So Eleanor had hidden the first of the earrings there.

But the girl in her latest dream had long dark hair and she'd found the second earring in one of the inner chambers of the caves. Eleanor tightened her grip on the pouch in her pocket, and as she did, she heard Angus's voice in her ear.

Her name is Piper. She believes in the power of the stone arch enough to bury her dreams and fantasies beneath them. And she knows about our secret cave. When she finds the second earring, the Stuart Sapphires will continue to find their way home. Trust me, Ellie...just as you did on the night we ran away.

The mists had cleared from the lake. With Angus's words still clear in her mind, Eleanor began the short climb down the cliff face to the cave, just as she'd done so many times with her lover before. She would leave the second earring for Piper to find, and then she would wait for Angus to send her more dreams.

1

PIPER SNAPPED AWAKE AT THE first annoying clang of her Donald Duck alarm clock. A long-ago birthday present from her sisters. They knew how she loved keeping her life in order and on schedule. Donald had gotten her to class on time through four years of college and three years at Georgetown Law School. He was still going strong. The clock had no batteries, no power source, and all it required to silence it was a strong, determined whack.

She gave it one. And since Donald provided no snooze option, she sat up in bed and rubbed her eyes. Then she ran her hand through her hair and automatically reached for the scrunchy she'd left on her nightstand. Her mind was already clearing and her vision would, too, in a couple of seconds. In the meantime, she tossed off the covers and reached for the gym shorts she always laid out at the foot of the bed. Swinging her legs to the floor, she pulled them on, then groped for the sports bra and T-shirt. By the time she'd managed socks and her running shoes, she could find her way to the bathroom to brush her teeth.

Her next stop was the coffeemaker in her kitchen. Unlike Donald, it required a power source, and thanks to top-of-the-line technology, it had already brewed a pot of strong coffee. The coffeemaker had also been a gift from her sisters. She poured a quarter of a cup and inhaled the fumes while she stretched and then slipped on the wristlet that held her apartment key. Finally, she took her cell phone off its charger and slipped it into her pocket.

Her morning routine never varied. But then variety wasn't her goal. Order and routine were. Life got messy. Piper had learned at an early age that controlling the parts she could gave her more time to fix up the messy ones.

And lately, her professional life had gotten very messy.

Not yet. Firmly, she blocked the thought while she blew on the coffee and managed two swallows that burned her mouth and nearly cauterized her throat. It was a sacrifice she made each morning to the caffeine goddess.

Then she headed for the door of the flat she leased above a ritzy women's clothing boutique in Georgetown, shut the door, tested the lock, then hurried down the steps and along the short alley to the sidewalk. At 6:00 a.m., the street was still mostly free of traffic. Mr. Findley who ran the coffee shop down the street was washing his windows, while a customer sat at one of the outside tables reading a paper. The sun was up and the humidity tolerable. The scent of stale beer and fresh bread baking mingled in the still air. Perfect.

She ran because it was an ingrained habit from her

high school and college years, when she'd been on cross-country teams. But she also ran because it was the best way she knew to clear her mind and get ready to face the day.

Which promised to be another busy one. Her current job as a research assistant to prominent law professor and celebrity defense attorney Abraham Monticello was one she worked hard at. She'd accepted his offer right out of law school because it would look good on her résumé and because it offered her a unique chance to get a background in criminal law.

It was turning out to be unique, all right, and it was causing her to question her career choice. Her main reason for choosing law as a profession was that she believed in justice and in the power of the legal system to help people find it. But recently.…

No. Not yet.

While she took the first block at an easy pace, she used a visualization technique her aunt Vi had taught her when she was very young. First, she pictured all the chaos of her upcoming day and her self-doubts being sucked into a bottle in much the same way Aladdin's genie had been sucked into the lamp. Then she jammed the cork in with the same energy she'd used to whack Donald.

Whenever things got really bad, she let herself remember the really chaotic time in her life right after her mother died. She'd been three, her older sister Adair four, and Nell had been a baby. They'd been too young to really understand the loss—except that their mother wasn't there anymore. And neither was their father. He'd hidden away in his studio and used his art to escape from his grief. Then their Aunt Vi had moved into the castle with them, and life had finally taken on some order again. That's probably when her love of routine had taken root.

As she reached the end of the second block, Piper shifted her focus to the details of her surroundings, taking the opportunity to speed window-shop in the stores that stretched along the street. She saw changes in the displays and made a mental note to take a closer look at a pair of red sandals—when she had the time. And she'd have to *make* time to call Nell and tell her that her first published children's book, *It's All Good,* was still on display in the window of the bookstore.

When her younger sister had last visited, she'd made a good friend of the owner and now Nell's story was selling well in Georgetown. Piper had to admit she was impressed. Nell had inherited their father's creative talent, except she'd chosen writing rather than landscape painting as A. D. MacPherson had.

But she certainly hadn't inherited their father's reticence. Currently, Nell was using a federal grant to travel across the country, offering writing classes to children in underprivileged schools, and at the same time, establishing a network for her own writing.

As Piper turned down a residential street, her muscles began to warm and perspiration sheened on her forehead. She settled into a rhythm. If Nell was surprising her, her older sister Adair had truly shocked her.

During the past eight months, Adair and their aunt Vi had turned Castle MacPherson, their family home in the Adirondacks, into what was becoming a very successful wedding destination spot. Adair had always been an idea person, and when they'd been growing up, Piper and Nell had been more than willing to go along with most of her schemes. But whenever Adair's plans had gone awry, it had always been Piper's job to do the cleanup, which usually included negotiating with Aunt Vi, and on some occasions, even with their father.

No wonder she'd always been drawn to the practice of law. What did lawyers do except clean up the messes people got themselves into?

Only this time, the mess was of her own making.

Not yet. She was not going there yet.

The biggest surprise from the castle was that her sister and Aunt Vi had discovered one piece of their several-times-great grandmother, Eleanor Campbell MacPherson's, priceless missing dowry: a sapphire earring that had reputedly been worn by Mary Stuart on the day she'd taken the throne. And during the same weekend, Aunt Vi had gotten engaged to Daryl Garnett, who ran the domestic operations unit of the CIA here in D.C. Even more astounding was that Adair, the practical queen of the five-year plan, had fallen in love, too. With Cam Sutherland, of all people.

Piper ran in place at the corner until the traffic cleared, then found her stride again. She hadn't seen any of the Sutherland triplets since her father had married their mother seven years ago. The MacPherson sisters and the Sutherland triplets, Reid, Cameron and Duncan, went back a long way to a summer of play-dates when the boys had opened up a whole new world of games—bad guys versus good guys, sheriff and posse, pirates and treasure, along with rock-climbing on the cliff face, a place where she and her sisters had been forbidden to play.

Then the Sutherlands had completely disappeared from their lives until they'd returned to the castle on the day their mother, Professor Beth Sutherland, married A. D. MacPherson beneath the stone arch. Since she had an eye for detail, Piper had duly noted that the scruffy, annoying Sutherland boys had morphed into tall, gorgeous and hot young men.

Especially one of them. Duncan. He'd really caught her attention that day with that tall, rangy body, the dark unruly hair and the mesmerizing green eyes. She'd felt those eyes on her during the ceremony when they'd been standing with their parents beneath the stone arch, and she'd felt a kind of tingly awareness that rippled along her nerve endings and heightened all of her other senses.

Intrigued, she'd met his gaze directly, and for a span of time, her vision and her mind had been totally filled with him and nothing else. Only Duncan. Heat had flooded her, melting her, muscle and bone, right to her core. The experience had been so new, so exciting, so terrifying. No one had ever made her feel that way before—or since.

Not that she'd had to worry about it. The triplets had flown in for the wedding and had returned to their respective colleges that night. She and her sisters had done the same the next day. Just as well. A man like Duncan Sutherland would likely wreak havoc on a girl's life, something she didn't have time for. She had enough problems to deal with in her work life.

Work. Her mind veered back to the coming day.

No. Not yet.

Increasing her pace, Piper ran full out for the next two blocks—pushing herself into a zone where all she had to do was enjoy the speed and the wind whipping past her face. The next corner marked the halfway point of her run. As she circled to head back, she moved into a slower rhythm and allowed herself to finally uncork the work bottle and face her demons.

Mentally, she made a list, one she'd been making

almost every day lately. Good news first. She loved working for Abe Monticello, and up until a few months ago, she'd loved everything about the job. The only irritation she'd had to face was one of her fellow research assistants, Richard Starkweather. He wanted to date her and was having difficulty taking no for an answer. But she could handle that.

And working for Abe Monticello was more than worth a minor hassle with a colleague. He was a larger-than-life man with a larger-than-average talent. At sixty-five, he had the sharpness of mind, the looks and the creative imagination of a man half his age. If he'd *been* half his age and unmarried, Piper might have fallen in love with him.

Everything had been perfect until Abe had been hired to handle the appeal in a highly publicized case. It involved a man on death row who'd been convicted of murdering a young woman, but suspected of killing several others. Many, including the FBI, believed Patrick Lightman was the serial murderer the press had dubbed the RPK, or the Rose Petal Killer.

Piper had been thrilled when Abe had assigned her to do the research for the appeal and write a brief. She'd worked on Lightman's case for two straight months. She'd studied the court recordings, read the media coverage and she'd viewed the crime scene photos of Suzanne Macks, the woman he'd been arrested for killing. Her killer had taken the time to arrange a little picnic setting. A white sheet had been spread across the floor of the living room of her apartment. Suzanne had been lying on top of it, her eyes closed, her hands folded across her chest and her long dark hair fanned out from her head. Rose petals, hundreds of them, had been strewn everywhere.

The Rose Petal Killer had left all of his victims exactly that way.

Everyone had believed Lightman guilty. The jury had taken only an hour to bring in a verdict.

But Piper had uncovered exactly what her boss had been hoping for—several procedural errors in the trial. She'd done the job and she'd done it well, but the hardest thing she'd ever done in her life was to hand her findings, along with the brief, over to her boss. Then a month ago, Abe had used what she'd written to successfully argue the case before the appeals court. And Patrick Lightman had been set free.

A man who'd been convicted of viciously murdering a young woman and who might very well have murdered seven others was walking the streets and could possibly kill again. Piper figured it was the biggest mess she'd ever gotten herself into.

For a couple of weeks, the media had created a circus surrounding the release of the Rose Petal Killer. Abe had taken all the heat. He was the one who'd received hate mail.

But she was the one who had the nightmares. In them, she pictured Patrick Lightman out on the streets, following another young girl with long dark hair. If Lightman was the Rose Petal Killer, he could even now be selecting his next victim. And Piper would be responsible.

Abe had taken the time to have a heart-to-heart talk with her. He'd reiterated his belief in the basic right of every citizen to a vigorous defense. The law always had to be applied meticulously and fairly in order to ensure justice. Piper believed that, too. In theory. But she was discovering there was a world of difference between theory and practice. What if Patrick Light-man killed again?

The only answer Abe had on that one was that pros-ecutors and defense attorneys couldn't afford to let the job get personal. Then he'd encouraged her to throw herself into the next case, one he was set to argue in court within the next month, and he'd invited her to sit in the second chair. It meant more work, but it would get her mind off Patrick Lightman. Just what Abe had intended it to do.

Time to put it all back in the bottle. Picturing the process once again in her mind, Piper turned the final corner and sprinted for the entrance of her alleyway. At least the reporters had never bugged her at home. Piper took the stairs to her apartment two at a time. If she hadn't let her mind wander back to work, she might have been more aware of her surroundings. As it was, her feet were both planted on the landing be-fore she fully registered that the door to her apartment was open. In fact, it had been propped open with the ladder-back chair from her kitchen table.

By that time, she'd glanced into the room and what she saw froze her to the spot. Hysteria bubbled into her throat and blocked a scream. Someone had staged the scene perfectly. Her coffee table had been shoved to the side. A white sheet had been thrown across the floor the way a picnic blanket might be spread across a patch of lawn. Strewn across the white cloth were hundreds of rose petals. Enough to appear as if they'd rained out of the sky. And red enough to look like blood.

The only thing that was missing was the body of a young woman with long brown hair, her hands crossed over her chest, the scene she'd pictured several times in her nightmares.

Piper pressed a hand against her chest. She had to think. She had to breathe. And she had to get away from here. Still, she wasn't sure how long it took her to tear her gaze away from the rose petals and get down the flight of stairs. She ran then, and she didn't stop to use her cell phone until she'd dashed into the coffee shop down the street.

IT WAS DUNCAN SUTHERLAND's day off, and to make sure he enjoyed every minute of it, he'd scheduled a 7:00 a.m. tee-off time. Although he preferred a low-key, laid-back approach to life, there were some deadlines that had to be met. And a tee-off time was sacred. Plus, he needed a break from work. Ever since accused serial killer Patrick Lightman had been set free, Duncan had been reviewing the FBI's files during every minute of his spare time. He'd been the lead profiler on Lightman, and he was determined to put the man back in jail. There had to be something in the files that had been overlooked, some detail or angle that he hadn't seen yet.

The first phone call came just as he was about to step into the shower.

A quick look at the caller ID told him it was bad news. His brother Cam never called except to report trouble or ask a favor. Either one might interfere with the perfect day he had planned. Cam's last call had been a favor. Duncan had transported a veterinarian from Montana to upstate New York to reunite him with his ex-wife.

He let the phone ring four times, then gave up and answered. "Trouble or favor?"

Cam laughed.

So it would be a favor. "I'm teeing off in an hour,"

Duncan warned. "And what time is it in Scotland anyway?" His brother had taken some time from his job at the CIA to run off to Scotland with Adair MacPherson. They'd recently become unofficially engaged and they were going to deliver the news in person to their respective parents, who were both on a working vacation there.

"Relax. I just wanted to know if you'd given any more thought to going up to Castle MacPherson and poking around in the library?"

"Some." Cam had been nagging him about that ever since he'd shown him the sapphire earring that Adair and Vi had discovered in the stone arch. His brother believed that someone had been sneaking into Castle MacPherson for nearly six months, and they still had no idea who the intruder was. But the nocturnal visits had started right about the time the *New York Times* had run a feature article on the castle and those missing jewels that Mary Stuart had reputedly worn at her coronation. Cam's theory was that the visitations had something to do with the missing jewels. That would have been his own best guess.

"You're the profiler in the family," Cam said. "If anybody can get some handle on who the intruder was, it's you. You always had a knack for getting into people's heads."

As the youngest of triplets, Duncan supposed that he'd developed that knack as a survival skill. And it had been part of what had drawn him to the FBI's Behavioral Analysis Unit. The other part of it had been what had drawn all three of them into some kind of law enforcement—the arrest of their father for embezzlement. They'd been nine when it had happened, and Duncan still carried the image in his mind of the three of them standing in front of their mother as the police handcuffed their father and led him away. Duncan also remembered what he'd felt—a fierce kind of happiness that David Fedderman couldn't hurt their mother anymore.

"He's still out there," Cam continued. "And the rest of Eleanor's dowry has to be at the castle somewhere. You don't want to miss out on a chance to find it, do you?"

It was Duncan's turn to laugh. As the middle triplet, Cam had always felt the need to compete, especially with Reid, the first born. "You should try that 'miss out on a chance' tactic with Reid. You could always get him with it when we were kids."

"I intend to," Cam said. "But serving on the vice president's Secret Service detail is keeping him hopping. Besides, the strategy will work more effectively after *you* find either the necklace or the other earring. Help me out here."

"Not on your life. My philosophy has always been to not take sides when it comes to the two of you and your competition." Waiting it out until the dust settled had always worked well for him.

"It was worth a shot. But you can't tell me that you don't want to find part of Eleanor's dowry. You were fascinated by those sapphires when you were a kid."

A brother, especially one with CIA training, knew what buttons to push. The truth was Duncan had been thinking about visiting the castle. The summer he was ten and they'd had daily playdates with the MacPherson girls, he'd spent hours studying Eleanor's wedding portrait, and he'd memorized the legendary jewels. Two thumbnail-sized sapphires hung from each earring and one of the jewels on the necklace rivaled the Hope Diamond in size.

There was a story there that hadn't been told. Tradition held that the jewels had been Eleanor's dowry, but there was no record of what had happened to them until the first earring had shown up less than a month ago when lightning had struck the stone arch and loosened some stones. Someone had hidden it. Who? And why? Those were the questions that drove all of his investigations.

"So—will you go?" Cam prodded.

Duncan shifted his thoughts back to the conversation and stalled. "I thought that you and Adair had run off to Scotland to see what you could dig up about the sapphires on that end."

"That's our plan, but the rest of Eleanor's dowry is at the castle. And I still think there's something in that library that holds the key."

Once again, he had to agree with Cam's assessment. The security had been beefed up at the castle, and the local sheriff was sending regular patrols now.

"The air is a lot fresher up there than it is in that basement you work in at Quantico," Cam said. "It'll be fairly quiet. No wedding is scheduled, just a photo shoot for some fancy architecture magazine. Daryl will be visiting Vi on the weekend. The two of you might be able to get in a game of golf."

Daryl Garnett was Cam's boss at the CIA and he'd recently become engaged to Vi. He was also a scratch golfer. Leave it to a brother to know your weaknesses. Duncan glanced at his watch. The minutes to his tee time were slipping away.

"If I tell you I'm planning on going up there this

weekend, will you go back to your fiancée and our parents and leave me alone?"

"You've got it, bro. My job with you is done," Cam said, and clicked off.

It wasn't until Duncan was stepping out of the shower a few minutes later that the second call came. And it meant he'd have to cancel his tee time and perhaps even his trip to the castle. There was a chance that the Rose Petal Killer had selected a new victim.

2

DUNCAN SHOWED HIS BADGE TO THE young uniformed officer standing on the landing of the small apartment then ducked his head to step inside. The space was small—one room where a minimum of furniture had been artfully arranged to separate the eating area from the living space. The floor between the couch and fireplace was completely covered by a white sheet sprinkled liberally with bloodred rose petals very much in the style of the Rose Petal Killer.

He'd get back to that in a moment. For now he took in the other details. A tiny kitchen was tucked into an alcove and a door directly ahead led into a bedroom the size of a closet. No surprise that the place was so crowded, considering all the people in it. Two of the men he didn't recognize. They were carefully dusting surfaces for prints. The other two he knew on sight. They stood just inside the bedroom. One was Detective Mike Nelson, who'd given him the call when he'd stepped out of the shower. Duncan had consulted on a case of Mike's the year he'd been hired to work at Quantico and they'd been friends ever since. The other man he recognized as Abe Monticello, whose head, like his own, was nearly brushing the ceiling. He was the reason that Duncan had missed his golf game.

Abe hadn't called him personally; instead, he'd called his sister, who happened to be Duncan's boss.

It had been a rough month for Adrienne Monticello. The division she commanded at Quantico had worked on the Rose Petal Killer cases, and her brother had been responsible for setting Patrick Lightman loose. Since she considered Duncan to be the division's expert on the RPK, Adrienne had asked him to go over to Georgetown and give her his personal take on the scene. Mike Nelson had called him, too, and asked if he could stop by.

It didn't surprise him at all that Abe Monticello had wanted the FBI involved in this from the get-go. He was a smart man and very savvy about handling the press. Someone had broken into the apartment of one of his research assistants and staged a scene that matched the romantic little sets that the Rose Petal Killer had designed for his victims. Abe would want to step into his favorite role—the white knight, charging in to save the day.

Both Adrienne and Nelson had called him because they wanted the answer to one question. Was this the work of the real Rose Petal Killer or a copycat? He imagined Nelson would prefer the former. The detective, along with everyone else in law enforcement, would like to get Lightman back behind bars.

Abe Monticello wanted the answer to be "copycat" because he'd spent a lot of time in front of TV cameras during the past few weeks speaking in defense of the legal system and the way it worked to prevent the violation of every citizen's rights. The speech might not play so well if Patrick Lightman started murdering slender young brunettes again. Or threatening to.

Well, you couldn't please everyone, and Duncan already had a feeling about which man would be happier about his opinion. His insights into the criminal mind were usually right. His mother had told him when he'd joined the FBI that his interest in behavioral science had begun with his trying to figure out what had motivated his father to become an embezzler.

David Fedderman had been born to wealth and privilege, but he'd abused both. In his position at Fedderman Investments, a firm that his grandfather had founded, he'd run a successful Ponzi scheme for years until it had collapsed and Fedderman had been arrested on several counts of fraud.

Of course, his father's arrest and eventual incarceration hadn't been the end of the story. His mother had had to battle Fedderman's parents for custody, and as soon as she'd won, she'd legally changed all their names back to Sutherland and accepted a position teaching at a liberal arts college in Chicago. As to figuring his father out, that hadn't been much of a challenge. David Fedderman had been one of those men for whom running a con and living life on a constant adrenaline rush was worth more than family or wealth. It had been worth risking everything. He was still serving time in a federal prison, and Duncan would have bet good money his father was still running scams.

Analyzing what he was seeing in front of him was a lot more challenging. The way the white sheet was spread was fairly accurate, the edges folded in to make what looked like a perfect square. The Rose Petal Killer had been meticulous about that. In the tiny room, the sheet filled most of the available space between the couch and a TV stand against one wall. Duncan dropped to one knee and caught the edge of the sheet between his thumb and his forefinger and rubbed. Then he studied the rose petals. They all looked fairly fresh.

Nelson spotted him first and walked to the back of the sofa. "Thanks for coming, Sutherland. Take your time."

He didn't need any more time to answer the question he figured was foremost in Mike's mind, but he'd learned a long time ago that the information he provided would be taken more seriously if he strategically delayed the delivery. "Any sign of a break-in?" he asked.

"No. She was out for a run when it happened. Claims she locked the door and took the key," Nelson said. "The only person who has a spare key is the woman who runs the dress shop downstairs. We'll question her as soon as she opens up."

The lack of evidence of a break-in was consistent with the RPK's pattern. The widely accepted theory was that his victims let him in. But that hadn't happened in this case.

"We didn't find any evidence that the lock was picked," Nelson continued. "But a pro wouldn't have had a problem with it."

And a duplicate key made from a wax impression was also a possibility, Duncan mused. A robbery ring recently arrested in nearby Baltimore had accessed house keys by distracting parking valets at high-end restaurants. The customers would return home after an evening of fine dining to find their houses stripped. A stalker with the patience and skills of Patrick Lightman might have used a similar method to gain access to his victims' homes.

It was when he was replacing the edge of the sheet that Duncan spotted the thin envelope that lay just beneath. He pinched the corner of it to draw it out.

"I want to know if Ms. MacPherson is in danger," Monticello said.

As Duncan glanced up and met the older man's eyes, his mind was racing. "Ms. MacPherson?" Piper wasn't a common name and he recalled that Piper MacPherson had gotten her law degree from Georgetown Law School.

"Yes," Abe said. "She works for me. I want to know just how much danger she's in."

Abe hadn't mentioned her first name yet, but Duncan was beginning to get a feeling. Then Piper strode into the room and confirmed it in spades.

He hadn't seen her in seven years, not since they'd stood beneath the stone arch at the castle and listened to their parents exchange vows. But every detail of her appearance slammed into his mind and pummeled his senses. The slender frame, the long, long legs that extended from narrow ankles to running shorts, the compact curves, slim waist and the dark brown hair that hung in a ponytail. He'd never been so aware of a woman as he'd been the day of the wedding. Or now.

"Whoever did this isn't the Rose Petal Killer," she said as she walked with economical grace toward Nelson and Monticello.

The voice with its low pitch and huskiness rippled along his nerve endings. It was the kind of voice that tempted a man to come closer. A whole lot closer. He imagined the mythical sirens who'd lured sailors to their deaths might have had voices exactly like hers. Which was why he'd kept his distance on their parents' wedding day. He'd been about to graduate from college and had his sights set on the FBI. And their parents' marriage had made the MacPherson girls family.

"Of course it's not," Abe Monticello said.

"The FBI is here to determine that for us," Nelson said.

Duncan stayed right where he was. For a moment he still needed the distance, but he knew the second she became aware of him. He could see the tension ripple through her, and even as she turned, he braced himself. Seven years was still a long time.

But as he looked into those amazing amber-colored eyes, once again he felt the impact like a blow. Desire sprang up, primitive and strong enough to nearly have him rising from his crouch. Then he felt his mind empty as suddenly as if someone had pulled a plug. All he could see was her. All he wanted was her.

For seven years, he'd tried to convince himself that what he'd felt that day was a fluke. A onetime event. And he'd succeeded in compartmentalizing it.

But he knew now exactly what he'd known then. Piper MacPherson was it for him. The only one. For seven years he'd compartmentalized that, too. He'd tried to convince himself that she was family, and that meant hands-off. But as he continued to sink into the depths of those golden eyes, Duncan had a feeling that the lids on all those compartments had been blown clean off.

"You," she said.

In Duncan's opinion, she'd summed up his situation nicely. And what in the hell was he going to do about it?

PIPER CLOSED HER EYES. There was always the chance that she was hallucinating. Or her habit of visualizing was getting the best of her. But when she opened her eyes again, Duncan Sutherland was still crouched on the floor of her apartment.

For an instant, she certainly hoped it wasn't longer than that. She felt just as she had when she'd stopped short in the open doorway of her apartment and seen the rose petals strewn over the white sheet.

Except that it wasn't just shock she was feeling. And her blood hadn't turned to ice. Instead, it seemed to be sizzling through her veins like an electrical current, melting bones and paralyzing muscles so that she wasn't sure she could talk. Or move.

"What are you doing here?" she asked.

"This is FBI agent Duncan Sutherland, Ms. MacPherson," Mike Nelson said. "He works for the Behavioral Analysis Unit at Quantico. I asked him here because he worked on the Rose Petal killings."

"I know Duncan," Piper said. Okay, she was breathing and talking. In a couple of seconds, she'd get her thoughts back on track. Should she try stuffing him into a bottle? Would he fit?

A young uniformed officer appeared in the open doorway. "Sorry, sir. She got away from me."

Piper managed to drag her eyes away from Duncan and glanced back at Nelson. "He was kind enough to get me coffee, and the caffeine helped me think." And she *was* thinking again. Finally. She waved a hand at the sheet. "I came up here to save you some time, Detective. This isn't the work of the Rose Petal Killer."

"Tell me why not," Duncan said.

Bracing herself, Piper turned to face him and managed to take one step closer to the edge of the sheet. And him. "Because the rose petals are so fresh. I read all the files. He used to buy the flowers over the course of days and save them up."

"Too many roses purchased at one time, one place, might have drawn attention. Plus, there was some speculation that he bought them over time as little anonymous gifts for his victims," Duncan said. "And if they saved them, he used those older petals."

She narrowed her eyes. She'd read those very words in the files she'd worked on. And those details had never been released to the press nor had they made it into the court records. Duncan had worked on the cases, all right. Of course he had. He might even have consulted with the police on the Suzanne Macks murder.

"What else is different?" Duncan asked. "Take your time."

She shifted her gaze to the sheet. "I should have done that instead of panicking." She sank to her knees to get a better look. But what she was looking at and what she was feeling were two different things. She was close enough to touch him now. She could certainly smell him—sunshine and soap and something else that bumped up that sizzle in her blood.

Focus.

Ruthlessly, she shifted her attention fully to the details she'd only glanced at before. The edges of the sheet were tucked in to form a perfect square in the available space. That was right. No wrinkles. The RPK had always been neat and precise.

Suddenly, she frowned. "There are fold marks in the sheet, as if it's been newly purchased."

"Good point," Duncan said. "What else?"

Lifting the edge of the sheet, she rubbed it between her thumb and forefinger. "This is wrong, too. The texture is too rough. The thread count should be higher. He always used Egyptian cotton."

"You did read the files," Duncan murmured. "You worked on the appeals brief, didn't you?"

After taking in a deep breath, Piper met his eyes and nodded. She'd prepared herself to find anger, maybe condemnation, censure at the very least. And why not? She'd set a killer free. And now she was facing a man who'd probably worked very hard to bring that killer to justice. But what she saw in the clear green depths of Duncan's eyes was understanding.

Something moved through her then, something she couldn't begin to name. But even as her gaze lingered on his, those green eyes darkened and triggered very different feelings. The rush of desire, the flood of heat, was intense and immediate, as if a button had been pushed. The impulse burst into her mind of just grabbing him, shoving him onto that sheet and rolling with him across it as she stripped him out of those clothes.

No. That couldn't happen.

But the thrill of what that might be like mingled with the accompanying shock that she'd actually thought of doing it. Wanted so badly to do it.

Here.

Now.

If they'd just been alone.

But they weren't. She dragged her gaze away from him and back to the sheet with its bloodred petals. What in the world was wrong with her? No man had ever made her think this...crazily before.

"Ms. MacPherson did an amazing job on the appeal," Abe Monticello was saying. "I've invited her to take second chair in the trial I'm scheduled for in a couple of weeks."

"She did an excellent job," Duncan agreed. "Thanks to her, a shoddy lab was shut down. For a while, our hardworking law enforcement agencies will be very careful about the way they collect and store evidence, and judges will think more precisely about what kind of evidence to admit into the record."

"Before we throw a ticker-tape parade, let's remember that the amazing appeal set a serial killer loose on the streets," Nelson added.

"So put him back in jail," Abe said. "In any case, our experts seem to agree that this incident is the work of a copycat."

"Not so fast. Before we jump on that bandwagon, we'd better take a look at this." Duncan lifted his hand, and out of the corner of her eye, Piper saw the thin envelope he held between two fingers.

"I found this tucked under the sheet." As he spoke he opened the unsealed flap and pulled out a piece of cream-colored vellum, the kind that a formal announcement might have been printed on.

He turned it so that she could see what was written in block letters. THE NEXT TIME, YOU'LL BE THE ONE LYING BENEATH THE PETALS.

It was only as Duncan read the message aloud to the other two men that the meaning began to sink in. A sliver of fear worked its way up her spine, but a little flare of anger chased it away. She shot to her feet. "Leaving a note was never part of the RPK's pattern. Who would do this?"

"Someone who's angry because we won our appeal," Abe said. "So it's clearly not Patrick Lightman. He's got to be very happy with the work we did."

"Well, someone definitely isn't," Nelson muttered.

"Agreed. Your job is to find out who's threatening Ms. MacPherson," Monticello said.

Duncan rose to his feet, but whatever he might have

added was forestalled by the commotion at the door of her apartment. Turning, she saw her colleague Richard Starkweather stride through the still-open door.

"Piper, thank God you're all right." He started toward her.

Duncan quickly stepped in front of her. "Who are you?"

Richard frowned at him. "Who are you?"

"He's all right," Abe said. "Richard Starkweather is one of my research assistants."

Because Duncan was completely blocking her view, Piper edged to his side. Two men now flanked Richard, a uniformed officer and Detective Nelson.

"What are you doing here?" Nelson asked the question that was foremost in Piper's mind.

"I came to see if Piper was all right. It's all over the news that the Rose Petal Killer has struck again." He gestured toward the petal-strewn sheet. "They're running footage of the crime scene on all three local news stations. It's even posted on YouTube. When I recognized Piper's apartment, I had to come over here to make sure she was all right. Surely you can understand that, Officer."

"Detective," Nelson corrected.

When the TV blared on, Piper turned to see that Abe was using the remote to find a news channel. The moment he did, they were all viewing a video clip of the scene in her apartment. It was exactly what she'd encountered when she'd returned from her run. There was a shot of the room that took in her kitchen, the open door to the bedroom, all the way to the fireplace. Then the picture on the TV screen narrowed to a close-up of the petal-strewn sheet. She felt a sliver of ice work its way up her spine.

A reporter's voice was saying, "This was the scene early this morning when attorney Piper MacPherson returned to her apartment. Our source tells us that Ms. MacPherson worked on the appeal that set accused Rose Petal Killer, Patrick Lightman, free. Will she be his next victim?"

Mike Nelson pulled out his phone. "I'll find out how they got that video clip."

"Whoever set up this little scene could easily have shot it on his cell phone before he left," Duncan said. "Then he could have attached it to an email. Starkweather just said it's accessible on YouTube."

Abe switched channels and caught another replay of the tape. A reporter gave the same information in a voice-over.

Piper made herself look carefully at it this time. "Someone shot the scene from the open doorway, then stepped inside for the close-up of the sheet. But why would anyone do this?"

There were three full beats of silence before Duncan directed a question to Abe. "Who knows she worked on the brief? So far you've kept a tight lid on that."

"Intentionally," Abe said. "No one from my office leaked it."

"Well, somebody found out," Duncan said. "And whoever did this is angry enough at her to paint a target on her back."

Great, Piper thought. She could picture it clearly in her mind. How could a day that had started out so normally become a nightmare so quickly?

3

TWO HOURS LATER, DUNCAN STOOD in the alley gazing at the wooden staircase that led to Piper's small apartment. Finally, he was alone.

Monticello had left first, waiting only until Piper had showered and changed so that he could personally escort her to work. Most members of the press who'd finally tracked down Piper's apartment had scurried after Abe's limo.

Mike Nelson had lingered longer. His men had talked to Piper's landlady, who owned the high-end dress shop beneath Piper's apartment, but the spare key was hanging from a rack in her office. One of the police department's tech men had tracked down the email message that had been sent to the TV stations. Both it and the attached video clip had been sent from a stolen smartphone. The owner hadn't even noticed it was missing.

The uniformed officers had questioned shop owners, but the incident had taken place hours before most of them had unlocked their doors. When Nelson had left, he'd taken everyone and everything with him—

crime scene techs, the uniforms, the sheet and the rose petals. Back at the precinct, Nelson and his partner would begin the tedious job of trying to track down where the roses and the sheet and the vellum note paper had been purchased. Tedious work, but it might pay off. They might get a description, even a name.

Duncan had hung around, instead of getting a late start to his golf game, because he did some of his best thinking as he wandered through a deserted crime scene. The quiet, the lack of other people, helped him to see things more clearly. He was frequently called in to consult on cases to do exactly what he was doing now. Lingering, noticing the small details, theorizing. He agreed totally with Piper. It wasn't Patrick Lightman who'd done this. Adrienne was checking on the man's alibi, but there were too many things about the scene that didn't fit into the RPK's M.O.

So who had done it? And why? Those were the key questions any profiler asked.

First, the perpetrator was smart. He'd had to gather data on the Lightman case and on Piper's schedule. And to pull it off as a media event in such a short amount of time, he'd had to have contacts at the local new stations.

No matter what angle Duncan viewed it from, he didn't think it was the work of a copycat who was planning to kill other women in the "style" of the RPK. His gut told him that the "who" was someone who had a personal vendetta against Piper. But whoever was trying to get to her was going to have to go through him.

Duncan wasn't sure when he'd made that decision. Perhaps it had been when he'd been studying the rose petals strewn across the sheet and Abe Monticello had mentioned her name. For just an instant, he'd seen the image of her he'd carried somewhere in his head all these years. He'd seen her lying beneath those petals.

Or perhaps it had been a decision that had been made for him seven years ago, when he'd stood under that stone arch with her. He was Scottish enough that he couldn't ignore the power of legends.

When he made the decision, it was irreversible. And it would lead to complications. While she'd been kneeling next to him studying the little picnic scene, he'd wanted his hands on her. And once he started down that path....

When his cell phone rang, he wasn't surprised to see Reid's number on the caller ID. That meant that the news about Piper had made its way to Scotland. And when there was trouble, Cam always made the first call to Reid, the oldest brother.

"I'm assuming you've got Piper's back," Reid said.

"Yes. I assume that our family in Scotland got the news and contacted you."

Reid laughed. "Sibling jealousy just never completely fades away. If it makes you feel better, no one has contacted me. I'm in France again with the VP and I caught it on the evening news. I thought I'd check with you before I got the call. I knew Piper was living in D.C., but I wasn't aware that she was working for Abe Monticello or that she was working on the RPK case. Your paths didn't cross during the trial, I take it."

"The FBI refused to share anything for that appeal."

"What's going on?"

"Wish I had a better handle on that." Then Duncan gave his brother a condensed version of what had happened and what they knew or theorized so far. While it helped to run through all the essentials again, it increased his sense that Piper could really be in danger.

"Could be it's someone who's unhappy with the fact that she helped to set Lightman free."

"That's a long list, but the police will have to start with Suzanne Macks's family, especially her twin brother, Sid." They'd been through quite a bit already. So if he could find anything that would narrow the list and eliminate them....

"I assume you have a plan," Reid said.

"Working on it."

"If I were you, I'd consider getting her the hell out of Dodge. Working on the vice president's security detail, I don't often have the luxury of doing that when my guy becomes a possible target."

"I'm considering that." The problem was to get Piper to agree.

"I'll leave it in your very capable hands, and I'll call the Scotland group to let them know that you're handling it."

After glancing at his watch, Duncan glanced down the alley, trying to see and think about it the same way the man who was threatening Piper's life had. She'd told Nelson that she ran at the same time every morning. That didn't surprise him. Her route took her past the shops on the street. Turning, he stepped out of the alley and glanced up and down the street. It was bustling now with both cars and pedestrian traffic. At six o'clock, she would have been easy to spot from a variety of locations. A regular routine made a serial killer's work easy.

The perpetrator hadn't had much to carry in, Duncan mused as he turned to walk down the alley and climb the stairs. The sheet, a couple of plastic bags filled with petals and the note. Everything could have been easily tucked into one bag. Maybe a backpack or a shopping bag. He recalled Piper's observation that the sheet had been new with the folds from the original packaging still apparent. She had a good eye for detail.

On the landing he crouched down to examine the lock. Duncan found nothing to contradict Nelson's judgment that it hadn't been tampered with. He took a slim tool out of his pocket, and twenty seconds later he was inside the apartment. Then he pantomimed moving the coffee table aside, shaking out the sheet. Thirty seconds. Adjusting and tucking the edges to replicate a perfect square took two minutes. Scattering the petals ate up another thirty. Tops.

He gave himself another thirty to examine the scene in his mind and thirty after that to make adjustments. Then he backed up to the door, took his cell phone out of his pocket and took a video, first panning the scene, then zooming in on the sheet and the petals.

It took him another minute to prop the ladder-backed chair against the door. Halfway down the stairs, he glanced at his watch. Seven or eight minutes from start to finish. Ten if the guy let nerves slow him down. But nothing else in the apartment had been disturbed. Whoever it was had come for one purpose only. To set up the scene, record it and get it on TV.

Mission accomplished.

Then he remembered the bag or whatever the guy must have used to carry in his props. If it had been a shopping bag, it hadn't been in the apartment. And it wasn't needed anymore.

On a hunch, he stopped by the Dumpster at the end of the alley. Duncan held his breath, ignoring the mix of odors he released as he lifted the lid. A Macy's bag lay right on the top, and inside he found a sales slip and the plastic covering for a single sheet.

Bingo.

He had his phone out, intending to pass the information along to Mike Nelson, when a long dark sedan pulled up to the mouth of the alley and his boss stepped out.

Adrienne Monticello was a tall, slender blonde with long curly hair. Today, she wore it pulled back into a ponytail. She had the same camera-ready good looks as her brother and she knew how to dress to enhance them. Her jacket and slacks were purple, her shoes designer. Gold winked at her ears and on her wrist. Although he knew she was in her mid-fifties, she could pass for a decade younger.

She whipped her oversize sunglasses off as she approached, and her expression was worried. "You aren't answering your phone."

"I don't like to be interrupted when I walk through a crime scene." And that's how she'd figured out where to track him down. The fact that she'd left the office to do so didn't bode well.

"Abe called me. He says you don't believe that Lightman was involved in this."

"He wasn't."

She studied him for a moment, and then nodded. "He's worried about Ms. MacPherson. He's been watching the TV coverage at his office, and they've located a photo of her from law school. They're running it along with the little petal scene."

"And Abe noticed that she's the Rose Petal Killer's type. Slender, long brown hair," Duncan added. Serial killers often had a type. Some even went for females who were left-handed or played a certain sport in high school. There'd been one who'd even chosen his victims because of the number and sequence of vowels in their first and last names.

"It isn't just Abe who's noticed it. The press is announcing it to the world about every fifteen minutes or so."

Not good, Duncan thought. That put an even bigger target on Piper's back. One that might tickle the fancy of Patrick Lightman. "Where is she right now?"

"In Abe's offices. He wants protection for her."

What he wanted, Duncan suspected, was for his big sister to help him out of the mess he'd created when he'd ignored her advice and taken the Lightman case.

"I thought you might have some ideas," she said. "Piper MacPherson is your stepsister, right?"

"Yes," Duncan said. "My mother married her father seven years ago, but we've never shared a home." And his feelings for her were definitely not brotherly. "You're having Lightman watched. Does he have an alibi?"

She nodded. "They didn't see him leave his apartment."

"I'm betting there's someone else who has a beef with Piper." He told her about the Macy's bag and the rest of what he was thinking. "It could be Sid Macks, Suzanne's brother." The young man had appeared on all the talk shows he could get himself booked on to protest the release of Lightman and the miscarriage of justice.

"Yeah. He confronted Abe a couple of times outside his office, but he never made any personal threats. He didn't seem the violent type."

"Maybe he or someone else is doing this to get Lightman's attention focused on Piper, hoping he'll do the dirty work."

"Shit. You're making me remember why I hired you. You can really get into the twisted way someone like Lightman would think." She glanced up at the apartment building. "Maybe it's a onetime thing. And maybe you're being paranoid about Lightman. He should be grateful that she helped get him off of death row."

"Hard to bank on that with a crazy psychopath."

"Hannibal Lecter had a soft spot in his heart for Clarice."

"Lecter was a fictional character. Lightman's not. But I may have a plan to keep her out of harm's way for a while." Duncan supposed it had been forming in his mind from the moment she'd walked into her apartment that morning.

"Then it was worth tracking you down in an alley," Adrienne said.

"The problem will be selling it to her."

Adrienne smiled at him. "I can't imagine the day when you won't be able to sell something to a woman."

AT A FEW MINUTES PAST SIX THAT evening, Piper started down the back stairwell in the building where Abe Monticello rented office space. She was wearing dark glasses, and she'd tucked her hair into an old golf cap her boss had dug out of one of his desk drawers.

A disguise.

Abe and Richard were, at this very moment, exiting through the front of the building, thus distracting the few die-hard reporters who had hung out all day hoping to interview her about the Rose Petal Killer's visit to her apartment.

No use telling the media that it hadn't been the real RPK who'd broken into her home and strewn those flower petals around. Some official spokesperson from the D.C. police department had already tried to clarify what had happened. And although the clips had aired all day on the twenty-four-hour cable news stations, first impressions were lasting. And whoever had taken that original video clip and released it to the press had created a dilly of a first impression.

Within hours some enterprising reporter had located her graduation photo from Georgetown Law and she'd become the celebrity of the moment, the latest face that could be blamed for letting Patrick Lightman out of jail.

Duncan had said that she had a target on her back. And by the end of the day, she'd felt it grow brighter and heavier by the moment. It hadn't helped one bit that every time she thought about the target, she thought about him and what she'd imagined doing to him and with him on that sheet in her apartment.

Seeing him again had blown open a floodgate of feelings that she'd successfully buried for years. The intense attraction she'd felt for him at their parents' wedding should have been history.

Piper started down the last flight of stairs. All day she'd tried to convince herself that what she'd felt when she'd seen him that morning had been a fluke. A one-time phenomenon that had been caused by the adrenaline rush of coming home to that terrible scene in her apartment.

But try as she might, she couldn't seem to get Duncan Sutherland completely out of her mind. Even as a child, she'd liked him the best of the triplets. He'd helped her out of an embarrassing situation once. She could still remember it as if it were yesterday. They'd been playing pirates, and Nell had drawn the short straw, which meant that she had to play the captured princess and sit in those dumb caves in the cliff face for hours on end until someone rescued her. Boring. But even though Reid had offered his help, Nell had looked frightened at the prospect of climbing up the cliff face to get to the cave. So Piper had volunteered to take her place.

She'd gotten there just fine because she and Cam, who'd been the pirate that day, had climbed up from the beach. For a while she'd amused herself by poking around in the small string of caves, three of them in total, but after a couple of hours, she'd known them like the back of her hand. Bored out of her mind, she'd decided to rescue herself. But when she'd started down the cliff face, she'd frozen.

When Duncan had arrived to "rescue" her, he'd found her just below the cave, clinging to the rocks. He'd told her he'd be right up, and when he was beside her, he simply told her that he'd go first and tell her what to do.

And he'd done just that, coaching her through it, telling her where to put her hands and feet. He had to have sensed her fear, but he'd never mentioned it or teased her. More importantly, he'd never ratted her out to his brothers or her sisters.

Duncan Sutherland was a man who could be trusted. She only wished she could trust her boss as unconditionally. But something was stopping her. Frowning, she strode down the hallway that led to the alley door. At five o'clock, Abe had called her into his office for a little heart-to-heart talk. He was worried about her safety. There might be other incidents.

Then he'd given her the really bad news.

He wanted her to take some time off. Maybe take a trip just until the media found something else to focus on. When she'd objected and pointed out that she was sitting second chair for the Bronwell trial in two weeks, he'd told her that he'd had to reconsider that decision. Richard Starkweather was going to take her place.

Her already much less than perfect day had become a whole lot worse.

Not that she could fault the logic of Abe's argument. The media circus that had surrounded him right after Lightman had been released had begun to die down. And the break-in at her apartment had stirred everything up again.

Just as seeing Duncan Sutherland had stirred her up again.

No. She was not going to think about him. What she'd felt had been a fluke.

She had bigger problems, not the least of which was the implied death threat on the vellum notepaper. Thus, her Greta Garbo-like exit down the back staircase. Her ride home, arranged by Abe, would be waiting at the end of the alley. And maybe, just maybe, her improvised disguise would allow her to sneak into her apartment unnoticed.

She turned the knob on the alley door. A relaxing bath, layered with bubbles and accompanied by a glass of icy white wine, would help her to think. There'd be other trials. And other setbacks. Piper MacPherson didn't believe that getting depressed or discouraged was ever an effective way to handle life's rough patches.

She was never going to become her father's daughter. He'd avoided life for years after her mother had died. She believed in facing life head-on. She'd figure out a way to deal with the rose petal incident and she'd win back the opportunity to sit second chair with Abe.

The instant she stepped out of the building into the

alley, she stopped short and every thought or plan she had in her mind disappeared. All she could do once again was stare.

Duncan stood leaning against the hood of a very shiny red convertible. The kind that was meant for the open road and speed. Not at all the kind of car she'd expected the quiet, studious Duncan Sutherland to drive.

Neither of those adjectives seemed to apply to the man leaning against the sexy car. He looked as big as he had in her apartment that morning. And his effect on her senses was just as intense. She could see more of him now. A lot more. Broad shoulders tapered down to a narrow waist and then long, long legs crossed at the ankles. With each passing second, the sizzle in her blood grew stronger, hotter.

He'd changed into a black T-shirt and jeans that made him look just a bit dangerous. His face, with its slash of cheekbones, broad forehead, unruly hair and strong chin, was nearly movie star perfect. That was the image of him that had kept sneaking into her mind all day, even when she'd been talking to Abe and losing her dream assignment.

When she met Duncan's eyes, they had the same effect on her senses they'd had that morning, sending a shot of heat that hit her dead center, then radiated right out to her fingers and toes. Okay. The way she was reacting to him was not a fluke and not the result of an adrenaline rush.

Terrific.

As if she hadn't had enough to deal with today. A nut who wanted to scare her, a boss who wanted to protect her, not to mention himself, and now this.

It was only then she realized she wasn't moving.

It was the second time today Duncan Sutherland had stopped her cold.

Time to put an end to that. She'd talk to him and send him on his way. Striding forward, she forced a smile. "We've got to stop meeting like this."

Duncan threw back his head and laughed. Her straightforward, no-nonsense approach was one of the things he'd always liked about Piper. And he was grateful for it now since it had effectively brought him back to the present. For a moment after she'd stepped out of that alley door, she'd wiped his mind clean.

"What are you doing here?" Piper asked as she reached the hood of his car.

He had to think for a second. Looking at her was slowing his thought processes down. But the reason was the same one that had brought him to her apartment that morning. "Your boss called my boss and asked for a favor."

Her brows shot up. "Favor? What kind of a favor? And why would your boss owe Abe Monticello a favor?"

"Family thing. My boss is Adrienne Monticello. She's Abe's younger sister. I suspect she grew up trying to get him out of trouble, and old habits die hard. They're both worried about you."

Duncan watched her absorb the information. While he absorbed more of her. The pantsuit was a pale gray linen with a slim fit that tapered down to narrow ankles and killer heels. When he slowly swept his gaze back up to her face, he saw by her frown that she didn't like his answer, but she got it.

"You're my ride back to my apartment."

"Yes." For starters. He wouldn't tell her his entire plan, not while they were standing in an alley and they hadn't yet discovered who'd set that nasty little scene that morning.

She shifted her gaze to the car and ran her hand over the hood. "Nice ride."

"Nice disguise."

"I had to improvise." She tipped her sunglasses down as she met his eyes. Duncan took the hit dead center and he struggled to keep his thoughts from scattering again. When she pulled the cap off and a rich cascade of dark brown hair tumbled out, he gave up on thinking of anything but the way the sun showered over her long, loose curls, lightening some strands, darkening others. He reached out and wound one of those curls around his finger. He couldn't be sure who had moved, but they were close enough that their fingers had suddenly tangled on the hood of his car. Close enough that he could see a ring of lighter gold surrounding the deep, rich amber shade of her eyes. And he could smell her. Spring flowers—he hadn't forgotten the scent.

If he lowered his head, he could finally taste her. Something he'd been wondering about all day. No. Longer than that. He'd been wondering about her taste for seven years.

Piper's mind was racing almost as fast as her heart but she couldn't seem to latch onto a coherent thought. When she'd started toward him, she'd had a plan. She was going to handle the Duncan problem by politely accepting his ride home and then sending him on his way. And now her fingers were linked with his and the heat from that flesh-to-flesh contact was zinging through her blood.

She could try to blame it on the car. If she hadn't run her hand over the hood, she wouldn't have gotten this close. But a good defense attorney would tear that excuse to shreds and claim she'd put her hand on the hood because she'd wanted this to happen—that she'd been thinking of touching him ever since she'd seen him in her apartment that morning.

Guilty, she thought. And, dammit, now that his mouth was only inches from hers, she wanted to taste him, too.

No. She had to think.

Breathe. The air she gulped in burned her lungs.

Say something. But the desire she was feeling was so huge, so consuming, she couldn't get any words past the dryness in her throat.

They touched nowhere else except where their fingers were linked, but he might as well have been touching her everywhere. And she wanted him to so badly.

With whatever brain cells she had left, Piper figured she had two options. Run or do what she really, really wanted to do. And why not? It had taken a Pandora to open that box and an Eve to sample that apple. Maybe she just needed to know how big a problem she was dealing with. A good attorney built her best cases once she'd read through the discovery. Gripping his shirt with her free hand, she rose on her toes and pulled his mouth to hers.

She might have made the first move, but once she had, Duncan Sutherland was no slouch in the kissing department. The scrape of his teeth had her gasping, then moaning as his tongue seduced hers. Those hands, quick and clever, were everywhere, enticing, exciting. She couldn't get her breath, didn't care if she ever did.

She thought she'd known what to expect.

The jolt was no surprise. But how could she have

known it would knock her off her feet? Or had he lifted her?

The heat, too, she'd been prepared for. When a man could make your blood sizzle with a look, heat was a given. But she hadn't imagined it would have the power of a blast furnace. Or trigger a need to crawl right into him until she dissolved.

Excitement was too tame a word for what was pounding in her blood.

Greed didn't even come close to describing the desperate hunger she was feeling or the urgent need to satisfy it.

Here. Now.

Had she said the words out loud?

Had he?

ALL DUNCAN KNEW WAS THAT HE couldn't think. She flooded his senses, blocking out everything else with her taste, her textures, her scents. He couldn't separate them. Couldn't possibly name them all. Couldn't resist taking more, asking for more.

When she wrapped her arms and legs around him, as much demand as invitation, he was helpless to do anything other than take them both deeper. No other woman had ever made him feel helpless. Now she was taking him places he'd never been before, making him feel things he'd never felt before.

And why had he waited so long to let her do it?

Here. Now.

The idea of laying her on the hood of his car and quenching the desire, the need that had gone from flame to inferno in seconds, flashed brilliantly into his mind. He wanted, wildly wanted to turn the image in his mind into reality.

Here. Now.

But he couldn't. With the words still thrumming in his mind and pounding in his blood, he reached deep for control and found it. Easing away, he settled her against the car's fender before he stepped back. His pulse was still racing. His heart slammed like a hammer against an anvil in his chest. And he still wanted her. He had to figure that wasn't going to stop any time soon.

So he had a problem. An even bigger one than he'd anticipated. "That isn't what I came here to do."

"Ditto." She'd folded her arms across her chest, but she was no longer using the car for support. When he noticed he still was, he stepped away.

"We have to figure out a solution to this," she said.

"Agreed."

"I have to think."

Duncan thought the time for that had passed.

"So." She walked around to the passenger door and opened it. "You can take me to my apartment, see that I'm safely locked in and then go away."

Duncan slid behind the wheel and then drove them out of the alley into D.C. traffic. He could go along with one out of three of her directives. But he figured he'd have a better chance of making his case in her apartment.

4

PIPER STOOD IN HER KITCHEN watching Duncan open a bottle of red zinfandel. He'd picked it up with the pizza on the drive back to her apartment.

"We have to talk. You have to eat," he'd said by way of explanation.

She couldn't argue with either point. And she figured she needed to save up her energy. If she was going to argue with Duncan about anything, it was going to be about what she was sure he wanted to "talk" about.

The mind-blowing kiss they'd indulged in.

In an alley. A very public place.

She'd made the move, but at least they knew what they were up against. And she hadn't been the one to call a halt to it. She'd always been able to before. That aside, they had to find a solution. They both worked in D.C. They were adults. And they wanted each other like gangbusters. No way they could ignore the elephant in the room.

She made her living arguing cases, negotiating solutions, and if she'd learned anything from law school and from working for Abe, it was the value of a pre-emptive strike.

So while they'd driven home, she'd tried to review her options. But it was damn hard to weigh them objectively while they'd sat so close in that tiny car. Every time he'd shifted gears, his arm had brushed against hers, and each time it had, "here" and "now" had blinked on and off, little neon letters in her mind.

Now he filled all the spare space in her kitchen. She could even smell him above the spicy aroma of the food.

He'd given her no chance to send him away as he'd cut a path through the little throng of reporters that had been waiting at the mouth of the alley. And she had to admit that she was happy not to have had to enter her apartment alone tonight.

He poured the dark red wine into two glasses and handed her one. "I have a proposition for you."

"Ditto," she said. She just had to figure out what it was. Exactly.

"Mind if I go first?"

"Go ahead." The only thing better than making a preemptive strike was learning what your opponent had in mind and then adjusting your strategy.

"Cam has been bugging me to take a few days off and go up to the castle to see what I can figure out about the rest of Eleanor Campbell MacPherson's missing dowry and about that intruder he believes was breaking into the library. I want you to come with me."

Surprised, Piper stared at him, her mind racing. Duncan Sutherland knew a bit about making preemptive strikes himself, it seemed. "Why would I want to do that?"

He sipped his wine, and then smiled at her. "Because your sister Adair already found one of the earrings. Don't you want to see what you can do if you set your mind to it?"

She tilted her head to one side to study him. "My sisters and I aren't much motivated by sibling rivalry. And I have a lot on my plate right now."

"Agreed." He finessed two slices of pizza out of the steaming box and handed her one on a plate. When they were both seated at the small table, he continued. "Look, I know that Monticello wants you to keep a low profile for a while. Part of that is because he is what he is. He doesn't want the spotlight focused on anyone else but him. But part of that is motivated by genuine concern for your safety. He's worried about you. And what happened today—you can't take that lightly. My boss isn't taking it lightly. What argument could I make that would convince you to come up to the castle with me for a while?"

Piper lifted her glass and swirled the contents. She took a careful sip before meeting his eyes. "Not a one. I don't believe in running away from problems."

Okay, Duncan thought. He'd struck out on his first and second strategies. The missing sapphires and the safety factor. It struck him quite forcibly that he didn't know as much as he needed to know about Piper MacPherson. Therefore, he'd used the wrong approaches so far. A first for him and totally due to the fact that for the last seven years he'd tried to avoid thinking about her, period.

So he did what he'd avoided doing for seven years. Biting into a slice of pizza, he put himself in her shoes, the same technique he used on the cases he profiled. She was tired. There were dark circles under her eyes and a little worry line on her forehead. The worry line struck a chord in his memory. When they'd played together as children, she'd always been the worrier about one or the other of her sisters. Protective, too.

And today of all days, why wouldn't she be tired? She'd been instrumental in writing a brief that had let a convicted murderer go free. Monticello's personal hunger for media attention had protected her so far, but now she was suddenly being credited with putting Patrick Lightman on the streets. And someone didn't like that at all.

She didn't like it, either. He'd seen both guilt and regret in her eyes that morning when Abe had been bragging about her brilliant brief. He'd recognized it at the time, but there'd been other things on his mind, including handling his response to her.

He took another sip of his wine. There had to be a better way to convince her.

As silence stretched between them, Piper picked a piece of pepperoni off of her slice and ate it. "Abe is so concerned about my safety that he replaced me as second chair on the Bronwell trial."

"That sucks." The case had made all the papers and hit the national news nearly a year ago. Alicia Bronwell, the trophy wife of one of D.C.'s most highly paid lobbyists, had been accused of slowly killing her much older husband with arsenic. When Abe snatched away Piper's opportunity to participate in the trial, that had to have been a blow. On a day when she'd already sustained a pretty good one.

But it didn't escape him that the loss of the Bronwell trial was foremost in Piper's mind—not the fact that someone might be intending to harm her. The woman had courage. He'd noticed it when they'd been children. There'd been one day in particular when they'd been playing a pirate game on the cliffs. Duncan recalled finding her clinging to the rocks, frozen with fear. She'd climbed down to the beach with him—in spite of the fact that she'd been scared stiff.

She selected a slice of green pepper.

"Monticello offered you second chair as your reward for the work you did on the Lightman case."

When she met his eyes, he saw the anger. "Yes. Then he took it away and gave it to Richard."

Duncan's eyes narrowed. "The guy who barged in here this morning."

"Yes. And he'll take full advantage of the opportunity. Richard's good at that."

"You've had a hell of a day. First a nutcase who wants to annoy and scare you at the very least and, worst case scenario, wants you dead. Then your boss reneges on his offer."

"If you're trying to cheer me up, you're failing."

"I'm not here to cheer you up. I'm just laying a foundation for the case I'm going to make. Isn't that what you'd do with a jury?"

She lifted her glass and studied him over the rim. There was a challenge in her eyes, and they didn't appear as tired anymore. "Go for it, Sutherland."

"Seems to me you have two choices." Holding up a finger, he talked around another bite of pizza. "You can stay here in D.C., deal with the press and hide away in your boss's office while you wait for the guy who staged the scene this morning to make his next move."

She sipped her wine and waited for him to continue.

"That *is* your current plan, right?"

"Close enough."

His eyes narrowed suddenly. "Don't tell me you're

going to try to find out who set up the little scene this morning."

Her eyes widened full of innocence. "Okay, I won't tell you that."

He grinned at her and had the pleasure of seeing surprise flicker over her features. "It's exactly what I would do. But I have a better proposition for you."

The second he saw the pulse flutter at her throat and the color of her eyes darken, Duncan knew he'd chosen the wrong word. *Proposition* had other connotations, and they were both now thinking about the possibilities. They were alone. And it would be so easy to just propose that they finish what they'd started in that alley. Better still, he could shove the pizza aside, pluck her out of that chair and do what he'd wanted to do since they'd walked into her apartment.

Except that wasn't what he was making a case for right now.

"Why don't you help me put Patrick Lightman back in jail?"

She narrowed her eyes, studying him. "Why do I have to go to the castle to do that?"

"Because I'm having all the FBI's files on him delivered up there. My current assignment at work is to review all of the RPK cases and find something that will allow us to charge Lightman again. Cam has been bugging me to go up there and get a feel for the intruder who may come back. So my proposition is— come with me to the castle and help me find what I need in the files."

"Are you serious?"

"I am. I can work there just as easily as I can work in my office at Quantico. My boss thinks it's a great idea, and your boss will be happy if you're safe and out of the public eye for a bit."

She frowned at him. "You've put a sugar coating on it, but it sounds like you want to whisk me off to the castle so that you can babysit me."

He met her eyes very steadily. "I don't think that you can afford to take what happened this morning lightly. To pull off what he did, he had to have stalked you. And I don't think he's through yet."

"Scaring me is not going to work."

"You've made that clear." He selected another slice of pizza, and leaning back in his chair, stretched out his legs. They nearly reached the back of the couch. "You know this place reminds me of a dollhouse." He chewed a bite of his slice, then said, "And you eat like a doll. Don't you like pizza?"

She picked off a mushroom and popped it into her mouth. "I love pizza. But when I'm playing the role of jury I like to give the argument my full attention."

"Okay, scaring you is the stick part of my strategy. The carrot part is that I really want you to work with me on the RPK files. You found things in the trial transcript and in the case files that got Lightman off. That means you have a damn good eye. I saw the proof of that right here this morning. Thanks to you, I think I found the bag the guy used to carry in a brand-new sheet from Macy's." He elaborated on the search Nelson was doing. "I could really use your help. There's something in one of the cases that I'm missing. And I want Lightman back in a cell."

So did she. "I'm not ashamed of the work I did on the case."

"I wouldn't be either. Under all the bombast and drama, Abe Monticello serves an important function in the justice system, and in the end all of us will be safer. You did your job and you did it well."

He could make her feel so many things. The approval in his tone triggered warmth that intensified when their fingers linked again. She felt the pull, the same one she'd felt when their hands had connected on the hood of his car. Her gaze shifted to his mouth, and she felt the pull even stronger than before. They were alone. All she had to do was lean across the table, close the small distance between them, and she could feel more—more than anyone had ever made her feel. And there was more that he could make her feel.

Here. Now. She simply couldn't prevent those words from coming to mind every time he was this close.

"There's a connection between us," Duncan murmured.

There was definitely something between them. She glanced down at their joined hands. She could try to pull her hand away. She might be able to. She might not. He might let her, but he might not. Each possibility brought a separate thrill.

Here. Now.

She met his eyes and saw that he was thinking the same thing. All one of them had to do was make that small move. But she saw something else she recognized, because it matched exactly what she was feeling. Wariness.

Watching each other, they drew their hands back at the same time.

Duncan closed his fingers around his wineglass. "If you agree to come to the castle with me, we can explore the connection. Or not. No pressure. That part's up to you. Bottom line, I'd really like your help."

Piper was surprised that her hand didn't tremble

when she used it to lift her glass. She needed a sip of wine because her throat had gone dry as dust. He was going to leave whatever was going on between them up to her?

Maybe. She wasn't sure she entirely trusted him on that score. As far as no pressure went…there was pressure each time she looked at him.

Duncan leaned forward. "I've never made a case to a jury before. What's the verdict? Will you go with me to the castle?"

She had her mouth open, ready to answer when footsteps pounded on the staircase outside. Duncan was already at the door when someone knocked.

When he opened it, all she could see beyond Duncan's large frame was the face of her visitor, and she recognized it immediately. "Mr. Findley." She crossed to the door. "Duncan, this is Mr. Findley. He runs the coffee shop across the street."

"A deliveryman left these with me earlier today. I promised I would bring them up when you got home. But I wanted to wait until the reporters finally gave up and went away."

"Thanks." But it wasn't until Duncan turned that she saw roses. They were bright red and arranged in a glass vase. Fear knotted in her stomach.

Mr. Findley was already retreating down the stairs as Duncan closed the door.

"Those are not from the RPK," Piper said. "They're from whoever set up that little scene this morning. And he's beginning to annoy the hell out of me."

Duncan took a vellum card out of an envelope and held it out to her.

THE NEXT TIME YOU'LL BE THE ONE LYING BENEATH THE PETALS. THESE PERHAPS.

"The person who sent this note could be just as dangerous," Duncan said.

"I don't want to run away from this. I want to catch him and make him pay."

Duncan set the flowers down, then turned to face her. The anger she saw in his eyes was such a close match to her own that some of her tension eased.

"We're going to catch him," he said. "He's already making mistakes. He left behind that Macy's bag, and he used a florist for this. Mike Nelson will check it out. In the meantime, why not play with his mind the way he's trying to play with yours?" he asked. "Just think of what he'll feel like if you're not here to get the next message or flower delivery. If you come away with me to the castle, it's going to annoy the hell out of *him*."

She studied him for a moment, but the decision had been made. "You're damn good at making a case, Sutherland. I'll pack a bag."

AT FIRST PIPER WASN'T SURE what had awakened her. Not Donald Duck, a fact she discovered when her hand whacked the flat top of the nightstand. And she couldn't see a thing. The lights from the street always filtered in through her bedroom curtains.

By the time her mind had slogged its way through the missing alarm clock and the pitch blackness that surrounded her, lightning flashed outside and the brief illumination chased away her disorientation.

She was in her bedroom at Castle MacPherson. Thunder rumbled. Rain splatted.

Ah, the sounds of home, she thought. Turning on her side, she angled her head toward the windows so that she could see the lightning sparkle and dance across the sky. Nature's fireworks.

For better or worse, she'd let Duncan talk her into coming here. And he hadn't wasted any time doing it. He'd called Aunt Vi to let her know they were coming, and his suitcase and golf clubs had already been in the trunk of his car when he'd finessed her suitcase in between them. Either he'd been very confident that he'd be able to talk her into going with him or he'd been prepared to leave without her. She suspected the former.

And she couldn't fault the argument he'd made. Or the bait he'd used. Offering the opportunity to put Patrick Lightman back behind bars had been the perfect lure. He had to have known she would jump at it. She suspected that he was very good at his job.

But if Duncan Sutherland thought he was going to have everything his way every time, he would be in for a surprise.

The rain was pouring down now, the thunder crashing overhead. The details of their exit from D.C., while pushing the speed limit through a series of small towns in Pennsylvania and New York, were coming back. Duncan had kept the music loud and tuned to a station that played and replayed the top twenty. The fact that only a few of the songs were familiar to her told her that she'd been working too hard. It had been after midnight when they'd reached the castle, but Aunt Vi had greeted them at the door and hustled them off to waiting beds.

She'd slept like a rock until now. Nearly 5:00 a.m. according to the illuminated dial on her watch. Throwing the covers off, she crossed to the sliding doors that led to one of the castle's many balconies and opened them. The rain was growing softer already and the lightning had dimmed to erratic flickers in the slowly graying sky. Even as a child, she'd loved the storms that rushed in over the mountain lakes, unleashed their fury, and then blew away. They seldom lasted long.

But then, few things in life did. Everything was temporary. The important thing was to live in the present the best way you knew how. And Duncan had given her the opportunity to do that on a couple of levels. She enjoyed solving problems, the planning, the execution, even the point at which you claimed success and then could put them behind you. For years now, she'd structured her life around projects. Finish college, get into Georgetown Law, make law review. Since she'd worked for Abe, it had been one case after another.

This was the first break she'd had in a long time. Not that it was a break, really. She had two projects to work on. Find something that would put Patrick Lightman back in jail, and decide what to do about the intense, almost primitive attraction she and Duncan were feeling for each other.

She knew what she wanted to do about Duncan. And every time she got near him, she wanted to do it on the spot. No other man had ever tempted her that much or that urgently. But keeping her heart unentangled and fancy-free had been part of her game plan from the time she'd first noticed that boys weren't so scruffy and annoying. During her college and law school years, she'd enjoyed a few relationships with men, but she'd never let them intrude on the rest of her life. If she and Duncan—what was the word he'd used? *Explored*— that was it. If they decided to explore what they were feeling, things were bound to get messy. Not only was there the family angle, but an attraction as consuming as the one she and Duncan were feeling might not be easily corked in a bottle.

Placing her palms on the balcony railing, she stared

out over the garden as the sky slowly lightened. In the distance, she could see the dark gleam of the lake, quiet now and smooth, and she could see the stone arch. Two floodlights had been installed as part of the tightened security on the castle after a man going by the name of Nathan MacDonald had planted a bomb behind some stones in the arch.

Of course, she and her sisters had buried something very different there—a metal box that contained their goals and dreams. Piper grinned at the memory. It had been years since she'd even thought of the box that their mother had once kept her jewelry in.

When they were just kids, it had been Adair's idea to write out their goals and dreams on slips of paper, put them in the box, and by burying it behind loose stones in the arch, tap into the power of the legend.

Piper's addition to the scheme was that they each use different colored paper to ensure privacy. Then Nell had assigned the colors—yellow for Adair, blue for Piper and pink for Nell. For years they'd made a habit of sneaking out of the house late at night, digging up that box and slipping in new goals. The last time they'd done it had been on the night that their father had married Beth Sutherland.

Something stirred at the edges of her mind. If she hadn't thought of the box in years, she certainly hadn't thought of that night. But little flashes were coming back to her now. She and Nell and Adair had snuck out of the castle close to midnight with a bottle of champagne and pads of their appropriately colored paper. They'd raced a storm to the stones—and won. They'd toasted their success and their father's wedding with the champagne, and then at Adair's suggestion, they'd all agreed to write down an erotic encounter involving their ideal fantasy man.

That part she remembered. But with all the champagne she'd drunk that night and the fact that she'd buried the memory for so long, the details of her fantasy were fuzzy. She knew one thing. It had been the first and only time she'd ever written anything about a man and buried it in the stones. She felt a little stir of unease.

Hours earlier on that same day, she'd met Duncan's eyes beneath those stones and she'd felt things she'd never experienced before. Had she been thinking of him when she'd written out her fantasy? Turning, she paced into her room. He'd certainly been on her mind that day. But she'd managed to avoid him. And he and his brothers had left to fly back to their respective colleges shortly after the ceremony. So she probably would have thought of anyone *but* him when she was composing her erotic fantasy.

Or she might have been thinking *only* of him. A mix of emotions moved through her—anticipation, excitement, panic. Lots of the other goals she'd tucked into that box had become a reality—starting with the medals she'd won in her elementary school's yearly spelling bee and right up to and including her law degree at Georgetown.

Before she decided exactly what she and Duncan would *explore,* it would be good to know what she was dealing with. Discovery was essential before you built a case for trial. Gathering all the facts was equally important in making any intelligent decision. Ignorance could come back and bite you hard.

And there was no time like the present to find out exactly what her fantasy had been all those years ago. Turning back into her room, she found sweats and shoes in her suitcase and pulled them on. For a second, she thought of running down the stairs to the foyer and disarming the security system Vi had shown them.

But there was a quicker way to the stone arch. She wasn't enamored of heights, especially if she had to climb down instead of up. But after the summer when the Sutherland boys had been focused on playing pirates on the cliffs and she'd discovered her fear, she'd worked on it by frequently climbing down to the garden from her balcony. Of course, her sisters had been with her then to silently cheer her on. And it had been a while since she'd practiced…

Her stomach took one, queasy roll as she threw her leg over the railing. Then she used the thick vines covering the stones to climb down. By the time she reached the ground, she was breathing hard and grinning in triumph. Then, in the growing morning light, she raced to the stone arch to find the metal box she and her sisters had buried their dreams and fantasies in.

5

As PIPER REACHED THE CLEARING, the eastern sky was lightening and just the rim of a red sun could be seen peeking out over the tips of the pines across the lake. The stone arch that Angus—Eleanor Campbell MacPherson's husband—had built lay at the far end of the garden. It was about ten feet long, eight feet or so wide and the ceiling arched to about ten feet. The fact that it had stood for more than two centuries testified to her several-times-great grandfather's engineering and construction skills. It had even withstood a lightning strike about a month ago.

It didn't take Piper long to find the box. The stones that concealed it in the niche were loose, as if they'd recently been replaced. By Adair, no doubt. Her older sister had been living here at the castle for more than six months. It was a good possibility she'd dug up the secret container they'd stored their fantasies and dreams in. It was about the size of a cigar box, made of metal, and it had a little padlock about as secure as one that came on a young girl's diary.

In fact, it had, if she remembered correctly. One of

Adair's. After wiggling the box out of its niche, she sat down on the flat rocks that formed the base of the stone arch and placed it in her lap. Just looking at it jogged a few more details loose. Nell had wanted to know how erotic their sexual fantasy could be.

"No holds barred." That had been her answer to her baby sister. And she'd been thinking about Duncan when she'd said it. It was coming back to her now. Once they'd exchanged that look while their parents had spoken their vows, she hadn't been able to quite put him out of her mind.

She couldn't put him out of her mind now. The chemistry between them was so strong, so primal. The stuff that sexual fantasies were made of. As she ran her hand over the box, she could have sworn the metal grew warmer. She examined the tiny padlock and saw that it had rusted through, so she removed it.

Lifting the top, she found the contents just as she remembered—three separate compartments, each holding different colored paper. Picking up the folded blue sheets on the top of her pile, she opened them.

The heading read *My Fling With My Fantasy Man: Sex on Demand*.

She felt her heart skip a beat. Then and now. Those were the words that said it all when she'd imagined the sexual fantasy that she wanted to bring to life with Duncan Sutherland. Oh, she might have buried the memory away, but if anything, it had just grown stronger.

At nineteen, it had described her ideal sexual fantasy period. She'd been in her sophomore year of college, and all her friends had been raving about the benefits of having a friend they could call on for sex on demand. *Buddy sex* was what they'd called it. It was convenient, no fuss and no bother.

Piper skimmed the first page. She'd gone way beyond what her friends had talked about. And like any good prelaw student, she'd defined her terms and embellished them as she'd argued the benefits. Sex on demand with a willing partner was simple, straightforward and didn't require all the time-consuming trappings that went along with dating and romance. It further prevented complications from spilling over into the other more important aspects of your life—like your work, your goals, your dreams.

The "sex on demand"—she was finding that aspect on the page in spades. She recalled just how fast her pen had moved over the blue paper trying to capture all the images she'd had in her head of having sex with him anytime, anyplace and in any position. By the time she'd finished skimming the second page, her heart was racing and her whole body had heated. She'd even written about making love with Duncan in that cave he'd rescued her from.

An image of doing just that flashed brilliantly into her mind. It was followed by another—the two of them standing in the alleyway at the back of Abe's office building. They'd come very close to having on-demand sex right on the hood of her car. Earlier that day, when they'd been in her apartment kneeling together on the floor, she'd imagined having sex with him right on that petal-strewn sheet.

She couldn't seem to look at him without thinking, *here* and *now*.

What if she could have sex on demand with Duncan—no holds barred? The idea thrilled her.

And why not?

She pressed a hand to her heart to make sure it didn't beat its way right out of her chest. Coming up here to the castle with him certainly hadn't been something she'd planned on. But a girl was a fool not to take advantage of the opportunities that life offered.

Then a thought struck her and an alarm bell jingled at the edge of her mind. She shifted her gaze back to the subtitle and skimmed the pages again. Discovery—that's what she'd come here for. And good discovery triggered questions. In this case a couple of very big ones.

The alarm bell went from jingle to clang. What if what she'd written down on these pages was influencing, perhaps even dictating, what she was feeling now for Duncan? What if the stones and the legend were playing some kind of role in making her want Duncan so badly?

She felt panic surge and shoved it down. She'd never solved one problem in her life by panicking. And it wasn't like she'd actually kissed Duncan in the stone arch. All she'd done was lust after him—very imaginatively and in great detail.

You had to actually kiss someone beneath the stone arch before the legend kicked in. She could argue that major distinction to any jury of her peers and win.

And sex on demand with Duncan was perfect as long as it had no strings, no expectations—all the good points her college buddies had raved about with "buddy sex." It would be the perfect arrangement for them while they were here. She could make that case to Duncan. And she couldn't imagine him having a problem with it.

A sound, a bell jingling, had her glancing up and she saw Alba, the dog her aunt had brought home from a shelter, approaching. They'd met briefly when she and Duncan had arrived the night before. If Alba had been sent to find her, that meant that her aunt Vi was up and Duncan might already be up, too.

She folded the sheets of blue paper, carefully tucked them back into the center compartment, then set the now useless padlock back in place. Then she put the fantasy box back where it been for the last seven years. She might not have figured out what she could do about the rest of her problems, but she'd definitely decided what she wanted to do about Duncan Sutherland.

WHEN DUNCAN WALKED INTO THE kitchen, he found himself greeted by the scent of freshly brewed coffee and a warm hug from Viola MacPherson. Now she was his mother's sister-in-law, but he would always remember her as the warm, loving woman who'd baked cookies and applied first aid on that long-ago summer when he and his brothers had spent nearly every day at Castle MacPherson while his mother researched the MacPherson family in the castle's library.

Minutes later, he was seated at the table in the sun-drenched kitchen and she was setting platters of scrambled eggs, bacon and her homemade scones in front of him. Then she poured herself a cup of tea and sat down across from him.

"Shouldn't we wait for Piper?" he asked as she loaded a plate for him and then one for herself.

"You'll starve if you wait for her. Eats like a bird. From the time she was a little girl, she's been a grazer. When she finally comes in from the stone arch, she'll go for coffee first and pick at half a scone. Then she might have a banana."

"She's out at the stone arch?" He was halfway out of his chair when Vi signaled him back down.

"She's safe enough. I sent Alba to her. Our dog may be deaf, but she senses things."

"Cam told me about Alba's talents." His brother's theory about an intruder visiting the castle's library for six months had been largely due to Alba's barking in the middle of the night. But the security on the castle, and especially the library, had been tightened since then. And he'd taken the time to check it out last night.

"She hasn't sensed anyone visiting the library lately, I take it."

Vi shook her head. "Things have been very quiet here since you delivered our last bridegroom and saved the day. No lightning strikes. No bombs. The most exciting thing we have planned all weekend is a photo shoot tomorrow morning."

As he dug into his eggs, Duncan reviewed the theory that Cam had given him, picturing it in his mind—someone sneaking in after everyone had gone to bed, making himself at home in the library and taking his—or her—time to search it thoroughly. It spoke of someone who was very patient. But it also indicated someone who had good reason to believe that he would find what he was looking for. Cam's theory was that the intruder had been searching for the location of Eleanor's sapphires. Then two things had happened. First, Adair had found one missing earring, and for the past month access to the library and the castle had been shut down. Not only had the intruder's easy-come, easy-go nighttime visits been cut off by a new security system, but Cam and Daryl had installed cameras and added laser light technology to the alarm system in the library.

Whoever the intruder was, he couldn't be happy with either development. And he was probably trying to find another way to gain access to the castle and the library. That's what Duncan would do. So there could very well be a storm brewing from that direction.

"How long has Piper been out there?" Duncan asked as he reached for his coffee.

"Probably since first light. Although I hope she got some sleep first." Vi sipped her tea. "From the time they were little, all three of them used to make midnight visits to the stone arch to share secrets, make plans, dream dreams. They even used to write their goals down. They buried them in a box in the stones so that they could tap into what Adair always called the 'power of the stones.' They used to leave from Piper's room because they could easily climb down from her balcony." Vi's smile held a hint of nostalgia. "They didn't think I knew about that part."

"You kept pretty good track of your girls back then," Duncan said. And she still did. When he'd called the castle last night to let Vi know they were coming, she'd already been aware of the incident at Piper's apartment and the resulting media storm. He reached across the table and gave her hand a squeeze. "I'm going to keep her safe. And we're going to find out who's targeting her."

"I know. I talked to Daryl after I spoke with you," Vi said. "He thinks that getting her out of D.C. was a good idea."

The instant she mentioned Daryl's name, a pretty blush rose in Vi's cheeks. Duncan smiled at her. "It's always good to know that the director of the CIA's domestic operations unit thinks I'm on the right track."

Duncan lifted her hand to examine her engagement ring. "Daryl has good taste."

Vi sighed. "It is lovely, isn't it?"

"I was talking about you, but the ring is lovely, too. Have you and Daryl set a date yet?"

"First weekend of September. Adair has already put our names on the wedding schedule. Daryl flew into Albany yesterday on some kind of business, and since I'm attending and presenting at a big wedding fair at one of the malls, I'm going to join him for dinner, and then I'm bringing him back here for the weekend. He wants to be here for that photo shoot tomorrow with *Architectural Digest*. He's looking forward to meeting Piper."

"Is he worried about the shoot?"

"No. Daryl checked out the man who's coming. Russell Arbogast is a senior editor and writer with the magazine. They've been running a series on Scottish castles and they want to include a feature article on the replica Angus One built of his ancestral home. With Cam and Adair both gone, Daryl didn't want me to have to handle it alone."

"It's always good to have the CIA on the premises for backup."

Vi smiled at him. "The only person who might not be a happy camper this weekend is Piper. I can't imagine she's taking well to the idea of being boxed in and... bodyguarded."

Duncan sipped coffee. "I've asked her to help me with a case we both have an interest in. The Rose Petal Killer. We're going to see if there's a way we can put Patrick Lightman back in jail. The files are being delivered this morning."

"How clever of you. It's the perfect project for her. I can see why you're good at your job."

"I also told her about Cam's certainty that the rest of Eleanor's sapphires are somewhere on the estate."

"Daryl and I agree with him on that."

As he speared more bacon, Duncan asked, "Why do you think she buried one of the earrings separately?"

Vi sipped her tea. "You're assuming Eleanor did it?"

"They were hers. And she wore them in her wedding portrait. The fact that there's no record of them after her death argues that she's the one who hid them. Angus died first, so that lets him off the hook unless they hid them together at some point. Cam has my mom researching the Mary Stuart connection, but that photo they reprinted in the *Times* article argues heavily in favor of the tradition that's been handed down about their connection to Mary Stuart. They're worth a fortune now. But even back then, they would have had that added value. If I had something like that, I'd protect it."

"From what?" Vi asked.

He smiled at her. "Good question."

With a smile, she reached over and laid a hand over one of his in a gesture that he remembered from that long-ago summer. "You'll figure it out. That's what you do best."

A chime sounded, followed by muffled knocks on a door.

"That will be Russell Arbogast." Vi rose from her chair and carried her teacup to the sink. "He wanted to bring his photographer here for a tour prior to the shoot tomorrow."

At the kitchen door, Vi turned and waved her hands in a shooing gesture. "Go on out and check on Piper. She's probably fallen asleep. There were mornings when I'd find all three of them sleeping in that stone arch."

Duncan exited through the terrace doors and headed toward the garden path. He heard the jingle of a bell before he spotted Piper on the grass in front of the stone arch. The impact on his senses was instantaneous. Every muscle in his body tightened and hardened; heat flared in his center and then spun outward just as it had yesterday morning when she'd barged into her apartment, and yesterday afternoon when she'd stepped into the alley.

He had no control over the way his body reacted to her. He'd always preferred to have control where women were concerned, and he'd never had a problem before.

She didn't even seem to be aware of him right now. She tossed a stick and then waited for the dog to retrieve it, a game that both dog and woman seemed to be thoroughly enjoying. The jingling bell hung from the dog's neck as a precaution in case she wandered off.

There was a car parked in front of the house, a new black SUV. Aunt Vi's visitors, he assumed. He paused beneath a trellis covered in roses and turned his full attention back to Piper. She wore comfortable-looking sweats and sneakers. Her hair tumbled down over her shoulders. When she tossed the stick, then raced with the dog to get it, her hair flew out behind her like a flag.

It had felt like silk, sliding through his fingers when he'd kissed her, and he wondered just how long he could wait to get his hands in it again. He could cross the distance to her in seconds, he thought. And once he closed that distance and touched her again, he couldn't trust himself to stop.

He'd promised her that she would make the decision.

Not so much because he was generous or thoughtful, but because he was hesitant. Very few things made him feel that way. Oh, he made a practice of sitting back and studying all the angles of a situation before he acted. But once he knew what he wanted, once he saw the answer, he went after it.

He wanted Piper. He'd never wanted anyone as much. So she was unknown territory for him. He'd recognized that much seven years ago. The one thing he was certain of was that they were going to make love. The attraction between them was too intense for either one of them to walk away.

The problem was he couldn't see what lay beyond that. Pursuing a relationship with her would be like plunging off a cliff into a river without knowing what would happen next.

Duncan had always preferred to know.

The ringing of his cell interrupted his thoughts. Pulling it out, he noted the ID. Mike Nelson. A glance at his watch told him that the detective had probably just arrived at his office.

"Good or bad news?" he asked.

"A mixed bag," Mike said. "I checked out Suzanne Macks's family. All of them, including her brother, Sid, have a solid alibi for yesterday morning. He was working the night shift at a pediatric care unit. He left the hospital at seven-thirty. Of course, he could have hired someone, so we'll keep working on that angle. We're still checking Macy's stores. There are a hell of a lot of them in the area. But we've got a date from the sales slip, and someone may recall selling a single sheet like that."

"And?" Duncan prompted. Mike hadn't called him merely to report on progress. Duncan had called him before he and Piper had left her apartment last night to report the delivery of the vase of roses, and they'd left her key taped to the underside of her stair railing.

"I dropped by Ms. MacPherson's apartment on my way into the office."

Not good, Duncan thought. Mike lived in Maryland and a jaunt through Georgetown was not on his way.

"I figured I'd pick up the flower delivery and save a uniformed officer the trip. I got there about the time she'd be going out for her run just in case someone showed up. No one did."

"But…" Duncan prompted again.

"Someone had visited the place before I did, and they left another bouquet of red roses in front of her door."

"Was there a message?"

"'Till next time.'"

Duncan let out a breath he hadn't been aware he was holding. Whoever was after her wasn't letting up.

"I went in to collect the delivery from last night. Different florist shop. But the messages are written in the same block letters. I'll have someone check both stores out today. Thought you'd want to know."

"Thanks, Mike," Duncan said.

"Serve and protect. That's the job description," Mike said with a yawn. "I'll keep you updated. You keep her safe. She's taking a hell of a beating in the press here. Suddenly, she's the new poster girl for setting a serial killer free. Getting her out of town for a bit was a good idea."

Duncan was about to repocket his phone when it rang again. This time it was his boss.

"Adrienne, what's up?"

"Just checking in. I'm assuming you and Ms. MacPherson are together and safe."

"That was my assignment," Duncan said.

"I'm worried. The press coverage she's getting makes her out to be an even bigger villain than my brother. That can bring the crazies out of the closet."

Duncan watched as an overnight delivery service truck appeared in the drive that ended at the castle doors. Piper noticed it also and then seemed to notice him.

As she moved in his direction, he filled Adrienne in on the two flower deliveries.

There were several beats of silence on the other end of the line. He could picture Adrienne in her office pacing. Thinking. He let the beats continue.

"I never asked where you were going. And I don't want to know. Abe has already called me to find out where Piper is in case he needs to ask questions about the Bronwell trial. She hasn't been picking up her cell."

"Tell him to keep trying," Duncan said.

"Tell her to keep a lid on her location. It might have been someone in Abe's office who leaked the information that she was involved in the Lightman brief."

As the deliveryman in the truck walked toward him, Duncan thought of how easy it might be to figure out exactly where he was. And exactly where Piper MacPherson might have sought temporary refuge. "You're worried."

"All the media attention could get Lightman focused on her. Find something that will allow us to put him back in jail."

"Consider it done. I'm taking delivery on the files I shipped as we speak." Duncan moved toward the deliveryman so that he could sign.

"Thanks," Adrienne said.

Duncan repocketed his cell. Adrienne had come to him at her brother's request to get Piper safely out of the way. Now she suspected someone in his office might have played a role in what was happening to her. Did she suspect Abe?

An interesting question, Duncan thought. And one he'd been trained to find the answer to.

He'd also been trained about what to do with regards to his feelings for Piper MacPherson. Considering the danger she was in—the danger she could be in—he should put anything personal on hold. He thought about that as she walked to join him on the driveway, the dog at her heels.

He could keep her safe from whoever had left the sheet and the roses. He wished he could be equally certain about keeping either of them safe from what they were feeling.

She'd make a decent model, but if she couldn't find
the concentration to fill out her law school application, when a model had first come to the edge of
the garden. Though she'd be content to lose
Alba, she'd deserved an even pare of her
mind, she'd been . . .

6

"WHAT DO YOU THINK, ALBA?" Piper turned in a full circle for the dog's benefit before she faced herself in the mirror again. Alba was sitting at the foot of her bed, her head raised and cocked to one side.

"No comment, huh?" She could hardly blame the dog. All in all, it was a diplomatic response. She just wasn't a femme fatale. And her wardrobe components were sadly lacking. The jeans and Georgetown T-shirt she'd dug out of her suitcase were pretty much the cream of the crop. And the best word she could come up with to describe the outfit was *plain*.

"He didn't give me any time to pack. Plus, I was thinking comfortable clothes for poking around in the library and searching through files. My only salvation is that I do have a weakness for pretty underwear. Wearing boring and conservative 'law suits' can do that to a woman."

Glancing at Alba, she pressed a hand against her stomach to stop the nerves from jittering. She was babbling to a dog who couldn't hear her and taking way too much time to get dressed.

She'd made a decision, hadn't she? If she could find the courage to act on it. She'd already missed one opportunity when Duncan had first come to the edge of the garden. Though she'd continued to toss sticks to Alba, she'd been aware of him in every pore of her body. Her heart had started racing, breaths had been harder to catch, and the image had flashed brilliantly into her mind of just racing to him and jumping him right there beneath the rose trellis. It would have been wild and wonderful and *totally* unlike her.

But so exactly like her fantasy. With a sigh, she sat down on the bed next to the dog. "I have sex-on-demand on the brain all right. But I chickened out."

Instead of making her fantasy a reality, she'd picked up the stick, tossed it in a direction away from Duncan, and then raced Alba to get it.

Oh, she'd made a case for her cowardice. There'd been those two visitors who had arrived in the SUV a short time earlier. One had been dressed like a fashion plate, the other had carried a camera. If either or both were prospective clients, Aunt Vi would no doubt show them around. Piper was pretty sure that the sight of naked people coupling beneath the rose trellis wasn't on the regular tour. And something else had given her pause. When she'd allowed herself to take a quick look at Duncan out of the corner of her eye, she'd seen that she was probably alone in her thoughts about naked coupling. He'd been on his phone.

But then, he hadn't started his day reading a red-hot fantasy with him in the leading role. She had.

The jingle of a bell brought Piper's full attention back to Alba, who had settled her head on her paws and was studying her intently.

"Here's the problem. Duncan and I might not be on

the same wavelength. He seems totally focused on the work he came up here to do."

When she'd finally approached him in the driveway of the castle, he'd invited her to join him in the library and start working on the RPK files after she'd eaten something. Then Duncan had turned his attention back to the deliveryman and the stack of boxes he'd unloaded from his truck.

"Very businesslike. Very FBI. Maybe he's just doing what he said he'd do—letting me make the decision."

Alba merely returned her gaze.

Piper frowned. "Or maybe he's having second thoughts about the whole exploring thing."

Alba remained silent.

She sprang up from the bed and paced a few feet away. "Now *that* I can see. The main reason he wanted me to come here with him was to keep me out of harm's way." She turned back to face the dog. "All the Sutherlands have this protective streak that runs deep. A kind of inner white knight—rescue-the-damsel-in-distress thing. Only I don't need someone to rescue me. And I don't need someone to back out on a deal."

Alba raised her head, jingling her bell.

"Exactly. I may have some wardrobe problems, but I have the winning argument. Sex on demand. Anytime, anyplace, any way. It's the perfect relationship for us. Win-win." As she spoke, some of the images from her fantasies slipped into her mind, but she pushed them ruthlessly away. It was time to stop thinking about them and make them real.

"I'll just have to make my case. And I'm good at deflating counterarguments. C'mon, girl." She strode to the door and opened it. Then with Alba at her heels, she headed down the hall and started down the stairs.

DUNCAN STOOD JUST INSIDE THE first-floor entrance to the library. But it was not where he wanted to be. He'd been at loose ends ever since he'd watched Piper run up the grand staircase to change her clothes. And he'd checked his watch several times, wondering why she hadn't joined him yet.

Twenty minutes had gone by, but it seemed longer. After he'd sent the deliveryman on his way, he'd fixed a plate of food for Piper to graze on and put it in the library. Then Vi had invited him into the main parlor to meet Russell Arbogast and his photographer Deanna Lewis. Both had seemed fascinated by Eleanor's portrait and the sapphires. Duncan sensed Arbogast had been less than pleased with the news that they wouldn't be allowed access to the library during their photo shoot. But Vi had smoothed over the news by showing them Angus One's secret cupboard.

Cam and Daryl had decided that no one outside the family would be allowed access to the library until they figured out exactly who'd been visiting it secretly. And that particular mystery was part of the reason he'd come to the castle, Duncan reminded himself.

He stifled the urge to look at his watch again. It was time to focus on work.

Closing the door behind him, he stepped farther into the long, narrow room and tried to clear his mind. Once Piper joined him that could be problematic. Intellectually, he might have decided to keep his distance, but when she'd walked up to him in the driveway, he'd had to stuff his hands in his pockets to keep from touching her. Right now, he wanted to go find her.

Ruthlessly, he pushed that thought aside and made himself focus on the library as if it were a crime scene. The room was two stories high with an iron-railed walkway running around the second level of bookshelves. Cam's theory was that after successfully gaining access to the castle, the intruder had entered through the door he'd just closed. The sunlight filtering in through the sliding glass doors that opened to a terrace on this level and a balcony on the floor above didn't do much to penetrate the gloom. In the middle of the night, the intruder would have needed a flashlight—a high-powered one.

As Duncan strode down the length of the room, the scent of dust and leather assaulted his senses. Piper's father had locked the room up after his first wife's death, and the last person who'd made any use of the room had been his mother when she'd done her research that summer nearly two decades ago. Books stuffed the shelves both horizontally and vertically. Others had spilled into piles on the floor. If someone had come here with the intention of finding some clue to the whereabouts of Eleanor's jewels, it would be a formidable task. Even with a small crew of helpers, it would take time to search through all the books on both floors.

But Cam believed it had been one intruder, someone who'd begun that search in a very careful and organized fashion. The only evidence he or she had left behind had been in disturbing the dust on the lower shelves along one wall from the outside terrace doors to well past the fireplace.

Duncan studied the shelved books as he walked back the way he'd come. He noted the way the dust had been disturbed and in some cases cleaned away. Then he walked around the entire perimeter of the room. None of the other shelves looked disturbed, and he estimated that in six months, the intruder had methodically looked through less than one third of the library's collection. Which meant he could have more than a year's work ahead of him.

That argued for both patience and determination. But it also indicated the same kind of obsession that most serial killers had when they stalked their prey. Whoever had paid regular visits to this library wanted those sapphires and they wouldn't give up. Obviously, someone believed that the priceless jewels were still here on the grounds somewhere and that there was some kind of clue—a map or drawings, a diary perhaps, that would reveal the location. Or locations. Maybe they'd even suspected that the sapphires might have been concealed in one of the books. People frequently used books as hiding places. All Eleanor would have had to do was hollow out the center, tuck her dowry inside and place the book on a shelf with all the others.

But she hadn't. Still, she might have hidden a map or a drawing into one of the books. The fact that one of the sapphire earrings had shown up would only fuel the person's determination. Obsession was never good news. In fact, there was a strong possibility that what he was beginning to feel for Piper might be headed down that path.

The question was, did he have any chance of preventing that? An impossible question to answer when he didn't know if he could keep his hands off her once she walked through that door.

Work, he thought as he shifted his gaze to the seven boxes of files that he'd had the deliveryman line up along the wall. The only strategy he had open to him was to keep them both focused on the work they'd come here to do.

PIPER STOPPED ON THE LANDING the second she saw that her aunt Vi was in the foyer, and she wasn't alone. She recognized the couple who'd arrived earlier in the SUV, and she took a minute to study them. The man was tall in his late thirties with sandy-blond hair and handsome, photogenic features. His suit was Italian, she guessed, and probably tailored especially for him. The pretty brunette standing next to him was wearing jeans, a T-shirt and carried a very professional-looking camera.

Alba growled at her side.

Vi glanced up the stairs and made a quick hand signal to the dog that silenced her. Then she smiled. "Piper, you're just in time to meet Mr. Arbogast and Ms. Lewis. They're from *Architectural Digest*. They're doing a feature article on the castle, and they'll be doing a photo shoot tomorrow."

The man smiled up at her, and by the time Piper reached the group, he had his hand already extended. "Russell Arbogast. This place is such a find." His smile was warm as were his eyes, and the slight accent added to his charm. "We've been running a series on Scottish castles, and when we came across the article in the *Times,* we called your sister immediately to book a shoot. I'm so glad we did. The photos they ran don't do it justice. Deanna here will remedy that."

"Yes," the woman said. Her smile was just as warm as Russell's.

Piper might have extended her hand to Deanna, but Russell hadn't let go of it yet. Not that he was holding it captive. His grip was light, the sensation was pleasant. Piper couldn't help but recall how different her reaction had been when her fingers had accidentally tangled with Duncan's on the hood of his car.

"We're going to do the official shoot tomorrow,"

Russell continued. "I like to make a preliminary visit just to get an overview. And Deanna here likes to take candid shots so that she can more efficiently map out the plan for her assistants. Your aunt has given us a tour, and we understand you're here with Mr. Sutherland on a working vacation. Perhaps after Deanna and I get settled in at the Eagle's Nest in Glen Loch, we could set up a time for an interview. I'd love to be able to include some of your memories growing up here in my article."

"I don't see why we can't arrange something," Piper said.

"Good." Russell gave her hand a quick squeeze before he released it. "Good. I'll be in touch."

After closing the front door, Vi turned to her. "They love the castle. I can't wait to tell Adair. She'll be thrilled. She set up the whole thing." Then she glanced at her watch. "Goodness. I have to get started if I'm going to get to Albany in time for my presentation at the bridal fair. Duncan's in the library with those boxes he had delivered. He's turned off the security for the terrace door so that you can work in there."

Vi scooped up a sweater and her purse from a nearby table. "Lock the door after me and key in the alarm when I leave."

Piper found herself doing just that. Then she narrowed her eyes. It wasn't like her aunt to just hurry off like that—without offering her coffee or homemade scones or something. But Vi MacPherson was no dummy. Could be she'd picked up on the attraction that was sizzling in the air between Duncan and her. So she was giving them some privacy.

"Time to put it to good use," she murmured to the dog as she led the way down the hall. When they reached the library door, the dog pattered on past her into the kitchen and Piper watched her stretch out in a patch of sunlight.

Okay, the verdict was unanimous. She and Duncan needed privacy. Hadn't she already decided how to put it to good use? Straightening her shoulders, she opened the door and stepped into the library. Books were everywhere, spilling off the shelves into random piles on the floor. Dust motes fought for space in the shafts of light that poured in through the tall windows and sliders. And she could see Duncan's silhouette at the far end of the room. He was seated at a desk, his back to her. And still she felt the incredible pull on her senses.

She looked at him and she wanted. It was that simple. That primitive. Her throat went dry as dust. And she wasn't even aware that she'd started walking toward him until she passed the fireplace.

"I've lined up the cases my unit has been able to attribute to the RPK," he said without turning.

Piper stopped and glanced at the boxes that were lined up neatly along the wall between the fireplace and where he was sitting.

"I thought I'd start with the most recent. You can start at the beginning and we'll meet somewhere in the middle."

"Good plan," she said. And he'd started without her. The lid on the box closest to his desk was open and he had file folders stacked beside him.

"Vi said you didn't have breakfast so I fixed a plate for you," he said. "You must be hungry."

She was, but not for food. Still, when she glanced over and saw the tray her heart did a funny little bounce. It held a carafe of coffee, two cups, a plate of her aunt's scones with honey and a couple of bananas.

She'd taken care of herself for years, ever since she'd left the castle to go to college. But Duncan wanted to feed her. Pizza and wine last night, bananas and scones this morning. She moved to the table, picked a banana up.

"While you eat, I want to talk to you about us."

The words, the way he'd said them, had her forgetting all about the banana. A replay of the scenes of the morning flashed through her mind. Duncan standing in the driveway telling her to join him when she was dressed. Duncan informing Russell Arbogast that she was here on a working vacation. And now, Duncan providing breakfast and lining up her work for her. Clearly, the plan was to keep their relationship strictly professional.

To hell with that.

And he still wasn't looking at her. She glanced down at the banana and stifled the urge to throw it at him.

"Okay," she said. "Let's talk." They were going to do a lot more than that.

He turned to look at her. She stopped short when she saw he was wearing glasses, and everything inside of her went into a meltdown. They made him look even sexier, which just wasn't fair. She could hear her brain cells clicking off.

"Take those glasses off. They're killing me."

"Killing you?" He took them off and set them carefully on the desk.

Piper felt her knees again. "I have a few things to say to you." At least she had when she'd been talking to Alba. "White knight," she managed.

"White knight?" Duncan swiveled his chair toward her and stretched out his legs. "You're going to have to explain."

Okay, the glasses were gone, but that incredible body was still there. And right now, just looking at him with those long legs and the hands steepled together had her tapping into all of her mental reserves.

She fastened her gaze on his face. "You and your brothers have all inherited the white knight gene. You like to ride to the rescue and save damsels in distress." She paused to point the banana at him. "You don't have to take care of me or feed me. I can take care of myself and I make my own decisions. I agreed to come up here and work with you on the Lightman files and look for those sapphires, but we also agreed on something else. I get to decide if we're going to explore what's... what's happening between us."

He opened his mouth, but she jabbed the banana in his direction again. "I know what you're going to say. I'm in danger, and if we decide to pursue what we started when we kissed in the alley yesterday, we might get distracted. It might be safer and more productive if we just put that all on hold until we can figure out who's sending me flowers and find another part of Eleanor's dowry. Plus we have to find something that will put Lightman back in jail." She waved her free hand at the boxes. "Have I hit the highlights?"

A little uncomfortable and totally fascinated that she'd read him so clearly, Duncan could see why Abe Monticello had hired her. She had a knack for summation that would be a boon to any trial lawyer. Then she stepped fully into one of the shafts of light from the glass behind him, and he became almost as fascinated by the way the sun played up the different colors in her hair.

"Well?" she prompted.

"What?"

"Are you following me?"

He put some effort into gathering his thoughts. "Except for the white knight part, everything you've said has crossed my mind." In fact, the ideas had been spinning on a nonstop carousel ride through his head since she'd crossed the driveway to him that morning. "I'm worried about you." He told her about the phone calls he'd received from Detective Nelson and his boss. "The person who staged that little scene in your apartment is not giving up. I don't want to put any added pressure on you."

"How's this for pressure? I can't stop thinking about getting my hands on you."

"Ditto." And the only way he was preventing himself from doing just that was by clamping them around the arms of his chair.

"Then why are we talking?" She glanced down at the banana she'd been pointing at him and suddenly tossed it over her shoulder. "I'm betting it's a lot more distracting to think about having hot monkey sex than it is to actually have it."

Monkey sex. Duncan's mind took one long spin.

"You said it was going to be my decision. So, I'm proposing that for the time we are here at the castle, we simply offer each other sex on demand."

"Sex on demand?"

"Yes. My college roommates used to rave about their buddy-sex arrangements. Today, I think they call it friends with benefits. We just make sex available to each other whenever we want it. It's perfect for us and our current situation. No strings. No expectations. Anyplace, anytime, any-way-you-want-it sex."

Duncan felt his mind take another spin. He was

skilled at getting into people's minds, but Piper's had to be the most fascinating one he'd ever encountered.

"If we can do it anytime we want, maybe we'll get it out of our systems. At the very least, I can think about RPK or the jerk who sent me those flowers instead of how I'm going to keep myself from jumping you."

When he said nothing, she frowned at him. "Well, what do you think?"

He registered the annoyance that laced her tone, but thinking had pretty much gone by the wayside. Not that it had done him much good so far. Thinking was what had kept him hesitating. Thinking had kept him away from her for seven long years. "Is there a difference between monkey sex and buddy sex?"

It took a full two beats for her to answer him. Then a grin lit up her features. "I can't say I'm an expert at either." She stripped out of her T-shirt as she walked toward him. "There's only one way to find out."

He couldn't take his eyes off the red lace bra. Until she pulled down her jeans and he saw the matching bikinis. And any brain cells still working clicked completely off when she climbed onto his lap and took his mouth with hers.

He had no choice but to wait out the first jolt. Then he greedily absorbed the second and third as she threaded her fingers through his hair and began to use her teeth on his lips—teasing, tormenting, torturing.

Nipping on his earlobe, she whispered, "I've been wanting to do this since I walked into the room."

Ditto. He wanted to say the words out loud, but her mouth was busy on his again.

"Oh, mmm," she murmured as if she'd just discovered a flavor she'd been craving.

He certainly had. *You,* he thought. *Only you.*

Sensations simply battered him and he relished each one. The softness of her thighs pressed against his waist. Her scent, feminine and filled with secrets. The low husky sounds that hummed in her throat and sizzled straight to his loins. The scrape of her nails as she flipped open the buttons of his golf shirt, then tugged it loose from his pants.

Together, they stripped off his shirt. Then her hands were on his flesh, inciting, arousing, demanding. Each trace of her fingers, each press of her palms brought a pleasure so intense, a weakness so delicious that he began to ache. She was aggressive in a way he'd never imagined or dreamed. She bewitched him in a way no other woman ever had.

When she drew back enough to slip her hands between them and tug open his belt, his fingers tangled with hers to free him. She found him, caressed him, and he lost his breath and probably part of his mind.

"Now," she said.

Her command triggered explosions inside of him. He thought he'd been prepared, but anticipation and reality were worlds apart. He covered both lace-covered breasts with his palms, heard the quick intake of her breath, felt the thunderous beat of her heart. And need clawed through him. She'd had a point about the white knight analogy, he thought. For the first time in his life, he'd wanted to just sweep a woman away on his charger to a place where he could keep her safe and make her his. More than that, he wanted to pull her to the floor and ravage her the way a warrior might claim the spoils of war.

But first, he wanted more. He needed more.

"My turn." He could barely hear the sound of his voice above the pounding of his blood, but he slid his hands down to her waist and stood, bringing them both up and out of the chair. In one quick step, he braced her against the bookshelves and began to take what he needed.

EVEN THOUGH HIS HANDS MOVED like lightning, each quick, impatient caress sent a separate thrill rocketing through her. This was the part she'd never gotten to in the fantasies she'd penned. How could she have known?

More. Had she said it or merely thought it?

His hands moved between them to flip open her bra. Then he lowered his mouth and devoured. Each flick of his tongue, each scrape of his teeth brought a sharp, edgy shaft of pleasure.

Too much. Too much. Her heart had never beat so fast. Her body had never pulsed with so much life. But even as she reeled in a tidal wave of pleasures, all she craved was more. More.

Suddenly his mouth was gone. So were his hands.

She dug her nails into his shoulders and dragged in a breath. "Don't stop."

But he was already carrying her away from the bookcase and suddenly her feet were on the floor.

"I want to slow things down," he said.

"Why?" She gripped his shoulder and rose up on her toes. "Fast was great."

He framed her face with his hands. "Because I've waited seven years, and you did say something about any way I want it?"

When she nodded, he drew them both down so that they were kneeling and facing each other. "Let me show you." He combed his fingers slowly through her hair, drawing it back from her face. "I've been wanting to do this since the day of our parents' wedding. You had your hair all twisted up in a fancy knot and I wanted my hands in it. I wanted to taste you, too." Lowering his mouth slowly to hers, he did just that. But not the way he had before. His lips barely brushed against hers before he traced their shape with his tongue. And just like that, he opened up a whole new world of sensations.

There was none of the flash and fire she'd felt before. Just softness and a glorious warmth that seemed to be turning her blood thick. Each time the heat threatened to flare, he would withdraw and change the angle of the kiss as if he were searching for the perfect position and was determined to find it. Her mind began to spin. Each time he changed the pressure of his mouth, heat, glorious waves of it, shimmered right through to the marrow of her bones. When her muscles went lax and her hand dropped from his shoulder, he lowered her slowly to the floor.

"Can't think," she whispered.

"Don't," he murmured against her mouth. "Just feel."

Starting with her throat and shoulders, he took his fingers and mouth on a journey down her body. Tasting, teasing, tempting. Sensations swamped her. Each one carried her further and further beyond what she'd ever imagined. Shouldn't she have known that the brush of a fingertip over the tip of her breast would make her tremble? Or that the scrape of a fingernail at the back of her knee could make her moan? Or that the feathering of his breath at her waist would make her heart skip and race? No one had ever made her want or need this way.

Fire and ice rippled over her nerve endings at the

same time that a flame flickered to life in her center and sent sparks spreading in a slow burn through her system. When he slipped a finger into her, she gasped his name as the unspeakable pleasure rushed through her. Then she fell weightlessly, bonelessly, and even as she did, he used his mouth on her and sent her soaring again. And again. There was nothing, no one but him. He could have asked anything of her. She would have refused him nothing. But all he did was give her more.

WHEN HE DREW BACK, HE WATCHED her in the thin shafts of sunlight as he hurriedly dealt with the rest of his clothes and slipped on protection. Her skin was sheened with moisture, her hair spread out on the floor, her eyes dazed and on his.

"Now," she whispered.

That one word shredded whatever thin grasp he still had on his control and triggered a series of explosions inside of him. The craving that had been building for so long had become so huge that he wasn't going to survive another second unless he filled her.

When he did, she cried out from the shock, from the intensity of the pleasure, and he felt his control snap. As he drove into her in fast, desperate thrusts, she matched him move for move. Heat became intense. Glorious. The pace was fast. Furious.

They were in a race, one that everything depended on, and they were neck and neck. The speed was insane, the pleasure outrageous. They both cried out as they reached the finish line together. He heard his name blend with hers before reality faded completely.

WHEN PIPER FINALLY OPENED HER eyes, she was lying on the floor of the library staring up at the ceiling two stories above. Her mind was gradually swimming back to reality, and she wasn't sure she could move. It wasn't just the fact that Duncan's arm and leg were pinning her down. She'd just never felt so relaxed, so spent. So…right?

No. Quickly, she pictured her bottle and corked up that little idea. Sex on demand was the perfect fantasy. No strings. No expectations. That was the deal she'd made with Duncan and herself.

At least she hoped they'd both agreed to it. She'd done most of the talking before she'd climbed onto his lap and conversation had pretty much ceased. She wasn't even clear on how much time had passed since she'd first entered the library. Minutes? Surely not hours. The slant of the sun through the windows hadn't shifted that much. And the dust motes had returned to their slow dance.

Still, she couldn't work up the will to move. She'd never noticed before that the ceiling was intricately carved and painted with some sort of scene; she couldn't imagine a more delightful way to have discovered its beauty. She felt her lips curve at the thought. So at least some part of her body was working.

Duncan stirred at her side. She angled her head, pleased to discover that it was also working, and met his eyes. For just a moment, she lost track of time again and there was just the two of them. Nothing else. No one else. She could have lain there just like that for a long time.

Too dangerous, she thought and searched for something to say.

Duncan beat her to it. "Do you think that qualified as monkey sex?"

She blinked, and then smiled at him. "I highly doubt that monkeys know how to do what you just did."

"Thanks, I think." He kissed the tip of her nose, then drew back to study her for a moment. He'd never felt so relaxed with her before. He wasn't sure he'd felt this comfortable with any woman. "You surprise me." Stunned would have been a more accurate word, he thought. And when he saw the slight frown flicker over her face, he gave her a quick hug. "In a good way." In every way. She'd been wild in a way he'd never imagined. And more responsive than he'd ever dreamed. "I don't think I'll ever look at this library—or any library—in quite the same way again."

The smile lit her face again. "Me, neither. So…are we in agreement?"

"About what?" For a moment he'd become totally focused on the way the light played over her features.

"About my proposal—sex on demand. It's the best solution to what's happening between us. It'll keep everything simple and neat."

Duncan traced a finger along her jaw line, felt her tremble. "You like simple." He liked it himself. Especially in his personal life, he'd always preferred it to complicated. But whatever they called it, he knew that what he'd just begun with Piper MacPherson was going to be as complicated as hell. He lifted the strap of her bra, rubbed the red lace between his finger and thumb. Who would have thought that beneath those conservative suits she was wearing something this… provocative?

"Duncan." She raised her hands to clasp the sides of his head, then waited for his eyes to meet hers. "I need you to focus on this because we have a lot on our plates.

We should get at least this part settled, and I have the feeling that half of your mind is on something else."

"It is," he said. "But I can multitask." There was some satisfaction in seeing her eyes widen as he fished into the pocket of his jeans to get another condom, then sheath himself in it. "If I recall, our deal is sex on demand, anytime, anyplace?"

"Yes."

"Okay then." He settled himself between her legs and then entered her in one smooth stroke. "This time it's going to be a long, slow ride."

And it was.

7

TAKING A HIKE HAD BEEN Duncan's idea. Piper had been motivated to agree when she realized that after making love three times, she would have been perfectly content to lie curled up with him on one of the couches in the library until they'd recovered enough for round four.

The sex on demand she'd fantasized about at nineteen was supposed to be convenient, not addicting. One of its benefits was they should actually be able to get some work done. So far they hadn't made much headway in the Lightman files. So it was probably a good idea to take a break and clear their heads.

It was one of those perfect days in the Adirondacks. The sun was high in the sky, the lake a perfectly matching blue below them. By the time she'd showered and changed, Duncan had already packed their lunch into a backpack and was waiting for her on the kitchen terrace. The man was meticulously organized.

His pace was brisk, but in spite of the fact that his legs were longer, she had no problem keeping up with him. The path he'd chosen was a familiar one that wound upward through the woods to the cliff face bordering the lake.

"Have you visited those old caves lately?" Duncan asked.

"No." She'd run along the cliffs frequently when she was in high school, but she'd never climbed down to revisit the caves after that summer he and his brothers had visited. She shot him a sideways glance. Maybe he'd forgotten how she'd frozen on the cliff face that day. "It was never one of my favorite places. If you'll recall, playing damsel in distress wasn't exactly my cup of tea."

"I do. After the first time we played pirates there, Reid and I tried to talk Cam out of playing it again. We thought it was too dangerous for you girls."

"Good thing you didn't tell us that. And I take it you didn't convince Cam, either."

He laughed as they came to the part of the cliff path that cut inland through the woods for a bit. "Not much chance of that. Cam was attracted to adventure and danger even back then. And Reid and I were certainly not immune to it. Plus, we got to take turns killing Cam in order to win back the treasure and rescue little Nell. Not a bad day's work. We did reach a compromise on the safety issue. After the first time, Reid made sure that Nell always drew the short straw and then offered to climb with her to the cave before you or Adair jumped in to protect her yourself."

Piper thought back, seeing the game through a different lens now. "As I recall, Reid spent a lot of his time that whole summer making sure that Nell was safe."

Duncan nodded. "Six was a little young to be rock climbing, not to mention some of the other things we did, and it turned out to be good practice for him. Even at ten, he already knew he wanted to go into the Secret Service. Now he's working on the vice president's detail."

She heard the pride in his voice and asked, "When did you know you wanted to be FBI?"

There were a couple of beats of silence before he glanced sideways at her and replied. "I probably decided the day the FBI came to our house and arrested my father for embezzling from his family's investment firm."

Surprise had her stumbling. But Duncan gripped her arm just in time to help her regain her balance. "How old were you?"

"Nine. It was the summer before we all came here. My father had always put his business as his first priority, especially after my brothers and I were born. He traveled and entertained a lot. He even kept an apartment in Manhattan. Every time he came home for any length of time, he would make my mother very unhappy."

He took a bottle of water out of the backpack, handed it to her, then fished another one out for himself. "I'd hear her crying in the middle of the night, and I felt helpless because there wasn't anything I could do."

She studied him as he sipped water. "Makes sense that you'd want to protect her. So you admired the FBI agents who took him away and wanted to grow up to be like them."

He began to walk again, this time veering off the path to take a shortcut to the cliffs. "I may not have been fully aware of it at the time, but I wanted to know what made someone do what my father did. Not just the stealing part. Greed is one of the things that makes the world go round. I wanted to know why he made my mom cry."

Understanding moved through her and tightened something around her heart. "So you were attracted to behavioral sciences."

"Ultimately." They stepped out of the trees into the sunshine. A few feet away, the earth fell away in a sheer drop to a strip of sandy beach below. "Sorry to put a dent in your white knight theory."

He hadn't. But she was prevented from pointing that out to him when her cell phone rang.

He put a hand on her arm before she could answer the call. "I meant to tell you before. Don't let anyone know where you are—not even your boss. I'll explain."

A glance at her caller ID told her that it was Abe. Guilt moved through her when she realized that she hadn't bothered to check her messages since they'd arrived at the castle. That wasn't like her at all. "Hello?"

"Piper, where are you?"

It wasn't Abe but an annoyed Richard Starkweather, her coworker. And he was using Abe's cell phone. "Hi, Richard. Is Abe all right?"

"Where are you? I stopped by your apartment to check on you last night and you didn't answer. So far, I've left three messages on your cell." There was concern in his voice, but beneath it, she heard a trace of annoyance.

"I've been…busy."

"Very busy," Duncan murmured in a voice only she could hear. She made the mistake of meeting Duncan's eyes and the glint of laughter had her choking back on a laugh.

"Where are you?" Richard asked again.

"Where's Abe and why are you using his cell phone?" she countered.

"Abe asked me to call. We need your help on the Bronwell case. You have to make yourself available. We need to know where you are."

Piper kept her tone patient. "Richard, you were in the meeting I had with Abe yesterday afternoon. I'm taking a few days off at Abe's request. As far as the Bronwell case goes, I turned over all my files to you. It's all there. Why aren't you using your own phone?"

"Because you haven't returned any of my calls. Obviously, you were avoiding me. If I have questions, I need to get a hold of you."

She bit down hard on annoyance. "You've got hold of me now. What do you want?"

"How long will you be out of town?"

"Until the publicity fades and Abe thinks I can return." But in her head she said, *Until I can take over second chair again. Then you won't have to ask me any questions.*

"Sorry, I'm losing the connection," she said aloud. Then she broke the connection and took a long drink of her water.

"You don't like Richard," Duncan said.

She paced away, and then whirled to come back to him. "Actually, I think it's the other way around. In Richard Starkweather's view, I have two strikes against me. He was Abe's right-hand man until I was hired, and then I refused to go out with him. Several times."

"What was the I'm-so-concerned-about-you act he put on in your apartment yesterday?"

"That was about impressing Abe."

"Some men don't take either rejection or competition well. Does he dislike you enough to stage that scene yesterday morning and send the flowers?"

Piper stared at him. "Good heavens, no. Why would he?"

"To get you out of the way so that he could take over second chair at the Bronwell trial. My boss, Adrienne, suspects that someone in Abe's office may have leaked the fact that you wrote the brief—to either the Macks family or to one of the other victim's families. No one in my office was aware of your involvement. I didn't even know you worked for Abe."

"I can't believe that Richard would do something like that," she said.

"Abe's a suspect, too. It's very convenient that the media is focused on you now and not him. He can go forward with the Bronwell trial with a cleaner slate, so to speak."

"That's ridiculous. Abe would never do anything like that."

"Maybe not. But until we figure out who staged that scene in your apartment and is sending you flowers, my boss would like to keep your location a secret, even from your coworkers."

"How? This is my home. Even Richard could guess that I might come here."

"Yeah." Duncan smiled slowly. "I've given that some thought. I didn't mention it to Adrienne, but it might work to our advantage if our RPK imitator does follow us up here. In D.C., it's fairly easy to remain anonymous. Up here, strangers are remarked upon. Earlier today, I spoke with Sheriff Skinner in Glen Loch and filled him in on the situation. He's putting the word out through Edie at her diner. He claims she's his best investigator."

Piper didn't like the fact that their conversation had started the nerves dancing in her stomach again. "I want this all to be over." She shifted her gaze down to the lake and let the view diffuse some of her anger. "But I'm not going to run any farther than this."

Duncan got that. He'd seen that quality in her when she'd been eight and he'd come upon her clinging to the cliff face for dear life. His heart had nearly stopped. But she'd held on until he'd been able to reach her, and she hadn't panicked. Then she'd followed his directions like a trooper as they'd climbed down together.

He placed his hands on her shoulders and turned her to face him. "You'll be fine here. Thanks to whoever it was paying nocturnal visits to the castle library, the security is currently CIA approved, and Vi says that Daryl Garnett will be here for the weekend because of that photo shoot. As head of the CIA's domestic operations, he's the best when it comes to white knights. But so are you."

She frowned at him. "What are you talking about?"

"That time you had to play damsel in distress in the cave all afternoon? You did that to protect Nell. And you told a bald-faced lie when you claimed that you'd always dreamed of being rescued."

"Maybe."

"Whoever this guy is who's sending you flowers, he picked the wrong person to mess with. But I suggested we come out here to get your mind off everything else for a while. And I have an idea of just how we can do that."

She stared at him. "You want to have sex here?"

With a grin he glanced around. They were on the steepest part of the cliff and while there was no one in plain sight, anyone with a good pair of binoculars or a camera with a telephoto lens could see them. "Tempting, but that's not what I had in mind."

Instead, he swung the backpack off his shoulder and sat down. "I thought we might share some lunch before we climb down to explore those caves."

"You want to climb down to the caves." She walked over to him and took one of the sandwiches he held out. "Why?"

He sat down on the grass near the cliff edge and gestured for her to join him as he pulled out his own sandwich. "I want to check something out." He explained his theory about it being Eleanor who'd hidden her dowry.

She took the time to chew and swallow the first bite of her sandwich while she mulled it over. "You're profiling her."

"I suppose I am in a way. I'm looking at what we know and trying to theorize what might have happened."

"Okay, I see your point. Eleanor wore the sapphire in her wedding portrait, and there's no record, either visual or written, of their existence after she died. So it's logical to think she'd be the one who hid them. It also stands to reason that if she split the earrings and hid just one of them in the stone arch, she hid the two other pieces of her dowry elsewhere. Otherwise, why split them up in the first place?"

"Exactly. And if she hid one of them outside the castle, it seems logical that she'd hide the other pieces somewhere else, also."

"Very logical," Piper said around a second bite of sandwich. "That's why we're here. You figure Angus would have known about the caves. This was land he chose. It stands to reason he would have explored all of it. Heck, it didn't take you and your brothers more than a week to find them. So Eleanor would have known about the caves also. You showed them to Adair and Nell and me the same day you discovered them."

"Right."

"But if any part of the Stuart Sapphires is in the caves, surely one of you would have found it."

"We scoured both of those caves, but we were looking for some kind of treasure box, not something as small as a leather pouch."

"Both of them?" She turned to meet his eyes. "Didn't any of you ever look in the third cave?"

Duncan stared at her. "There's a third cave down there? We only knew about two. How did you find a third one?"

"Boredom is a strong motivator. The tunnel leading to it was pretty much blocked off by a boulder in the second cave. I couldn't budge it, but I managed to squeeze behind it. The third cave is the biggest one and it was empty. But then I wasn't focused on finding Eleanor's dowry at the time. Finish your sandwich and let's climb down and take a look around."

PIPER'S ARMS WERE ACHING AS she wedged her fingers in between two rocks and searched for the next foothold. She could do this. She wasn't a scared eight-year-old anymore.

"To your left," Duncan called from below her.

In true white knight style, he'd pointed out the narrow rock ledge about one hundred feet below them, and then he'd insisted on going first and she'd let him. She was betting he'd already reached it. He'd been halfway there when she'd swung her legs over the edge. But she didn't dare look down to check his progress.

"A little more to the left," Duncan called.

Her shoe found the opening, then slid out. The sudden shift in her weight had her fingers gripping the rocks and her heart leaping up to lodge in her throat.

"You've almost got it," Duncan called.

What was the matter with her? This wasn't any different from climbing to the ground from her balcony. Except there weren't any vines and it wasn't soft ground that she would land on if she slipped.

"Don't worry. The ledge is directly below you now. If you slip, you won't fall far."

Good to know. If he was telling the truth. She glanced up at how far she'd come and realized that it would take as much effort to go back up as continue.

And wasn't that exactly what Macbeth had realized during his famous dagger speech?

"Shakespeare always comes back to haunt you," she muttered.

"What?" Duncan called up.

"Nothing." This had actually been easier when she was eight. And with that depressing realization came a surge of determination.

Muscles straining, she jabbed her toe into the crevice and lowered herself another foot.

"Directly below you, there's a flat rock you can step on," Duncan called.

The instant her foot connected with the narrow ledge, she heard a rumble above her. Pebbles and small rocks clattered down. The first one hit her knuckles so sharply that she nearly lost her grip. Another bounced off her shoulder, and as she glanced up, a third grazed the side of her head. She had to blink dust out of her eyes, but for a moment, she thought she saw a figure on the cliff above. By the time she blinked again, Duncan was at her side, his arm around her waist, his voice murmuring. "On three, we're going to jump. The ledge is just below us. Ready?"

She managed a nod as more dust and stones rained on them.

"One...two...three."

The drop was short, the landing hard. Then he pushed her into the low-ceilinged cave, using his body to block the debris still rattling down.

"You all right?" he asked as the noise subsided. His arms were wrapped tightly around her and her back was against stones. For a moment, she simply held on. She'd move as soon as her heart stopped pounding. Just one more minute.

She made herself breathe. In. Out. "I'm fine." Other than feeling like Chicken Little, she was. Still, she clung for one more moment, trying not to think of what might have happened if he hadn't climbed up to get her. "I have to admit that white knights come in handy."

But it would be very dangerous to depend on one too much. She met his eyes. "I'm pretty sure I saw someone on the top of the cliff."

"Me, too." Then he put a hand over her mouth and for a moment they both listened hard. The shower of rocks and pebbles had stopped. All she could hear in the silence was the call of a gull.

Duncan whispered, "Stay here."

Then he rose and moved to the mouth of the cave. The moment he stepped out onto the ledge, she rose to her feet, but he stepped back in before she could reach him.

"There's no one up there now, but if we go out on that ledge or try to climb up, we could be sitting ducks. I figured we'd have more time before someone tracked us here." He pulled out his cell, and then swore under his breath. "No signal."

"Well, as I see it, we have two alternatives. We can take our chances surviving more rock slides and climb down to the beach. Not my favorite plan. Or we can go ahead with our original idea," she said. "We did come here to search the cave and look for Eleanor's dowry. And since we risked life and limb to get this far, I say we forge ahead."

Duncan gave it some thought. The woman had guts and she was giving voice to his own instincts were telling him. "Whoever we saw up on the top of the cliff may decide to follow us."

"And run the risk of revealing himself or even getting caught?"

"Point taken." He pulled a flashlight out of his backpack and handed it to her. "You lead the way."

"This may be a tight squeeze for you. We're both bigger than we used to be."

"I'll manage."

Piper switched on the light and swept it over the walls. The area they stood in was roughly five feet deep, perhaps seven wide. The tunnel they entered offered even less space, and while she could walk upright, Duncan had to hunch over.

"Just a warning," she said. "If I see anything that moves, I'm screaming."

Duncan chuckled. "But you won't be running away."

"Correct." She stopped dead in her tracks when the tunnel widened into the second cave. "This is different."

Over her shoulder, Duncan saw the large boulder and the rocks of various sizes that now partially filled the space. Beyond the pile up of debris was an opening that appeared to be another tunnel.

"Look." She stepped to the side and ran her flashlight over everything so that Duncan could see. "That big boulder was blocking the tunnel to the third cave the last time I was in here."

"It's been almost two decades," Duncan said. "Plenty of time for things to shift around. You still game to lead the way?"

"Absolutely." She placed a hand against the wall to brace herself as she negotiated the fallen rocks toward the other tunnel.

Duncan had to hunch down when the ceiling abruptly lowered, and before long, the tunnel began to slope upward. In his mind, he tried to picture where they were headed in terms of the land above them. Just when he'd decided they were walking roughly in the direction of the castle, the tunnel took a sharp turn to the left, then widened abruptly into a larger room that allowed him to fully stand for the first time.

"Here's the third cave," she announced as she moved the flashlight slowly around the space.

He spotted the small pile of rocks at the same instant that she froze the beam of light on it. The pile lay near a good-size boulder that had shifted and evidently tumbled loose from the arch of yet another tunnel directly across from the one they'd stepped out of.

"I never saw that tunnel before," she said. "It must have been completely blocked."

"Alba found the leather pouch containing the earring in a pile of rocks that had tumbled loose when lightning struck the stone arch," Duncan said, urging her forward. They both dropped to their knees and began sorting through the pile near the side of the boulder.

Then they began to work on the stones that were loose at the sides of the newly opened tunnel. Each one they dislodged seemed to loosen more.

"Got something," Piper said. The sound of her voice echoed in the space. When she pulled it out, Duncan recognized the leather pouch immediately.

"It matches the one that your aunt Vi and Adair found the first earring in," he murmured.

Piper set it between them on the stone floor and then met his eyes. "Your theory. Maybe you should do the honors."

"No. You're the one who found it." Another part of Eleanor's dowry would be inside, he was certain. But he still held his breath as she folded back the flap of leather and reached in. Even in the dim light, the gold of the earring glistened and the sapphire glowed. She lifted it out and offered it to him. When he clasped his hands around hers, the stone flashed even brighter, and Duncan felt that same, strong, sure connection to Piper that he'd first experienced on his mother's wedding day. Time seemed to stand still.

Then they heard a clatter of rocks.

"Shhh," Duncan breathed in answer to the question in Piper's eyes. Only time would tell if the noise had been caused by some of the rocks they'd loosened on their journey or by someone who'd followed them.

Seconds passed—five, ten, fifteen. Just as he was about to breathe again, there was a second scrape and clatter of stones. He leaned closer to whisper, "Someone's in the tunnel we just came through."

If he'd been alone, he would have doused the light and waited at the side of the opening they'd just stepped through. But he wasn't alone, and he wanted a better tactical advantage and more data before he initiated a confrontation.

He took the earring out of her hand and secured it in the leather pouch. Then he slipped it beneath his T-shirt and tucked it into his back pocket. Finally, he picked up the flashlight and rose to check out the tunnel the stones and boulder had tumbled from. It was smaller than either of the ones they'd walked through. But for now, it would offer some cover.

"We'll have to be quiet. C'mon." He spoke the words lower than a whisper, but she rose and gripped his outstretched hand. Ducking his head, he led the way into the cramped space. Being quiet was easier said than done. But he let out the breath he'd been holding when he noted the rocks that had tumbled loose near the entrance gave way to smoother stones in a matter of a few yards. The bad news was that he couldn't see a curve in the tunnel yet, and he had no idea where it would take them.

But he could swear he felt the warmth of the sapphire through the thickness of the leather that enclosed it. Pausing, he glanced back. They'd come far enough that he could no longer see the room they'd left. But there was another clatter of rocks. He moved on, and within a few steps, the beam of the light illuminated the curve he was hoping for.

Drawing her around it, he spoke in a hurried whisper. "I'm going to have to turn off the flashlight, but first, get the gun out of my backpack."

She didn't hesitate a beat, but handled the task with the same ease and efficiency that she might have exerted if he'd asked for his water bottle. When he held out his hand, she placed the gun in it. "Now, switch places with me."

Once she had, he turned off the light, pitching them into total darkness. And waited. While they did, Duncan put himself into the mind of the person or persons who'd followed them into the cave. Whoever it was had to know that Piper wasn't alone. If it was the person who was sending the flowers and the death threats, why would he or she make this move? Setting that minor avalanche of stones off the cliff—*that* he could see. But following them in here seemed reckless. Desperate.

For now, he and Piper had a slight advantage. They weren't moving. And there was a very good chance that their pursuer still was.

At first the silence was so total that Duncan was sure he could hear the beat of his own heart. Then he heard what he'd been waiting for—the sound of more rocks being dislodged.

But which ones?

In his mind, he pictured the route they'd taken— the first pile of stones had been in the second of the caves he and his brother had played in as kids. So that's where their pursuer must have been earlier. That meant he had to be in the cave they'd just left, the one that Piper had discovered, where they'd found the earring.

Close, Duncan thought. He listened hard.

Nothing. No more rocks shifted. And there was no conversation, not even a whisper sounded. Then the darkness in front of him lightened fractionally. Whoever it was had seen the tunnel and was shining a light into it. Beside him, Piper placed a hand on his back to indicate she'd seen it, too, but she remained perfectly still. Perfectly silent.

A lone pursuer, Duncan guessed, who was weighing options. And listening for a sound—just as he and Piper were. To go forward or retreat? Pursuing them any farther was risky. Especially if your quarry knew you were coming. And in the silence, he had to at least suspect they did.

Rocks tumbled again. Behind him, he heard Piper suck in a quiet breath. But the darkness was total once more. The next sound of stones came from farther away. Still, Duncan didn't move and neither did she.

He'd counted to twenty when Piper breathed. "He left."

"That's the good news."

"What's the bad?"

"We can't go out the way we came in. Whoever it is could be waiting. And that's not the worst scenario."

"It can get worse?"

"He could suspect we're listening, and he could have retreated just to throw us off. Even now, he could be doubling back. That's what I'd do." He took her arm and urged her in front of him. "I'll bring up the rear just in case."

8

With one hand pressed against the wall of the tunnel and the other out in front of her, Piper concentrated on putting one foot in front of the other, testing each step as she went. Just think about that, she told herself. Worry later about who might have followed them into the cave and why.

The stones beneath her palm were cool to the touch, some smoother than others. She couldn't see a thing. And this tunnel could dead-end in front of them in a Hollywood minute.

Don't think about that. Instead, she pictured what the two of them must look like. With one hand clamped to her shoulder, Duncan was totally relying on her to lead the way. The perfect image of the blind leading the blind. Much better to think about that than to worry about the fact that his other hand was probably gripping that very large gun she'd found in his backpack.

Seconds ticked into minutes, and she felt as if they were moving at a snail's pace. But Duncan said nothing, and he didn't have a problem with telling her what to do. She heard a whack, then Duncan's quick intake of breath.

"Hit my head," he breathed. "Need a minute."

She used the time to reach up. The rocks overhead were only inches away, which meant that Duncan had to be practically crab-walking. In the short silence that stretched between them, she heard only the sound of their breathing.

Then came the faint sound of rocks hitting other rocks.

"He's in the cave we just left," Duncan whispered. "When I see a light behind us, I'll let you know."

Oh, good, Piper thought. One more thing to be nervous about. What would they do then? Run?

No, she wasn't going to go there. In her mind, she corked up all the worries and started forward again. She was just going to pretend she was on her morning run—which she hadn't had a chance to get in yet.

In the next seemingly endless stretch of minutes, she imagined that she was passing the shoe store, the bookshop. All routine except she found that the floor of the tunnel was climbing upward more steeply. The walls had begun to press in, and they were suddenly not just cool to the touch, but damp.

"The walls," she whispered. "Touch them."

His hand left her shoulder for a moment. "Wet. But we're not headed toward the lake."

"No." This time she was the one who whacked her head hard. Stars spun in front of her eyes as she sank to her knees.

"You all right?"

"I think so."

Duncan's arm was around her, and she felt his chest pressed hard against her back. Panic bubbled up. Whatever she'd rammed into had come up fast. Had they finally reached a dead end? She blinked once and then twice. It wasn't just stars she was seeing. Ahead of her light penetrated the absolute darkness. And when she glanced down, she thought she could just make out her hands on the floor of the tunnel.

In the silence, they could hear the scrape of something against stone. A shoe? A shoulder?

But escape was in front of them. Piper was sure of it. "There's got to be an opening up ahead," she breathed. "It'll be faster if we crawl."

Crawl they did. The incline was sharper now, but they were making better time. Rocks scraped against her hands. And she had to slow her pace twice to get the sweat out of her eyes. But the light ahead grew steadily stronger and suddenly she could hear the sound of water above the pounding of her heart.

The area around them suddenly widened, and the shaft of light pouring in from above was blinding. She was still blinking against it when she heard Duncan grunting behind her. Turning, she saw he had his shoulder against a rock the size of a small boulder. In seconds he had it blocking the space they'd just crawled through. "Just in case," he gasped.

Then he gripped her waist and thrust her toward the opening above them. It wasn't large, but the fresh air nearly made her giddy. She spotted the root of a pine. She clamped one hand over it and dug the fingers of her other into the soil. Breathing hard, she pulled, twisted and muscled her way onto her belly. For one long moment, she was tempted to just lie there on the ground.

But Duncan still had to get out. His push on her foot gave her the extra boost she needed to crawl all the way out. Rolling, she shoved to her feet in time to see the backpack appear in the opening. Then Duncan wiggled out. *Good grief,* she thought. Was he some kind of superhero? He gave her no chance to catch her breath. Instead, he said, "Help me with this one."

Together, they rolled the largest of the nearby rocks to cover the hole they'd crawled out of. "I don't think they'll get past the other blockade, but just in case."

Piper bent over, braced her hands on her knees and concentrated on taking deep breaths. She was on her second one when Duncan grabbed her hand. "Where are we?"

She had to take a second to get her bearings. They'd climbed out of a wall of rocks that rose high to form a ledge. That, plus a glimpse of the pond beyond and the thundering noise of water falling, told her exactly where they were. "Tinker's Falls."

Duncan gaze swept the small clearing. "The pond. That's where we used to play water polo."

"It's where you and your brothers used to play 'Drown the MacPhersons,'" she said drily. "And imitate various superheroes by diving off the rock ledge."

"We were ten."

"You were jerks," she said.

As he reacquainted himself with the space, he'd already begun to get into the mind of the person who'd followed them. "How far away are the cliffs and the lake?"

She was still dragging in air, fighting for oxygen as much as he was, but she knew exactly what he was thinking. Jerking her head toward the thick wall of tall pines to their left, she said, "Three minutes, tops. You think we can cut through the woods and beat him back there? Catch him?"

"That's the plan. Are you game?"

Her answer was to tighten her grip on his hand and lead the way into the woods. The trees stretched high into the sky, blocking out any breeze and perfuming the air with their scent. In spite of the fact that there was no clearly delineated path, she set the pace at a jog, zigging and zagging between and around thick tree trunks. Twigs snapped underfoot, and brambles snatched at their clothes. Together they leaped over a fallen log that blocked their path.

THREE MINUTES, SHE'D SAID. As they continued to tick by, Duncan pictured the chain of tunnels and the caves beneath them. If their pursuer had turned back at the first boulder he'd shoved into place, he could be almost back to the ledge by now. But there was always the chance that he'd wasted time trying to shove it aside. Duncan could only hope for the latter. That kind of desperation, obsession, would be consistent with the profile he'd already tentatively posed in his mind.

The pines were suddenly thicker, the brush denser. Piper slowed their pace, but she didn't change direction. "Not far now," she promised.

Seconds later, they stepped into full sunlight again, only a hundred yards or so from the place where'd they'd eaten their sandwiches earlier. Keeping her hand gripped tight in his, he raced with her to the spot just in time to see a figure climbing down the rocks toward the thin ribbon of sand that bordered the lake. He gauged the distance, weighing the possibility of pursuit.

"Go," Piper said, her breath coming in huge gasps.

"No." He couldn't leave her alone. Not until she was safe again. He'd already been too careless today. "There'll be another time." He was going to make sure of it.

The figure below reached the sand. He was wearing a hooded sweatshirt that prevented them from getting a good look at his features. Without glancing up, he raced off along the lakeshore in the direction away from the castle. Seconds later he disappeared around a sharp curve in the beach.

Suddenly, all the fear that he'd pushed aside when they'd been in the tunnels and while they'd raced through the woods hit him again. With one rough move, he pulled Piper around to face him.

Her face was streaked with sweat and dirt, her hair tangled. And it struck him so hard that for a moment everything else faded. He could have lost her. He streaked his hands from her shoulders to frame her face. The instant he lowered his mouth to hers, he fell away from the fear and into her. And he wanted to fall further. With her mouth hot and avid on his, he wanted to keep on descending into a world where there was only the two of them.

Some lingering awareness of their surroundings had him gripping her hips and carrying her into the cover of the woods. At the first tree that blocked his path, he stopped, pressed her against it and felt his mind shatter like fine crystal. For several seconds, he forgot everything but the strength of that tight, lithe body molded to his, the movement of her mouth. And he couldn't seem to get enough of any of it.

He drew back and felt his lungs burn as he dragged in air. Some of the oxygen made its way to his brain. There was an important reason he should get her back to the castle. But he couldn't quite latch onto it. Not when she plunged her fingers into his hair and sank her teeth into his shoulder.

"I want you," he managed. "I need to touch you."

"Magic words," she murmured and dragged his mouth back to hers. Their thoughts were completely in tune. And for one moment, his hands seemed to be everywhere, tough, impatient, relentless. The speed, the roughness, delighted even as it spurred her on.

Something ripped. Her clothes or his—she couldn't be sure, but her hands found flesh at last. His skin was burning, damp and so smooth. His body was so tight, his muscles bunching under her hands. Hunger spiked. Greed dominated. She simply couldn't get enough. Using teeth and hands, she feasted.

Her breath caught as he dragged her to the ground. Then they rolled, legs tangling, mouths and fingers searching, groping, bruising while they fought with their remaining clothes. As desperate as he was to taste and to possess, she rolled with him again. Their minds and desires were fused, locked on the same goal. Each second of delay, each obstacle they overcame—jeans, shoes, even those precious moments when he had to find the condom and sheath himself, brought its own separate, torturous thrill.

Duncan felt his muscles quiver as they rolled again. There had never been anyone he'd craved this way. Every inch, every curve, every tremble, every throaty whisper of his name only fueled the fire that had been building since he'd touched her last. Need sliced him, its razor-sharp edges cutting into his throat, his loins, his heart. He raised his head, meeting her eyes as he drove into her.

He felt her clamp around him and shuddered when she came. But he fought a vicious battle against his own release, dragging her up with him so that he was kneeling, her legs still wrapped around him. Then he gripped her hips, his fingers digging into her.

"Stay with me, Piper."

He wasn't sure he'd even said the words out loud. But those amber eyes opened, and he could see himself in their depths. She thought only of him. He thought only of her as he coaxed her into a rhythm, biting back the need to race until he knew she was with him. Only when he felt her clamp around him again, only when he heard her cry his name on her own release did he let himself fall with her.

DUNCAN COULDN'T BE SURE how long they lay sprawled there on the ground. She was in his arms, stretched along his length, and the feel of her, the fit of her body pressed to his was…right. Just as he'd always known it would be. What was new, what was spreading not like a fire but like a warm river through his blood, was the thought that he could have been happy to hold her just like this for a very long time.

And he couldn't afford to do that right now. Two sensations drove home that realization. One was the leather pouch pressing into his backside. The other, more annoying, was the insistent vibration of his cell phone against his left thigh.

In one smooth move, he shifted, lifting her onto his lap as he leaned back against a tree. She fit her head into the crook of his shoulder in a gesture he found so endearing that for another moment, he simply held on to her, ignoring his phone.

"This isn't working," she said.

Alarmed, he pressed a finger under her chin, tilting her head so that he could look into her eyes. "I know I was rough. Did I hurt you?"

"No. Even if you had, I'd let you do it again in a

second." She drew in a breath, let it out. "Just as soon as I catch my breath."

"What exactly isn't working?"

His cell phone vibrated again. He ignored it.

"That's what's not working," Piper said. "You're ignoring your cell phone. And I can't even think straight yet."

"Have to say, we're in the same boat there."

"The whole idea of the on-demand-sex fantasy is that it compartmentalizes sex so that it's less distracting. That's why I fantasized about it all those years ago. I wanted simple. We should be able to keep our eyes on the goal and do the work we came here to do. But you're currently ignoring your cell phone. And I haven't even checked mine yet. Plus, we just narrowly escaped from someone who may have wished us bodily harm."

She sighed and leaned her head against his shoulder again. "It should have been the perfect solution for us, but I can't seem to be near you without wanting to rip your clothes off."

Duncan laughed. He couldn't stop himself. She'd hit the nail on the head. And when she gave up and joined him, he squeezed her in a friendly hug. "Look on the bright side. Since we're both pretty much naked, that problem seems to be solved temporarily."

She gave his shoulder a punch. "Not funny." But the shared laughter was still clear in her voice. "We have to get serious and figure out who followed us into the cave and why."

"Those *are* the questions of the day," Duncan said. And they were enough to sober both of them.

"I think we can cross your favorite suspects, Abe and Richard, off the list," Piper said.

"Agreed." He couldn't picture either one of them scaling down those rocks so effortlessly. And how would either of them have found the time to come to the castle? "They could have hired someone, mind you."

"Why? If your theory is right, they've achieved their goal. I'm out of town. Richard's sitting second chair. Why follow us? But…"

"But what?"

"What if we're looking at this from the wrong angle?" She raised her head enough to meet his eyes. "They're not the only ones who might have wanted me out of D.C. Maybe the whole point of that staged scene and the flower deliveries was to get me back up here to the castle?"

"I'm listening," Duncan murmured.

She rose from his lap and began to pace. "What if this is all about Eleanor's dowry?"

Duncan narrowed his eyes, following her train of thought. "The sapphires could very well be playing some role in this. Cam's theory is that whoever was visiting the library had some kind of inside information, something that makes him or her believe that the library holds the key to the location of Eleanor's dowry. But then lightning struck the stone arch and Adair found the first earring before he could unlock the secret."

"Had to be a bummer for him," Piper said.

"It gets worse. Cam set up extra security so he couldn't visit the library anymore. It's not a stretch to think that the library guy starts thinking there might be some link between you and your sisters and the rest of Eleanor's sapphires."

"Or he could see us as competition. Adair found the

first earring. Could be he's afraid Nell or I will beat him to the rest."

He had to admire the way her mind worked. Shifting the lens and looking at it from that angle made a great deal of sense. "Very possible. But then my guess is that the library guy wouldn't want you up here. So I'm still not convinced he was behind the scene in your apartment. But it's certainly in his interest to keep tabs on you now that you're here. And if he followed us from the castle earlier, he heard everything I told you about my theory of where that earring might have been hidden. But I don't think he could know for sure that we found it."

"So the guy in the hooded sweatshirt could be the library guy."

"I like it as a theory. Whoever he is, he's obsessed with finding Eleanor's sapphires. But we can't discount other possibilities. The guy who's sending you death threats could have easily caused that little avalanche. My suspicion is that he's someone who's really angry that you let Lightman out of jail. And he wants you to suffer at least part of what the victims suffered before they died. The fact that you left your apartment may have made him even angrier. Why not kick a few stones down on you? Or someone else could have followed us out to the cliffs, someone we haven't thought of yet. The key to being a good profiler is that you can't jump to premature conclusions."

"Great. You've already pointed out there's a target on my back. Now I can worry about the number of people taking aim at it."

Standing there naked in the slants of sunlight, she looked like Diana the Huntress. Was that why it hit him so hard again? All he knew was that she was beautiful in a way that made his heart take a long tumble. That was dangerous. Almost as dangerous as the image he'd planted in both their minds. And he had to keep focused on the fact that she was in danger.

Rising, he went to her and took her hands. "I want you to picture it. I want both of us to imagine the worst and hope for the best. We can't be certain yet that there isn't more than one thing going on here. In fact, I have a definite feeling that there is."

When his cell began to vibrate again, he released her so that he could retrieve his jeans and dig it out of his pocket. He checked the ID. "Adrienne."

"You're not answering your phone," she said.

"I am now. Good or bad news?"

Adrienne's sigh spoke volumes.

Duncan tipped the phone so that Piper could hear the bad news. "I'm letting Piper listen to what you have to say."

"The men I've assigned to keep tabs on Lightman have lost him. He hadn't made an appearance outside his place all morning. When my men checked his apartment about an hour ago, there was no sign of him. Last visual they had on him was yesterday around dinnertime."

Duncan's mind was racing. Maybe he'd been too quick to dismiss Lightman as the person who'd staged the scene in Piper's apartment.

But it was Piper who spoke the suspicion out loud. "Lightman is smart. He could have bought the wrong kind of sheet and used fresh rose petals just to throw us off."

Or to simply play with her mind, Duncan thought. He squeezed her hand as Adrienne continued, "If Lightman is targeting you, Ms. MacPherson, he'll have done his research. He'll know that your home is at Castle MacPherson."

"Keep me posted," Duncan said, and disconnected. Then he raised the hand he was holding to his lips. "I know. You're not going to run."

She met his eyes. "You're not going to try to change my mind?"

"Waste of time. I'm a Scot. We're thrifty. And I'm not sure it's the best option."

"I just wish our prime suspects were still Abe and Richard."

He grinned at her. "Me, too."

She released his hand and began to gather up their clothes, tossing his to him as she sorted through them. He was watching her pull her jeans on when she met his eyes and the Diana the Huntress look was there again.

He felt his heart tumble again.

"If Lightman comes after me, he's in for a surprise."

She was right about that. She was a very surprising woman. But he didn't intend to let Patrick Lightman anywhere near her.

9

THE ROAD TO HELL WAS PAVED with good intentions. Less than two hours later, Duncan pictured his most recent one being crushed by the wheels of his car as he parked it in front of Edie's Diner. The restaurant sat on the main street of Glen Loch, and its wide front window offered customers a view of the lake and Castle MacPherson across the water. From what he could see, the place hadn't changed. His mother had brought them to Edie's frequently during the summer that she'd worked on her book at the castle.

The setup inside was typically fifties and provided seating at tables, in red leather booths and on stools along a polished white counter. Beyond that, the kitchen was open to view. People, locals as well as tourists, could come to Edie's for the food and the latest in news and gossip. As he recalled, both were the best in town.

He and Piper had come for neither. They'd come to talk to Patrick Lightman.

Sheriff Skinner's call had come a half hour after they'd gotten back to the castle. By that time Piper had checked in with her aunt Vi and passed on the news about the earring, and Duncan had used the number Cam had given him to fill Daryl Garnett in on the discovery, as well as the person who'd followed them into the cave. Cam's boss didn't like it any more than he did. Daryl assured him that as soon as Vi finished her wedding presentation at the mall in Albany, they'd drive straight back to the castle.

He and Piper had been about to resume their work on the Lightman files when the castle phone had rung. Skinner's message had been brief. A man had just walked into his office and asked him to arrange a meeting with Piper.

The man had identified himself as Patrick Lightman.

Skinner had insisted that they meet at Edie's Diner. After turning off his car's engine, Duncan reached over the gearshift and linked his fingers with Piper's. "You don't have to go in." Earlier, he'd argued vehemently and unproductively that he could take the meeting for her. He'd already contacted Adrienne and informed her of Lightman's whereabouts.

"I'm going in. This is my chance to see him in person. He could say something, do something that will put me on the right track to sending him back to jail. Plus, I want to know why he's come all this way to see me. And why he's doing it in this public way."

That was one of the questions he'd given some thought to on the drive into town. "Cam has a great deal of respect for Skinner. Meeting here at Edie's will broadcast Lightman's presence to the entire local community. Within an hour of the time Lightman leaves the diner, everyone in town will know who he is and why he's here. If he's planning on staying in Glen Loch, everyone will have his description and be on the look-out for him."

"But it was Lightman's idea to approach Skinner rather than just knock on the castle door," Piper pointed out. "He doesn't have to report in to the sheriff. He's a free man."

"He's also a brilliant man. This way, if he hangs around no one can accuse him of stalking you. Even if that's his intention. We could be playing right into his hands."

Piper shook her head. "No. It doesn't fit his pattern to be so public. He's not here to stalk me. And he's not as smart as he thinks he is. He may be playing into our hands." She smiled at him. "He's a meticulous planner, but I'll bet he didn't expect me to bring an FBI profiler with me to this meeting."

His lips curved slightly. "You're trying to make me feel better about this."

"I'm trying to make me feel better, too." On im-pulse, she framed his face with her hands and pulled his mouth down for a quick kiss. But any temptation she felt to prolong the kiss and feel even better was halted by the sound of a voice hailing them from across the street.

"Ms. MacPherson?"

The man striding toward them was the handsome blond man who'd visited the castle that morning. Piper used the few seconds that it took her to climb out of Duncan's car to gather her thoughts and search for a name. "Mr. Arbogast. From *Architectural Digest*."

"Russell, please." His smile beamed. "I'm so happy to run into you like this. I was trying to get hold of you a couple of hours ago, but no one picked up the phone at the castle."

"Duncan and I were out for a while."

Russell nodded at Duncan. "Good to see you again, Mr. Sutherland. You're Piper's stepbrother, right?"

When she felt Duncan stiffen, she said, "Why did you call?"

"I hoped to schedule that interview you promised. That way you could give me your take on growing up in the castle that Angus MacPherson built for his true love. I'm particularly interested in the stone arch and its legend. We've made arrangements to do a feature on the old Campbell castle in Scotland, and we were thrilled to discover what must be the original stone arch in the garden."

"Really?" Piper asked.

"We're as certain as we can ever be about something like that. I could tell you all about it if you'd join me for dinner. I hear there's a lovely little restaurant over by the college with a porch that overlooks the lake."

"Ms. MacPherson has other plans for dinner," Duncan said. "And we're on our way to a meeting right now."

The next thing she knew Duncan was pulling her across the street. "Tomorrow," Piper called over her shoulder. "We'll talk when you come to the castle tomorrow morning." And she was relieved when Russell's smile didn't waver.

As they walked up the steps to the diner's entrance, she spoke in a low undertone to Duncan. "You were rude to him. He's doing an article on the castle that could be instrumental in building Adair's and Vi's destination wedding business."

"Until we figure out exactly what's going on here, you are not having drinks and dinner with a stranger."

She shot him a sideways glance. "I would have insisted that you come along. And one of the perks of on-demand sex is that there's no reason to feel jealous."

"Well, as you so correctly pointed out in the woods, this sex-on-demand thing isn't as simple as it seems on the surface. We clearly don't have the hang of it yet, so we'll just have to keep practicing."

"You *are* jealous." The idea of that thrilled her to the bone. It made the nerves that had been growing tighter in her stomach ease.

With his hand on the doorknob, all Duncan said was, "Ready for this?"

"Yes."

He pushed through the doors. Piper immediately noticed the scent of fried onions, grilling meat and coffee, and the sounds of an old-fashioned jukebox pumping out country music. In the kitchen, Edie, with her cloud of tightly curled red hair and a pair of reading glasses perched low on her nose, turned a welcoming wave into a thumbs-up gesture before she turned back to flip a burger high in the air. There was a smattering of applause from the customers at the counter.

"Corner booth to your right," Duncan murmured before he steered her in that direction. The booths surrounding it were empty, partly due to the fact that at two-thirty, the lunch rush was over and partly due to the "Reserved" signs on the tables.

Piper spotted Sheriff Morris Skinner first. His hair had gotten a bit thinner and grayer, his midsection a little thicker since she'd seen him last, but the smile was the same. The other man with a smaller build sat across from him. Piper couldn't prevent the knot of nerves from tightening again in her stomach.

When they reached the booth, Duncan slid in beside Patrick Lightman and she took the space opposite beside the sheriff. It was such a smooth maneuver, boxing in Lightman and putting her across from him— Piper couldn't help but wonder if Duncan and Skinner had planned it out in advance. Or perhaps it was bred into the gene pool of men who had been born to protect and serve.

Then she pushed the errant thought away and focused her entire attention on Patrick Lightman.

"Ms. MacPherson, I'm so happy to make your acquaintance." He stretched out a hand.

Skinner gripped Lightman's wrist and set it back down on the table. "Hands to yourself. That was part of our agreement."

"Sorry." Lightman kept his eyes steady on Piper's.

They were intense and very blue. And they'd registered no surprise at Duncan's appearance. Since she'd taken her seat, he hadn't looked at anyone but her.

"Why exactly did you want to meet with me, Mr. Lightman?"

A thin smile curved his lips but didn't reach his eyes. "I wanted to thank you."

If he was hoping for a "you're welcome," he was plumb out of luck. In the silence, Piper continued to study him. The man looked just as he had in his photos and in the shots of him that the press had captured during his trial, except now he wasn't wearing glasses. In his late thirties, he was five-foot-eight or so, with the wiry and toned build of a jockey. Sandy brown hair fell in bangs over his forehead, and his face was on the pudgy side. If she'd passed him on the street, she wouldn't have given him a second look.

During the trial he'd worn black-framed glasses. They'd emphasized the nerdy, geek aura that Lightman exuded even now. Something tugged at the edge of her memory.

"Where are your glasses?" she asked.

He patted a hand on the pocket of his jacket. "I don't need them for everything."

"You didn't make a trip all the way up here just to say thank you," Skinner prompted.

Lightman's gaze never wavered from Piper's. "You've saved my life, and I thought I might return the favor."

"Are you saying her life is in danger?" Skinner's tone was mild, but Piper could feel the tension in his body.

"Whoever staged that little scene in your apartment doesn't wish you well, Piper."

His use of her first name sent a cold sliver of fear down her spine. Piper ignored it. "I know you didn't stage it."

"I may be able to help you identify who did."

"How?" Skinner asked.

"He's also been stalking me." Lightman shifted his gaze to the sheriff for the first time. "I recognized him. I'm going to reach into my pocket. You know I'm not armed."

Skinner nodded. "Go ahead."

Lightman pulled out his cell phone, a smartphone with a good-size screen, and placed it at the far end of the table. "I happened to have shot this little video clip."

He carefully pulled out his glasses and put them on. This close, Piper could see a designer logo on the side of the frames.

Out of the corner of her eye, she saw that Edie was polishing the nearby corner and no doubt picking up every word of their conversation. A couple of customers at the counter were also within earshot, not that they gave any indication they were eavesdropping. The jukebox had switched from Shania Twain to Katy Perry.

Reaching out, Lightman pressed something that set the video on the cell phone screen in motion. Piper immediately recognized the street in Georgetown where she routinely took her run. Just as she calculated that he must have shot it from the coffee shop two buildings down from her alley, she saw herself appear and head up the street.

"You were there," she said, forcing her voice to be steady as she tamped down on another sliver of fear. "You were watching me. Why?"

"You saved my life," he said. "The Macks family has been harassing me ever since I got out of jail. Have you seen them on TV? And they're bothering my friend Abe. I figured it was only a matter of time before they got around to you. You were the one who saved me, so I was keeping an eye out for you. I pay my debts."

"How did you know Ms. MacPherson was responsible for your release?" Duncan asked.

"Abe told me. Watch. This is the important part," Lightman said.

And it was. She was barely out of the picture frame when a figure appeared on the sidewalk wearing jeans and a hooded sweatshirt and carrying a shopping bag. He moved quickly, disappearing into the alleyway she'd just jogged out of. The video followed his progress as he hurriedly climbed the steps that led to her apartment. Then it lingered as the man inserted a key and stepped through the door.

"That's the same person I've seen walking up and down my street," Lightman said. "And he'll follow me if I let him."

"Do you know who it is?" Duncan asked.

"No. Sorry, but I didn't get a clear shot of his face when he came out." To prove his point, he swiped a finger across the cell phone and they watched the man hurry down the stairs, pause to toss a shopping bag into a Dumpster and then jog up the street in the same direction Piper had taken. Once again, the hood prevented a clear view of his features.

When the screen went blank, Piper met Duncan's eyes. She could tell he was thinking the same thing she was. The person they'd spotted running on the beach below the caves had also been wearing a hooded sweatshirt. Coincidence?

Piper shifted her gaze to Lightman. "What else can you tell us about him?"

Over the top of his glasses, he met her eyes. "He's about five feet, ten inches, slender build, weighs about a hundred and thirty. My guess is that it's Suzanne Macks's brother, Sid."

"You must have followed him. Where did he go?" Duncan asked.

"He used the Metro. I don't." Lightman shuddered slightly. "Too crowded. Too many germs."

"How long was he in the apartment?" Duncan asked.

"Five minutes or so." His eyes remained steady on Piper's. "After he left, I went up to check and to see what he'd done."

Lightman pressed something on his cell. More video followed, but Piper would have sworn that it wasn't the same one that the TV stations had played and replayed. The angle was different, and it remained totally focused on the sheet with its display of rose petals.

When the screen went blank again, Sheriff Skinner

spoke. "Why didn't you come forward and give those video clips to the D.C. police?"

"They wouldn't have paid me any heed. They didn't do anything when I complained about the Macks family—or about the guy watching my apartment. So I decided to bring them directly to Ms. MacPherson. I figured they'd listen to her."

"Would you send those video clips to my cell right now?" Skinner took out a card and pushed it toward Lightman, then waited for the man to push the buttons.

"Thanks," Skinner said when the transmission was completed. "I'll see they get to the police in D.C. How did you know where to find Ms. MacPherson?"

"Abe's office told me she was out of town for a few days, and I figured she'd probably come up here. It was a lucky guess."

"Thank you for your help," Piper said as Duncan slid out of his side of the booth. "I appreciate your making such a long trip from D.C. Have a safe journey back."

"Oh, I'm not leaving Glen Loch." Lightman took his glasses off, replaced them in his pocket and picked up his cell phone. "Didn't the sheriff tell you? I'm staying at a charming bed-and-breakfast, the Eagle's Nest." He kept his eyes on her as he slid out of the booth. "Till we meet again."

Piper absolutely hated the fact that she had to suppress a shudder. Duncan remained standing until Lightman had exited through the diner's doors. The instant he sat down again, he took her hand in his and gave it a squeeze.

Edie hurried over and delivered three mugs of coffee. "What a creep. These are on the house. If I had my way, I'd have put something stronger than coffee in his." She dropped a hand on Piper's shoulder and gave it a squeeze. "Don't you worry. We'll keep an eye on him."

"She will, too," Skinner said. "As will I. Are you buying his story?"

Duncan answered first. "Not entirely. He's not telling us everything he knows. And Sid Macks has an airtight alibi for the time Lightman was shooting that video."

"I don't believe Macks staged the scene in my apartment," Piper said. Then she told Skinner about the two vases of flowers that had been delivered and the message on the second one.

"He used the exact words that were on the third card," Duncan said.

"But if he's the guy behind all this, he's breaking pattern," Piper said.

"And who's the guy in the hoodie?" Skinner shifted his gaze out the window to where Lightman had settled himself on a park bench. "I'll keep my eye on him. While we've been chatting, my deputy Tim has been checking out Lightman's room at the Eagle's Nest. It'll be wired by the time he's finished. Other than that, my hands are tied. Lightman's a free man."

"Thanks to me," Piper said.

Duncan took her hands and held them so tight, Piper was afraid he was stopping the blood. Startled, she met his eyes and she saw anger, this time hot enough to nearly singe her skin.

"He wasn't hanging out over at your apartment to say thank-you. My theory is he was stalking you and ran into some competition. I want to get you away from here. Now."

Before she could even open her mouth, Skinner

spoke in a voice that didn't carry. "Not the place to make a scene."

He was right. And she and Duncan could hardly take the discussion outside when Lightman had decided to sit down on a park bench across the street and enjoy the view of the lake. Still, Piper had to bite down hard on her tongue. It gave her some satisfaction to see that Duncan was struggling also.

When he spoke, it was in a very low tone. "A serial killer has taken a fancy to you. He's followed you up here and he intends to stay."

She could see the argument he was making. She did fit the description of the RPK's victims. And the fact that Lightman had taken pictures of her the day before made her skin crawl. But she couldn't run. Where could she go?

Pitching her voice very low, she asked, "What if he's telling the truth?" Impatience flickered across Duncan's features, but he eased the pressure on her fingers enough for her to turn them and grip his. "Or at least a partial truth. Why would he pick me as his next victim? He'd have the spotlight turned on him full force and he'd lose his good friend Abe as his defense attorney."

"Go on," Duncan said. He was listening now.

"Even if he was stalking me, he isn't anymore. If he were, why seek the spotlight like this? Why come all the way up here, contact the sheriff and offer to turn over those video clips? That isn't the RPK's profile. He's gotten away with what he has because he stays in the background. No one ever sees him. If I were to end up on a sheet with rose petals strewn over me now, he'd be the prime suspect."

"She's making sense," Skinner said.

Duncan was aware of that. She was making perfect

sense. And she was doing what he should be doing—
getting into Lightman's head and thinking the way he
was thinking. The RPK was very smart, and while he
might have been tempted by the idea of targeting Piper,
might even have been considering it, he wouldn't have
come up here, notified the sheriff and moved into the
bed-and-breakfast. Would he? Duncan wasn't sure.
Usually, he was. "He was on your street, watching your
apartment, yesterday morning."

"Maybe out of concern. I did help to get him out of
jail. The crazy thing is he might even be trying to do
the white knight thing," Piper said.

Duncan's lips almost curved. "Let's not get carried away." He glanced at the sheriff. "Even when we
were kids, Piper never liked to play the role of damsel in distress. White knights riding to the rescue are
not her thing."

He admired that about her, he thought as he studied
her. It was part of what had always attracted him. He
also liked the way her mind had zeroed in on the facts
and then arranged them into a persuasive argument.
He could see what she was saying about Lightman as
clearly as she did. The problem was that his emotions
were blurring everything. If he wanted to keep her
safe, he had to keep his mind as focused as hers was.

He turned to Skinner. "Can you verify Lightman's
whereabouts shortly after noon?"

"No. My first contact with him was just before I
called you at about one-forty-five, give or take a few
minutes. That was right after he made his request for
a meeting. I can see when he checked in at the Eagle's
Nest."

"Do that."

The sheriff made a quick call and got the answer.

"Ada says he checked in at one-fifteen, took his bag up to the room and then asked for directions to my office. Why do you want to know?"

He told the sheriff about their adventure and their discovery in the caves.

At the end of it, Skinner said, "So another piece of Eleanor Campbell MacPherson's dowry has surfaced. I assume you've secured it."

"It's in the Fort Knox-quality safe that Cam had installed," Duncan said.

Skinner took a sip of coffee. "And it could have been Lightman who followed you into the caves. But you say the person you saw was wearing a hooded sweatshirt. I know they're pretty common apparel, but could it have been the guy Lightman filmed going into Piper's apartment?"

"Both are possibilities. The hooded sweatshirt guy could have taken a lucky guess and followed her up here just as Lightman did," Duncan admitted as he cursed himself silently. The problem was that he hadn't been thinking straight since Piper had walked into her apartment yesterday morning. If he had, he might have found a safer place to take her. Although where that might be, he didn't know.

"Or the person who followed us into the cave could be the person Cam believed was paying regular visits to the library," Piper said, then explained what she and Duncan had theorized about in the woods.

"Or someone new," Skinner mused. "The Stuart Sapphires have brought fortune hunters out of the woodwork before. And the news that you've discovered a second earring will leak out soon enough." He glanced around the diner. "Anything that's said in this place goes viral almost immediately."

"So we're back to a whole cornucopia of suspects. Happy thought," Piper said.

"Plus, there are those people from *Architectural Digest* planning on their photo shoot tomorrow." At Duncan's raised brows, Skinner shrugged. "The town has been buzzing about it for weeks. They're staying at the same bed-and-breakfast as our friend Lightman. The woman left early with her camera to take location shots around the lake. I can check on that. The man has been exploring the village, talking to the locals, visiting the library. He's even visited the college. When do you expect Vi and Daryl Garnett to be back?"

"Roughly around dinnertime," Duncan said. "They're going to leave Albany right after Vi's presentation winds up."

"I told Vi I'd stop by tomorrow for the photo shoot. But I could send someone out to the castle until they arrive tonight," Skinner offered.

"I think we'll be fine until the CIA arrives." Duncan offered his hand to the sheriff and then rose. "Thanks for your help—and for the information."

Lightman was still sitting on the park bench taking in the view when they stepped out of the diner.

"I'd still like to get you away from here," Duncan murmured as he escorted her to the car and opened the door.

Lightman turned, beamed a smile and waved.

Stifling the sick surge in her stomach, Piper muttered as she slid into her seat and clenched her fists in her lap. "There's a part of me that wants to run. But running never solves anything."

She was right, he thought, as he joined her in the car. That's what his mother and A. D. MacPherson had done after that summer when they'd first met. They'd fallen in love, then they'd run away from it and waited for a decade to act on what they'd felt.

"Let's go back to the castle and take a closer look at those files," Piper said. "I helped let that monster out and I'm going to put him back behind bars."

Duncan took one of her clenched fists in his hand, raised it to his lips and kissed it. "*We're* going to put him back behind bars."

10

STRETCHED OUT FULL LENGTH ON one of the leather sofas in the library, Piper slept with the same focused intensity that she worked. Duncan leaned back in his chair and watched her, fascinated. A short time earlier, he'd opened the sliding doors to the terrace to alleviate some of the stuffiness of the room, and the only sounds that interrupted the silence were the breeze stirring the pines and the occasional call of a bird. Alba slept in the one remaining patch of sunlight she could find near the open doors.

He and Piper had worked for nearly two hours on the RPK files before she'd taken one to the sofa and stretched out with it. For about five minutes she'd lain on her stomach, propping herself up with her elbows. Then her head had simply fallen onto the report she'd been reading and she'd dropped into sleep as abruptly and thoroughly as an infant.

She hadn't moved an inch since. It was little wonder that she was exhausted. They'd had quite a couple of days. And though they hadn't discovered anything yet in the files, they'd each made their way through two more boxes.

Better than that, he'd gotten a feeling that they were going to find something in them. He'd been through the files before, of course. He'd started on them the day that the verdict had been handed down on Lightman's appeal. But he hadn't had even a trace of a feeling then.

What was different now was that he was working with Piper. And to his surprise, he was enjoying it. Bouncing ideas off her and talking about them was nearly as exciting as making love to her.

He'd always preferred to work alone. Even his brothers had been aware of that. During those times when he'd gone into the field, he'd had partners; that was standard protocol. But in his office at Quantico, he usually kept the door closed because he didn't like interruptions or idle chatter.

From the time they'd reentered the library, Piper had offered neither. Instead, she'd seemed as totally absorbed in the work as he. Whatever his motivations, Patrick Lightman had made a mistake by taking a personal interest in Piper. For a moment, Duncan's mind flashed to those seconds in the diner when Lightman had been playing the video clip, and he freed the anger that he worked hard to keep on a very tight leash.

He'd been right about the fact that Lightman had been stalking Piper. But she may have been right about the reason. Maybe in a twisted way, he did want to protect her. Maybe.

More than likely, Lightman was jealous that someone else was stalking her and had decided to get even. Either way, the man was going down. He shifted his eyes to the boxes of files. The answer was in them somewhere, and she was going to lead him to it the same way she'd led him to the sapphire earring.

But where else was she going to lead them both?

She'd made clear what she wanted. Simple, uncomplicated, no-strings sex—anytime, anyplace. The idea certainly held appeal. And it had held a lot of appeal for him in the past. Relationships demanded time. They also demanded risks, ones he'd studiously avoided. His mother had taken that risk. He believed that she'd truly loved his father, and when she'd had to face and accept the fact that he'd never loved her or his sons, he'd seen the price she'd had to pay. Then he'd watched her spend a great deal of her life trying to avoid taking that risk again.

So that summer, when he and his brothers were ten, she'd agreed to have a summer romance with A.D. Whatever one called it—a summer romance, a fling, an affair or no-strings sex on demand, the concept hadn't changed. Keep it simple.

The smart thing to do was to play it Piper's way and do just that. He could go to her right now and join her on that couch. In minutes, seconds even, he could wake her and arouse her. He could taste her and experience the thrill, the incredible generosity of her response, and he could sink into her and lose himself in her again. Just the thought of it was enough to have everything in him hardening. Yearning. They could be moving together in that lightning-fast rhythm that he could only create with her. The thought of it had him aching.

He wanted to touch her. He couldn't seem to get enough of simply running his hands over her skin. Softly and slowly. He imagined tracing that delicate cheekbone with his fingers, then the strong line of her jaw. In his mind, he already smelled the faint scent of summer flowers in her hair. Next he'd explore the slender line of her neck, then her collarbone and that surprisingly muscled arm. Those amber eyes would be open by then. He pictured them golden and clouded with sleep, watched them focus and darken as he turned her, straddled her on the couch, and continued to touch her.

As the images grew more and more clear in his mind, his blood began to pound and the ache inside of him intensified. She would reach for him, eager to make her own demands. That much he knew. So he'd capture those slender wrists, hold them over her head, and continue to savor the slow heating of her skin and the husky sound of her voice as she said his name.

He clamped his fingers on the arms of the chair as his mind flashed to another scenario. He imagined freeing her hands and lowering his mouth to hers. He was half out of his chair when his cell phone vibrated in his pocket. He slipped quietly through the sliding glass doors to the terrace. A quick glance at the caller ID told him it was his brother Cam.

"Problem or favor?" Duncan asked.

"Question. When were you going to get around to telling me that you found the second sapphire earring?"

Shit, Duncan thought. Connecting the dots in his head, he remembered that he'd told Daryl, and Piper had relayed the news to Vi. Obviously, one of them had passed the news along.

"Vi told Adair you and Piper found the earring in one of the caves where I killed you and Reid when we were playing pirates."

"The way I remember it, I killed *you* several times."

Cam laughed. "Funny, but I don't remember it that way. And Adair will back me up."

"Piper has a pretty accurate memory of what actually went on in those caves," he warned. "In fact, she found a third cave that you and I and Reid missed. That's where we found the second sapphire earring."

"A third cave. No shit. But you still haven't answered my question. Why am I hearing about all of this secondhand? Wasn't I the one who had the brilliant idea you should go up there?"

Duncan glanced back through the glass at Piper. "I've been a little busy." So busy that he'd forgotten to phone his brother about the discovery of a priceless earring.

"With Piper. I understand. Daryl filled me in on her situation and the fact that someone followed you into the caves. Adair's worried."

Duncan believed that. He also knew his brother's concern was the real reason for the phone call. "Daryl doesn't know yet about the latest development. Neither does Vi." He filled Cam in on Patrick Lightman's appearance in the village of Glen Loch.

"So you've got a mysterious guy in a hoodie sending threatening notes and vases of roses to Piper in D.C., someone else following you into our cave at the castle, a person who may or may not have been paying nocturnal visits to the library until we upped the security, and now a serial killer has joined the party."

Plus, he had this no-strings sex-on-demand relationship going on with Piper. Which was obviously distracting him. But what Duncan said was, "Those are the highlights."

"And here I thought that it might be Piper who was keeping you so preoccupied."

Duncan frowned. One of the plagues of growing up with brothers was that they could read you very well.

"Those secret sexual fantasies the sisters buried in that metal box can keep you busy," Cam said.

Duncan waited a beat before he took the bait. "Secret sexual fantasies?"

"Piper didn't mention them yet?"

"No." Duncan sat down on the stone wall that bordered the terrace and kept his gaze on Piper.

"Adair didn't tell me about what was in the box, either," Cam said. "But my curiosity got the best of me."

Duncan had to laugh. "There's a surprise."

"Hey, I'm trying to do you a favor here. I figure I owe you one after I asked you to bring that reluctant bridegroom back from Montana. And I like to pay my debts."

"I'm all ears."

"From the time they were little, Adair, Piper and Nell wrote down their private thoughts on paper, locked them in a metal box and buried that box beneath some of the stones in the arch so they could tap into the power of the legend."

"Vi mentioned that to me," Duncan said. "Not a bad plan."

"It gets better. On the night that our mother married A.D., they drank a little champagne and decided to write down their most secret fantasies. Sexual ones. And they put them into the box and tucked them back into the stones."

"Adair told you all of this?" Duncan asked.

"Not at first." Cam cleared his throat. "She was showing me where she and Vi found the first earring and we accidentally dug out the box. I was naturally curious, and when she ran off with the thing, I looked into the matter."

"What good CIA agent wouldn't?"

"Exactly. First chance I got, I read all of them. I knew which one was Adair's right away. And brother to brother, I'll give you a hint that might help you to identify Piper's. To ensure privacy, they each wrote their fantasies down on different colored paper. Adair's are the yellow ones. So you have a fifty-fifty chance that Piper's fantasy is written on either the blue or the pink paper. I'm thinking that a top-notch FBI profiler like you should be able to figure it out."

"Just where is this metal box?"

"Still buried in the stone arch. Adair wanted her sisters to still have the power working for them. Look for loose stones at the base about two feet in on the right. At the very least, they make very interesting reading," Cam prodded. "If you have the time."

Duncan continued to study Piper's prone form on the couch. She was still out for the count, and a quick glance at his watch told him that Vi and Daryl wouldn't arrive for another couple of hours. The timing was perfect.

What he said to Cam was, "Before I let you go, what have you found out on your end about Eleanor Campbell and Angus One and their elopement from Scotland? Russell Arbogast, the senior editor from *Architectural Digest,* says that he's seen the original stone arch on the Campbell family's estate."

"I'm looking at it right now. A.D. is painting it. Thanks to Mom's meticulous research, we're visiting the ancestral home of the Campbells, and she's even gotten the current owners to let her do some research in their library. The bad news is that about a hundred years ago, there was a fire. Many of the books were destroyed. But if there's something on this end about Eleanor's dowry, Mom'll track it down. In the meantime, enjoy your reading."

That was exactly what he intended to do, Duncan

decided as he disconnected the call. Moving quietly through the sliding doors, he closed them, turned on the security system and activated the cameras.

When Alba lifted her head, Duncan signaled her to stay and retrieved his reading glasses from the desk. Then he let himself out into the hallway and locked that door also.

PIPER SURFACED SLOWLY, drifting in that dreamy zone between waking and sleeping while sensations penetrated one by one: a low sound she couldn't quite nail down, the soft press of leather beneath her legs, something with an edge to it poking into her cheek. And a prickling at the back of her neck.

The prickling grew stronger. Someone watching her? The sound came again.

A growl.

Opening her eyes, she fought through a moment of disorientation. The library. She'd been working with Duncan and she must have dozed off. As she rubbed the back of her neck, she shifted her gaze to the desk where he'd been working earlier.

Gone. She didn't have to even glance around to see if he was somewhere else in the room. She would have sensed his presence, felt that low humming in her blood. Instead, she felt a pang so sharp, she had to rub the heel of her hand against her chest to ease it. Disappointment that he was gone?

And if Duncan wasn't here, whose eyes had she felt?

The growl sounded again, starting low and building into an insistent bark. Alba. The dog stood on her hind legs, pawing at the glass doors that led outside. Piper sprang up from the couch and ran to join her. Stroking the dog's head, she focused on the stretch of lawn beyond the low terrace wall. A storage shed sat near the line of trees that bordered the castle on this side. The doors were closed. To the left, she could just see the bright blue of the lake and the dark clouds that had formed on the opposite shore. To the right, more trees.

No one in sight.

Alba dropped to all fours and growled again.

"I agree, girl," Piper said as she stroked the dog's head. Someone had been at these doors looking in.

And that's when she saw them. She'd been so intent on looking at the space beyond the terrace that her gaze had shot right over the flagstones. Slivers of fear shot up her spine.

Red rose petals, hundreds of them, lay strewn across a white sheet. It looked as if it had been raining blood. She tried the door and found it locked. The security light on the pad was blinking. Duncan must have engaged it before he'd left. The cameras would have caught whoever had done this. She wouldn't do much about it now, any case. And she'd be damned if she'd let this creep scare her.

Alba growled again. Piper patted her head. The dog wanted to give chase.

"Me, too," she murmured. "But it wouldn't be smart. That's probably just what they want." And if Duncan hadn't slowed her down enough so she had to think, she might be out there right now.

A faint rumble of thunder sounded in the distance.

Where was he anyway? This time the fear was sharper. Had he seen the person and given chase himself? "Duncan?"

Whirling from the window, she raced the length of the library and opened the door to the hallway. "Duncan?"

No answer.

Once Alba joined her, she locked the library door and hurried to the kitchen. But she knew he wouldn't be there even before she entered. He would have answered. Turning on a dime, she ran back down the hall that led to the large foyer, calling his name again.

The only answer was Alba's bell as she followed.

At the foot of the stairs, Piper made herself stop. Pressing a hand to her chest, she took a deep breath. Silly to panic. What in the world was the matter with her? Duncan was a smart man. Not only that, he was an FBI agent. She thought of his big gun. He could handle himself.

But there was that person who'd followed them into the cave that morning. And there was Patrick Lightman, who seemed to have a knack for slipping away from surveillance any time he felt like it.

Squaring her shoulders, she climbed onto the first step. She'd just search the castle, room by room, until she found him. Alba whined and she turned to see the dog standing at one of the glass windows that framed the front door. When she got there, she scanned what she could see of the yard. The drive was empty.

Alba whined again.

Piper spotted Duncan then. Because her view was partially blocked by the garden, she could only see the side of his face and his shoulder. He was in the stone arch. Even as she watched, he raised a hand to brush it through his hair.

And he was wearing his glasses. Of course. Maybe he'd needed a change of scene. He'd probably taken a file out there to read. Maybe he was thinking the power of the legend would give him some insights.

"He's fine," she assured Alba. The degree of relief

she was feeling was ridiculous. And telling. It wasn't just that for a couple of minutes she'd been afraid for him. When she'd woken up in the library and found him gone, she'd actually missed him.

"No, no, no." Alba's bell jingled and Piper glanced down to see the dog was looking at her strangely. "I'm not talking to you." She paced to the stairs and back. "It's just the stress. It's been a long day. Starting with digging that box out of the stones and refreshing my mind about that sexual fantasy I wrote with Duncan in mind."

Alba had stretched out on the floor and tilted her head to one side.

"So, I decided why not? On-demand sex is simple, uncomplicated. The perfect solution to the fact that I couldn't stop thinking about getting my hands on him. And I was nineteen when I thought it up."

When she paused, Alba just looked at her.

"Okay, so I'm older now and supposedly wiser, and it still seemed like the perfect solution this morning. Maybe it would have been if it hadn't been for the person who followed us into the cave or the fact that Patrick Lightman, aka the RPK, has decided to be my BFF."

Alba was looking at her as if she were taking in every word.

Piper sank onto the floor in front of her. "It still is a good solution. I want him. He wants me. All I have to do is keep the complicated stuff in a bottle."

Closing her eyes, she pictured the bottle. Then she imagined the words that described what she'd been feeling in the library. Fear. That funny kind of emptiness. That incredible and scary yearning. And…she felt her heart take a little bounce. Okay—panic, too.

Those were the emotions that she could put a name to when she'd woken up alone. In her mind, she did what she could to separate each word into letters and imagined them disappearing into the bottle. Then she jammed the cork in.

"There." She opened her eyes and looked into Alba's. Leaning forward, she hugged the dog. "You're a good listener." She rose to her feet and reached for the door handle. "And now that I've sorted everything out, I'm in the mood for some sex on demand."

Thunder rumbled again.

11

DUNCAN HAD SPENT MOST OF HIS adult career getting into other people's heads. He was good at it. He enjoyed it. But he didn't think he'd ever looked forward to doing it quite this much. The metal box had been right where Cam had said it would be—a couple of feet into the stone arch on the right. No CIA or FBI skills involved. The stones were loose, as if they'd been recently replaced in a hurry.

Had Piper dug out the box? Was that why she'd paid that early morning visit to the stone arch?

It was the size of a cigar box, but sturdy. The small padlock hadn't even been fully closed. The compartments inside were filled with scraps of paper in three colors, just as Cam had said, and they all seemed to be folded. That argued that, in spite of the fact the sisters had shared the box, they'd valued each other's privacy.

A pang of guilt assaulted him, but it wasn't enough to make him close the box. If Piper had a fantasy that she'd buried in the stones, he wanted to know what it was. More, he wanted to fulfill it.

He took Cam's word that the yellow paper was

Adair's. And pink seemed to fit Nell with her blond curls and blue eyes. She'd even worn a pink dress on the day that their parents had wed.

And Piper was the middle sister; logically, she would choose or be assigned the middle section of the box. He assumed the fantasies the girls had penned were on the larger sheets of paper that lay on the top of the compartments. To test his theory, he lifted the blue one and selected one of the smaller scraps of folded paper beneath it.

I want to win the spelling bee on Friday.

A noble ambition, but not telling. He could imagine any one of the MacPherson girls being that competitive. Digging deeper, he selected another one.

One day I want to clerk on the Supreme Court.

Bingo, he thought. That could only be Piper. Then because he couldn't help himself, he opened a few more. The wish to master long division made him smile. The wish that she would one day become a black belt fascinated him. Had she achieved it? And how many other things didn't he know about her dreams and ambitions?

A lot, he thought as he stared at how crammed her compartment was. Not that her sisters were slackers. His admiration for the MacPherson sisters grew. There was a lot of academic research to support the fact that simply writing down one's goals dramatically increased the odds of achieving them. Kudos to the girls for tapping into that power, as well as whatever extra power the stone arch possessed because of the legend.

Inspired, he pulled out a pen, and using the back of Piper's wish to win a spelling bee, he wrote: "Keep Piper and the other MacPhersons safe." Then he folded it and buried the slip of paper beneath the others.

Only then did he pick up the folded blue sheets of paper on the top of the center compartment. "My Sexual Fantasy: Sex on Demand."

He skimmed the first page. It presented various settings and scenarios for making love, each one spur of the moment. On a deserted beach with the waves pounding on the shore, in a limo, on a coffee table, on a bathroom counter. There were more on the second page—some of which went beyond his own experience. He had to admit, he'd never made love to a woman in a phone booth—but then seven years had passed since this had been written and phone booths were hard to find. By the time he'd finished the last one, he'd had to use the sheets of paper to fan himself.

Each scene illustrated the excitement and convenience of sex on demand with someone you trusted. A buddy. At least one could even have been "monkey sex," he supposed. But the writer hadn't used those specific words. Still, they all fit the description she'd given him when she'd made her argument in the library.

Besides making him want to go back to the library and wake her up, reading the pages had also left a bitter coppery taste in his mouth. Who had she imagined doing all these things with?

As he'd read them, he'd thought only of her. And he wanted her again. Right now.

"You…you jerk."

He turned and found himself staring at Piper. Her image was blurred because of his reading glasses. And it wasn't Diana he thought of as he removed the glasses and set them aside. She looked like one of the Furies from one of those Greek tragedies that always ended badly.

The flash of lightning over the lake strengthened the illusion.

"You broke into our box."

He was surprised that more lightning didn't shoot out from the accusing finger she pointed at him.

"And you read them?"

Not only read them, but he'd been too caught up in them to hear her approach.

"You read them." It wasn't a question this time. And the tone was enough to have him getting to his feet. Growing up with three brothers, he'd learned there were serious disadvantages to being a sitting target.

"How did you know about them? Who told you?"

"Cam." He hated to betray a brother, but Cam was an ocean away and desperate situations called for desperate measures. He took a cautious step forward.

"Not so fast," she said. "You…you just put them all back where you found them. Right now."

Without another word, Duncan did as she asked. Keeping quiet had gotten him out of plenty of scrapes as a child. Letting Reid and Cam do all the talking had focused his mother's attention on them. Not that he'd gotten off scot-free—but a strategic silence had often lessened the punishment his mother had meted out.

He took his time, sliding the metal box back into its niche, then shoving the stones back in place. He figured that with each passing second her temper had to be cooling. That was what had happened with his mother.

"Now, step out here and fight like a man."

One look told him her temper hadn't cooled one degree. She was crouched, arms bent, hands flexed in a stance that he knew all too well. As she stood there waiting, several things flashed into his mind—*I don't want to hurt you* being the first. He rejected it. Being condescending and sexist was only going to dig him deeper into the hole he'd dug.

Besides, he always liked to err on the side of caution. "What degree of black belt?" he asked.

"Fourth." The fact that she smiled when she said it sent a shaft of fire straight to his loins.

Still, his rational side kept him standing where he was. Now was the time to offer excuses, explanations. Except that he had none.

"I'd apologize," he said. "But it would be a lie." The temptation to read her fantasy had been irresistible. Every bit as irresistible as the outrageous temptation to take her on in a fight.

He sprang out of the arch to land lightly on his feet in a stance that matched hers. Clouds had rolled in overhead, darkening the sky, but he saw the excitement in her eyes—not fear or panic but an excitement that fueled his own.

"What degree are you?" she asked.

"We should be evenly matched." He partially blocked the first blow. Still, it sang up his arm to resonate in his shoulder. Then he had to shift quickly to prevent a well-aimed kick from connecting with his chin.

She was fast and agile. He kept his moves defensive as he tried to assess her strengths and weaknesses. Which were damned few, he decided, as her foot connected solidly enough with his hip to send him stumbling back a few steps. Admiration streamed through him along with the zing of pain.

Overhead, the thunder clapped loudly.

He was going to have to go on the offensive. Or he might just end up on his back with her foot on his throat. The next kick, which sailed past his guard and into his rib cage, confirmed his decision.

After five sweaty minutes, he was breathing hard and she seemed to be just hitting her stride. The rain had begun to fall in needlelike pellets. They ignored it. He'd been absolutely correct in his prediction that they'd be evenly matched. Except that he was taller, heavier, and his reach was longer. He might even have used one of his advantages if he hadn't decided that fighting with her was almost as absorbing and enjoyable as making love with her. Then without warning, she slipped close enough to hook her foot behind his and flip him to the ground. He landed hard on his backside just inside the stone arch.

The instant before her foot came down on his throat, he grabbed her ankle and jerked her down on top of him. Then he rolled so that she was trapped beneath him. To his surprise, he found the struggle wasn't over. He had to use his full weight to keep her there as he pinned her hands above her head. And thanks to a bright flash of lightning, he read the intent in those golden eyes and shifted out of the way just in time to prevent her knee from connecting with his groin.

For seconds, neither of them moved. He was winded. A first for him. And she wasn't done. The heat of battle was still strong in her eyes. In the dim light, they gleamed at him as tawny and challenging as those of Alice's Cheshire cat. Duncan felt his heart go into free fall, and it seemed to be the most natural thing in the world to lower his mouth to hers. The instant their lips met, he felt what he'd known from the first. She was right for him. Just simply right.

He wanted to show her that there was lovemaking beyond what she'd described in her fantasies. And he wanted more from her than convenient buddy sex. So for both of them, he kept the pressure of the kiss light, letting his lips toy with hers, then drawing back just far enough to feather kisses along her jaw to her ear. The rain was loud now, pounding on the stones overhead and pouring in a thick sheet over both entrances to the arch. He couldn't hear her sigh above the noise, but he felt the quick expulsion of breath against his cheek and the beat of her pulse beneath his lips.

Then he returned to her mouth, nibbling first, then slipping his tongue in to taste. Her flavor was different, warm instead of hot, and as sweet as melting ice cream on a hot summer day. Unable to resist, he deepened the kiss, degree by degree, pulling them both under. His reward came slowly as he felt the tension drain slowly out of her. She gave him what she hadn't offered, even at the end of their fight. Pliancy and surrender. And he was utterly seduced.

DUNCAN. THAT WAS THE ONLY WORD she could form in her mind as his mouth toyed with hers. Her mind had emptied and filled with him. No one had ever kissed her like this, as if he had hours and hours to spend and intended to do just that. With his mouth alone, he weakened her, drained her and sent her floating. Pleasure ran through her like a slow-moving river that penetrated deeper and deeper into her system with each passing second.

He spoke at her ear. "Let go, Piper. Let go."

The echo of the words whispered through her head, and she did just what he asked. How could she not?

He released her wrists and began to touch her then, skimming his fingers down her arms, lingering at the curve of her elbow, then tracing her shoulders. He undressed her slowly, too, easing her shirt off, then drawing her shorts down, touching and tasting each inch of her that he uncovered. No part of her was ignored. Her nipples tingled from the brush of his fingers, the nip of his teeth. The back of her knees ached and the curve of her ankles throbbed with the memory of his caresses.

While the storm raged outside, she could focus on nothing but the slow, powerful one that he was so intent on building in her body. Each press of his fingers, each stroke of his tongue left a bright foreshadowing of the flash of lightning and the outrageous heat to come. But for the moment, his tenderness forestalled it, invading her, consuming her.

She was his. Only his.

The words swirled in a thick mist in her brain and hammered in her heart. It was as if he was trying to keep her just this way, trapped in pleasure. But he seemed to want to give her more, take more using his mouth and tongue alone to drive her to a climax.

The pleasure slammed into her like a bare-knuckled punch, going beyond anything she'd ever imagined, anything she'd thought she could endure. Shuddering, she hungered for more.

He gave her more. And took more. In the arch of the stone walls, she knew only him—the taste, the scent, the feel of him. She would have given him anything he asked. Each time she thought he would have to end it, he found a new way to send her up and over a new crest.

"More."

He drew her up then so that they were kneeling, body to body, eye to eye. Still gripping her shoulders, he mouthed the words, "I want more. I want everything."

The sound was inaudible above the noise of the storm. But her eyes flashed as brilliant as the lightning, in triumph, in need. They worked together then to get rid of the barrier his clothes presented. Once he'd dealt with the condom, she eased him back onto the stones and straddled him. He reached for her to grip her hips, but she forestalled him by capturing his hands.

"Take more," she said as she straddled him, then lifted her hips and took him inside. "Take all of me."

His fingers gripped her hips, but trembled as she began to move. "Take everything."

Eyes locked, hands linked, they rode the storm.

AFTERWARD, THEY LAY TOGETHER beneath the stones. The fury of the storm had passed, but the rain continued to pour in sheets off both ends of the short tunnel. There was a part of Piper that wished they could stay right where they were, tucked away from the world. She knew that was a dangerous thought. It was always a mistake to wish for more than you could have.

But she was pretty sure the mistake had already been made.

Reality check, she lectured herself. And it was then that she remembered just how she and Duncan had ended up naked beneath the stone arch.

He'd invaded not only her privacy, but the privacy of her sisters, as well.

Raising her head, she looked him dead in the eye. "If you think that counts for make-up sex, you're wrong."

His burst of laughter filled the space.

She frowned and poked him in the shoulder. "Not funny."

"I know. Sorry." More laughter bubbled up. "I've just never tried to sort sex into so many different categories. Maybe it's a difference between the male and the female brain. I'm still trying to sort out buddy sex and monkey sex."

"Right. Now it's my turn to laugh."

To Duncan it sounded more like a snort.

"They've done studies on how many times men think about sex during the average day. With all the time your brains spend on it, don't tell me you don't sort the experience into categories."

He grinned at her. "I can't speak for all men, but I usually think along the lines of good, better, best." She was lying half on top of him, her arms folded. He took a lock of her hair and twisted it around his finger. "At this very minute, I'm thinking *now* or *later*."

"Later." She shoved herself to her knees, intending to start searching for clothes, but she cracked her head on the side of the stone arch.

And that was when reality hit her. "No. Oh, no."

Something in her tone had him sitting up and reaching for her. "You're hurt. Let me see."

"No." She pushed his hands away, picked up his shirt and shoved it at him. "My head's fine. Or I thought it was. But I can't seem to think straight when I'm around you. I definitely wasn't thinking." She waved a hand. "Do you have any idea what we just did?"

"I have a pretty good idea."

"You never should have come out here to read my fantasy. I never should have followed you. This was not supposed to happen. What we've been doing can't work. We have to stop right now."

Her voice was rising. She was rattled and he realized it was the first time he'd seen her that way. He put his hands on her shoulders, but she twisted out of his grip. "Why don't you explain what the problem is— and fill in the details?"

She waved a hand. "You kissed me and I kissed you back."

"I've kissed you before."

"Not *here*. We just kissed under the stones. We made love *here*. That was not supposed to happen. A sexual fantasy is one thing. A great thing. But I don't want to have anything to do with the legend and its power. And I certainly don't want to fall in love with someone. Do you?"

"No." The answer came out quickly. It was the truth. He didn't want to fall in love with anyone. Something tightened around his heart.

"Good." She placed a hand against her heart and rubbed it. "We're in agreement. What we're doing. It has to stop now."

And what if they couldn't stop it? What if it was already too late? What if he'd already fallen in love with her? There were things he wanted to say. But before he did, Duncan had to work them out in his own mind. What he said was what he knew for sure. "We'll figure out a solution, Piper. You're good at that, and so am I."

But Duncan was careful not to touch her as they gathered up their clothes and dressed. And when she handed him the reading glasses he'd set aside, she was careful that her hand didn't come in contact with his.

The rain had slowed, and while they'd been safe enough in the stone arch during the Adirondack monsoon they'd just experienced, he wanted to get her back in the castle. He had to agree with her insistence that they put a halt to what was happening between them—because he'd lost track of everything while they'd been making love.

And Piper's life was in danger.

When they were ready to leave the stone arch, the rain had stopped completely, and the early-evening sun was throwing long shadows across the garden. He figured that Daryl and Vi would be arriving soon.

The sound of gravel crunching had them both turning toward the driveway as a truck pulled to a stop in front of the castle doors. The sign on the door read Margie's Flowers. Duncan noted that the location was Glen Loch, New York.

He got a bad feeling then, and he kept Piper behind him as they walked toward the man who climbed out. Before they even reached him, he unloaded a vase of red roses.

"For Piper MacPherson," he said with a smile.

"Do you know who placed the order?" Duncan asked as Piper took the vase.

The man shook his head. "My wife took the order over the phone. They paid extra for a speedy delivery. Not that they had to. We're mighty grateful for the business that Miss Vi and Miss Adair are bringing in to all the merchants in Glen Loch." Then he nodded to both of them and climbed back into his truck.

"I can call Sheriff Skinner," Duncan said as he opened the door. "He might be able to get a phone number or trace the credit card."

Saying nothing, Piper set the vase on a table in the foyer as she locked the door and reset the alarm.

Duncan wanted to touch her, to simply run a hand down her arm, to tell her that she'd be safe. More than that, he wanted to pull her into his arms, to tell her... The problem was there was too much to tell her. And it wasn't the time.

Instead, he reached for the note on the vase of flowers and opened it. The message wasn't written on vellum, but it was clear.

TILL WE MEET AGAIN. AND WE WILL VERY SOON.

The words told him what he'd already known. Time was running out.

_12_

"THERE'S MORE," PIPER SAID. "And you're not going to like it."

That's what she'd said the moment that she'd looked up from the note. Then she'd led him into the library. And she'd been right. He didn't like it at all.

Duncan silently cursed himself as he stood next to her and studied the rose petals that had been strewn over the white sheet on the terrace outside the library. He'd contacted Skinner and Adrienne. Lightman had been in plain sight all afternoon—sitting on the park bench and taking in the view of the lake. Richard Starkweather and Sid Macks were both still in D.C., their movements accounted for.

As he'd relayed the news to Piper, he'd wanted more than anything to simply pull her into his arms and hold her. But he didn't dare. Everything on the terrace had been pounded by the downpour, but even in the long shadows cast by the late afternoon sunlight, the wet rose petals looked like drops of blood.

And that could easily have been the case. It could have been Piper's blood he was looking at. He'd left her alone because his mind had been so full of her, so obsessed with her, that he'd gone out to the stone arch to find out what her secret fantasy had been when she was nineteen.

Idiot. He cursed himself again. No woman had even come close to turning him into one before. If he was going to keep her safe, it had to stop.

About fifteen feet separated the scene he was studying from the couch where he'd left her sleeping. And she'd been there alone when the psycho had set up the little tableau for her. A mix of emotions assaulted him as he stood there, imagining what she might have been thinking, feeling. He was furious with whoever was doing this to her and angry with himself that he'd left her alone. But overriding all of that was a cold fear that he wasn't doing enough to protect her, wouldn't be able to do enough.

Ruthlessly, he shoved the feelings aside. None of them were helping him.

"Take me over it again," he said, "starting with when woke you up."

As she did, he tried to put himself into the mind of the person who'd taken the time and the opportunity to set up the scene they were both looking at. Whoever it was had been in a position to see what was going on in the library. There were several positions in the woods where an observer might have stationed himself. He might have even chosen to use the garden shed for cover.

"And when I saw the petals," Piper said, "my first reaction was to rush out and give chase. But you'd locked the doors and keyed in the code. That slowed me down enough to think."

Thank God, Duncan thought. If he hadn't slowed her down… He reined his thoughts in.

"If Lightman, Richard and Sid Macks are out, that leaves Cam's library guy or the hoodie guy that Lightman captured on his phone."

"Right." It irked him a bit that she was able to focus more on analyzing the evidence than he was, so he followed her lead. "When I called Daryl, he and Vi were about a half hour away. He'll be able to download what the security cameras captured."

"I'm betting the guy's wearing a hooded sweatshirt, and we won't get a look at his face. He had to be out here waiting and watching. He would have spotted the security cameras."

"Yeah." Duncan reviewed what had led up to the rose petal shower in his mind. "The woods provide plenty of cover. While you were sleeping I opened the doors for a while. I even stepped out to take a call from Cam." He scanned the clearing again. He took his gun out of his backpack and tucked it into the waist of his jeans and continued, "There are lots of places he could have concealed himself. Even in the gardening shed. He could have heard my conversation, then watched me lock up the place and go out to the stones, and he grabbed the opportunity."

"To scare me or to lure me out," Piper said.

"Come with me." He punched the code into the pad, then slid open the doors and drew her with him out to the terrace. Alba followed.

After he re-armed the security, he closed the doors and they moved toward the shed. The door was closed, the padlock secure. Any hope of footprints had been erased by the fury of the storm.

"Whoever was here is long gone," Piper said. "Otherwise Alba would be barking."

Duncan turned to see that the dog hadn't ventured beyond the terrace, and she was digging at something. Pressing a hand to the small of Piper's back, he urged her back to the library doors. Together, they squatted down to see what had caught Alba's attention.

Duncan picked up the small round piece of plastic.

"She found a clue," Piper said.

"Some kind of lens cover. And there's a logo on it, something we can trace. Good girl." He ran a hand over Alba's head, and the dog rubbed against his side.

"She was the one who woke me. And she threw herself against the glass doors. She probably scared the wits out of whoever was out here." When she turned back to Duncan, their knees were nearly brushing. "So you can stop feeling so damn guilty about leaving me alone for a few minutes. You left Alba with me. And I can take care of myself." She used a finger to poke him in the chest and nearly set him toppling back on his heels.

Yes, he thought. She could. And even though she had that Diana-the-Huntress look back in her eyes, he was going to see that she had backup. And to do that, he needed to keep an objective distance. He raised both hands, palms up. "Agreed."

For now.

TWO HOURS LATER, PIPER STOOD in the main parlor of the castle stifling the urge to pace. Once Daryl and Vi had arrived, the men had formed a separate team. While she and Vi had made sandwiches for dinner, they'd worked in Adair's office. Through the open French doors, she watched them still huddled at the computer screen. Duncan stood looking over Daryl's shoulder. He took his reading glasses off, set them aside and pinched the bridge of his nose.

Something pushed at the edge of her mind, but she couldn't quite catch hold of it. Hoping to get another push, she continued to study the two men. They were still running through the pictures from the security cameras. She'd been right about the rose petal person wearing a hooded sweatshirt. The cameras hadn't caught more than pieces of his face. Daryl was using some software program to come up with a composite picture.

What she could clearly read in the body language of the two men was that they weren't having much luck. The lens case Alba had found belonged to a portable telescope with a powerful lens. Not something that could be easily found at a chain store. Daryl had assigned someone in his office to try to trace where it might have been purchased. It proved someone was keeping a close but distant eye on the castle and its grounds.

No big news there.

There hadn't been any useful updates from D.C., either. The only relatively interesting piece of news had been provided by Sheriff Skinner. The vase of roses that had been delivered from Margie's Flowers had been called in from a D.C. florist, and it had been paid for with a stolen credit card over the phone. The call could have been made from anywhere.

She stood there for a few more minutes studying the two men, but whatever was struggling to get foremost into her mind had slipped away again. And she'd found herself just staring at Duncan. He was doing exactly what she'd asked. Keeping his distance. He hadn't touched her since they'd left the stone arch. They were in agreement that they'd chosen the right solution.

So why was she feeling so…restless? Worse, why was she second-guessing herself? Turning on her heel, she went to the kitchen where she knew she'd find her aunt.

The room was filled with the scent of freshly baked cookies, and Vi was pulling a tray out of the oven. The scent and the memories it triggered immediately eased some of her frustration. "Can I help?"

As if in answer, the teakettle began to shrill.

"You can help me load the tea cart. I think the men could use a snack."

"They've formed their own little investigative team," Piper muttered as she made the tea and then loaded cups onto the cart.

"They're worried about you," Vi said.

On the way to the refrigerator, Piper took a cookie off the cooling rack. "I'll be fine. I just…"

"What?"

She turned back to face her aunt, cookie in one hand and a pitcher of cream in the other. "I just want my life to go back to normal. Is that so much to ask?"

Vi took the cream and placed it on the cart. Then she met Piper's eyes. "And what would normal be?"

"My job. My routine. Everything was fine until… dammit." She bit into the cookie, and barely tasted it.

Vi said nothing.

Piper took another bite of cookie, then set it on the counter. "Your cookies used to fix everything," she complained.

Vi stepped forward then and ran a hand down her niece's hair. "What is it you want to fix?"

"I liked my life just fine. It was exactly the way I

wanted it to be. Everything was on track. Until the Lightman case. But I was going to handle that. I still can. But seeing Duncan again has mixed up everything, and I've just made it worse."

Vi took her hands. "How have you made it worse?"

"I just wanted him so much. He wanted me, too. So I came up with a plan that would solve the problem. We're adults, so why shouldn't we have this temporary arrangement? No promises, no strings. It was working. It was great."

"Until…?" Vi prompted.

"I kissed him in the stone arch." There. She'd said it.

Vi squeezed her hands. "And you think he's your true love."

"No." But wasn't that exactly what she was afraid of?

Don't panic.

"He can't be. What we feel for each other is desire." Something that red-hot and primal couldn't be love. "It's chemistry. It'll go away. In the meantime, I told Duncan we have to stop. I mean, it would be dangerous to keep indulging ourselves when there's so much at stake."

Vi nodded. "Yes, the biggest stakes of all. You're afraid of losing your heart. Do you know how Duncan feels?"

"No." Panic surged. "But he agrees with me that we need to step back. Quit while we're ahead."

"He said that to you?"

She lifted her chin. "Actions speak as loudly as words."

Vi placed a hand on Piper's cheek. "Even when you were little, you always had the best arguments. I wish I had a dollar for everything you ever talked me out of."

Piper frowned at her. "What are you saying?"

Vi smiled at her. "That you'll figure this all out. And when you come up with a solution that satisfies you, you'll convince him."

"FRESH BAKED COOKIES," Vi announced as she and Piper entered the main parlor with the tea cart. By the time she had filled the cups, the men had joined them. Daryl sat on the love seat next to Vi. Piper sat on the sofa. And as Duncan pulled out the desk chair and placed it closer to the tea cart, something tightened around her heart. Oh, he'd heard her argument loud and clear. He was keeping his distance, and he looked perfectly happy to do so.

She tried another cookie. Chocolate chip were her favorite, but they tasted like sawdust. She'd made the right decision, she told herself. Break it off before it could get riskier.

And just as soon as they figured out how to put Lightman back in jail and how to stop the crazy person who was sending her flowers, they could both go back to D.C. and make a clean break of it.

"These are spectacular, Vi," Duncan said as he reached for another cookie.

Obviously, they didn't taste like sawdust to him. She picked up her cup of tea and set it right back down.

"I wish we had something more to celebrate," Duncan said. "The good news is one of the security cameras got a couple of partials on the face of the person who tossed rose petals all over the terrace."

"I've sent it to one of my top technicians," Daryl said. "He's working up a full face composite and he'll run it through a facial recognition scanner. However, not everyone is in the system."

"We'll be able to check it against members of the Macks family and the family members of other victims of the RPK," Duncan said. "It will take some time. Which we might not have. Daryl and I were talking about it while we worked."

Daryl waved a hand. "And I agree with Duncan's analysis, so I asked him to fill you in."

Piper's stomach sank. He was totally working with Daryl now. She'd gotten just what she'd asked for. What she'd demanded.

"Until we know for sure, I think we have to assume we're working with three different problems here. Number one, we have Lightman in town—a man motivated by his own self-interests. Then we have the guy in the hoodie who set up the scene in Piper's apartment and keeps sending her vases of roses and threatening notes. And third, we have Cam's library visitor."

"The last two could be the same person," Piper said.

He met her eyes for the first time. "True. But I believe the person who followed us into the caves this morning is interested in the sapphires." He paused to glance up at Eleanor's portrait. "And his determination to have them has become obsessive. Following us into that cave was risky. He may not know for sure yet that we discovered the second sapphire earring, and he could very well see Piper as competition. Or he could believe she found it, and he's furious with her. He may very well have showered those rose petals outside the library today, with the purpose of luring Piper out and eliminating her."

Her stomach didn't sink this time. It froze. "We've already established that I have a very large target on my back. But I'm not leaving the castle. Running away will not solve this."

"His behavior today indicates that he's not only willing to take risks to get what he wants, but that he has an ability to seize the moments that present themselves. That makes him much more dangerous than someone who has to plan everything out in advance."

She met his eyes. "I'm not running."

"Duncan doesn't want you to run," Daryl said. "He wants to cancel the photo shoot tomorrow."

"No." Vi and Piper spoke in unison.

"That's just another kind of running away," Piper argued. "And the castle can't just shut down because I made the mistake of coming here."

Vi rose and joined her on the sofa. "Adair set the shoot up months ago. And we have a wedding scheduled next week. I also have two appointments with prospective clients tomorrow. Plus, Daryl has already vetted the magazine and Russell Arbogast and Deanna Lewis."

"I have some men digging deeper on both of them as we speak," Daryl said.

"There'll be strangers on the grounds," Duncan said, speaking directly to Piper. "This person almost lured you out of the castle when there were just the two of us here. There'll be more opportunities tomorrow." He shifted his gaze to Vi. "And the shut-down wouldn't be permanent. We just need more time to gather information."

Piper gripped Vi's hand in hers. "We've got top-notch agents from the FBI and the CIA here in the house and Sheriff Skinner plans to be present for the photo shoot. Aunt Vi and I are smart. We won't do anything stupid. And we have Alba."

Daryl gave Duncan an I-told-you-so look. "Then we'll have to go with Plan B."

"Not until you run it by us," Vi said.

"No negotiations on this one," Daryl said in a flat, no-nonsense tone. "If we're going forward on schedule tomorrow, Piper is confined to working in the library all day, and she's going to wear a wire just in case somebody gets past the security."

"Fine," Piper said. "I'll wear a wire and work on the Lightman files."

Duncan looked as if he was going to say something. But he didn't. Something tightened around her heart.

"You ladies should get some sleep," Daryl said. "Duncan and I will clear the tea cart. Then we'll work a little longer, but tomorrow is going to be a long day."

She'd won her case, Piper thought as Duncan followed Daryl out of the room. She wasn't running away. But it was the argument she'd made earlier when they'd been in the stone arch that was bothering her. Once this was over, she'd make another case to Duncan. Because she wasn't going to let him run away, either.

13

DUNCAN KNEW THAT HE WASN'T going to sleep. He didn't have to waste time lying in his bed and staring at the ceiling to figure that out. So at midnight, instead of following Daryl up the wide staircase to the second floor, he'd slipped out of the castle to walk on the castle grounds. The storm that had thundered through earlier had left a clear sky peppered with stars. With the moonlight, there was plenty of light to see by as he made his way through the gardens.

He rarely experienced restlessness or felt at loose ends, but those were exactly the feelings that had been plaguing him since he'd seen those rose petals strewn outside the library. He could deal with the cold hard fear that had settled like one of Angus One's stones in his stomach. But the other two were more problematic. Because they'd been triggered by Piper.

He could have holed himself up in the library and distracted himself with the Lightman files, but that wouldn't have brought him any closer to solving his problem. When he reached the stone arch, he stepped into it and then turned. What he saw first was the gardens, then the castle and the gleam of the lake below, all surrounded by the darkness of the mountains and the trees.

Angus One could have built the stone arch anywhere on the estate, so he must have taken care with the selection of this spot. He also must have stood here many times, with Eleanor's hand in his, looking at what they'd created together. And they'd risked everything to do it.

Over the years, he'd never given much thought to the legend of the stone arch. Why would he? At ten, he'd been much more fascinated by the missing sapphires. Even when he'd stood here and heard his mother make her vows to A.D., it hadn't been the legend he'd thought of. Once he'd looked into Piper's eyes, he hadn't been able to think much at all.

That's what had scared him off. He was a rational man and she had the power to make him lose his control over that. In fact, he'd never been able to rationalize what he felt for her. Not then. Certainly, not now. He wanted her, needed her to a point way beyond reason.

Was that love? And what did she feel for him?

Those were the questions that had sent him into default mode. When she'd demanded that they break everything off, he'd agreed because he understood her decision. He hadn't lied to her or to the others when he'd said that the person who'd strewn those petals on the terrace was unpredictable, and therefore dangerous. Perhaps even more dangerous than Patrick Lightman. The RPK was a creature of habit, pattern, bound by ritual. The person who had followed them into the cave that morning wasn't. Duncan needed to put Piper's safety first.

And by going along with her, he'd slipped comfortably back into his own pattern—being cautious and staying on the sidelines. Nothing of what he was seeing right now would have been here if Angus One and Eleanor had been either cautious or predictable.

To hell with rationality, he decided as he stepped out of the arch and strode toward the castle.

When he reached her room, Duncan slipped in quietly and closed the door behind him. Moonlight poured through the closed balcony doors. The tangled sheets spoke of restlessness, of a battle hard fought and won. So like his Piper. Now she lay curled into a ball with one arm tucked beneath a pillow, her breathing even.

He recalled watching her sleep before and wanting her mindlessly. That hadn't changed. What had changed was the very different rush of emotion he experienced now. For a moment he saw what it might be like to see her like this every night and every morning, and something inside of him opened.

Moving soundlessly, he slipped out of his shoes and clothes before he joined her on the bed. When he drew her close, she pressed herself against him and settled. He kissed her first on the cheek and then very softly on her mouth. Her lips were warm and softened by sleep. Her taste was almost familiar now. He let himself absorb the sensations, drift with them.

He heard the moment she awakened, a sound of pleasure, a quick gasp of surprise. Her nails dug into his shoulder as she drew back and opened her eyes.

"Duncan. We said… We agreed." But she didn't push him away, and her body remained soft against his.

"I can't sleep for wanting you, Piper." He whispered the words against her lips. "Let me touch you. Show you how much. Just for tonight."

She didn't have the strength to say no. How could

she form the word when his mouth was nibbling at hers? And she'd been dreaming of this, wanting him to come to her, yearning for the pleasure of his mouth, his hands on her.

But this wasn't a dream. His heart beat fast and steady beneath her palm, and the pulse of it echoed her own. She wanted to touch him, to offer him as much pleasure as he was giving her. So she did, testing the strength of his shoulders, feeling those smooth muscles flex beneath her hands.

There was no need to hurry or rush. Time was a gift they offered each other as they lay loving each other in the moonlight. Steeped in him, she whispered requests and murmured in pleasure when he granted them. Should she have known how tenderness both given and received could make her aware of every pore and pulse of her body?

Even when he moved over her and made a place for himself between her legs, there was none of the speed and the fury that they'd brought each other before. She absorbed every detail of him, the gleam of those dark eyes, the strong lines of that warrior face. Framing it with her hands, she drew it closer until their lips melded, parted and then touched again. She would remember seeing him this way forever. Her throat ached when he linked his fingers with hers and pressed their joined hands into the tangle of sheets.

She spoke only his name as he slipped into her and filled her completely. The sound aroused him unbearably, but he kept the pace slow and easy. With their minds and needs fused, she moved with him and gave everything.

As desire built, her taste darkened, her body shuddered for more. So he gave her more. As he felt her crest, he clung to control and guided her up and over the next climax. And the next.

And when he knew she thought only of him, he finally gave his own needs their freedom and poured himself into her.

DUNCAN STOOD JUST OUTSIDE THE main foyer of the castle, in the hallway that ran back to the library and the kitchen. From his position, he could make sure that no one wandered back to the library area and still keep everyone in view. Deanna Lewis was halfway up the stairs taking shots of the stained-glass windows on the landing. She'd impressed him yesterday as competent and efficient. She carried a notebook with her and consulted it frequently, especially when she gave instructions to the two young assistants she'd brought along.

The trio had started with the main parlor and moved on to the formal dining room and the ballroom that was used for many of the wedding receptions. Currently, the two young men were outside the main entrance taking a break. Through the glass panels, he could see that Sheriff Skinner had engaged them in conversation.

Across the hall, he could see Daryl and Vi in the main parlor where Richard Arbogast was having tea. The senior editor had been disappointed when he'd learned that Piper wouldn't be available for an interview. When he'd once again tried to convince Vi to let his photographer take a few shots of the library, Duncan had almost intervened. But Vi had diverted Arbogast's attention by including him in a tour she was giving to a prospective bride and groom. They'd been fascinated with his knowledge of Scottish castles, and now Vi was rewarding him with homemade scones and stories about her girls growing up in a castle. He could see why she and Adair were building such a successful business.

So far everything was quiet. In D.C., Glen Loch and here at the castle. Daryl's tech man hadn't gotten back to him with any news about the composite photo yet. Patrick Lightman had appeared at the diner for a late breakfast, and then sat on a bench to take in the view of the lake, just as he had the day before. Currently, he was back in his room at the Eagle's Nest taking a nap. His snores were being recorded by Skinner's deputy.

Duncan couldn't have asked for a less eventful morning. But waiting on the sidelines for something to happen had never frustrated him so much. He could only hope that Piper was having more luck with the RPK files. Daryl had fitted her with a wire that was voice activated. Both he and Daryl wore a small earpiece, but so far Piper hadn't made a sound. Vi and Daryl had each checked in with her, but the news had been the same. Nothing.

He glanced back over his shoulder at the closed library door. She'd be safe enough there until everyone left.

"Mr. Sutherland?"

Duncan turned his attention to Deanna Lewis as she came down the main staircase. She was an attractive woman in her late twenties and she was dressed in the same comfortable jeans and T-shirt she'd worn the day before. "You could do me a big favor."

"And that would be?"

"There's a library here." She raised a hand. "I know Russell was told that it's closed to the public and not really ready to be photographed. But this is my first freelance assignment with a magazine of *Architectural Digest*'s prestige. If there's any way you could make an exception and let me take a few shots, it would really earn me points with my boss."

"I'm sorry, but the library is off-limits. After the death of the current owner's wife, it was locked up and unused for years," Duncan said. "I can't see why you'd want a shot of it."

"Because it's off-limits," she said. "Forbidden. I don't always want to be taking pictures for a magazine—I'm more interested in photojournalism."

Russell Arbogast entered the foyer. "Deanna, I'm going to pay a last visit to the stone arch with Daryl and Vi. Do you need any more shots of it?"

"I've got what I need, but why don't you take Sam and Carl? It will be good practice for them."

As soon as everyone left, Deanna turned back to Duncan. "How about letting me take a few shots of the library from the outside? I took some pictures of the grounds yesterday, but I'm not even sure where the library is located."

Duncan studied her. Her curiosity seemed genuine. But it also occurred to him that if she'd been taking outside shots yesterday, she might quite easily have found the library on her own. It wouldn't be hard to spot a library through the glass doors. If you used the telescopic lens on the camera, you could easily identify it from quite a distance away in the woods.

His own curiosity aroused, Duncan said, "I'll show you where it's located, but no shots through the windows."

She beamed a smile at him. "Deal."

PIPER CLOSED THE LID ON BOX number five of the RPK files and stretched her arms over her head. A glance at her watch told her that she'd been working on it for more than two hours. Nothing had popped.

Standing, she walked to the sliding glass doors that led to the terrace and swept her gaze around the clearing. She'd decided to work at the desk so that she could keep an eye out in case someone decided to throw rose petals all over the terrace again.

So far, no one had.

There was something, some detail that she was missing. Something important. Her first inkling had been at the diner yesterday when she'd been sitting across from Lightman. And twice later in the day she'd experienced that little mental nudge, but she couldn't latch onto it.

She needed to talk to Duncan. If he could just take her through the conversation they'd had with Lightman in that methodical way he had, she might remember.

Or she might just be making up an excuse to see Duncan again. He'd left her room before she'd awakened.

And that had hurt. She rubbed the heel of her hand against her chest where it still did.

Just for tonight.

That's what he'd said to her. He'd never promised her any more. In the beginning, even in the stone arch yesterday, she hadn't wanted any more.

She certainly hadn't wanted to fall in love with him. But that's just what she'd done. She rubbed her hand again over the ache in her chest. Now she would pay the price—the same price her father had paid for loving her mother. Loss.

She wasn't even aware that her vision had blurred with tears until she saw Duncan walk into the clearing outside the glass. Blinking, she recognized his companion as the photographer who'd been with Russell Arbogast the day before. Deanna Lewis. For one second, she was tempted to punch in the security code and step out to say hello. But they weren't walking toward her. Then she remembered, Russell had asked to take photos of the library, and Vi had told them it wouldn't be available. So what were they doing here?

Her mind had barely considered the question when Deanna set her camera down and pulled out her notebook. Duncan took it and put on his reading glasses to study it.

That's when the memory struck her like a barefisted punch.

Reading glasses.

Images flashed into her mind at fast-forward speed. The first pair she'd seen on him had been right here in the library. She recalled him setting them aside on the desk and also handing them to him in the stone arch. If she hadn't found them on the ledge, he might have left them behind.

Patrick Lightman had said he didn't need the glasses he'd worn during the trial all the time. But he'd pulled them out yesterday when he'd been looking at the video clip on his cell phone and replaced them later in his pocket.

The memory tugged hard this time. There was something she'd seen in one of the files.

Which one? Whirling away from the glass doors, she strode back to the boxes neatly lined up along the wall and squatted down in front of them. She'd been working on the fourth box yesterday when she'd fallen asleep. Crime scene photos of one of the RPK killer's earlier victims.

Piper sat down on the floor, located the file, and

removed the photos. Then she spread them out, examining each shot before she placed it on the floor. The RPK had staged his scenes so exactly and the details were so similar that it was hard to distinguish one from another.

But something in this particular one had stuck with her. The body lying in the center of the sheet had been shot from different angles, and a zoom lens had effectively captured close-ups of different sections of the scene.

She spotted it in the third photo—a pair of glasses lying just beneath the couch. They rested on the top of the lens frame with the temple wings spread out—just as if someone had set them down for a minute. Yesterday, Duncan had set his on the desk in the same way when she'd ordered him to take them off. And she could see it—just the shadow of a logo on the side. It was the same one she'd seen on the glasses Lightman had used in the diner and on the ones he'd worn during the trial.

In her mind, she tried to picture it the way Duncan would. Lightman working, totally focused on setting up his victim and getting the scene perfect. He slips off his glasses and sets them down and in adjusting the sheet they somehow slip beneath the edge of the couch. Or perhaps he slides them away to allow for a perfect fall of rose petals.

And then, in his focus on the crime, he forgets and leaves them behind.

Those glasses had to be in an evidence bag somewhere. Someone had probably assumed they belonged to the victim. They'd probably never been tested for prints. Or if they had, Lightman hadn't been a suspect then. Daryl could probably enlarge the photo and get a clearer image of that telling logo. There was a very good chance that Patrick Lightman could now be connected to at least one of the RPK's other victims.

She glanced at the other boxes. Maybe Lightman had left things behind more than once. Excitement had her surging to her feet. She had to tell Duncan. Thank heavens he was still in the clearing. Punching in the code, she disarmed the alarm and then raced onto the terrace.

"Piper, no. Go back."

The shouted words had her freezing in her tracks. But only for a second. When she saw him crumple to the ground, she raced forward. There was a buzzing in her head as she dropped to her knees. "Duncan."

He didn't answer, and he was lying so still.

"What happened?" But when she glanced up at Deanna Lewis and saw the gun, she knew. "You shot him."

"Not yet," she said in a pleasant tone. "Too much noise. I used a very high-powered Taser. And I have to thank you for coming out. You distracted him just enough. I was having a problem convincing him to let me come into the library."

Duncan wasn't dead. That thought helped clear her mind, and she remembered she was wired. Daryl would have heard everything once she started speaking. He'd be on his way right now. She just had to stall.

Piper forced her gaze away from Duncan and away from the gun to meet the young woman's eyes. The hate she saw there nearly had her taking a quick step back. "Why are you doing this?"

"Why? Because Eleanor Campbell MacPherson's sapphires don't belong to you. And you can't find them before I do. So you have to be eliminated."

Eliminated? For the first time the realization hit

her that the woman she was looking at wasn't entirely sane. *Obsessed*—that was the word Duncan had used. "You're the person who was visiting the library, aren't—?"

Piper broke off when she saw Deanna shift the barrel of the gun toward Duncan's head.

"Stop talking. I'll use the gun on him first and then on you unless you agree to come with me now. Your choice."

No time to wait for Daryl. "Don't shoot Duncan." Piper rose to her feet. "Spare his life and I'll take you to the sapphires. They're what you want, aren't they? They're why you visited the library, trying to find some clue to their location?"

"They belong to us. They always did. And now it's our mission to find them. Not yours."

"I'll do more than go with you. I'll show you where they are. Duncan and I found a second sapphire earring in the caves. I can take you there."

Deanna hesitated for just a moment. "I followed you and I looked. If it was there, you took it away."

"We heard you following us, so we hid it well. To protect it." It was such a huge lie that she wondered how her nose didn't grow like Pinocchio's. And Piper was pretty sure it wouldn't stand up to logical scrutiny. Why on earth, if they'd found the sapphire earring, would they have left it behind? But Duncan's theory was that the woman she was looking at right now was obsessed with getting hold of Eleanor's dowry. And she was just as obsessed with getting her away from Duncan. "I can show you exactly where. The necklace may be there, too. We didn't have time to search for it."

"All right."

Piper didn't even allow herself a breath of relief before she turned and headed toward the cliff face.

TOO MUCH PAIN, DUNCAN THOUGHT. It swam in his head and streaked through his muscles with an intensity that nearly blocked out the fear. He couldn't move. He could barely think. *Piper.* Each second that ticked by, Deanna Lewis was getting her farther and farther away from the castle. Eyes closed, Duncan put all his effort into getting control over his body.

He opened his eyes first, blinking against the blinding sun. But he knew that he was recovering when the fear began to push out the pain. The second time he opened his eyes, he was able to raise his hand to shade them. And he knew a brief flash of relief when he saw Daryl, Vi and Sheriff Skinner rush out through the sliding terrace doors from the library.

He'd managed to sit up by the time they reached him.

"Deanna Lewis," he managed.

Daryl squatted down beside him. "Don't try to talk. Piper let us know they're headed to the caves."

"Caves," Duncan repeated.

"Piper told Deanna that you and she had left the earring hidden there. She even suggested that the necklace might be there also."

Brilliant, Duncan thought. But when Deanna found out it was a lie, the strategy could prove lethal for Piper.

"You think she's the person you saw running away wearing the hoodie," Sheriff Skinner said.

Duncan managed to nod and didn't like the way his head swam.

"When Piper asked her, she didn't deny being the

person who paid all those patient visits to the library," Daryl said.

"She's not patient anymore," Duncan said. "Arbogast?"

"I got a man babysitting him and the two young photographers at the stones. They're not going anywhere, and my deputy is on his way out here. He called me a few minutes ago to tell me that Lightman isn't in his room. Seems the snoring that's been going on for the last couple of hours has come from a mini tape recorder Lightman set up."

"I'll follow along the cliff path," Daryl said, rising.

Duncan grabbed Cam's boss by the ankle. "She won't hesitate to kill Piper. If the profile I've been building is right, there's a good chance she blames Piper because she didn't find the jewels first. The kinds of risks she's running—like revealing herself today— mean she's very dangerous. She may not even be worried about being caught."

He could talk again, breathe. He made his way unsteadily to his feet.

"What's the plan?" Daryl asked.

"We're going to the cave through an alternate route. You got a flashlight?"

Daryl patted his pocket. "Always. Along with my gun."

Duncan fished in his pocket for his own. "This way." He could only pray that he and Daryl would make it in time.

14

DON'T PANIC. PIPER REPEATED the phrase in her head,
keeping the pace fast as the path wound upward to the
cliffs. The sun was behind them, casting long shadows
in front of them, so she knew just where Deanna was
without looking back. She'd given some thought to
running. But as fast as she was, a bullet was faster.
And if she did outrun it, crazy Deanna might decide
to go back and shoot Duncan while he lay helpless on
the ground.

Talk. That was her safest alternative, Piper decided.
It might save both of them from panicking. At the very
least, it would keep Deanna from wondering why she
and Duncan had decided to leave a priceless earring
in the caves.

"Why were you visiting the library?" Piper asked.

"Because there had to be something there. Some
clue to the whereabouts of the Stuart Sapphires. Anyone could have figured that out once the *Times* ran
that picture of Mary Stuart wearing them side-by-side
with Eleanor Campbell MacPherson's wedding portrait.
And there hasn't been a trace of them since Eleanor

died. They have to be here. We just needed more time. Your sister found the first one and cut off our access to the library."

"You're sure that Eleanor's dowry and the jewels Mary Stuart wore at her coronation are the same?"

"I'm sure. We've seen the original of the picture the *Times* ran, and we've seen the portrait of Eleanor. And the Stuart Sapphires were never Eleanor's dowry. They were a gift to our family. And she stole them. Just as you're trying to steal them now."

They weren't Eleanor's dowry? Could that be true? Or was crazy Deanna just spinning a fantasy? Piper had to hope that Daryl was getting everything down. They'd reached the part of the path that cut deeper into the woods. The light around them dimmed and the scent of pine filled the air. Out of the corner of her eye, she thought she saw a flash of movement about fifteen feet to her left. Not Duncan. He couldn't possibly have gotten here this quickly. Daryl?

Whoever it was, she had to keep Deanna's attention totally focused on her. So she stumbled and fell.

The sound of the gun discharging was so loud it made her ears ring, and she felt the heat of the passing bullet on the skin of her arm.

"Get up," Deanna said. "And don't try that again."

"I won't." But Piper took as much time as she dared shoving herself to her feet while she scanned the areas in her peripheral vision. To her left, and much closer to the edge of the woods and the cliff face, she saw exactly what she was hoping for—another shadow moving from tree to tree. She purposely led the way on a slant to the right, saying, "The cliff face isn't far, and the caves should be right where we come out through the trees."

Then she prayed that Daryl would have time to get there first.

DUNCAN FELT HIS HEART STOP WHEN the sound of a bullet exploded in his earpiece. If he hadn't just dropped into the small cave behind Tinker's Falls, he might have raced into the woods. As it was, the instant Daryl dropped beside him, he moved to grab the edge of the opening, intending to climb out again.

Daryl grabbed his arm. "She's okay."

Through the ringing in his ears, Duncan made out the voices again.

"If you try to trick me again…if you try anything, I won't miss the next time. I wanted you to come up here so that I could eliminate you. And I will if you don't take me to the sapphires."

"I'm not going to trick you, Deanna. We're only about a hundred feet away from the cliff face, and I'm going to show you where the sapphires are."

Duncan let out a breath. She was not only okay, she was letting them know exactly where they were and she was refocusing Deanna's attention on what she was after.

"You okay?" Daryl asked.

"Yes." If Piper could keep her head, so would he. She'd lead Deanna to the third cave, the one where she'd found the earring. In his mind, he pictured their climb down the cliff face and the route they would have to follow to get to the third cave. He and Daryl had a shorter distance to cover, but the narrow tunnel would slow them down.

Quickly, he gave Daryl an overview of the terrain. "Watch your head," he warned as he dropped to his knees and led the way into the first tunnel.

"YOU CLIMB DOWN FIRST," Deanna said. "When you get to the cave, step to the side of the ledge, but keep in sight. I won't hesitate to shoot."

She might not have to waste a bullet, Piper thought as she looked down and gauged the distance to the ledge.

"Now," Deanna urged.

Piper took as much time as she dared sitting down on the edge of the cliff and dropping her legs over. There'd been no sign of the figure she'd seen in the woods. Daryl, she was hoping. Maybe he'd had time to climb down to the cave.

Best-case scenario, he was waiting inside right now, and all she had to do was get to the ledge. In her mind, she tried to remember the instructions Duncan had called up to her. Was it only yesterday? Turning onto her stomach, she searched for and found her first toe-hold.

Think. If Daryl wasn't there, she was good at finding solutions. She'd figure a way out of this. She searched for and found another place to set her foot. First she had to get down to the cave. Pushing fear and everything else aside, she focused her full attention on the climb. One minute, two minutes went by. Every muscle was straining, and she could feel sweat dripping down her back, but she reached the point where the stones had cascaded down on her.

There wasn't far to go. If she could just reach the ledge, she knew the caves and tunnels. She might be able to get away. Deanna had followed Duncan and her to the third cave, but Piper knew the way out. Deanna didn't. Clinging to the rocks, she twisted her head and made herself look down. Too far. She couldn't drop yet. She had to get closer.

Glancing up, she saw Deanna start down. The woman was both agile and fast, and Piper didn't dare rush. When she was finally within jumping distance of the ledge, she glanced up again and saw that Deanna was only a few feet above her, braced against the cliff face with her gun out.

"Drop to the ledge, but stay where I can see you," Deanna said.

Holding her breath, Piper let go of her death grip on the rock she was holding and dropped. She had time to glance into the cave, and her heart leaped. She'd been right. Someone was indeed standing in the darkness just inside.

When Deanna landed lightly on the balls of her feet, her gun hand steady, the shadowy stranger moved quickly, striking Deanna on the head. She fell like a rock, her camera smashing on the rocks, her gun sliding over the ledge and clattering down the cliff face. Then Piper found herself looking into Patrick Lightman's blue eyes.

Her mind began to race nearly as fast as her heart. Details registered in flashes. The gun in his hand, blood oozing from Deanna's head and staining the stones. She had questions—so many that her head ached with them. And Lightman could answer some of them. "Patrick, what are you doing here?"

"I followed you and Ms. Lewis, of course."

"Why?" The biggest question at the back of her mind was if Patrick Lightman was the shadow she'd seen in the woods, where were Daryl and Duncan?

Had Duncan been injured more seriously than she'd thought? Wasn't the wire she was wearing working?

"I told you in the diner yesterday that you were in danger," Patrick said in a calm voice. "She didn't wish you well. She'd been studying your movements in D.C. for a while."

"She was the person you filmed wearing the hooded sweatshirt. The one who set up that scene in my apartment?"

"Yes. I actually admired her style until she did that amateurish job, but then I knew I had to put a stop to it."

"Why didn't you tell us all that yesterday? Why did you throw suspicion on Sid Macks?"

"Because I hadn't decided what to do about Ms. Lewis yet." Then he smiled at her, and the glee in his eyes had the panic inside of her threatening to break free again. "After all, she does fit my profile."

Keep calm. Keep him talking. And think. "I don't understand. Why would you have to do anything about her?"

His smile faded abruptly and some of the calmness faded from his voice. "Because she had decided to stalk you, and you belong to me. The ones who came before you—they were nothing. All they did was to bring me to you. You've been mine ever since you set me free. No one else can have you."

Piper recognized what she was seeing in his eyes. Not merely madness, but obsession. And she remembered what Duncan had said. True obsession destroyed rationality.

But Duncan would be thinking in a rational way. He couldn't think any other way. The certainty of that helped her focus. She'd made sure to say quite clearly where she and Deanna were going. And Duncan would never have followed her along the cliff path. He would be with Daryl even now entering the caves from the other entrance at Tinker's Falls. And he'd be expecting her to lead Deanna into that third cave where they'd found the earring.

Now she wouldn't be leading Deanna anywhere. So she had to keep Patrick Lightman talking.

"Do you know why Deanna was following me in D.C.?"

"Not at first." He glanced down at the very still body of Deanna Lewis. "I checked into her background and learned that she was a photographer. So I thought she wanted to hurt me by stirring up all those nasty stories in the press again. But after she staged that scene in your apartment, I knew she wanted to hurt you. And I was right."

"You followed her up here."

"I followed you both up here. I protect what's mine. I overheard her talking on her cell phone this morning and telling someone that she intended to make her move today to eliminate you. She suspected that you'd found the second earring and that you were searching the library for the location of the necklace. It made her furious. She knew that you were being protected by the FBI and the CIA and she was still going to find a way to hurt you. So I did what I had to do."

"Do you know who she was talking to?" Piper asked. "Did she say why she wanted to eliminate me?"

Lightman shrugged. "The sapphires. She believes they belong to her. Just as I believe you belong to me." He raised the gun and pointed it at her. "I'm a little more wary of the FBI and the CIA than she was. I'm sure they'll be along shortly, so we'll climb down together. Ready?"

READY WAS THE LAST THING HE was, Duncan thought as he and Daryl finally reached the cave where he and Piper had found the earring. He'd kept the fear and anger on a very tight leash as he'd listened to that maniac talk about his obsession with her. Instead, he'd focused his energy on crawling as fast as he could through the narrow tunnel near the falls. But the thought of her having to climb down to the beach with Lightman had his fear threatening to take control.

All he could think was that he hadn't said nearly enough to her last night and he'd kept his distance all day. He hadn't told her what she'd come to mean to him. He hadn't told her he loved her. So they had to get to her in time. And they still had two tunnels and a cave to go.

Crossing the cave where they'd found the earring, he'd stepped into the next tunnel with Daryl close behind when he heard Piper's voice again. "They're going to know I'm missing by now. Sheriff Skinner will be looking all along the lake for Deanna and me."

"We'll have to take our chances," Lightman said.

"My sisters and I played a lot in these caves when we were little," Piper said. "I know another way out."

Duncan met Daryl's eyes as silence stretched for three beats.

"Tell me about this other way out," Lightman finally said.

"This is the first of three caves connected by tunnels that finally reach to ground level. We'll come out in the woods near a waterfall."

Two more beats of silence.

"I'll hold the flashlight," Lightman said. "Lead the way."

"She's bringing him to us," Duncan whispered to Daryl. "We have to beat them to the center cave."

Piper spoke over him. "The tunnel to the first cave is short. And there's this big boulder in the middle cave that we'll have to get around. It'll take some time. And the second tunnel is longer."

Duncan immediately held a hand up to Daryl. She was talking as much to him as to Lightman, reminding him of the layout. Signaling him? She was right about the fact that the first tunnel was the shortest. He spoke softly again to Daryl. "I think she has a plan. We'll get as close as we can to the end of this tunnel and still keep out of sight." Then he pulled out his gun. Daryl did the same.

PIPER FORCED HERSELF TO breathe in and out slowly, evenly, as she led the way to the center cave. She could only hope that Duncan had read between the lines of what she'd been saying to Lightman. More, she hoped her plan would work. To give it just a little more credibility, she slid on some of the loose stones underfoot and slapped her hand against the side wall of the tunnel. "Watch your step," she said to Lightman.

"Watch yours," he said back to her.

The fact that he was holding the flashlight and her body blocked much of the light slowed their progress. If he'd given it to her, she might have used it as a weapon. But Lightman was no dummy. So she was going to have to use what came to hand. When they stepped into the center cave, he swept the light around, throwing long shadows on the walls before he let it come to rest on the opening of the next tunnel.

There was enough spillage for her to get a good look at the large boulder that had once blocked off most of the tunnel. There were plenty of pebbles and rocks at its base. Without giving herself the chance to think any further, she strode toward it. The instant her foot struck some of the stones, she let it slide out from beneath her, then fell, making sure to hit her head as hard as she dared against the boulder on the way down. She heard the sound of the impact, saw stars, and fell so that she landed on her side. Before he could get the light fully aimed at her, she wrapped her fingers tightly around a rock the size of a baseball.

"Get up. You tried that same trick to distract Ms. Lewis. It won't work with me."

"Hit…my…head." The beam of light blinded her, but it pinpointed his position. It also allowed her to see the gleaming chrome of the gun. She sat up, careful to keep the rock out of his sight.

"Get up," he repeated.

He wasn't going to come any closer. By the time she threw the rock, he'd have a bullet in her. Then she heard exactly what she'd been hoping for, a slide of rocks in the tunnel behind her.

Lightman shifted his gun and the light toward the tunnel's opening. Piper used all her strength to hurl the rock at him. She heard the sound of it hitting flesh and bone before two shots rang out nearly simultaneously. She saw Lightman pitch to the ground and heard the crash of his flashlight. Then for a moment everything went black.

"Stay down." It was Duncan's voice.

She was perfectly happy to obey the order. Her head ached. Every bone in her body ached.

"I'll take care of Lightman." Daryl's voice now. She saw two shadows rush out of the tunnel. "You see to Piper."

Aiming his flashlight at her, Duncan dropped to his knees. "You're bleeding. Did he shoot you?"

"I'm fine." She touched her forehead gingerly and felt the blood. "I did that to myself. I had to make it look good when I fell."

She had, Duncan thought. Too good. He'd heard her head connect with that boulder. He used the flashlight to check her eyes, but the pupils weren't dilated.

"Lightman isn't shot, either," Daryl said. "Looks like she knocked him out cold with a rock."

The relief that rushed through Duncan erupted in a laugh as he sat down beside her and scooped her onto his lap. "I don't know why I was worried about you." Then he lowered his mouth to hers and, trembling, he found everything. Everything.

"If you two want to come up for air for a minute," Daryl said, "I've got some more good news."

"What?" Duncan raised his head, but he didn't loosen his hold on Piper.

"Lightman has some interesting items in his backpack—a white sheet, several plastic bags filled with rose petals. I'd say this stuff, along with what I recorded from the wire on Piper, should be enough to send him away for a very long time."

"Are his reading glasses in there?" Piper asked.

"They are," Daryl said.

"They're going to connect him to at least one other RPK victim." Then she told them what she'd discovered in the file. "They have to be in an evidence bag somewhere, and they may have his prints on them. I'll bet he doesn't even remember he left them behind. And you may even be able to trace his purchases. Those are expensive designer frames."

Daryl glanced over at her. "You sure you want to practice law? I could use someone with your eye for detail in my office."

"The FBI could use her, too," Duncan said.

"I can't get a signal on my cell," Daryl said. "How far is it to the outside of this place?"

"Fifteen feet or so through that tunnel," Duncan said.

"I'll let Sheriff Skinner and Vi know that we're all safe and sound, and I'll check on Ms. Lewis."

For a few minutes after he was gone, Piper stayed right where she was with her head pressed into Duncan's shoulder. Just a few more minutes, she told herself. She'd be fine in just a few more minutes.

"It's my fault," Duncan said. "I convinced you to come up here. And I brought her around to the library."

She raised her head and looked him straight in the eye. "Enough. Stop that right now. I agreed to come up here, and I'm the one who broke the rules by rushing out to tell you about my discovery in the files. There's enough blame to go around. And I'm really, really tired of dealing with irrational people today. Those two were total fruitcakes. What I need more than anything else is for you to kiss me again."

When he tightened his arms around her and lowered his mouth to hers, she poured herself into the kiss. He was here holding her, and she felt her fears drain. She'd needed this. And she needed more. So much more. She wanted…

Daryl cleared his throat when he reentered the cave.

When Duncan broke off the kiss, he said, "I've got Deanna Lewis secured. She took quite a blow on the head. Skinner's notifying the trauma center in Albany. He's already called in the state police. They're on their way to the cliff face right now."

Duncan helped Piper get to her feet. "I have to call my boss. She'll probably want someone from the FBI office in Albany to take Lightman into custody. Can you make it out to the ledge?"

"Sure." Every bone in her body ached when she got to her feet. The adrenaline rush was over. But Patrick Lightman was trussed up like a turkey, and she and the people she loved were fine.

15

THE LATE-AFTERNOON SUN SLANTED long shadows over the patio at the back of the kitchen as Duncan put steaks on the grill. He felt as though the day was never going to end. He'd wanted to talk to Piper alone, but one thing after another had interfered, the latest being a celebration dinner that Vi had insisted on. Sheriff Skinner had been invited to stay, and then the men had been assigned to grill duty while the women made salad.

Daryl stepped out of the kitchen with three beers. "The ladies are chilling champagne, but I told Vi we'd start off with these."

Sheriff Skinner took one of the offered bottles. "I propose a toast to a job well done."

Duncan took one of the bottles and raised it. "It's not over yet." His eyes strayed to Piper inside the kitchen. She was tearing lettuce into a bowl. And for a moment he felt the same thing he'd felt when he'd slipped uninvited into her bedroom last night—just an inkling of what it might be like to see her do that ordinary task again and again.

"You're referring to the fact that Deanna Lewis wasn't working alone," Skinner said.

"We listened to her say 'we' and 'us' several times while we were crawling through those tunnels," Daryl said. "And Lightman overhead her making a phone call to someone telling them that she planned to eliminate Piper."

"I think Russell Arbogast is in the clear," Skinner said. "His credentials seem genuine, and he claims he knew nothing about Deanna Lewis's reasons for taking on the job of photographing the castle. But he says she was the one who pitched the idea to him, and the portfolio she showed him of her freelance work was impressive. Her résumé checked out."

"When Arbogast first approached Adair and Vi, I ran a thorough background check on him," Daryl said. "I should have dug deeper on Deanna Lewis, but my impression was the same as Arbogast's. There was nothing there to raise any alarm. I have someone working on her now."

A hissing noise from the grill made Duncan glance back at his steaks. "Whoever Deanna was referring to and talking to on her cell has to be connected to both her and the sapphires. She told Piper that they were given to *their* family, and that Eleanor stole them. I've called Cam. He and Adair, along with A.D. and my mother, have been visiting the Campbell estate. It may be that Deanna Lewis is a descendent of the Campbell family, or she may believe she is. The story that's been passed down is that Angus stole his bride."

"So, some descendent of the Campbell family might believe that she had no right to the dowry and therefore stole them?" Skinner asked.

"That's one theory." Duncan sipped his beer. "Cam's

going to see what he can find out. Deanna also claimed that the sapphires weren't Eleanor's dowry. If not, how did she come into possession of them? My mom is already trying to trace how the jewels made their way from Mary Stuart's coronation to Eleanor Campbell MacPherson."

"In the meantime, the state police are tracing the calls on Lewis's phone, and the trauma center will let you know the moment she regains consciousness," Skinner said. "The bad news is that due to the severity of her injury, that may not happen anytime soon. She's slipped into a coma."

Which meant that Deanna was a temporary dead end when it came to information. Duncan flipped the steaks. "There's still someone out there who is after Eleanor's dowry."

"Any ideas about him or her?" Skinner asked. "You're the profiler."

"I'm thinking, I'm hoping, that Deanna's partner is more rational," Duncan said. "Whoever decided that Eleanor must have hidden the sapphires had the same basic idea that I did. The plan to search the library for some clue to the location of the jewels is exactly where I might have begun. And he was patient. Deanna wasn't. But until we track that person down, we can't be sure any of the MacPherson women are safe."

"They're going to be as safe as we can make them. And we may have answers soon." Daryl put a hand on Duncan's shoulder. "In the meantime you and Piper have taken a dangerous serial killer off the street, you've captured one of the persons who was sneaking into the library, and you've found the second of Eleanor's earrings. Any one of those things is worth a good steak any day. Even if we have to eventually wash it down with champagne."

"I can drink to that," Skinner said. The three men raised their bottles in a toast.

PIPER THOUGHT THE MEAL WOULD never end. Not that she didn't enjoy the steak and the champagne. It was just that since they'd come back from the cave, she hadn't had a moment to think or to plan. Or to talk to Duncan.

There'd been so many people, asking so many questions—first the state police, then the FBI. Her cell phone vibrated just as Daryl leaned over to top off her champagne. Reporters had been bothering her all afternoon, but she'd let them all go to voice mail. She glanced at the caller ID—Abe Monticello. Rising, she said, "I have to take this." Then she walked out onto the patio. If Richard Starkweather was using Abe's cell phone again, she was going to—

"Piper. The story's just breaking on the news here in D.C. Thanks to you, Patrick Lightman is going back to jail. Are you all right?"

Not Richard, but Abe.

"I'm fine. What do you mean thanks to me?"

"The FBI has released an official statement that you were instrumental in the arrest, and that he was trying to abduct you when you took him out with a rock. You're a heroine. Don't you watch TV up there?"

She turned back to stare at Duncan. "We've been busy." Especially Duncan, she suspected.

"I need you back here in the office on Monday. Now that you're out of danger, I want you to take over second chair on the Bronwell trial. Richard can't seem to do anything with the files you left him. Will you come back?"

"Yes," she said. "But there's something I have to take care of right now."

Then she strode into the kitchen and right over to Duncan's chair. "That was Abe Monticello. Evidently your boss called my boss and I'm supposed to report back to work on Monday. Now that I've been instrumental in the arrest of Patrick Lightman, I've gone from villain to heroine in the twenty-four-hour news cycle. So I'll be an asset sitting second chair in the Bronwell trial."

"You will. But you don't sound happy about it," Duncan said.

"I am." She just wasn't as happy as she'd thought she'd be.

"This is what you wanted, isn't it?" Duncan asked.

"Yes, it is." She remembered standing in the kitchen the evening before, telling Vi that this was exactly what she wanted. Her old life back. She'd wanted what she'd had before her apartment floor had been turned into an imitation of a crime scene. She'd wanted normal. And she still wanted to work for Abe. With all his flaws, he was the best teacher she could have at this stage of her career. But…

Piper glanced around the table and noticed three sets of interested eyes on them. She shifted her gaze back to Duncan. "We have to talk. Now." Then she turned and walked back out on the patio. When Duncan joined her, she led the way to the far end, then whirled to face him.

"We have to get this settled now once and for all. I know that you played a role in Abe's decision to call me."

When he opened his mouth to speak, she held up a hand. "Don't try to explain. And I know I should be thanking you. I am thanking you. It's what I wanted."

"The thing is, I don't need you to play white knight. I can take care of myself." And that was true. It just wasn't what she'd wanted to say.

Duncan studied her in the dimming light. She looked like a huntress again, and if he hadn't already fallen in love with her, he would have right in that moment.

Beyond one of her shoulders, he saw the sun, a large orangey-red ball, sinking slowly toward the lake. In a matter of minutes, it would be gone. And it reminded him of how quickly time passed. And of how much you could lose out on if you hesitated too long.

"I agree. You can take care of yourself, and we do need to settle this." He took her hand and drew her quickly along the path that wound through the garden. He didn't stop until they were standing beneath the stone arch.

"Okay," he said. "I think it's only appropriate to settle everything in the place where everything began between us."

"Yes." Her gaze strayed to the spot on the right side of the arch where the metal box was hidden. Then she clasped her hands together. "You're right. Everything did begin here. With that fantasy I wrote out. And…I think…I…"

Duncan narrowed his gaze on her. Had he ever seen her at a loss for words?

She twisted her fingers together and met his eyes. "I know what you're going to say. It's just…I…"

It was only the second time he'd ever seen her rattled. He'd be a fool not to take advantage of it. Stepping forward he took one of her hands and linked his fingers with hers. And just that contact had his own tension easing a bit. Keeping his eyes steady on hers, he raised her hand to his lips. "You don't know what I'm going to say, Piper. Because I'm winging it here. I don't have your way with words. But I didn't bring you here because of that fantasy you wrote all those years ago."

"You didn't?"

"No. I brought you here because I thought it was the best place to explain exactly what I want. I'm taking a page from your book, and Angus and Eleanor's book. I want to tap into every bit of the power of the stones, just as they did."

When she simply stared at him, speechless, Duncan felt one flutter of panic. But there was no way he was going to back down or revert to sitting on the sidelines. No way. "I love you, Piper."

When she continued to stare at him, the panic fluttered again. "I know you like things neat, but I can't promise you that. And I can't promise you that I'm not going to want to take care of you. Because I intend to keep doing that for a very long time."

She still said nothing, but even in the shadows, Duncan caught the sheen of tears in her eyes. Panic did more than flutter this time. It spiked through him like a spear.

When she opened her mouth to speak, he tightened his grip on her fingers. "You are not going to talk me out of this. Don't even try."

"Okay."

"Okay?"

Her smile spread slowly, and fear and panic flowed out of him just as easily as the one tear that rolled down her cheek.

"I didn't want this to happen," she said.

"Ditto." He smiled at her. "But it has. So we have to deal with it. Don't run away, Piper MacPherson."

"No, I won't. And we will deal with it, Duncan Sutherland." She rose on her toes and used her free hand to bring his face down to hers. "Together. Because I love you, too. So kiss me again beneath the stones. Might as well tap into as much of that power as we can."

He did, and as they both sank into the kiss, the stones surrounding them sighed.

* * * * *

NO ONE NEEDS
TO KNOW

BY
DEBBI RAWLINS

Debbi Rawlins grew up in the country with no fast-food drive-throughs or nearby neighbors, so one might think as a kid she'd be dazzled by the bright lights of the city, the allure of the unfamiliar. Not so. She loved Westerns in movies and books, and her first crush was on a cowboy—okay, he was an actor in the role of a cowboy, but she was only eleven, so it counts. It was in Houston, Texas, where she first started writing for Mills & Boon, and now, more than fifty books later, she has her own ranch. . .of sorts. Instead of horses, she has four dogs, five cats, a trio of goats and free-range cattle keeping her on her toes on a few acres in gorgeous rural Utah. And of course, the deer and elk are always welcome.

1

FROM HER PERCH ON THE PORCH railing at the Sundance ranch, Annie Sheridan took what she called a memory shot. If she'd had her beloved old Nikon she'd have pulled it out and centered the lens on the familiar faces of her hosts, but the spectacular sunset against the Rocky Mountains would have been the star. Only to the casual observer, though, which Annie most definitely was not.

She'd become an expert at the art of watching from a distance. It didn't even bother her that much, not anymore. Two years into exile, she'd grown used to being the strange woman who ran the Safe Haven large-animal sanctuary, the one who never came to parties unless there was something her shelter needed—a favor, a donation, an adoptive home. Of course everyone in Blackfoot Falls knew who she was, and it would have stunned her if the residents of the small town hadn't made up at least a dozen stories to explain her hermit ways.

No one, she was sure, would ever come close to the truth.

She sipped from her glass of white zinfandel, a rare treat along with the scrumptious steak and baked potato she'd had earlier. The last time she'd eaten at a party was…in another life.

That sobering thought had her off the railing and heading toward Barbara McAllister and the cluster of family that surrounded the Sundance matriarch. If Annie let herself yearn for anything these days—outside of more money for Safe Haven—it was the friendship of this clan. The three brothers—Cole, Jesse and Trace—were always willing to lend a hand during an emergency. Jesse had saved many a poor animal's life, or given a horse or a llama or a potbellied pig a new home with his rescue airlifts.

Then there was Rachel and her boyfriend, Matt, so giddily in love. In the past six months two of the three McAllister brothers had hooked up. And now with Rachel taken, that only left Trace on the loose. Something the Sundance dude ranch guests, all of them single women in their twenties or early thirties, were trying to remedy.

Rachel had made several attempts at befriending her, though Annie had kept her distance. But boundary lines that had once been set in stone were becoming more flexible.

"Are you getting ready to leave?"

Annie smiled at Jesse's girlfriend. The whole reason Annie was socializing at all was due to unassuming, crazy-generous Shea. Taking a break from her high-security job as a computer programmer, she'd come to Montana over the Christmas holidays to help at Safe Haven. But she'd come back to Blackfoot Falls because of Jesse. That she'd turned out to be the sanctuary's most influential volunteer and backer was a miracle.

Annie sighed with real regret as she nodded. "I have chores."

"Need help?"

"Not from you, although thanks for offering. You stay right here and enjoy yourself with that man of yours."

Shea blushed as she slipped her hands into the pockets of her dark gray trousers. "I'm glad you stayed so long. Jesse said you've never had dinner here before."

"You know how things are. Always something to do, what with every female animal at the shelter pregnant."

Shea laughed. "Not every one."

Annie set her glass on a big tray, knowing no one would mind that she didn't stay to clean up. "It's been a nice party."

"It has," Shea said, with more than a little surprise in her voice. "I usually hate parties. Never know what to say. But with the McAllisters it's different." She leaned in a little closer and lowered her voice. "Yesterday, I talked to Sadie from the Watering Hole for almost half an hour."

"Whoa, look at you, Shea. You haven't even lived here a full month yet and you're already one of the in crowd."

"Jesse tries to include me in things because he knows I'm oblivious," she said in that matter-of-fact tone that still made Annie smile. "Not with gossip, though. He doesn't do that."

Perhaps because he'd heard his name, the man in question sidled up to Shea and snuck his arm across her shoulders, but kept his gaze on Annie.

"I'm flying out to Missoula on Tuesday," Jesse said, "so you might want to put together a shopping list."

She perked up because it was about a hundred miles to Missoula, and she could get things there that weren't available in a small town like Blackfoot Falls or even the bigger Kalispell. Northwestern Montana was gorgeous, but it was mostly land and lakes and mountains. "I'll get on that tomorrow."

"With all that loot you two have been raking in," Jesse said, "it'll be hard to decide what to buy first."

Annie smiled at his teasing. He was the only other person who knew how much of the influx of money had come either directly from Shea or from donations she'd wrangled. Annie pulled her keys out of her pocket. "Trust me, most of it is spent and we had no trouble doing it. Unbelievable how many things need replacing or fixing at that sorry shelter."

"Your cabin, for instance?" Shea said.

"My cabin is fine, thanks." Annie addressed Jesse again, wanting to change the subject quickly. "I'll send a list home with Shea." She looked at her. "I'll see you tomorrow morning?"

"Of course."

Annie fiddled with her keys as she backed up in the direction of her truck. "Great. See you then." She said quick goodbyes to most of the McAllisters along with many thanks, but before they could even try to convince her to stick around for dessert she climbed into her old green pickup.

No matter what she did or how long she left the windows open, the cab always smelled like horses. She didn't mind. Horses had been a comfort to her all her life, and even though they were an amazing amount of work, especially this time of year, she couldn't have wished for better company.

Horses didn't care that she was on the run, that she'd messed up her life beyond repair. They loved her, anyway.

It didn't take long to reach Safe Haven, and the first thing she did was check on the animals in the stable. She had an abandoned stallion that was starting to pick up some weight and get a little shine to his coat, and she added some grain to his feed trough. She spent longer checking on the mares, both of them with full teats but only in the prep stage of foaling, so there was time.

An hour later, she was finished with the barn chores and walked the couple hundred feet to the cabin everyone was so obsessed with. Inside, the overhead light sputtered to life, giving her a shadowed view of her home.

No, it wasn't much, but it served its purpose. She could run her computer, plus she had a coffeemaker, a microwave, a toaster oven and a minifridge. Hell, she'd lived for years with less at the Columbia University dorms. The tiny claustrophobic bathroom wasn't a big deal anymore, though she missed having a tub. But the shower got reasonably hot, and she'd replaced the cracked mirror. And the toilet…well, that could use replacing, too. But not until the emergency supplies were stocked and the tractor had a new engine.

Once upstairs in her loft, she turned on the lamp by her bed, and only then realized she should have changed out of her good jeans and one nice shirt before she'd done chores. No use worrying about that now, though. It was late for her, and the alarm would go off before first light, so she pulled on her nightshirt, and by nine-thirty she was under the covers reading a paperback thriller.

A chapter in, her eyelids started sinking. Thankfully, sleep wasn't hard to come by anymore. The key was to keep herself in a constant state of exhaustion. She'd become an expert at that, too.

FOR THE SECOND TIME IN AN HOUR, Tucker Brennan found himself more focused on the view of the stables outside his window than the business at hand. There were several wranglers busy with chores, just like on the rest of his ranch. He would have preferred being out there building up a sweat instead of sitting in his office, filling his day with the business of running the Rocking B.

His Monday morning had gotten off to a rough start. He'd slept through his alarm, then spilled coffee on his lap during breakfast. Maybe he should have gone out last night. There were a number of women he could've called who wouldn't have minded a last-minute invitation. But it was never that easy, was it?

"There's a fundraiser for City of Hope next month."

Tucker turned his chair so he faced his personal assistant, who was seconds into an eye roll. Darren smoothed over the near-gaff by clearing his throat. Tucker didn't let his own frustration show, knowing full well this probably wasn't the first time Darren had brought up this particular agenda item. Or the second.

"It's at the McDermott?"

"Yes. Black tie," Darren said. "The Dallas Symphony Orchestra will be performing before the gala."

Tucker clicked over to his May calendar where Darren had already highlighted the date. He had three other formal events in May and the thought of another one didn't appeal. "Send them a check, please. Personal."

"Match last year's?"

It had been sizable. "Yes."

They continued to go down the list of requests, which seemed to grow exponentially year by year. While Darren did most of the correspondence concerning the ranch operations, Tucker liked to write personal messages where it counted. Like the one to an old warhorse of a rancher from Idaho who was about to retire. With no heir, he was going to auction off sixty thousand acres, along with his cattle and horses and all his equipment, and Tucker meant to purchase a great deal of the stock.

He barely acknowledged Darren leaving the office and

set to work composing a letter to the rancher, handwritten, just like the old days, because Cotton and his late wife, Lula, had sent out Christmas letters every year until she'd passed away in 2009.

Just as Tucker started the second paragraph, a notification popped up on his computer. He went to delete the intrusion with one quick click, but the words stopped him.

He saved his screen and switched to Google, where he'd set up dozens of alerts a year ago, having no faith whatsoever that he'd ever hit pay dirt. He'd gotten hundreds of hits because there wasn't anything all that unique about the chosen keywords, but he never skipped a one. This particular alert was for the name *Ann,* even though the object of his search had been born Leanna Warner. The other keywords were *horses* and *fundraising.*

Tucker wasn't even sure why he'd bothered, because that was too close to Leanna's true history. But he'd been thorough and he never let himself get his hopes up. He clicked on the link.

A blonde woman sat in the corner of a photograph. She wasn't looking at the camera, but to her left. Saving the photo, he brought up the Warner file he kept under a separate password. He'd gathered everything he could about the woman a year ago, right after his brother, Christian, had given up his tough-guy act and confessed that he'd been hoodwinked.... By a slick fundraiser who was tall and slender and had a face that made men do foolish things.

Leanna was a card-carrying member of the Association of Fundraising Professionals with an office in Park Slope. She'd started out with a big firm, eventually opening her own office.

She and Christian had done quite well building up a sizable fund to benefit a number of charities. Only, none of the dividends reached the account. Instead, the investment profits had disappeared. Vanished. So had Leanna Warner, but only after the New York district attorney's office, acting on a complaint, had gone after Christian.

While there was a lot of circumstantial evidence putting the money in Christian's hands, there was no proof, no paper trail. Not that the D.A.'s office had stopped looking. They had made it clear Christian would remain a person of interest until they found Leanna and took her testimony. In the two years since the embezzlement, including the year Tucker had been conducting his own investigation, there hadn't been a single clue as to her whereabouts.

Tucker still wasn't sure there was one now. The pictures he had of Leanna showed an elegant, sophisticated New Yorker. She'd been one of the Manhattan hungry, seeking her fortune and status among the elite. If her plan had been to cut and run, she'd done herself a disservice. With her looks and the confidence she displayed on the two videos he'd found of her, she could have gone far.

Greed had a way of making fools of even the most promising.

Trouble was, he couldn't be sure that the woman, identified simply as Annie, was Leanna Warner. If she'd only turned a little more toward the camera… Besides, this woman looked as if she'd been born in Western gear.

He ran one of the old videos and froze it when he had a decent view of her profile. He pulled up the two images so they were side by side on his monitor. For a long time, he just flicked his gaze from one to the other, and dammit, there were similarities. The odds were not high that he'd found the missing Warner, but it would drive him crazy not to know for sure. More importantly, he owed this to Christian.

Tucker didn't have to look up the number for George Morgan, a family friend who also happened to be a private investigator in New York. He'd been on the case from the moment Christian had told Tucker about Leanna Warner, and while George had found out about her past, he'd had no luck finding the woman herself.

"Tucker. It's been a while."

"Too long," Tucker said, leaning back in his chair, staring at the new picture as if her position would change if he looked hard enough. "I'm calling about Leanna Warner."

George took a second. "Did something happen?"

"Maybe. I might have uncovered a picture, although I wouldn't count on it. If it is her, she's living in a flyspeck town in northern Montana, working at an animal sanctuary."

"You want me to go check things out." It wasn't a question.

"I'd like that, yes."

"I'm slammed at the moment but I can go in a couple of weeks." Met with silence, George added, "Or I can recommend a couple of other investigators if you'd like."

That changed things. Tucker hadn't realized how invested he was in finding Warner until this photo had cropped up. Locating her might not solve all the issues he had with his brother, certainly wouldn't fix things between Christian and their mother, but it would be a significant start. "Maybe I'll fly out there myself. It's probably a fool's errand, but if it is her, I'll make damn sure she doesn't run again."

"You know, there's no guarantee that bringing her to the district attorney will be enough to clear Christian's name."

"I know." Tucker stared out the window, trying to organize his thoughts. "I won't be hasty. I'll take a look around. See if I can dig up something tying her to the money."

"I don't know.... Sure it can't wait two weeks?"

He smiled. "I won't do anything risky. In fact, I have

the perfect cover. My foundation funds sanctuaries and shelters."

"Or you can have a look, confirm it's her and, while you wait for me, take some time to go fishing. Montana has some great streams and lakes."

Tucker laughed.

George did, too. "I know. What was I thinking? You're so much like your old man. He never took time off, either."

"Listen, do me a favor. When you can, dust off those Warner files, huh? It's been a while. Let's see if we missed a connection somewhere along the way."

"That I can do fairly quickly."

After they hung up, Tucker looked at his April calendar.

It was jammed, of course. The Rocking B ranch, started on a shoestring by his adoptive grandfather, built into an empire by his late step-father, was over 500,000 acres. They raised cattle, horses and crops, and there were twelve working oil wells on 160,000 acres of backcountry land. Although he had managers to handle the day-to-day business, the buck stopped with Tucker.

It wasn't easy for him to make the trip himself, but he'd manage. If he rearranged his schedule, he could go the following Monday. That time frame would give him a chance to refresh himself on Leanna's history and find out what he could about Safe Haven and the town of Blackfoot Falls.

He called Darren in, and they began the work of shuffling appointments. There wouldn't be any problem, except for one—he dedicated Tuesday nights to dinner with his mother. If he flew out Monday, he doubted he'd be back in time.

Irene lived on the ranch in a private suite of rooms, but they didn't cross paths that often. She had her own social circle that kept her reasonably busy, but she was still grieving for her husband, who'd died eighteen months ago.

Tucker spent his weekends in Dallas proper taking care of social obligations, and worked the rest of the week at the ranch. She probably wouldn't say much, but of all the things Irene did, she most looked forward to their weekly dinner. He hated disappointing her, but it couldn't be helped.

While Darren went through item after item, Tucker kept staring at the pictures he'd pulled back up on his computer. He might want to blame his younger brother for being so gullible, but that didn't mean Tucker wouldn't help him clear his name. There was more at stake here. Christian had gotten the short straw when they'd been children, and while Tucker's own guilt was great, it was nothing compared to their mother's.

He couldn't afford to wait for George. Tucker needed to see this "Annie" for himself. And if she was the woman who'd left Christian holding the bag for her crimes, delivering her to justice might help bring his erstwhile family together again.

As ANNIE SIPPED HER COFFEE, she checked the big blackboard above her desk. On it were the days of the week, the scheduled volunteers, appointments, deadlines...basically her life in chalk.

Mondays were always fun, at least in the early afternoon when Melanie Knowles brought a group of high school students to volunteer. Melanie had convinced the principal and the school board to give the students academic credits for their participation. Each time a group arrived in the small yellow bus, they had an hour of instruction—everything from animal husbandry to money management—before being assigned tasks.

Melanie and the students had even started a major project on their own that would benefit the shelter for years to come.

Thank goodness, because Safe Haven wasn't in nearly good enough financial shape to handle anything outside the basics of feeding and caring for the animals. But at least they'd made significant headway by turning the operation into a not-for-profit organization that was finally eligible for grant money and more substantial donations. All thanks to Shea. She'd helped Annie with the paperwork, but her participation meant much more. Shea was the name and face of Safe Haven.

Just remembering the days before Annie had asked Shea to serve as Safe Haven's chairman of the board made Annie tense. The future of the sanctuary had been at stake. Annie couldn't use her real name on any government document. Since she was an unpaid volunteer, she wasn't noted at all.

The rest of the board positions had been filled with longtime residents of Blackfoot Falls, and they were one hell of an ornery bunch. Their first meeting would be next week, and wasn't that going to be a corker. Annie would be there to run things—Shea had made her promise—but with an official and legal board of directors, Safe Haven would continue even if Annie had to disappear in a hurry.

That thought sent her mood plummeting. Better get busy before she had too much time to brood.

It wasn't light out yet, but she'd have to start the first round of feeding shortly, so she booted up her computer and checked her email. She didn't get much. A few volunteers liked to keep in touch between visits, some ebills had to be slotted for payment. Shea had sent pictures of yesterday's party that she'd posted on the Sundance website.

The fourth one nearly stopped her heart.

It was a picture of her. For anyone to see. Including the New York district attorney.

TUCKER WAS ALREADY IN THE sunroom, waiting for his mother to join him for lunch. He never minded spending time with her, but he wished he could do something more to lift her spirits.

Finding Leanna Warner would help. Irene wanted so badly to bring Christian back into her life that Tucker would do just about anything he could to make that happen. Proving Christian's innocence was no guarantee that he'd see past the pain of being abandoned as a child and give his mother and Tucker another chance. But it was Tucker's best shot.

Tucker had gone through his own pain and doubt during his parents' bitter divorce, but he'd been the lucky one. He'd ended up with his mother, a man he admired as his new father and a legacy of wealth and privilege to live up to. Christian had been the bargaining chip for Rory Andrews to grant Irene her divorce. She'd never dreamed that Rory would vanish, would subject Christian to a nomadic life following the horse-racing circuit and running from debts.

That Christian had gone to college and received his master's in finance was a testament to hard work and determination, because there'd been no support from his dad.

Now, to have this cloud of suspicion over his reputation was another kick in the teeth Christian didn't deserve.

Every time Tucker thought of the grief Leanna Warner had brought down on his family it angered him further, but he'd never been one to act rashly. By the time he turned that woman in, he'd make damn sure his brother would be exonerated completely.

Irene entered the room with her head high, and a smile on her face. It was all for show, but sometimes he thought the facade was the only thing keeping her going. That and hope.

THE MORNING WENT BY IN FITS and starts, and Shea was late. Her phone was going straight to voice mail, which meant she probably hadn't remembered to turn it on again. Annie had gone back to the computer several times, just to make sure she wasn't freaking out over nothing, but she wasn't. Her picture, along with her first name being associated with Safe Haven, was plenty to worry about. Shea would know how many hits the site had logged, and that page in particular. A high number would be more reason to run as quickly as possible. A low number meant it was far less risky for Annie to stay.

God, she wanted to stay.

The irony wasn't lost on her. She'd been so intent on becoming a mover and shaker in Manhattan that she'd gotten herself into the worst trouble she could imagine. Now, she was desperate to live in a cabin that made her first New York apartment look roomy, and had fallen in love with a life of pitching hay and nursing everything from piglets to Brahma bulls. But she'd better stop romanticizing the sanctuary and her life, because that would make running even harder.

"Annie? Can I ride Candy Cane after class?"

Shaken out of her slide toward panic, she smiled at one of her favorite students—a small girl for a senior—who was deeply infatuated with horses. "You have a ride home?"

Stephanie nodded. "My mom said I could stay for an hour if it's okay with you."

"You bet. Candy needs a little exercise."

The girl ran back to the work of mucking out one of the birthing stalls as Annie heard a car crunching over the gravel driveway. Her heart beat furiously as Shea parked her truck.

"Sorry I'm late. I ran into Doc Yardley and we got to talking. But I remembered to bring the—"

Annie grabbed the bag of medicine from Shea's outstretched hand. "I need to speak to you," she said. "Inside. I'll be right there."

Shea's expression had gone from pleasant to worried, but instead of shooting back questions, she simply closed the truck door behind her and headed for the cabin.

Annie trotted to Melanie, who was helping one of the kids distribute feed to the goats. "Can you watch things for me? Something's come up."

Melanie, who had once considered becoming a vet, agreed at once.

It struck Annie hard that she knew so much about this quiet woman who'd made such an impact at Safe Haven and with her students. In fact, Annie knew a great deal about many of the people in this quaint Montana town. She'd meant to avoid all this. To keep to herself. Getting involved hadn't been part of the plan, and this was why.

She forced a smile for Melanie, then turned, wanting to run to the cabin. But it wasn't that far, and she could use the extra minute to calm herself. Since she'd seen the picture, she'd worried about a million things that could go wrong, but she hadn't bothered to think through what she was going to tell Shea. As little as possible, yes, but where was the line?

Shea looked up from the kitchen area when Annie walked inside. She was making a fresh pot of coffee. Annie wished she had something stronger.

"What's wrong?"

"I need to ask you a favor."

"Okay."

Annie studied the woman she'd gotten too close to. "The picture you posted on the Sundance website, the one with me in it? I need you to take it down. Please."

Shea didn't react, not even a lift of her eyebrows. "All right," she said calmly as she sat in front of Annie's computer. Shea typed very quickly. Logging into the Sundance website, it took only a few clicks to find the photo and delete it.

Annie sighed with relief. "Did you put it up this morning?"

"No. Last night," Shea said, returning to the desktop picture of the corral at sunset. "Late. Just before midnight."

Twelve hours. Annie's face had been freely available for twelve hours, but then the odds of someone from her past checking out the Sundance dude ranch website were miniscule. She didn't think facial recognition had come far enough along to have identified her from her somewhat fuzzy profile. Still, the smart thing to do would be to get out. Now. Just in case. "Do you know how many hits that page had?"

Shea typed a bit more. "Eighteen."

Eighteen wasn't bad. Eighteen could be just folks from town and some of the guests.

"I won't do that again," Shea said. "I didn't realize you disliked having your picture taken. I apologize."

All Annie had to do was nod, and that would be that. Shea wouldn't pry or tell anyone, with the possible exception of Jesse. They'd chalk it up to Annie's reclusive ways.

But this was Shea, who had given her time, her skills, her money and her friendship without any expectations. She never overstepped, respecting Annie's privacy in every way. Which would make leaving her in the dark the easiest thing ever.

The ache in Annie's chest was no reason to talk, to say aloud the secrets she'd been holding close for so long. In her old life, she'd been anything but an introvert. And she'd never met a camera she hadn't liked. "I used to be a professional fundraiser," she said, and those few words, that small admission, revved up her heart rate again. Made her flush with heat and fear and relief.

Shea went to the coffeepot and took out two mugs from the cupboard above.

Annie closed her eyes and tried to calm herself. By the time Shea put both cups of coffee down, Annie felt ready to begin. "I was good at it. I liked the work, even after the economy tanked. I made raising money for good causes my personal crusade. Not just because I was paid to do it, but because I knew that even in the worst of times, when people donated it made them feel better."

"Your effectiveness hasn't diminished at all," Shea said. "I can't believe how fearless you are in approaching everyone you see and how favorably most of them respond."

"People want to help. Well, most people." Annie briefly closed her eyes. "There are also those who understand the motives behind charitable giving, and use that information to steal and destroy people's faith and good intentions."

"What are you saying?" Shea looked at her plainly, expecting the truth. She wasn't naive, although some people mistook her manner for innocence.

"I worked with a partner who turned out to be one of the bad guys. Unfortunately, I didn't realize he'd been embezzling funds until it was far too late to do anything."

"Oh, Annie," Shea whispered, and Annie had to turn away so she wouldn't tear up.

"I had to leave my home. My everything."

"Surely no one would believe you were involved. That's ridiculous."

"Oh, but they could." Annie thought the bitterness had left her, but it still simmered inside. "I found out second-hand that one of my clients felt something wasn't right and approached my partner. He wanted to withdraw the money from the fund and invest it himself. My partner gave him the runaround and the client went to the district attorney."

She set her cup aside, rubbed her hands together, then down her jeans. The cabin was so small, there was no room to pace, but she couldn't sit still. She pulled herself up until her butt was on the edge of the sturdy table she used for everything from sewing to eating, then began to squeeze the beveled wood with her hands.

"The story hit the papers with the allegation that my partner was responsible but I might be involved after the fact. It was only a matter of days before I'd be subpoenaed by the state to tell them what I knew. Unfortunately, that amounted to nothing. I was as shocked as anyone when I saw that money was missing. All of the investment profits had been siphoned off. The seed money was still there. I went to an attorney, a good friend from college, and he flat out told me that I'd better have something on my partner. With charities involved, he felt certain someone would go down, and it could very easily be me."

Annie flexed her hands and tried to relax her body along

with her speeding thoughts. She'd never intended to tell Shea so much. Only, she'd been holding on to her silence for so long it was easy to keep talking, to spill everything. But the next part...

The next part was hard to think about, let alone say out loud. Besides, she wanted Shea to continue working with Safe Haven. To continue being a friend. "I'm not proud of what I did, but all I could think to do was run."

Shea sipped her coffee, clearly in thinking-things-through mode. When she looked at Annie again, her blue-gray eyes showed only concern. "I'm so sorry you had to go through that. It must be horribly difficult. Do you have a large family?"

"Mom, Dad, my younger sister. I left them a letter explaining so they wouldn't think I was dead. But I can't call."

"You must miss them."

Annie sighed. "Every day." She jumped down from the table and looked Shea in the eye. "Please, you have to keep this between us."

"Of course."

"Thank you." Annie maintained eye contact, hoping Shea understood that meant not telling Jesse. "And thanks for taking down the picture without even asking why."

Shea, who wasn't a toucher, put her hand on Annie's arm. "Whatever I can do to help, all you need is to ask."

Annie wanted to hug her, but just nodded and led the way outside, remembering in the nick of time to get the bag of equine medication. Despite the chance someone from her past had seen her on the internet, she felt lighter than she had in years.

"I INVITED HIM TO COME LIVE here," Irene said, just before she sipped her bourbon and sweet tea.

Tucker put down his fork. "What did he say?"

She sighed. "No."

He wasn't surprised. "He's got a life in New York. Friends."

"But we're family." Irene's voice had gone rough, which wasn't unusual however much he wished she could accept the situation.

"Christian needs time, Mom. It hasn't been long since he found out his father refused to let you see him. Most of his life he thought you didn't want him."

"You stopped being angry ages ago, and Rory Andrews stayed away from you out of spite."

"I had Dad. And you. I was lucky. Christian only had Rory and whatever stories he made up." Funny how Tucker never thought of Rory as being related, much less his biological father. His hazy memory of the man didn't even seem real, more like a fictional character in a story Tucker had read as a kid.

"You know I wanted to keep both of you." She took another drink, and this time it wasn't a mere sip. Soon she'd ask him for a refill, and he'd give her one. The drinking wasn't a problem, though it could head that way if she wasn't careful.

But how could he blame her? Tucker's own guilt weighed on him, and he'd been a child during the divorce. Was that the reason his desire to find Leanna Warner had become a borderline obsession? Why he'd been tempted to go early, to hell with his commitments?

No, he had to play it smart. He'd already baited the hook by suggesting the possibility of a large donation to Safe Haven. He'd put time between the email he sent and the day he was to arrive. She wouldn't be suspicious because no one looking for her would give her that much time to run. She'd accept that he was exactly who he claimed to be—a rep for a benevolent foundation.

All he had to do was be patient, observant and ready to take her down.

WELL PAST MIDNIGHT, TUCKER stretched his neck before he looked again at the papers he'd spread over the desk in his bedroom. Every one of them related to Leanna Warner, and every one of them intrigued him in a way that was keeping him awake despite his exhaustion.

She didn't quite add up. Her parents had been and continued to be social climbers. Joseph Warner was an attorney who'd worked for one of the most prestigious firms in New York, but he'd never made partner. His wife was an assistant manager at a design firm, again, second tier, but living among the elite.

According to Christian, Leanna had fit in so well with the wealthy young Manhattan scions and entrepreneurs that he'd been shocked to find out that she was a fundraiser. When he'd looked closer, though, he'd seen that her "designer" clothes and accessories were clever knockoffs. It was her personality and flair that let her get past all the normal barriers.

Christian would know about that kind of thing because he was in the same boat. His finance degree had gotten him only so far in a city that thrived on connections, but his audacity had helped make him a hell of an investment manager. No wonder the two of them had decided to team up. They each wanted a lifestyle that was just out of reach.

Reading the background material was helpful, but he had to check his bias at the door. If he let his emotions take the reins there was a risk he'd miss something important, or jump to conclusions. But there was no denying that Leanna was extremely clever.

On paper, she seemed the least likely person in the world to have stolen money. But if she'd had nothing to do with the fraud, why disappear? The logical conclusion was that she'd wanted to let Christian take the fall—except she hadn't tied him to any real evidence. One transaction record, even an email referring to an offshore bank account, could have put Christian squarely in the bull's-eye. Instead, Leanna had been forced into a life of hiding and his brother had just enough of a stain on his reputation to cripple his future.

Though she'd made off with over $500,000, she'd left each charity's seed money in the account, which, he suspected, was a clever way to avoid notice. At least until the whistle was blown, and then things had happened quickly. She probably hadn't had time to clean out the rest of the funds. But who could be sure of her reasoning?

So many discrepancies and oddities made it difficult to figure out her end game. Good thing Tucker was a patient man. He wouldn't make the mistake of acting rashly. If she had something that would nail her, he'd find it. Then turn her over to the D.A. gift-wrapped all nice and pretty.

He turned off the computer and gathered his materials. Most of what he had were printouts, but there were also several articles from New York newspapers, two yearbooks, four different brochures that Leanna had created and a short stack of photographs. The alarm was going to ring in under six hours, and his agenda was full all the way through Sunday. He wished he wasn't committed to the Rangers game, but it was more business than pleasure, so no choice there. It had been a long time since he'd been to a game for the fun of it.

He stripped down to his boxers and climbed between the sheets. As tired as he was, he should have been out like a light, but images of Leanna…Annie…kept spinning on a loop that wouldn't quit.

3

ANNIE LOVED THIS TIME OF YEAR. She breathed in the cool spring air and squinted at the Rockies still wearing their lacy snowcaps. Safe Haven didn't have many cows or calves to monitor. Even if they had she wouldn't have minded the job of running stock. Working out here in the big north field under the open sky seemed more like therapy than a chore.

She heard the pounding of hooves and forced herself to calmly turn in her saddle. Of course it was Will Woodruff riding out to take her place and not guys wearing suits and badges coming to slap handcuffs on her. Twenty-four hours had passed since Shea had deleted the photo, long enough to assume that if the wrong person had seen it, Annie would've been picked up by now. But not long enough to stop her from jumping at every shadow.

That didn't mean she'd let down her guard, but…she had to stop dwelling on it. The odds were in her favor and she'd decided to take the risk. In the meantime, she had a hell of a lot of animals and people counting on her.

"Afternoon, Annie. Anything I should know?" Will, who'd been a wild man in his heyday, a cowboy renowned for breaking the meanest horses and taming beautiful women, was in his sixties now and a valuable volunteer.

"Everything's fine. Anything exciting back at the ranch?" she couldn't help asking.

He looked at her as if she were nuts. "Not a thing."

They chatted for a minute, then she took off for home base, ready for some lunch before she moved on to chores in the barn.

Her first task after washing up and getting coffee was checking her email. A message from the Rocking B ranch made her pause. After reading the long email three times, she still pinched herself, just to make sure she was conscious. Then she went to the Texas ranch's website.

Looking at the list of grants and gifts the philanthropic arm of the Rocking B had shelled out through the years made her break into goose bumps. Those people didn't mess around. When they gave a worthy nonprofit funding, they gave enough to matter.

With shaking fingers, Annie bookmarked everything, then got out her cell phone. Good thing Shea picked up or Annie surely would've burst.

TUCKER LOVED TO FLY, AND EVERY time he went up in the Cessna, he thought about his father. It had been Michael Brennan's idea to send Tucker to flight school. The old man had been progressive in his thinking, and the ranch showed it.

The CJ2+ had earned its keep, despite the hefty price tag. It seemed as if Tucker's attention was always needed yesterday and flying gave him the freedom to respond immediately. It would be good to have the plane nearby when he met Annie Sheridan. There was always a chance that she'd want to give herself up. He wasn't counting on it.

The email exchange hadn't been as illuminating as he'd

hoped. Although he found it interesting that Shea Monroe was so invested in the workings of Safe Haven that she'd authored most of the correspondence.

A quick search of Monroe's name had prompted Tucker to send a link to George. He confirmed that she had high security clearance and was connected to some government programs that could be worth a fortune if sold to the right party. Tucker found it hard to believe that Leanna Warner would go to a backwater town like Blackfoot Falls without a good reason.

He shook his head, knowing he'd passed the point of no return given all he'd invested in that one vague online photo. Although the fact that the picture had disappeared without a trace, even in the computer's cache, was suspicious in itself. Fortunately, he'd saved it to his hard drive.

Annie's emails had focused on logistics, informing him of the airfield in Kalispell, the nearest moderately sized town that had accommodations and car rentals. He'd booked a room at the Hilton Garden Inn, reserved an SUV.

The closer he got to Montana, the more he thought about meeting the woman who had taken over a large portion of his brain. She confused him. Intrigued him. While he'd done his fair share of tricky negotiations with savvy competitors, he had the feeling his skills would be tested to the limit.

He'd have to be on his toes. Remember what lurked behind the beautiful face. And not for a second forget what she'd done to Christian.

ANNIE LOOKED UP FROM THE TABLE where she'd stacked copies of the Safe Haven board meeting agenda. Time had decided to slow down to a snail's pace, giving her a wonderful opportunity to let worry overshadow every bit of potential good that might come from Tucker Brennan's visit.

Safe Haven was too small. There were only a handful of permanent part-time volunteers. Because of their remote location, even if she could attract more help, they had to be local, and she'd already dried that well.

No, the problem was, most every animal sanctuary she'd researched had a visitor's program and a welcoming atmosphere for potential adopters. She couldn't even try to have guests because there wasn't a hotel in Blackfoot Falls.

She'd hated telling Brennan he'd have to fly all the way from Dallas, then drive to Safe Haven. And she sure hoped he'd like the food at Marge's, because that was his only choice. She just wished he would get here already.

No; in fact, what she really wished was that he would stop by, hand her a huge check, then go. Although she'd researched his credentials down to his alma mater, strangers made her nervous. Brennan lived miles away from her old stomping grounds in Manhattan, but there was always a chance that he knew someone who knew someone....

God, she had to stop thinking like that. Instead, she collated, stapled, put paper into file folders. In the end, it ate up ten minutes. Ten. And Brennan wasn't due for another hour or so. She'd never survive.

She could change, but no, she'd wait. The clothes she had on—work jeans, old tee, boots—were perfectly fine for day-to-day. It didn't matter that she smelled like a barn. But she would prefer to spiff up a little for the big shot with a checkbook. Nothing too fancy, just better jeans and a clean shirt.

Talk about a different life. In the beginning, she'd missed shopping like crazy, but she'd adapted. Learned to cook a little. She'd have killed for a pricy latte...okay, still would. But there were advantages to living on this very thin wire. She'd also learned to sew, and was grateful for the training because she'd had to patch up more than a few animals. Safe Haven survived due to the kindness of a few key players, like the vet, Dr. Yardley, who donated what time he could. Mr. Jorgensen from the feed and hardware floated loans for grain and other supplies. In fact, the whole sanctuary was built out of goodwill and patience, but Mr. Brennan could change all that.

Thanks to Shea, Annie had seen the difference an infusion of cash could bring to a two-bit operation like Safe Haven. But she remained cautious. Hope was only a friend in small measure. She didn't dare put herself in a position where she might fall into another pit of despair. It had taken her almost a year to climb out of the last one.

A quick knock at the door was followed instantly by one of the school kids ducking his head in. "Pinocchio's gotten stuck in the fence by the water pump."

All thoughts of Tucker Brennan vanished as Annie grabbed her gloves, followed the boy out of the cabin and ran as fast as she could.

THE DRIVE WAS PLEASANT, considering the circumstances. Tucker had only been to Montana for business, and never this far north. Looking out at the Rockies and the acres of lush land brought back memories of his early days when he'd still been learning about ranching from the ground up.

His father had made sure he'd done every job the Rocking B had for a cowboy. It had been hard work, but worth as much as his college years. His apprenticeship had given him more than just hands-on experience; it had given him perspective.

He barely noticed the town of Blackfoot Falls from the highway. It was like a thousand others across the country with a local diner that served great home-cooked meals, a bar that offered cheap beer, pool tables and country music.

All he cared about was that it was thirty miles from the Safe Haven turnoff.

Finally, he saw the big wooden sign that marked the entrance to the sanctuary. He was early, hoping the surprise would give him a slight edge. He liked to take stock of people when they were flustered. They revealed more than they knew.

So he slowed the rented SUV to keep the dust down as he headed for the main buildings. He passed one pasture with a half dozen horses, none of whom were particularly bothered by his vehicle. They looked pretty decent for rescue animals.

The fencing was sturdy, if old-school, about what he'd expected. According to the info he'd gathered on Safe Haven, there had been a few corrals, a barn, two stables and a cabin standing when Annie took over. Clearly, she'd made improvements.

His pulse revved as he neared the buildings. In one glance, he'd know the truth. But the truth alone wouldn't be enough. He'd have to use every moment he could to catch her vulnerable and get the evidence he needed. Even if it took a couple of days.

He pulled into a small parking area. There were several trucks lined up, mostly pickups, a tractor that had seen better days and a short yellow school bus.

Behind it was the cabin that had to be Annie's living quarters. She hadn't been kidding when she said it was small. But the working buildings gave a good first impression. Well spaced, old, but taken care of. In back of the barn he saw a small crowd of folks standing in a semicircle, as if they were watching a fight. Something pretty fierce, if the dust coming from the center was any indication.

He jumped out of the SUV, his inner alarm bells ringing. As he approached the crowd, he saw that the onlookers were kids—high school age—and two adults, a middle-aged woman pressing a hand to her throat and a petite twenty-something holding the arm of one of the teenagers, preventing the boy from moving forward. They all looked worried.

And then he heard it. The cry of a panicked, bleating goat.

He jogged the last few feet until he could muscle past the outer ring of spectators. It was a pygmy goat whose horns were tangled up in some high-tensile wire. Despite the name, pygmies weren't that much smaller than other breeds of goats, and the situation was dangerous. The woman trying to free him was taking a hell of a risk. Goats were notorious for their fear response. They kicked and struggled so fiercely they sometimes died from their hearts giving out.

Tucker knew the best thing to do was let the goat be and hope he tired himself out in time for intervention. Because a person trying to save one could well end up needing a doctor.

The woman making that mistake was Annie Sheridan. He had to admit she made quick work of cutting free the wire, but he could see she'd been battered and bruised. Her blond hair was damp with sweat, her face smeared with mud and blood.

The kid next to Tucker was a big beefy guy whipping the side of his leg with a pair of thick gloves.

He nudged the boy, who did a double take. "Lend me your gloves."

"Annie told us not to step in," he said. "It could be dangerous."

"I understand."

The boy looked him up and down, then handed him the pair. Tucker slid them on as he shouldered his way closer to Annie and the struggling goat.

She had just managed to cut the second to last wire curled around the goat's right horn when the back-leg kicking started again. Tucker ducked what could have been a very unfortunately placed hoof, then lunged forward, one hand on the back of the animal, the other grabbing on to his horn.

"What the... Get out of here, you idiot!"

"Cut the damn wire." Tucker was holding the goat's head back, just enough to unbalance him so he couldn't lean on his front legs. "Now."

Annie, grunting as the goat's body slammed her in the side, got the final wire cut.

Tucker had to use both hands to steady the terrified creature, while Annie quickly and efficiently cleared away the loosened wire fragments from his other horn.

The goat was free now, but he didn't know it, and Tucker didn't want to release him until Annie was out of the way. But she was too busy shouting at him to move to see that his position was stronger.

It was someone from the crowd that finally got her attention. An older man ran up, yelling, "Annie, get the hell out of there."

She did. Quick on her feet even with that prodigious frown on her face.

Tucker stopped looking at her and focused on making his own exit. It took a highly uncoordinated jump straight back, after which he nearly fell on his ass, but the goat did the right thing and ran toward the barn.

"What the hell were you thinking?"

For the first time, he got a good, clear look at the woman who'd just yelled at him, her fury uncompromised by her dirty face or her breathless exhaustion.

He didn't answer. He was too busy accepting the fact that he had found Leanna Warner.

4

"WELL, THIS IS PERFECT," Annie said, shaking her head. "Of course you're Tucker Brennan."

"And you're Annie Sheridan."

She nodded, made an abortive move to shake his hand, but her gloves were still on and her body had decided to alert her to a whole symphony of hurts and burns. What she would feel like when the adrenaline faded was going to be torture. "Welcome to Safe Haven," she said. "You're bleeding."

He followed her gaze down to his arm where there was now a rip in his shirt. There was blood, but while the cut was long, it wasn't deep. "Damn. I like this shirt."

"Sorry about that." She looked him over, just beginning to appreciate that the man in front of her was in a league she didn't come across anymore. The McAllister brothers were prime examples of tall, dark and handsome, no doubt about it. The sheriff and Matt Gunderson, too. But Brennan had a different kind of good looks.

Even with the rip in his shirt and those hefty gloves, she could picture him sipping champagne at a ritzy social event as naturally as riding the range. He wasn't New York fancy, though, which became very clear when he tugged off the gloves. There were some calluses, and he had a tan that wasn't perfect enough to have come from relaxing at the spa.

He was a gentleman rancher, certainly…with thick dark hair, a strong face and intense green eyes, all of which she shouldn't be noticing. He was doing his own inventory of her assets and liabilities, and she couldn't begrudge him. Though if he'd been another man she might've found his close scrutiny a bit creepy.

"Let's head to the cabin," she said. "I can patch you up there."

"I'll be fine. You, on the other hand, are a mess."

"Um, yes." She couldn't help but smile as she glanced down at herself. "Yes, I am." It could've been worse had she already changed to her good clothes. She looked over her shoulder toward the barn. God bless them, the kids had already returned to their chores. Although they'd be leaving soon. "Actually, I need to make sure Levi is tending to Pinocchio before I do anything else. We can get you a cloth to put on that cut, if you think it can wait."

"Yeah, this is nothing." He waved dismissively. "I'm assuming Pinocchio is the unlucky goat."

She nodded, leading him across the mix of packed dirt and gravel that became a muddy pit during rainy season. "He's a curious guy, and he never seems deterred by the messes he gets himself into."

"Goats can be difficult."

"Every animal in Safe Haven can be difficult. I think they sign some kind of agreement before coming here." She gestured vaguely. "Prelude to the tour. This is where we house the goats and chickens. We have twenty-two goats as of yesterday. We're always on the hunt for new families for them, but only for milking and breeding, not for meat."

On a shelf by the door, she picked up and folded a clean

rag from a pile and handed it to him. He pressed it against the cut, hissing a little.

Annie figured he would be fine for the next ten minutes or so. He was a rancher, so he understood that her first responsibility was to the stock. "The chickens, they kind of came with the place. Sometimes I'll wake up to new hens, more so roosters that people have dropped off."

She watched Tucker scope out the barn. Feed was safely stored behind big fences. The coops were spacious and well maintained. The goats had new water tanks from a central well, which had been the most expensive improvement since she'd taken over. No more lugging pails. Cleaning troughs? That job would never disappear. But then, that was something the high school kids helped with.

"That must be Levi," Tucker said, looking toward a bale of hay where the older man sat petting Pinocchio gently as his wife, Kathy, worked on cleaning the goat's wounds.

As Annie slowed her step, Tucker did, as well. No need to spook Pinocchio any further. Not that the other animals paid that any mind. Chickens wandered and pecked, making a racket that had become white noise to Annie. Some of the other goats were nursing or filching scratch from the hens. There were stalls for resting and birthing, and stacked bales of hay for the baby goats—kids—to find their legs.

"It's a great setup," Tucker said.

"We're always at capacity." Looking on, she sighed. "That's what's hard. So many in need, and we try not to overcrowd the barn. I've tapped out the locals for the most part. Though we're lucky to have an animal rescue pilot living nearby. Jesse has taken special cases to better-equipped shelters."

"How's Pinocchio doing?" Tucker asked, speaking to Levi and his wife.

"Banged up some," Kathy said, "but he'll be fine once

he gets his calm back. He's a devil, this one. If he wasn't so darn adorable we'd have pitched him out ages ago."

Both Levi and Annie laughed. "The day you pitch out an animal is the day we close up shop," Annie said. "You're worse than all of us."

Kathy's kids had left the nest. She and Levi, a former teacher, had been married for thirty-two years. She'd grown up in cattle country, and her wiry body was fit and strong. At sixty, she could still lift a fifty-pound bag of feed without breaking a sweat.

Her husband was just as sturdy. He didn't let his arthritis stop him. "What the dickens were you thinking, jumping into that mess?" he asked, frowning up at Tucker.

The slow curve of his mouth and amusement in his eyes said he wasn't normally spoken to in that manner. "I saw an opening. I took it."

"Could have got yourself killed." Levi shifted his stink eye to Annie. "And you sure as hell know better. Just who do you think would take over for you if you got hurt bad? You need to think of that before you rush in next time. We can't save everyone," he said, his gaze softening as he turned back to Pinocchio. "Much as we'd like to."

Annie wanted to change the subject quickly. The last thing she needed was for Tucker to think she was irresponsible. She couldn't very well yell at Levi for speaking the truth, but did he have to be so blunt with Brennan standing right there? Grasping for the quickest exit she could think of, she winced, touched her side and breathed a soft, "Ow."

Tucker's attention flew to Annie. Her face didn't show the pain she had to be feeling. But she could be hiding something serious beneath those well-worn clothes. "We should get you fixed up," he said.

She nodded, and all he could think of was that seeing

her pictures and even the videos had not prepared him for this striking woman. He'd known she was tall, but in heels she would just about reach his height of six-one. Even with the grime smeared across her cheeks, he could see she had smooth, creamy skin. Her lack of concern for her appearance finally struck him. She'd given him a rag but hadn't taken one for herself.

Once she wiped off the mud, he wondered if her eyes would still look so blue under those thick lashes. And her hair was…interesting. He'd bet she cut it herself, but it somehow made her look more appealing. Her beauty was a perfect cover, all right. Of course Christian would have been captivated by her. Hell, any man would have.

She cast a final look at Pinocchio, then turned for the door. Tucker paced himself so he could get a look at her from the back. Long and lean, she walked with utter confidence. Another puzzle to work out. Why? Why had she run, only to end up working her ass off out in the middle of nowhere?

He got a quick look at the stable as they passed by. The younger woman he'd seen earlier approached Annie with a smile. "You okay?" the woman asked.

"Fine. Banged up a bit. But fine." Annie turned briefly to Tucker. "This is Melanie Knowles. She teaches at the local high school and is responsible for bringing the kids you've seen out here. Mel, this is Tucker Brennan."

He shook the woman's hand, but she was clearly too concerned about Annie to bother with him.

"You need some help?" she asked, nodding at the already blooming bruise forming on Annie's forearm.

"I'll be fine. All the help I need is that you and the gang are here."

"We've got you covered," Melanie said, then nodded

at him and circled back to the stable, where more of her charges were waiting.

Annie had developed a slight limp as they finally made their way into the cabin. He reached to hold the door at the same time she did. The awkward dance ended with her the victor. Then she nearly ran into him when he stepped inside and stopped dead still.

This was more like a line shack than a cabin. A crappy line shack at that. There was a beaten-up table in the center of the small room, three mismatched chairs pushed under it. A counter held a microwave while a toaster oven and a big coffeepot flanked the sink. On the sideboard sat a computer, and above that was a large chalk duty roster that listed volunteers, chores, memos and reminders. Under the sideboard was a dorm fridge. A leather recliner had been pushed so far up against a wall he doubted there was any chance of it actually reclining.

Stairs led up to a loft, which he imagined was her bedroom. The only other door had to be the bathroom, and that was it. He could probably fit the entire place into his walk-in closet at the ranch.

She touched his arm to sneak around him, making him jump. "Sorry. The bathroom's back there. Why don't you go in first and wash up? You should probably take off that shirt and let me have a go at that cut."

Tucker nodded and made his way to the bathroom, maneuvering around the table. He noticed a brass lamp, the only decorative object on the lower floor. There were no pictures, no trinkets, no nothing. He assumed the cupboards were as sparse as everything else. It would have made a perfect home for a monk. But hard for someone who had things to hide. With no space to spare, she'd have to get creative.

He'd sure like to get a look upstairs. If there was anything tying Leanna to her past, she'd keep it close when she was most vulnerable.

The bathroom was so small it made his jaw drop. The toilet desperately needed replacing, and next to that was a very tiny shower. There was enough room to turn around. That was it. The plastic curtain was too long for the bar, and he couldn't picture any woman he'd ever known who would last two days in this miniature house.

The pedestal sink looked old with its stains, but clean. Underneath, there was a medical kit, and above, a wooden cabinet with a small mirror.

His hand hit the shower enclosure as he took his shirt off. Putting it on the closed toilet, he soaped up. He checked his torso for bruises and cuts, but there was only one on his upper right hip, and while it was getting ugly, he'd survive. The cut on his arm stung, and it started bleeding a little, but it was shallow and would stop soon. No stitches needed, although an aspirin would be welcome.

Using one of the fresh-smelling towels, he dried off, grabbed his shirt and the medical kit and went back to the main room. "It's all yours," he said.

Annie opened her mouth but didn't speak. Instead, she stared at his bared chest. He knew he wasn't anything like one of those six-pack guys in catalogs, but he kept himself in good shape. The way she blushed surprised him, but then again, this was ostensibly a business meeting.

"I made some coffee," she said, finally, and that's when the aroma hit. "You'll find everything you need, unless you want cream. I do have some goat milk in there, though."

"Thanks."

He watched her go, feeling huge and clumsy in this small room, although he normally wasn't. But as he investigated, finding mugs along with plates and glasses and utensils, he realized how organized Annie had to be to make things work.

What was the use of running away with the money if this is how she had to live? There weren't two mugs that matched, or two plates. Everything looked secondhand. The fridge had very little to say for itself—the milk, a couple of bags of greens, some condiments, two beers way in the back. A tiny freezer section held a couple of frozen burritos and ice trays.

It wasn't surprising that the most abundant food in the cabin were packages of ramen noodles. This was worse than a dorm room.

She came out of the bathroom with her T-shirt untucked. She'd lost the pink on her cheeks, but she wasn't back to meeting his gaze. "Please sit," she said, kicking out one of the chairs.

"Can we have coffee while we do this?"

"Yes." Her demeanor changed with that one word, her face somehow expressing real pleasure without having to smile. "Of course."

So, without the smudges on her smooth cheeks, her eyes were still that incredible blue. He liked her mouth, as well. Full lips, well-defined and naturally pink. She wore no makeup, and she sure didn't need any.

He tensed when he realized what he was doing. Twenty minutes since he'd met her and he was already getting distracted by her looks. Christ.

She blinked, then lowered her lashes. "Go ahead," she said, with a jerky tilt of her head that had him cursing himself for staring too long. "I'll get the supplies sorted, then fix myself a cup."

Together, they made it through the dance of moving with only one open path. She almost avoided his chest, but that one brush of her shoulder made them both freeze as if they'd done something illegal. Annie cleared her throat, and he managed to ignore the contact.

He sat down with his coffee and tore open a package of gauze while he waited for her to fill her mug. The situation was perfect for his purposes. Sudden intimacy with a relative stranger was something no one could plan for. He would find out more about Annie in the next ten minutes than he would being shown around the sanctuary. But only if he stopped allowing himself to be distracted. She was a stunner, no argument there. Knowing how she'd used her looks to dupe his brother made him more the fool if he fell victim.

Along with her coffee, she brought a wet cloth and clean towel to the table with her. A pair of scissors, antiseptic and other first-aid needs had already been laid out. He watched her eye his arm, her top teeth toying with her bottom lip. She winced a second before she swabbed him with alcohol, and so did Tucker.

Far from the cool distance of someone used to causing pain, her expression was the picture of concern. A sharp inhale through clenched teeth, a soft, "Sorry," as she used a second swab. Once she covered the cut with gauze, her shoulders relaxed, and she was again the confident woman in charge. What he couldn't tell yet was if her empathetic response was completely false.

"Thanks," he said. "Now you."

"Oh. No. I can handle it."

"I doubt it," he said, watching her reluctance turn into another blush. "I was there."

When she finally responded it was with a weary sigh. "Okay, but I know it's nothing." She slowly got to her feet, looking as if she'd rather be walking barefoot on hot coals. "It's my back. I got caught on a wire."

He turned in his seat as she stood directly in front of

him, his eyes level with her leather belt. Now that he was looking for it, he could see spots of blood on her shirt. She lifted it carefully, exposing a long stretch of what would have been perfectly pale skin. Instead, there were two sizable bruises that were coloring in darkly.

"I don't know," he said, in no way faking his own concern, which made him uncomfortable. "Maybe you should get these checked out. It looks bad." He touched the worst of it with careful fingers.

Annie inhaled sharply. "If you'd stop poking at it."

"I'm trying to make sure there's no internal hemorrhaging."

"I'm fine. I've had worse."

"This one's over your kidney. It could be dangerous."

"I know there's no real damage," she said, lifting the shirt higher, but now with evident tension running through her. "I know because I was kicked by a horse years ago. So, the cut?"

"Right," he murmured, the word coming out low and slow as her bra strap came into view. It was the least fancy bra imaginable. White, no frills. A sensible bra that had no business looking like that against her pale flesh. Just as he had no business noticing.

The bruises hurt him to see, and the cut was no picnic, but it was impossible not to notice the rest of her body. The sleek elegance of her lines, the curve of her waist, the indention of her delicate spine. This close, her scent came through. Yeah, she was no rose petal, not from a foot or so away, but from inches, she smelled like a ripe peach. Damn his senses for the traitors they were. He murmured another curse.

"What? Is it that bad?"

He cleared his throat and moved his gaze to where she'd been bleeding. Now that he had some focus, he saw it wasn't a bad cut, on par with his own, but there was no way she could have taken care of it herself.

Tucker got a swab at the same time he pulled himself together. "No. It's fine. But it's gonna sting like hell."

"Go for it."

He did, and this time, their roles were neatly reversed. He winced—especially with the feeling so present in his memory—although he didn't apologize or make any noise at all. His job was to be efficient. Observant. He had a rare opportunity in front of him, and he was so busy thinking with his dick it was slipping away.

"This was some introduction, huh?" Her laugh was high and nervous. "I'm really sorry—"

"Do not apologize. I completely understand." Good. Back to business. "I saw a quarter horse that looked ready to foal. How many mares are pregnant?"

She seemed to relax even though he was taking the second swab to her cut. "We've had two births so far, both healthy. Besides Glory, one more is close enough to get her own birthing stall, and another one is showing. That's it, because we're keeping the mares separate, but they're the last of a large herd that was kind of dumped on us. Most of them were taken to a horse sanctuary in Wyoming, but we've got the rest.

"Thankfully, they're pretty healthy now. Some—" She stopped when his fingers touched her skin as he worked to adjust the gauze before taping it. "Some of them were undernourished," she continued. "And the vet was here a lot in the beginning. We've got a line on new homes for a couple of the stallions, which is amazing. It's going to be hard to place them."

"I'll take a look at them, if you like. I can't promise anything, but I know some people who might be interested, and they're not too far away."

"Yeah, distance is a problem for us. I'd appreciate any help you can give."

"Okay," he said. "You're all set. Are you sure there's nowhere else you might need help? I can get Melody in here, if that's more comfortable."

"Melanie." Annie dropped her shirt. "And no, but thank you. If you're up for it, we can take a real tour. You can bring your coffee with you, or we could finish it here if you'd rather." She gave him a quick smile, then handed him his shirt.

He stood, slipped it on and angled away to tuck it in. When he faced her again, she was drinking her coffee, her gaze focused on something other than him.

Was she thinking of another life? Of future plans? She understood that the Rocking B Foundation gave sizable grants and gifts. It could turn this little operation into something to be reckoned with, and considering they had access to aircraft, the potential for animal services was huge. Or maybe she was just thinking about how the foundation money, along with the stolen investments, could build her a dream home right across the border in Canada.

"We can walk and talk," he said. "That is, if you're not too sore. But I'd like to grab another cup of coffee."

"There's no such thing as too sore working a ranch. I guess you already know that."

Not the way she did. He'd been part of a big machine. Yes, he'd had to learn all the grunt work jobs, then those that took skill. But very few times had he faced the cold of a winter morning alone, when every animal in sight was counting on him for food and shelter and care.

There was nothing simple about sanctuaries. He'd investigated a hell of a lot of them. Each time, there was one individual or couple who were the lifeblood and soul of the operation. Those who gave up any sense of a normal life to the welfare of the animals.

She'd been doing it almost on her own for two years. He didn't have the faintest idea why. Penance made no sense. Not when she could go back to New York and really make things right. How was it he hadn't anticipated her working like a dog? What had she done with the money she'd already stolen?

"You know, I've got to make a couple of phone calls." He checked his watch, then made sure he looked at her when he added, "Would it be okay if I met you in the stable in about twenty minutes?"

There. A flash of panic that was gone in the blink of an eye. Just long enough for him to see her gaze fly to the loft and back. She didn't want him here alone. Not for anything. But he simply waited her out.

"Sure. No problem. I'll see you there."

"Thanks. I won't be long."

Annie picked up her coffee mug, then set it in the sink without taking another sip. She hesitated at the door as if she was working out what to say to him, but in the end, she stepped outside. He watched her walk down the path, his phone to his ear.

The minute she was out of sight, he headed straight up the steps. His heart was beating too quickly, but there was nothing he could do about it. He wasn't used to subterfuge. He'd always believed in facing his problems head-on. But this case was the exception to all his rules.

He saved the obvious for last, moving quickly around the room, looking at the floorboards, the wall for any possible nook where she could have something stashed.

With no paintings and no closet, there wasn't much territory to explore, but he took his time. The dresser was filled with clothes, packed tight. Still, he pulled each one all the way out to look underneath the drawer. Nothing.

The bed was intact, as far as he could tell without stripping it completely, but underneath…

Coffee cans. Four of them. And an old-fashioned suitcase. That's what he opened first, checking his watch, appalled at how long everything was taking. She could come back any second, and she'd have every reason to call the cops on him.

The suitcase was full of paperback books and music CDs. He checked every pocket twice, flipped through the books and popped open the CD cases, but he didn't find anything noteworthy. Disappointed, he shoved the case back under the bed.

He hit one of the cans of coffee, and just to be sure, he checked. It was unopened coffee. So was the next, and the next.

The fourth one had an unsealed envelope. Inside, it was a single sheet of paper with a typed number and password. He was certain the number was for a bank account. There was also a driver's license in the name of Alison Bishop, with a picture that sort of looked like Annie, and a roll of cash thicker than his fist.

After he took a picture of the license and the account number, he put it all back under the bed just the way he'd found it. Then he got the hell out of there before she caught him red-handed.

5

THE KIDS WERE GONE, AND WITH them, Melanie. It was relatively quiet outside, as quiet as it ever got around Safe Haven. Annie was grateful because she had to calm herself before she went in to see the pregnant mares. They didn't need her fear and worry, and no one would ever convince her that animals didn't respond to human energy, good and bad.

It made perfect sense that Brennan would need to make some business calls, that he'd like to be alone when he made them, and also not have to worry about the background noises that were inescapable on the property.

She'd already decided that the website photo had not blown her cover. She'd researched Brennan and he was legit. Even Shea had done some of her magic and given him the thumbs-up.

Besides, a man like Brennan wasn't the type to go snooping. And even if he did, he wasn't going to look inside coffee cans stored under her bed, for God's sake.

Some deep breathing made her wince, but it also helped calm her down long enough to dismiss her concerns about him discovering her real identity. Which left her wide-open to worry about everything that had actually gone wrong since he'd arrived.

Annie had known for a while now that wishes and daydreams were a waste of time. That didn't stop her from wishing that she could start the day over, or at the very least ask Tucker to leave and come back tomorrow.

She didn't even dare think that nothing else could go wrong because that was just inviting catastrophe. She still had on her stinky, now bloodstained and torn work clothes. The man she so desperately wanted to impress had walked in on her making a fundamental mistake in caring for animals—one that could have cost them both physically, and certainly may have cost her financially. What foundation wanted to invest in a sentimental idiot?

Then, to make everything a billion times worse, the libido she'd managed to stifle for two long years had decided to rejoin the party by filling her mind and body with so many hormones she could barely see straight. She'd actually had to bite back a moan when he'd touched her.

Thank God he'd put his shirt back on. It didn't erase the memory of his muscled chest and the smattering of dark hair, or his small hard nipples or the perfect V from his broad shoulders to his trim waist. But at least she didn't have to dig her fingernails into her palm to stop from touching him back.

Dammit, now she wished she'd brought her coffee. And taken some ibuprofen. She thought about going back to the cabin, but they kept a bottle of aspirin in the stable med kit. She should have offered him something when she'd bandaged him, but with all that chest showing, she'd been distracted.

"Is everything okay?" Tucker asked from behind her. "Are you feeling dizzy?"

She must have jumped a foot. She hadn't heard him walk

across the gravel. He had to think she was nuts, stand-ing in the middle of the path, staring at nothing. "No, I'm fine. Sorry, just thinking about… We should go check on the horses."

"Right." He smiled, although it seemed a little forced and made her edgy. "FYI, in my younger days, I spent a lot of time in foaling stalls."

"Good, then you can help if it looks like things have progressed that far. I think Glory might foal tonight. She's been up and down a lot today, sweating like crazy. I wouldn't be surprised if her water's already broken."

"Is this her first?"

Annie shrugged, but she was relieved that the conver-sation was squarely in safe territory now. She could talk animals till the cows came home and feel fairly sure she wouldn't make a misstep. "Don't know. She arrived preg-nant and undernourished. We fattened her up, but it's im-possible to say what that period of malnutrition did to the fetus. So Doc Yardley is on call, and I'll be setting up camp out here tonight."

"You've done this a lot, then?"

"Often enough to know when to call for help." She stopped at the stable door. "I've been meaning to ask," she said, looking directly at him as the sun cooperated and moved from behind a cloud. The butterflies she'd never expected to feel again came back, but she couldn't afford not to watch him, because the issue had been bothering her since that first email. "You're the head honcho of the Rocking B ranch. Your foundation has a director by the name of Rafael Santiago. So how come you're here in-stead of him?"

Oddly, the question made him smile. A half grin, actu-ally, the right side of his mouth lifting for a few seconds. "I think it's important to do some things personally."

"You go to each nonprofit yourself?"

"Not all of them, no. This is a special case."

That made her blink. "Why?"

"Okay, I admit it." Tucker gave the impression of shrugging without moving his shoulders. "I may have had some other business in the area, but I figured this might be a nice break from the daily grind."

Annie laughed. "You picked a lousy place to find rest and relaxation, Mr. Brennan. I only have six permanent part-time volunteers. Levi and Kathy have been keeping an eye on the mares today, but they leave when the sun sets. I'm pretty much it until eight tomorrow morning, and I'll have my hands full. I can't even offer you dinner, unless you want a frozen bean and cheese burrito."

The half grin came back. "Hey, at least I got to wrestle a goat."

This time her laugh was accompanied by a sense of ease. "To each his own," she said, although she didn't for a minute think his answer was silly. Her last real vacation had been spent working at a horse rescue shelter in upstate New York.

"Come on," she said. "This is the primary stable, used for horses who need special attention. We've got plans in the works for a separate quarantine stable, but we don't have the funds yet. The economy hasn't helped us with a lot of donations. Although our board chair, Shea Monroe, has been doing wonders in that area. We've got several email campaigns running with more planned."

"It's Tucker," he said.

She blinked, stopped walking.

"Not Mr. Brennan."

"Oh, right." Annie walked him into the stable proper, making sure to move slowly, talk softly. "The stalls are twelve by twelve. That wall serves as the barrier to the half of the stable we use to house the newcomers. There are four stalls back there. The four in the middle are for those who are hurt, and we keep the nearest four for foaling. They're really too close to the doors but we don't have much choice."

Annie let him take his time looking around the big white structure. Considering it was almost twenty years old, the stable was in good shape. The man who'd originally built Safe Haven had come from Idaho, and he'd worked his tail off to save whatever horses he could.

Tucker walked past the pregnant mares to check out the other horses that were in sick bay. None of them were contagious, just needing special attention.

Levi and Kathy were inside the empty foaling stall next to Glory's. "Hey," Kathy said, keeping her voice low and calm.

"How's she doing?" Annie asked, taking a look at the mommy-to-be. Glory was a sturdy black quarter horse with a blazing white star on her forelock. She was lying down on her nest of fresh straw but her agitation was clear.

"She's fine," Kathy said. "We've got a bet going on what time her water'll break. I say ten."

"I think it's gonna be midnight," Levi said. "You gonna call Doc Yardley?"

"He's supposed to come by later, but everything's going okay. I can handle it."

"You know," Kathy said, "we can stay."

"No need." It was Tucker's voice coming from behind her, and Annie jumped, even though he'd kept the words soft. "I'll stick around."

"You don't have to do that," Annie said. "I can manage, and you just flew in today. Wrestling goats is exhausting."

His grin made her want to flip her hair back like a teen at the mall.

"I'd like to stay," he said. "We used to tell all our most embarrassing stories waiting for the foals. It was fun."

Annie turned to face him, wincing as she tried to cross her arms over her chest. If she'd had a brain, she would have iced some of the worst bruises before heading out to show off the sanctuary. She really needed to get that aspirin. "We've got a ton to go over tomorrow, including that ride across the property you asked for in your email. Besides, I don't recall telling embarrassing stories being an essential part of foaling."

His casual wink made her pulse leap. "You just haven't been to the right stables."

Kathy and Levi both laughed, but that got Glory struggling to her feet, so all attention went to her. As soon as she was standing, Annie entered the stall to comfort her. She moved slowly, holding up her hands and whispering the same soft nonsense she had since Glory had been brought in. She'd made a point of touching the mare a lot, letting the horse become familiar with her scent and her hands.

The foal was moving and there was no sign of excessive distress. With luck, there would be little to do but observe and clean up after the birth. As she left the stall, everything was quiet except for the familiar sounds of horses. Snorts and breathing, shifting straw, a soft nicker from Cocoa, who was waiting her turn to go into labor.

She walked to the open stable doors, knowing Tucker, Kathy and Levi would follow. As soon as they were far enough away to speak normally, Annie said, "You guys don't have to stick around. It's almost six."

Kathy looked from Annie to Tucker, then back again. "You're awfully stiff. Did you put something on your bruises?"

"I'm fine, Kathy. Thanks."

"I brought you that liniment for a reason," Kathy said.

"You've got us here for a bit. Go fix yourself up, and stop being a stubborn mule. You might be up all night, for heaven's sake."

Annie wanted to shoo her friends on their way, but Kathy was right. The ointment would help. "All right." She turned to Tucker. "Other than that cut, are you aching anywhere? Kathy makes up her own salve, which works wonders."

"Nope, I'm fine. But I'll watch out for Glory if you two want to get home."

Kathy didn't even respond to Tucker. Instead, she hustled Annie back to the path toward the cabin, which meant that she wanted to speak to Tucker without Annie hearing.

Resigned to her fate, Annie gave in to the ache in her hip as she headed for the jar of salve. It didn't help that it was so easy to picture someone else applying the ointment, someone who looked mighty fine without a shirt on.

TUCKER COULD HAVE USED something to ease the minor aches that had cropped up in the past hour, but he was more interested in paying attention to the couple who were about to give him a heartfelt testimonial. He hadn't gotten this far in business without being able to read people. In fact, that particular skill had been a primary factor in keeping the Rocking B strong through the recession and the drought.

Sure enough, Kathy, who looked tired but determined after the eventful day, approached him the moment she could. "Here's the part that isn't obvious, Mr. Brennan."

That stalled Tucker's arrogant assumptions in their tracks. An excellent reminder that he wasn't the only one who could read people.

"That girl," Kathy said, pointing in the direction Annie had disappeared, "has gone without basics so she could feed the horses. Not that she'd ever say a word. We didn't know in the beginning. But things started to add up. So some of us decided to bring treats, meals, coffee, because she won't take a penny for herself. Not a penny. Everything goes to the sanctuary."

Glory was making some real noise, so they moved inside. Levi turned on the bank of red lights, bathing the space in an eerie kind of beauty, which allowed them to observe but wouldn't disturb the mare. Her water hadn't broken, but she was nesting again, rearranging the straw as she prepared for the birth.

"She hardly ever comes to town," Levi said, his arms crossed over his broad chest, staring at the horse, not Tucker. "When she does, it's to get supplies or to find help in one form or another. Not for her, mind you, but for the animals."

"Any idea why?" Tucker asked.

"Why she gives so much, you mean?"

He nodded at Kathy.

"She doesn't talk about herself. We don't even know where she's from, really. She just showed up one day, volunteered. It wasn't two weeks later that Edgar, the man who built Safe Haven, went back to Idaho to be near his grandkids."

"Thanks for letting me know." Tucker gave her a nod. "But I'll warn you, as I've warned Annie. I can't make any promises. I have a board of directors myself, and I have strict criteria that has to be met before we can offer funding or grants."

"Oh, we know that," Levi said. "But we couldn't let you leave without telling you that you'll never spend a wiser dollar. It's not just the animals who benefit. You should see how much the high school kids are learning. Everyone who comes to volunteer at Annie's sanctuary is the better for it."

"I believe you," Tucker said. He had no reason not to.

For whatever reason, Annie had decided to play her role to the hilt. She clearly needed these people to be on her side. Just like Christian had been so enthusiastic about her before the money went missing.

Now that he'd found that account number, Tucker was even more certain that whatever Safe Haven was, it was also a cover for Leanna. Or a stepping stone to something bigger. He had some theories about the account number and the license in the coffee can. It had to be an exit strategy, but why hadn't she used it yet? Was access to the stolen money contingent on some future date? Was someone else holding the key? Another kind of partner, perhaps?

He needed to find time tonight to send the pictures to George, get him working on making connections, putting the pieces together. In the meantime, he had to keep his wits about him and look beyond his physical attraction. He'd run across some smooth operators before, but Annie was in her own league. She confused him. He couldn't nail down her motives or predict her next move. He felt as if he was missing one vital piece of information that would unravel all the mysteries.

Levi and Kathy shook his hand and made sure he knew where the birthing kit was. He watched them meet Annie halfway to their truck. Huh. He'd expected Kathy to touch Annie. A hug maybe, or at least a friendly hand on her shoulder. But they kept to their own personal spaces, and said their goodbyes with nods.

When Annie returned to the stable, the first thing she did was hand him a couple of pills and a bottle of water. "Ibuprofen."

"Thanks."

With a nod, she went to check on Glory, but from outside her stall. Tucker followed until he was close enough to smell a hint of liniment, which he didn't mind at all. He supposed it had a lot to do with his own history. The scents of a ranch were home to him, including the one that overshadowed the sweet peaches that lay beneath....

At the thought a bolt a lust shot through him, making him reel. It was crazy. Maybe he was too tired to be sticking around when everyone else was gone. He'd like to think he was made of stronger stuff, but his reactions were off. Just to get some distance, he went to check on the other pregnant mare.

The two empty birthing stalls still had shavings instead of pure straw. He walked deeper into the stable, really looking at the other horses. A sturdy-looking mustang had a bandage over one eye. Then there was a buckskin Appaloosa who seemed unaffected by the human comings and goings, but had some bandages on her flank. She reminded Tucker of a horse he'd ridden for five years, a great palomino who'd been so good-looking, no woman for miles could resist her.

"You can't see it from here, but Pretty Girl was quite a mess when she arrived," Annie said, indicating the Appaloosa. She'd come close, and Tucker kept his gaze on the mare. "She'd tangled with some barbed wire, and it took a lot to patch her up."

"You do it well."

"Nothing like on-the-job training. I put another pot of coffee on while I was at the cabin. I'm going to make us a couple of thermoses. How do you like yours?"

"Black is fine. If you tell me where things are, I could do that for you."

"That's okay. I think we have a wait. I'll be back in plenty of time." Annie started walking, but stopped before she stepped outside. "You promise you've done this before?"

"I swear." He put his hand up, and she sighed.

When she had rounded the path out of his sight, he let himself breathe again as he got out his cell to speed-dial George. Tucker updated him on the attached photographs, what he'd found under the bed, and then asked him to look for evidence that Annie might have been working with someone else. Maybe someone who was pulling her strings.

"You think she was coerced?" George asked, not sounding as surprised as Tucker might've expected.

"I don't know. I'm trying to look at every angle. Some things don't make sense about her. I'd rather we kept an open mind. If she's not the only one behind the embezzlement, I want to know. You find anything else since we talked?"

"No. That account number might just be the answer we're looking for."

"It might," Tucker said. "I'll call you when I can."

After he put his cell away, he found a couple of blankets in the area they used for supplies, and brought them up front. If they were going to wait, they might as well get comfortable. Besides, it was better to be as discreet as possible when mares were foaling. They could spook so easily.

He spread out the blankets against the wall in the stall next to Glory's, then went back to the supply area to gather everything they'd need for the arrival of Glory's foal. He couldn't see well with the red lights, but it didn't matter because the packaging told him most of what he needed to know.

The same could not be said about Annie. If he'd returned to his hotel room, he would've gone straight to his computer. Hell, he wouldn't have been able to wait that long. He had an iPad in his briefcase in the rental, and he'd have stopped way before Kalispell to reread every word in his files. Watch the videos, look at the pictures as if he didn't have each detail seared into his memory.

Thing was, he'd only been with Annie a few hours, so maybe him not being able to figure everything out wasn't all that strange. On the other hand, now was the time to turn every stone, including the ones that seemed least likely.

He thought about his mother spending Tuesday evening on her own. He'd asked if she'd made other plans, but he'd anticipated her answer. She would end up in her room, eating off a tray. She'd watch TV, mostly reruns of shows she'd liked when his father had been alive.

Tucker had heard her talk to him from time to time. As if he were in the next chair. Irene was lonely. What scared him was his suspicion that she wanted all the forgiveness she could get from Christian because she didn't plan on sticking around.

He rubbed his tired eyes, then stared at his watch until it came into focus. Annie was taking a long time. A whole lot longer than making a pot of coffee required. Maybe she was checking her hiding spots, making sure he hadn't been snooping. Great. He'd probably disturbed something that made her suspicious. For all he knew she'd grabbed her coffee can and run.

As if on cue he heard the rumble of an engine. He jumped to his feet, half expecting to see her taking off in that old green pickup, leaving a cloud of dust behind. As soon as he made it outside, he saw that it was a truck, a late-model four-door from what he could tell, coming down the road toward Safe Haven. He'd assumed they'd be alone for the rest of the night, but maybe the local vet was arriving to check on the mares.

Annie came around the edge of the path, stopping to stare at the oncoming vehicle. Tucker couldn't see her face, but her body stiffened and she brought the thermoses she carried up to her chest.

A moment later, she relaxed again. The truck was familiar to her. The vet, or perhaps a friend. Although Kathy and Levi had suggested that Annie didn't have many of those.

She shot him a look, and when he nodded, she changed course for the parking area. The big truck had settled next to the old green pickup. He watched four people climb out. Two men, two women. The men were both tall, one dark haired, the other light brown, both dressed as his own hands would be, but that didn't mean a thing in cattle country. He knew professors and CEOs who wore Stetsons and jeans on a daily basis. The smaller woman was a brunette, the other a redhead, also wearing jeans. Annie was taller than both of them.

Instead of continuing to stare like a tourist, he went back into the stable. Glory was on her side, huffing, uncomfortable, more obviously stressed. He watched for a bit, but he couldn't see enough from this angle to tell if there was cause for concern. She settled, though, so Tucker went to the birthing kit and checked it out, even though he knew exactly what he'd find. Subdued voices approached, and he walked outside. One guy held a cooler, and the other had a big picnic basket. A good distance from the doors, Annie and the two women waited. The closer he got, the more uncomfortable she appeared.

"Kathy called Shea, so they came with dinner and help if we need it. Doc Yardley is stuck on a call at another ranch, most likely for the night," Annie murmured, sweeping a glance from the newcomers to him. "This is Tucker Brennan."

"Shea Monroe," the brunette said, and held out a stiff hand, which he shook.

"Ah, yes, the chairman of the board," he said. "Pleasure."

Annie nodded at the guy holding the drinks. His hair

was shorter than his cohort, almost a military cut. "Jesse McAllister."

"The pilot. That's a great service you run," Tucker said.

"It's a co-op. I just fly where I'm told."

"And this is his sister, Rachel."

They greeted each other with smiles.

"I'm Matt Gunderson," the other guy said. "Hope we're not intruding, but according to Shea, you two are in for a long night."

"You're not intruding." Annie's words sounded sincere, but she wasn't looking at any of her friends, and the thermoses were back in place against her chest.

"Have we met?" Tucker asked, staring at Gunderson.

"Don't think so."

"Wait, you're a bull rider. I've seen you ride in Dallas. You won the nationals in Vegas last year."

Matt nodded. "That'd be me. Listen, I know you guys have to keep it down, make sure the mares are doing okay. We can just drop this stuff off and be on our way, unless you think you'll need a hand."

Annie looked up at that, first at Matt, then at Tucker. He couldn't read her expression, but if he had to guess, he'd have said she'd tell them to go. But then she looked at Shea, and her shoulders dropped. "No, stay. In fact, you guys can tell Tucker about town, and the new boardinghouse and stuff. I have to go check on Glory." Annie shoved one of the thermoses at him, then walked into the stable.

The surprise wasn't that he'd guessed wrong about her telling her friends to leave, but at the deep sense of disappointment he felt at Annie pawning him off. He tried to convince himself that his frustration was because of his investigation, but he knew that wasn't quite true.

6

ANNIE HAD KNOWN THAT LETTING people into her solitary life was going to be trouble. She just hadn't guessed the form it would take. She'd tried to make it clear that any generosity or kindness flowing her way should be directed solely at Safe Haven. People being nice to *her* made her want to scream.

It wasn't their fault. They had no idea who she was, what she'd done to her parents, to the people her stupidity had harmed. Even with what Shea knew, she probably still didn't get it. They all saw this person saving animals and figured she must be a wonderful soul, selfless to the core.

The only reason she hadn't chased them away was because of Tucker. Annie should have been prepared with some food and drinks. Despite all appearances, she hadn't been raised in a barn.

But at least she could trust Shea with Tucker. Unlike Kathy and Levi, Shea was more concerned with getting financing from Tucker's foundation than talking up Annie. As if she hadn't figured out their little ploy.

Glory was really sweating. She was on her feet and moving around, and as Annie watched, the mare's pla-

centa ruptured. Annie wouldn't leave again until the foal
dropped. Glory went down again in the middle of her nest.

Annie held her breath as the first signs appeared. Thank
God it was two front hooves and muzzle. Still, a lot could
go wrong.

"She looks good."

Annie exhaled, starting at Tucker's voice so close to
her. She had to stop doing that. She hadn't heard him or
sensed him enter the stable, let alone come right up to
stand by her shoulder.

She didn't reply, her focus entirely on the mare. The
contractions made her wince, but the baby was coming
on fast. Before it seemed possible, the foal was mostly
expelled, but Mom needed a few minutes to gather more
strength before the next push. When it came, there was a
beautiful soaking mess of a foal, and everything from that
moment on went like clockwork.

Tucker never interfered at all, but he was right there
when Annie took care of the umbilical stump and handed
her towels to rub the foal.

She had no idea what time it was when Glory set about
bonding with her baby, except that humans were no longer
welcome in the stable.

After a quick look at the other two mares and getting
cleaned up at the deep, old-fashioned sink, Annie led the
way out. She expected that everyone had eaten, or at least
to find the picnic basket and cooler waiting for them, sans
company. But that was clearly too much to hope for.

Matt opened the cooler and pulled out two beers. "Cause
to celebrate?"

Tucker took them both and handed one to Annie. "Text-
book," he said.

"Great. Let's eat." Shea headed to the parking lot, where

Annie saw they'd set up the food tailgate-style, complete with folding chairs.

Annie had to admit she was hungry. It had been an utterly nerve-racking day, and while her adrenaline was flowing now, she knew a crash was inevitable. Thankfully, it wasn't that late. Tucker could go home right after a quick bite, and she could at least try to get some sleep.

She had the feeling that no matter her degree of exhaustion, turning off thoughts of Tucker wouldn't be easy. So many things to process, not the least of which was the fact that every time he came within spitting distance, the flutters started up with a vengeance.

There were enough chairs for everyone, and whoever had set them up did her a favor by putting them in a large circle. The cooler was brought to the open tailgate of the pickup, alongside the basket.

"We've got sandwiches," Rachel said. "Roast beef, tuna and veggie on sub rolls. There's chips and carrot sticks—"

"And cupcakes," Jessie added. Annie doubted he meant to sound quite so excited.

"Cupcakes and beer?" Tucker shook his head. "You Montana folks are culinary daredevils."

Rachel snorted, but somehow made it ladylike. "We had a whole ten minutes to pull everything together because someone who should have reached out earlier didn't," she said, pinning Annie with a mock glare. "Oh, and there are cold sodas and bottles of water in the cooler."

Annie really liked Kathy, but she was going to strangle her. "Just how many meals were you planning on serving?" she asked. "It's late. You guys all have to go home so I can get some sleep."

"We didn't know that the horse was going to foal so early," Matt said. "And I heard there was more than one ready to go."

"We only have one other mare in the stalls, but there's no reason to think she's going into labor tonight."

Shea looked at her. "Would you prefer that we left?"

Annie knew Shea wasn't being sarcastic or touchy. "No, really. I just hate keeping you all out like this. Tucker flew in from Dallas this afternoon, remember?"

"Don't worry about me," he said. "I'll be fine. I confess, I could eat."

Annie touched his arm with her hand before walking over to the basket. "Thank you for your help today. It was unexpected."

He stared at where her hand had been, then met and held her gaze in the weird light cast by two lanterns. "It's been my pleasure. A very memorable day."

She had no idea what to say to that, and honestly couldn't tell if he was simply being polite or flirting. The flirting part was probably wishful thinking, which was nuts because what in the world was that going to get her? The two of them would never happen. No way in hell.

She swallowed hard. What she hated the most? The need was back, the desire to touch and be touched. And if anyone could satisfy that itch, it was a man like Tucker Brennan. She stepped back, away from temptation, and did everything in her power to not turn and run.

TUCKER GRABBED A RANDOM sandwich and bag of chips, way too aware of the woman beside him. He'd flirted with her. Hadn't meant to, especially in front of her friends. The blame went to the long day at least for now, but when he was alone again, he'd have to have a serious talk with himself about appropriate behavior.

As no one else was sitting, he went for the farthest chair, hoping Annie would sit opposite him. He wanted to watch her from a distance. He would've preferred to observe from outside the circle so he could concentrate on what was important instead of chasing his personal fascination with the enigmatic Annie. Instead, food was grabbed quickly and everyone sat, leaving Annie the chair to his left.

"How did you find out about Safe Haven?" Shea asked.

Halfway to a bite, Tucker paused, the question catching him off guard. He thought about asking her the same question. A woman with her security clearance and computer skills didn't fit in this cowboy world.

"My foundation manager," he said. "I'm not sure precisely where he ran across this particular sanctuary, but he does a very good job of finding worthy causes."

She nodded slowly. "Perhaps I can speak to him. I'd like to know how effective our online marketing is. It's difficult to choose where to spend money and energy when there's so little to spread around."

"I'll make sure to get you that information."

It turned out the sandwich was tuna, and it was good. He'd been so distracted he hadn't realized how long ago he'd eaten, and for a few minutes he did nothing else.

Annie was chowing down, too, and it should have been far less compelling to watch her hunched over her sandwich as if she were afraid someone would steal it. But she managed to make it look sexy in a way that was slowing him down as his pulse sped up.

Damn, but she was a beautiful woman. That was another conundrum. Beautiful women often seemed to use their looks to get what they wanted. It was difficult not to, when the world around them made it so easy. Beauty was a passkey to so much. Even as children, teachers treated cute kids differently, everyone did. He'd been a recipient of that kind of bias himself. And he knew for a fact Annie had successfully used her looks to deceive Christian.

Yet, here she was out in the middle of nowhere, surrounded by livestock when she could have hidden in a hundred easier ways. He couldn't imagine the number of men who would have been happy to hide her, to keep her safe.

When he looked down, he realized he'd not only finished his sandwich, but actually used his fingers to capture the last crumbs of his potato chips. After a swig of beer, he went back to the basket. "Anyone else want seconds?"

"I'll take another beer as long as you're up there." That was…Matt. The rodeo champ.

"You still riding the circuit?" Tucker asked, handing Matt his beer before heading back to his own folding chair.

Matt didn't answer straightaway. "Yeah," he said. "I've got things here in Blackfoot Falls that are taking precedence at the moment, but I'm still riding."

"You'd better be," Annie said. "We've been talking about having a charity rodeo for Safe Haven. Trouble is housing out-of-towners. There's an old boardinghouse that's going to be fixed up, but we'll probably have to hold the rodeo closer to Kalispell if we do it in the next year."

"It's not a bad drive." Tucker sat, consciously slowed himself down while unwrapping his next course. His hunger was easing, not gone.

"Too much beer drinking at rodeos to have people driving afterward," Annie said.

Having a conversation made observing her easy. Although the way he was getting caught up in the view was a problem. "True," he said. "But a rodeo is a good idea."

"From what I saw on your website, your ranch is riding out the drought well," Jesse said.

All Tucker's plans to keep Annie engaged, to keep himself separate from the group, vanished in a discussion about cattle and the weather, which then segued into ranching innovations. By the time the eating and drinking had come to its natural conclusion, he felt every hour he'd been awake, and every ache he'd earned from his goat wrestling.

None of them would let him help pack up the impromptu picnic, but he was allowed back into the stable to check out the newborn. Already standing on wobbly legs, the still-damp foal was a sight to see.

Next to him, Annie sighed softly as they stood in the neighboring stall, keeping as quiet as possible. She had to lean into him so he could hear, and the contact against his arm wasn't helping things. "We should go," she whispered. Her warm breath skimming the side of his neck sent a jolt of awareness straight to his groin.

He nodded, made his tread as light as possible on his way out, Annie walking alongside him. For some reason the others were still there, all standing near the pickup. His knee-jerk reaction was disappointment. Dammit. Wanting to be alone with her was fine, even wise if he wanted to get information, but not when it was personal.

"What's wrong?" Annie asked, as soon as they'd reached the others.

"That," Rachel said, nodding at Tucker.

Caught in the middle of a yawn, he snapped his mouth closed. "I'm fine."

"You might be right, but we don't want to take any chances. Safe Haven needs your money." Rachel grinned, but she wasn't lying. "Our place is close by. We have a spare room you can bunk in for the night. Then you can go back to the hotel first thing to change and whatever."

"I assure you, I've lived in isolated places my entire life, and I purposely had only one beer. I can drive."

Jesse shook his head. "You'll pass more deer, cattle and coyotes than cars on the way, but that's not the problem. You're tired from flying and driving. Why take the chance when we've got room?"

"Besides," Rachel said, "you should get a look at the Sundance before you leave. You'll be surprised."

"At?"

"All the beautiful women who are staying with us," Jesse said, and grunted when Shea elbowed him.

"Excuse me?" Tucker looked to Annie, who smiled, at least for a few seconds.

"They've turned it into a dude ranch," Annie said, and then he recalled the website where he'd seen her photo. She'd been at the Sundance ranch when it was taken.

"Wait a minute." Jesse was obviously annoyed. "That's not true. Our main concern is raising cattle."

Shea and Rachel exchanged glances, then stared at their feet to hide smiles. Clearly the dude ranch operation was a touchy issue, and as a cattleman himself, he understood. But that didn't concern him. What did interest him was the opportunity to find out more about Annie from these people. And Shea…perhaps he should know more about her.

"Sorry," Annie said. "It's a working spread, but the dude ranch part is helping to transform the area. More guests, more tourists, more cash flow. And more opportunities to spread the word about Safe Haven. It's all good."

Rachel laughed. "Trust Annie to squeeze in Safe Haven."

He didn't think about it for too long. He would have preferred having his things with him, but the chance to gather information, and frankly, to get to bed sooner, was too strong an incentive to say no. "All right. Thank you, I'll take you up on that."

"Thank God," Annie said, sincerity softening her voice. Her lips lifted in a tired but sweet smile. "I'd never have gotten to sleep if I was worrying about you driving all that way."

That he instantly thought of staying right where he was,

bunking down on the blanket in the empty stall, made him shake his head. He needed a good night's rest. Desperately.

IT WAS ONLY WITH TREMENDOUS will that Annie brushed her teeth before heading upstairs to bed. She'd watched as Tucker had followed Jesse's truck down the road to the Sundance, then she'd done a final check on the horses.

The short walk to the cabin had felt more like a mile, and she'd made herself prepare the morning's coffee before she hit the bathroom. Now she had to climb stairs, but then she'd be horizontal and nothing would come between her and sleep.

An hour later, she was seriously contemplating bashing her head against the wall because her brain would not stop.

At first, it had been okay thinking about Tucker and wondering yet again if he'd flirted with her. She'd debated taking care of her suddenly awakened body, which was something she hadn't done in so long, she wondered if she remembered how.

It was only after those thoughts that she was reminded why she'd stopped. Being in exile, being a fugitive, eliminated all possibility of having any kind of anything with any man. For an indeterminate period of time, up to and including forever.

It had taken her a solid six months of denial to get to the stage where she didn't think about sex anymore. No, okay, longer than that, but she hadn't caved since. Though she'd had close enough calls that she'd become very judicious with her reading material, and careful with her time around other people.

Some thought she was shy. No problem, shy worked, because most everyone kept their distance. At first, she'd thought the McAllister men were going to be a problem, but her fear was so great, it overwhelmed her sex drive by quite a bit.

She'd become celibate in every sense of the word, and then Tucker Brennan.

It wasn't fair. He was only going to be in town a couple of days. She'd never see him again, but if she kept thinking about him, remembering the touch on her bare back, the quickening of her pulse every time she saw him staring…

Bodies weren't meant to be turned off like empty refrigerators. She was only twenty-nine, but she knew without a doubt that somewhere inside her there was a clock ticking away. Exhaustion had always been her best defense, but here she was after a brutally tiring day, and he'd broken through over a year's worth of defenses with a few touches and a good smile.

Her life, her entire life, was dedicated elsewhere. She'd done her best to never think about what she'd left behind, what she was missing. She worked until her body couldn't take it anymore. Then she did it again.

Tonight was an object lesson. Letting herself get caught up in the real world would do her no good. Tucker Brennan was a potential check. Financing. That's all. She'd better drum that into her foolish mind, because there'd be hell to pay if she didn't.

The sad thing was that she'd have to pull back from Shea, as well. It had been an experiment, a test to see if she could open her life up a little.

The answer was a resounding no.

7

THE STRANGE ALARM JERKED Tucker out of sleep so hard he felt as if he had whiplash. And damn, he didn't even have a razor or a change of clothes with him. It seemed foolish to shower when he had to put on the same shirt to go to Kalispell before he could return to Safe Haven, but yesterday clung to him with the scent of straw and stubborn goat.

So he showered and dressed. He would have killed for a cup of coffee, but he wanted to check in with George first.

Luckily, the private investigator was already up despite the early hour.

"I don't have that much to report," George said. "I've started working on the account number, which isn't an easy thing to trace, my friend, but we'll get there. As far as the driver's license goes, the ID number doesn't match the name or address. So it's a fake, but from the picture it looks like a decent one. I don't know that it'll bring us much more information. I did send the photo you took to some people I know, but don't get your hopes up."

Tucker had figured as much and tried to tamp down his impatience. He was more interested in the possibility he'd raised yesterday. "What about the coercion angle? Any evidence she was pressured into taking the money?"

George hesitated long enough for Tucker to tense. "Nothing's changed," George said finally. "Not since I checked a year ago. Leanna had no known criminal associates or unsavory friends or family problems. If she took the money under duress, I haven't seen any evidence. Doesn't mean I won't be looking. We did have a different agenda back then, and I might have bypassed something crucial."

"All right." Tucker rubbed his eyes. "You have anything on the men in her life?"

"There were a few in college, nothing too serious. When she worked at Keystone as a fundraising assistant, she was with a man named Alex Phillips. They were a couple for three years. He moved to D.C. and is now a lobbyist for a New York telecom consortium. He's married and has a son. No arrests, no ties to any scandals."

"Okay," Tucker said. "And Shea Monroe?"

"That's still tough. She's worked on highly classified projects, and if I tug too hard on any of those strings we could be inviting more problems than we want. I did find out that she's still under contract for something big, but I have no idea what."

"Do what you can with that. And maybe start looking at Annie's family more closely. It could be one of them in trouble, I don't know."

"Look, Tucker..." Shit, George was using his fatherly voice. "We never thought we'd get this far, right? I mean, worse comes to worst, we let the authorities know, they come in, do their own digging. Running like that makes her look awfully guilty."

Tucker's breath caught at the cavalier words. "We already decided that finding her isn't enough to clear Christian. I need to dig more and understand what happened, before the D.A.'s office gets wind of this. My instincts are telling me we're missing a big piece. I'm not even going to mention anything to Christian, not until I know more. So, do your best, huh?"

"You know I will, Tucker."

"I appreciate it."

His next call would have to wait until after coffee, because Darren wouldn't be in yet. Irene wouldn't be awake, either. Though Tucker wasn't sure he wanted to speak to her at the moment, anyway. She still didn't know his trip out of town was a fact-finding mission to help Christian, and Tucker aimed to keep it that way for the time being.

Now, it was going to be coffee or death. Personally, he voted for coffee, and he knew the day was going to be a good one because the scent of a rich dark roast greeted him halfway down the big staircase.

He'd known he wasn't the first one up, but he had hoped that he'd recognize someone in the kitchen.

Instead, there were a lot of young women. Pretty young women at that. They were bustling about with an older Hispanic woman, making what looked like enough breakfast to feed an army.

"Well, hello there."

It seemed early for a greeting like that, especially coming from an attractive brunette whose jeans were so tight he wouldn't recommend she do much sitting. "Morning."

"Who are you, and when did you get in?"

Another stare, this from a woman with a spatula in one hand and a smile that reminded him of this year's Miss Texas posters. "Rachel didn't tell us there were any men coming to stay."

"That's because he's not here for a vacation." At Shea's no-nonsense voice, Tucker turned. She entered the kitchen frowning at the spatula girl. "Rachel asked me to tell you that you're all leaving for Glacier National Park in an hour, whether you've eaten or not."

Tucker could tell the other girls were intimidated by Shea. He doubted they had reason, although she'd been a big surprise. The woman who'd written emails about the financial viability of Safe Haven—who'd outlined their immediate plans for fundraising campaigns and upgrades to the facility—had come across as a smooth communicator, one who had the kind of social skills that went along with certain high levels of government contracts.

What he'd found instead wasn't so easy to classify. There was a bluntness about her that wasn't rude, just… raw. He wondered if she could be manipulated, say, by a woman in hiding waiting to make a last big score before darting over the Canadian border.

The bad thing was, the very traits that drew him to Annie were what made her role in the theft all the more believable. Hell, even knowing what he knew, Tucker had been drawn in and wanted to at least give her a chance.

"Morning, Tucker," Shea said. "Coffee?"

"Please."

"I assume I should put it in a to-go cup?"

"I have a few minutes." He smiled at her unguarded sigh. "I thought maybe we could talk."

With a resigned expression and a glance at the guests, she took out a large insulated mug, poured, then handed it to him. "Let's go into the other room."

He nodded and followed her past the dining area into a parlor with an expansive view of the Sundance and the snowcapped Rockies in the background. She leaned against a wooden post, which would have fooled him into thinking she was comfortable if he hadn't seen how she avoided his eyes.

"If you had any questions about Safe Haven, about the financials or the fundraising, I mean," she said, "I can probably help you. Because Annie's very private."

"Really?"

Shea toyed with her cup, slightly lifting one shoulder. "Most of us don't know much about Annie except for her work ethic and her commitment to saving every animal she can. The things that matter."

"She works extremely hard. I could see that yesterday."

"She's driven, you know?" Shea met his eyes, her caution fading. Perhaps acknowledging Annie's dedication had earned him an ally. "Or maybe she just prefers the company of animals. I get that. Mostly I do, too."

Tucker smiled at her candor. "There are days, a lot of them, when I'd have to agree."

"Well, as long as you know that she's worked miracles with virtually no assets. I can only imagine what she could do with proper funding."

"I assure you, I'll give Safe Haven every consideration. So far, I like what I've seen. Is there anything else you can tell me that would help sway the vote?"

She blinked, then narrowed her gaze. "Like what?"

So much for bringing her over to his team. "I don't know." He paused to think. "In your opinion, what's Safe Haven's biggest selling point?"

"Annie."

Exactly the answer he wanted. "Well, there's a problem with that," he said, letting his words settle, then studying Shea's worried frown. "We don't know if Annie will be here long. She could leave tomorrow and then who'd run Safe Haven?"

Shea relaxed. "Annie's not going anywhere."

"She might get homesick," he said, and Shea shook her head with a sadness she quickly masked. "Or find someone and get married. Have kids."

"No," Shea murmured quietly, her gaze downcast. "She won't."

He almost felt guilty for the pain he'd seen flash in her eyes. But he hadn't caused it, not directly. Annie had. He'd bet his Range Rover she'd confided in Shea. Maybe he'd just found Annie's Achilles' heel. Which was perfect because Shea was a lousy liar.

This was good news. So why did he feel like crap?

"Thanks for the coffee," he said, holding up the mug. "I'm going to gather my things and take off for my hotel. I want to be back at Safe Haven early. Please tell Rachel and the others I appreciate the hospitality."

"No problem." Shea finally looked at him with a small smile, and he didn't doubt she was glad he was leaving.

The ride to Kalispell was a straight shot, and soon enough he'd put on clean jeans and a fresh shirt, and was reading over his files as he went through a quick room service breakfast.

Now that he'd met Annie, the material he'd gathered had taken on new shades of meaning. From her days in high school to her equestrian victories on horses that belonged to other people, he could see so much of the woman he'd spent time with. The data on her family didn't suggest anything unsavory, but he still felt that was where George should focus. Because God knew, families could be tricky.

He finished reading every document in his extensive files, knowing he should have left already. But he needed to do this now, before he saw her again.

His gut was telling him there was something big missing in the picture of Leanna Warner and her disappearance. The idea that someone behind the scenes had forced her to run had taken hold in him, and he was ninety-nine percent certain he was reading that correctly.

All the things that made no sense about her—how hard she was working, why she kept herself distant and alone, even her failure to ensure Christian looked guilty to the feds—came together if she'd been coerced.

Annie Sheridan was hiding, all right, but not from justice. He'd wager a hell of a lot on that hunch. Christian had to know more. Maybe something he didn't even realize was important.

If he wasn't afraid Christian would tell their mother, he'd call Christian right away. But his brother was still too angry to be trusted. Or maybe that was Tucker. Lord knew he didn't blame Christian, but his brother was filled with a very old rage. Tucker wasn't stupid, he knew Christian had been playing Irene, using guilt to get money, then ignoring her until he needed more. But he'd chosen to stay out of it for his mother's sake.

Better to wait, to see what came of George's investigation.

Tucker put his iPad in his briefcase, along with an emergency set of clothes, just in case, and headed down to his rental. It wasn't right the way he was itching to see Annie again. But there didn't seem to be a damn thing he could do about it.

THE INSTANT ANNIE WOKE UP, she knew something was wrong. The light. There was light coming in from the window, and she'd set her alarm…had she set her alarm?

With a hammering heart she looked at the clock. Ten. Ten in the morning, and God, Glory and the new foal. The morning feed. She jumped out of bed and almost screamed as all the aches and pains from yesterday hit her like a sledgehammer. Wincing and cussing all the way through throwing clothes on, she barely looked at what she'd hauled out of the dresser. Limping downstairs, she washed up so fast she probably skipped half her face.

Forget coffee. She hurried to the stable, trying to get her

heart to slow down and her brain to speed up. She caught
her hip on the edge of the door as she swung herself inside
and it was a lucky thing because she would have fallen at
the sight in front of her.

Tucker Brennan stood at the entry to Glory's stall, his
head turned, his brow furrowed and a single finger over
his lips. "Quiet, he's eating."

"He's…?"

"The little guy," Tucker whispered. "He's been having some trouble this morning, but he's finally latched
on tight."

"How long have you been here?"

"About half an hour."

"The feed. I have to—"

"Levi and Kathy are out there somewhere, said to tell
you not to worry. They've got you covered."

She'd known the couple would come today, but they
typically didn't arrive until long after the early-morning
rounds. "I overslept."

"So I gathered."

"I never do. This is literally the second time it's happened, and the first was because of a power outage, but
then I bought a battery-run clock."

His smile was warmer than it should have been. They
were strangers, maybe would-be business associates, and
that smile was meant for a friend. Something they could
never be. "It was a long day yesterday. Come on over here
and take a look."

She crossed the short distance to the side of the stall and
made sure she didn't stand too close to Tucker. Especially
after she'd found her stride slowing as she ran an appraising gaze down the back of his body. He had on jeans and
a blue Oxford shirt. Sharp, clean and sexy as hell, and she

hadn't even bothered to brush her hair. Great. Bedhead was one of her better looks.

Then she saw the dark brown foal with his skinny, knobby legs splayed so he could get up under his mom. Glory was munching away, calm as you please. "Oh, that is a sight."

"There might be another one tonight," he said. "Cocoa's on her way."

"It's a factory in here," she said. "Something big must have happened eleven months ago to the day for two so close together."

"Statistical probability, but I know what you mean. We see groupings a lot. Pheromones, I imagine, in the herd."

She nodded, liking this. Just talking. It was easier when she wasn't looking at him. "I need to do my rounds, catch up with Levi and Kathy. You can come along if you like, or stay. After, I'm going in to make coffee. I hope you'll join me at the cabin."

"I'll come with you now," he said.

He didn't follow her into the other stalls as she checked on the rest of the brood, but he accompanied her to the barn, where the chickens ignored them but only because the goats wanted all the attention.

Pinocchio, it turned out, was doing fine, and deeply unconcerned about his battle scars. Kathy, who'd sadly lost her own land due to hard times, started out smiling at Annie, but that changed in a flash to something far harsher.

Kathy's hand went to her hip. "I hope you're hurting like Hades, young lady."

"Gee, thanks. Yes, I am."

Kathy's big hair barely moved as she nodded. "Serves you right for getting in that mess with Pinocchio. You should've let him work himself into a frenzy until he passed out. Then you could have cut him free, and not got yourself in trouble."

Oh, God. Annie knew everyone meant well but she did not want to hear the same thing for a month. "He also could have died."

The older woman sighed. "There are always risks. Pinocchio might've died, and that would have been sad, but if you got sidelined…"

"Point taken. I'll do better next time."

"Levi finally got that part in for the feed truck. Should be working by this afternoon."

Annie grinned at the news. "Fantastic."

"Now might be a good time for you and Mr.… Um, sorry, my short-term memory's shot, don't take it personal."

"It's Tucker," he supplied.

Kathy smiled. "You and Mr. Tucker should take a ride out. Show him the field."

Annie and Tucker exchanged glances and laughed.

"What?" Kathy frowned at them.

"Nothing, really." Annie cleared her throat. "Tucker is his first name." It was weird for her, sharing a private joke with someone. No, not someone…with him. "We will get a ride in, but first we have to go over the books." She squeezed Kathy's shoulder, then moved over to give one of the baby goats some attention. "When are you two planning on leaving?"

"Not until this afternoon. We worked it out with Will. You're covered tonight. For as late as you want. This meeting is important to all of us, so take the time you need."

"Thank you," Tucker said. "The attitude of the volunteers tells me a great deal about an organization."

"Well, sir, we're all simple folks from around Blackfoot Falls. We believe the sanctuary helps everyone. To my mind, a community should be judged by how it treats its most vulnerable creatures. We're doing what we know in our hearts is right."

"I agree," he said.

"And I need coffee. I'll see you when we're done inside." Annie started walking before Tucker could see her sappy grin.

HALFWAY TO THE CABIN, Tucker decided to change things up, take a chance. See what happened. "As long as you're covered here at Safe Haven, how about dinner tonight?"

Her inhale told him the suggestion had thrown her off balance. So did the pause in her step. She hadn't expected the invitation. For a moment there, she'd been frightened. He'd seen it, but only because he'd been paying close attention. So far, they'd kept things professional. Dinner could mean anything.

"I've been wondering what motivated you to take over the sanctuary. I don't know much about you, and it's always interesting to discover what leads someone to this kind of life. It's not an easy one. You have to want it badly to put up with all the obstacles. I thought we could talk about it over a meal."

The flash came again, only for a second, and more contained this time, but it was important that he push her. More than ever, he needed to get to the bottom of this mystery. If she had acted under duress, as he suspected, he had to know. Not that he was forgetting about Christian. His brother was still his priority, but if he could get to the truth, it would solve both their problems.

"You know what? Let's see how the day goes." She hurried the rest of the way to the cabin, held the door for him. "Why don't we have that coffee and go over the books? Then see where we are. I mean, you're going home tomorrow, so—"

"I've moved some appointments around. Thought I'd attend your first meeting tomorrow, meet the rest of the board."

She looked at him as if he'd slipped a rug out from under her feet. He supposed he had. Trouble was, instead of taking satisfaction in throwing her off kilter, it seemed he wanted to catch her before she fell.

8

THE HORSE ANNIE GAVE TUCKER TO ride had been named Ronald Weasley, by a committee of four from the high school. She assured him that at one time, the majority of the cast from the *Potter* series had been in residence, but that a lot of them, including Harry, had found homes.

She rode Candy Cane, who'd become something of a favorite among the staff. The names and explanations behind them had taken them past the first and second corrals. Annie was grateful for the distraction, knowing she couldn't put Tucker off for too much longer. After the ride was over, she planned to shower and change, sending him to town on his own. After all, it was foolish to take one vehicle when he'd be going back to Kalispell for the night. She'd meet him at Marge's.

She'd debated calling him with an excuse after he'd gone to the diner, but that seemed like a surefire way to kill any chance of getting foundation funds. A man like him was used to conducting business over dinner. In New York she'd done it more often than not. There was no reason for her to think he wanted to share a meal for any other reason. At least him driving ahead would give her time alone to figure out what to tell him.

When she'd first arrived in Blackfoot Falls, people were curious about her and of course they'd had questions. But she'd been vague and firm, and for nearly two years no one had pressed her about her past. God bless cowboys. Not that everyone didn't gossip about her—she knew they did. But that was fine.

Tucker had caught her off guard, that's all. Sure, he had money, but at heart he was a cowboy. She'd been ready to tell him every last detail about Safe Haven and all her plans. She wasn't comfortable telling him lies.

It was bad enough she'd donned Annie Sheridan like a new skin. On the few occasions anyone asked, she said she was from back east. True. When they asked her why she wanted to run Safe Haven, she said she'd always had an affinity for animals, horses in particular. Also true. Then she changed the subject. That wasn't going to work with Tucker.

"This is gorgeous country." Tucker rode in a way that made her feel like a klutz. "I'd forgotten what a real spring looks like."

She wasn't a klutz. In fact, she was a good rider. But Tucker had been born to the cowboy life.

"The drought has hit everyone in Texas hard," he said, his baritone laced with sadness. "It's a different landscape from when I was a kid. It breaks my heart."

"I'll bet," she said. "This is all Safe Haven land, you know. It doesn't belong to the state or the Bureau of Land Management. That's good, because we need the space. But we're not incorporated, and if there's a fire, unless it threatens buildings or livestock, it's only going to be managed, not fought. So the more snow and rain we have, the better it is for everyone. Thankfully, this far north, we still get a lot of snow."

"You have trouble with predators?"

"Much as any ranch out here. We've lost our share, but that's the way of it. The price for free range. Most of the cattle are just passing through, though. We're not equipped to take care of many, but people are quicker to take cows."

"That's good. What about the horses?"

She found herself urging Candy Cane to move faster. "We get a lot of abandoned horses. Too many folks have lost their homes, lost their property, including their ability to care for their stock. Cows are typically bought, but horses… There's a lot of sentiment around horses, even if the old-timers want to deny it. Nobody likes to send a horse to slaughter. Unfortunately, those same people aren't able to find them new homes. I'm sure it's the same story on your end."

"Every rescue shelter we support has a different set of circumstances unique to their location." Tucker looked around at the distant prairie, spread as far as they could see. "There are plenty of lakes here. Shade trees. Underground water flow. A horse might find a decent chance."

She nodded. "Good thing we have that because there's never a time we're not at capacity. Not a week goes by we don't have to turn someone away."

"That won't change if you get funding."

"It'll happen less. That's something to hope for."

He seemed to study her with a different kind of interest. "Safe Haven is lucky to have you. Whatever happens from this trip, the work you've put into this place is something you can be proud of."

"Thank you." Annie rode ahead a bit, trying not to let him see her confusion over the oddly ominous compliment. Had he already eliminated Safe Haven as a worthy nonprofit? Then why bother to stay for the board meeting?

Maybe they weren't ready for a gift yet. She'd run across

that in her fundraising efforts, where an organization would hold back money until certain goals had been met.

That would be a blow, but only because she was letting herself hope too much. Nothing was ever guaranteed. Especially when things looked brightest.

They weren't far from the field she wanted Tucker to see. Putting aside her worries, she let the excitement of this amazing project spur her forward. Candy Cane caught her enthusiasm and Weasley trotted along. The perfect breeze lifted Annie's hair, taking her out of her myopic panic for the first time since he'd mentioned dinner.

The day couldn't have been better. Green leaves and buds and early flowers were everywhere she looked, the scent of spring vivid, the sky an astonishing blue. Realizing she'd let this pass her by for half an hour reminded her to grab what she could while she could.

When Tucker caught up to her, she truly saw him, not as the man who could solve her financial problems or the nosy stranger who asked too many questions. He wasn't smiling or anything so obvious, but he looked happy. As if he belonged in Montana, at least for this day.

It was the contrast that made it so clear to her. Yesterday, this morning, Tucker had walked with an air of gravitas about him. Even when he joked around or drank beer from the bottle, he made an impression. You wouldn't want to tangle with this guy. She had the feeling if he went after someone, they wouldn't know what hit them until the dust had long settled.

"What's this?" he said as they got closer to the five-acre experiment. "How tall is that fence?"

"Seven and half feet. It's not finished, though. But we'll need to keep the deer out, so we had to go high."

"What's it guarding?"

"The future," Annie said, her voice tight with anticipation of his reaction.

When he looked at her, sparks lit up all through her, but she decided they were a result of the project, not Tucker. "Show me."

"Well, the view's not impressive. Yet." She urged Candy Cane into a burst of speed and led Tucker around the fence to the western gate. Of course, he could see through the wires, see that there was nothing but flat ground, not even plowed yet. But she wanted him to get a feel for how big the plot was, how big the idea was, so she slowed, dropped from her saddle and waited until he'd done the same.

They walked beyond the gate. "This is going to be a field of alfalfa," she said. "Five acres. Before the tractor engine blew, we'd just started to amend the soil, so it won't be ready for planting until next year. There are some issues with irrigation that need to be handled before we can truly make this work, but I know we'll do it. All old school. No motors, no generators. Just wind to push the water through."

"Huh," he said, mostly to himself, turning his head as if trying to picture what this land would look like in five years. In ten.

"If it works, which it will, it'll be the first of many plots growing feed. Not only to make Safe Haven more self-sustaining, but to help future interns learn about alternative agricultural methods. We want to train ranchers to be able to take care of their land using creativity to build and grow.

"This fence has been a large-scale project guided by the high school kids. They did all the fundraising and recruited the help they needed to get the fencing equipment. They're still working on it, and maybe it'll take more than a year, but I don't think so. We've discussed making it a cooperative, so that other ranches might be able to start rebuilding. But that's pretty far in the future."

When he turned to her this time, his smile made her blush. There was no doubt that Tucker was impressed. More than she'd hoped. "This is remarkable. Really outstanding. It was your idea?"

"I'd mentioned it as a faraway dream, but Melanie and the students, they ran with it. She's so committed to using the sanctuary as an educational resource that great ideas are all stacked up, just waiting to come to life. She's amazing."

"She isn't the only one."

Annie's cheeks burned. She ducked her head and tucked her hair behind her ear. When she looked up again, though, something had changed. The smile had frozen on his face, and his gaze seemed troubled. A second later, the grin lifted, and if she hadn't looked up at the right time, she would have missed it entirely. "Is something wrong?"

"Not at all," he said. "I'm very glad you brought me out here." He moved closer, and for a moment she thought he was going to touch her arm, but then he ended up running his hand through his hair. "You have any more surprises up your sleeve?"

"Nope. This was it."

He nodded. "Maybe we should head back, then. I've got some phone calls I need to make, and I know you have things to do. We'll figure out dinner arrangements on the way."

"Sure, no problem." Annie mounted her horse, unsettled and disappointed. The moment had been so perfect. What had changed? She couldn't think of anything she'd done wrong, but then, she wasn't always quick to see beyond her own enthusiasm. So much for her ace in the hole.

MARGE'S DINER WAS...A DINER. It wasn't crowded. Only two men sat at the counter sipping from white mugs. Tucker nodded to them as he passed on his way to a booth in the back. A waitress appeared, poured the men refills, then brought him a menu along with a curious smile.

Strangers had to be infrequent guests in Blackfoot Falls. The interstate was an hour away, and the town was small. And, except for the Sundance, didn't seem much like a tourist attraction.

He'd arrived early, but he didn't mind waiting. He was still worrying over a moment of clarity he'd had when Annie had shown him the five acres. She'd swept him away, as thoroughly as if she'd been a magician. Standing there, he could see her vision of the future, her commitment to changing her slice of the world for the better. For one powerful moment, he'd been ready to take out his checkbook.

And then it had hit like an unexpected tackle. She wasn't Annie Sheridan. He had no idea who she really was. Except that she had to be one of the best fundraisers he'd ever encountered. He didn't give his money away, not without a lot of forethought and reason, but she could have taken him for a completely different kind of ride.

He didn't doubt his intuition. He believed that there was far more to the story of Leanna's skipping town than Christian had said, because she wasn't the greedy, unscrupulous woman he'd described. Tucker had more faith in himself than to think his judgment was so far off. But that didn't change the fact that he didn't *know*. She could still be under someone's thumb, still need money to get herself out of a desperate situation. Although that was a stretch. Running an animal sanctuary was the worst way he could think of to raise a lot of cash. And her enthusiasm for the place… she hadn't been faking that.

He raised his gaze just as she walked through the front door.

She'd changed into a different pair of jeans, a fresh shirt. He couldn't help wishing she'd worn a dress, something more sophisticated that would have shown off her tall, lean body, the way she carried herself. She must have amazing legs.

He stood as she approached the table, then sat when she slid into her side of the booth.

"You're early," she said.

"I've only been here a few minutes. It's a nice place."

She grinned as she looked at the row of uniform booths along the window facing Main Street and the old-fashioned counter with black vinyl and metal stools. "It's the only place."

"There are more restaurants in Kalispell. We could go right now."

She picked up the menu, shaking her head. "Cocoa might foal tonight, so I can't even be here for long."

He picked up his menu, too, noticing straight off that they had a homemade beef stew featured. "You know, you never did answer my question about how you ended up in northern Montana."

She studied him, her lips pressed together and her eyes grave. "Serendipity. I'd heard about Safe Haven when I was traveling. I've always been into horses, and animal sanctuaries were a passion. When I came to Blackfoot Falls, I never intended to take over Safe Haven. That just sort of happened."

"Traveling from…?"

"Back east." She studied the menu, then smiled up at him. "I haven't eaten here much, but I do know about the popular dishes. The chicken fried steak is homemade, battered right here, and the burgers are supposed to be off the charts. Oh, and if you like crispy fries, Marge's is the place."

Instead of calling her on her subtle misdirection, Tucker found himself caught in her gaze. He leaned forward, aching to break down the walls that she'd built so well. There were no obvious lies in anything she'd said. She hadn't blinked or given any tells that he could see. It only made her more of an enigma.

God, but she was beautiful. His hand moved across the table until he almost touched her. It was a near-miss, stopping himself just before contact. There was too much he wanted from this woman to let his attraction subvert his plans.

Unfortunately, what he saw reflected in her eyes wasn't the hint of fear he'd been expecting, but a want he understood too well.

Her lips, pink and lush and unpainted, parted, revealing her white top teeth. If she were his, he would kiss her for hours, make them both crazy for more. But he wouldn't give in. Not until she was quivering in his arms.

Then again, maybe he'd do that as an encore. He doubted he'd have any self-discipline with her.

"You two need a minute?"

The intrusion made him almost knock his water glass over. Quick reflexes from the waitress saved the day, but the accident gave him time to regain his composure.

When he glanced across the table, Annie was looking anywhere but at him.

"Yes, another minute would be good," he said, checking the waitress's name tag. "You don't serve alcohol here, do you?"

"Nope," Karen said. "You'd need to go to Sadie's down

the street for drinks. But we've got great milk shakes. Our ice cream is awesome. Though you might wanna save that for dessert, because we've got fresh huckleberry pie just out of the oven."

Tucker sniffed the air. He could smell the pie. "I might just skip dinner altogether."

The young woman laughed. "Don't do that." She leaned in a little. "I'd go for the stew tonight. Or the rib eye. Can't go wrong with either one."

"Thanks, Karen."

Tucker was almost afraid to meet Annie's gaze again. Afraid of getting drawn in. He didn't seem to have many defenses against her. The ones he'd brought with him were toppling like dominoes with every new look.

Annie put away her menu, then folded her hands on the table, gripping them tightly. She looked at him, but only in quick snatches. "I did a lot of work around stables when I was young. Never owned a horse. Wanted to. My family thought it was a passing phase, something girls go through until boys come along. Not for me."

"None of the boys were more interesting than riding?"

"Not what I meant." She smiled. "I was a perfectly normal girl, went on dates, even had a couple of relationships, but my passion for animals, and horses in particular, never dimmed."

"Did you plan on running a sanctuary?"

"I wanted animals in my life. Somehow. And see? I got what I wanted. I may not have the life I'd imagined, but I'm where I need to be. Doing things that matter. I'm better here, in northern Montana. I'm the right person in the right place."

"Yes," he said. "I've met a number of people who have given up a lot to run animal rescues, and you're one of the most dedicated I've ever met. But—and you can tell me to mind my own business—don't you get lonely? It doesn't seem like you have many opportunities to meet new people."

"I'm not lonely at all," she said, sitting up straighter. Her jaw flexed a bit, then she exhaled and relaxed. "Alone doesn't automatically mean lonely, you know."

"I do."

"So what about you?"

"Hmm?"

"Are you married?"

"No." He laughed.

Her face lit with amusement. "Why'd you say it like that?"

"Like what?"

"Like it was an absurd notion. You don't care for the idea?"

"I think it's a fine institution. And when or if I meet the right person, I'll consider it."

Annie's left eyebrow quirked up. "Who would fit that bill, Tucker Brennan? A Dallas socialite, perhaps? Someone with a high-class education and Texas roots?"

"Really? That's who you think I am? That I'd be more attracted to a pedigree than a person?"

Her shoulders dropped a little, as did her head. "No. I was being a smart-ass. Pardon me. I don't know you, but from what I've seen, and what I know about how you ranch and your priorities, I'd say you'd want someone you could trust and respect. Someone you could admire."

"Don't we all?" he asked, the conversation hitting him hard for some unknown reason.

She smiled at him, and it was about the saddest thing he'd ever seen. "I think I'm going to try that stew. And take home a slice of pie."

He nodded, accepting the segue into safer territory.

But for the rest of the meal, the conversation felt strained. They laughed too quickly at things that weren't that funny. Pretended the sporadic silences were comfortable. Stole glances, ate quickly, tiptoed.

After he'd paid the check he realized he couldn't have said what the food tasted like. At the door he asked, "You parked on the street?"

Annie shook her head. "Behind the diner."

He touched the back of her elbow. It hadn't been a planned move, and once the connection had been made they both froze for a second. But he didn't drop his hand.

More importantly, she didn't step away.

They walked slowly. Country music rose and fell as people opened what he imagined was the door to the neighborhood bar. He didn't see one vehicle that wasn't a truck of some kind, or an SUV. And he only noticed that because he forced himself to think of something other than what it would be like to touch a hell of a lot more than her elbow.

Maybe it was the mystery that made him feel this powerful pull, but he doubted that was all. He remembered sitting in his Dallas bedroom at one point, her file spread in front of him, thinking that he might have liked her if she'd been the person she appeared to be.

Now that he'd met her, she was more that woman than he could have imagined. Hardworking, dedicated, kind, strong. It didn't hurt that she pressed all his personal preference buttons in terms of her looks, but this thing, it wasn't just physical.

He really liked Annie. More than he should, that's for damn sure. It was wrong to feel like this when she'd done so much damage to his brother, but he couldn't seem to help himself. So what, was he trying to justify his reaction to her, is that why he was finding it increasingly hard to believe she was capable of such a crime? Not an easy pill to swallow. Though both scenarios were troubling.

If what his gut told him about Annie was right, he had to seriously consider that Christian hadn't told the full truth about the embezzlement. Or flat out lied. Oh, man, that wasn't a possibility Tucker wanted to entertain at all. His mother would crumble.

But that changed nothing, because with every conversation, his certainty that Annie's guilt would be mitigated grew. He slid her a look that went unnoticed. With an upward tilt of her lips she was busy gazing at the clear blue sky. She loved Safe Haven, loved this small corner of Montana. Annie was doing good for the animals and the community without expectation of personal gain. It wasn't just him—the people who worked alongside her believed that.

Dammit, he wasn't wrong about her. And that wasn't his lower half talking.

She stopped, and it startled him, but then he saw the beat-up green truck of hers.

He moved around to face her, reluctantly releasing his hold. "Thank you for coming to dinner with me."

She shrugged. "As Shea would say, I really do want your money."

"Is that it? The only reason you came tonight?"

"Not completely. I admit, I find you good company. You were helpful yesterday, and I didn't properly thank you for that. Today, you asked intelligent questions, and I could see you care deeply about what your foundation does. You listened to me. Heard me. I appreciate that."

"You're fascinating. I would probably have listened to you read the phone book, although that wouldn't have been nearly as interesting as hearing about your plans for the shelter." He put his attraction to her out there, then watched closely, waiting for a small tell. A sign that she knew he was ripe for the picking, a perfect mark. One sultry smile and she could have him reaching for his checkbook....

"Thanks." She blinked. "I think."

He paused, knowing he should go. Right now. Just say good-night and walk away. "Annie," he said, his voice lower, soft enough for her to lean forward. "You're—"

She moistened her lips. "I'm...?"

He kissed her, half hoping to uncover the ruthless Warner woman who'd turned so many lives upside down. But it was sweet Annie Sheridan who kissed him back.

THE PRESSURE OF HIS LIPS STOLE far more than Annie's breath. She found herself leaning on him, as if to hold herself up and also to make sure this wasn't all in her head. He was solid against her, strong enough to carry her, and she'd been alone so long, shouldering everything.

A moment later, she parted her lips, opened her mouth in invitation, urging him to enter. He tasted incredible, nothing she could point to like beer or chocolate…it was more masculine than that. Maybe it was his clean scent— he'd showered and changed and this was him without hay and goats and horseflesh.

Her moan rose as he ran his hand under her hair. He cupped the nape of her neck, holding her steady while he changed his angle, and kissed her so thoroughly she shook with the need for more.

Gripping his upper arms, she made sure he didn't move while she pressed against him, her right breast, her thigh. His hand slid down her back, stilling in the small curve above her behind. Then he pulled her closer, and it was so overwhelming her head fell back as she gasped.

"No," he said, kissing her jaw, the curve of her neck, then back up until he found her mouth again. A quick nip on her bottom lip was followed by a thrust of his tongue, then a whisper of breath without touching at all as if they were trying out kisses to see what fit. Every one of them was perfect.

Each kiss and touch brought increased awareness that she was tasting Tucker, that the moments she'd imagined in her fantasies were becoming reality. She'd let him break the shell of her abstinence, and she knew the amazing shocks running through her body, making her squeeze her legs together, would cost her.

Dizzy with greed, she let the thought go, chased it away when she pried one hand free so she could touch his chest. If only she could reach under his shirt, feel his skin and hair and run her tongue over his nipples and hear the sounds he'd make.

Instead, like a cell door closing, approaching laughter slammed between them. She jumped away from him so quickly she almost tripped.

Tucker steadied her with his large hands. Thank God the lighting in the back lot was crap because her face felt as if it was on fire. The laughing people had nearly reached them, and she hoped they didn't recognize her.

"I should let you get home," Tucker said, releasing her completely.

She nodded. "The board meeting's at one o'clock. At Sadie's Watering Hole. The bar. It's impossible to miss, seeing as it's the only one."

"Ah, holding the meeting where there's alcohol. Attendance should be good."

She got the truck keys from her jeans' pocket. "Oh, you have no idea. The board members are…eclectic."

"I look forward to it. You don't need me to come in the morning? To Safe Haven, I mean?"

"You don't have to, no. I mean, if you want to…"

"I should use the time to take care of some business."

She looked at him, only then realizing she'd kept her head down since they'd stopped kissing. "Of course. Okay, then. I'll see you tomorrow."

He leaned forward as if to kiss her again, but she side-stepped him and grabbed hold of the truck door handle. Luckily, he caught himself in time and moved away so smoothly no one would have ever guessed his true intent.

"Night."

He distanced himself further. "Good night."

Her fingers shook when she tried to insert the key into the ignition, but she made it out of the parking lot without mishap. He was in her rearview mirror until she turned onto Main Street.

Regret didn't truly hit until she reached the highway.

FOR THE THIRD TIME IN THE PAST fifteen minutes, Tucker had to reread the email from his attorney. The memory of Annie in his arms kept intruding. Followed swiftly by re-crimination and doubt.

It was a quarter to eleven, mere hours from when he'd kissed her, and despite the work that was piling up and his assistant becoming increasingly hysterical over Tucker's botched schedule, he couldn't get his thoughts straight and figure this mess out. Because he'd crossed a line, for better and for worse.

First and foremost, there was no doubt in his mind that the woman he'd kissed was not some criminal mastermind who'd willfully stolen money that should have gone to char-ity. However, a lot of questions remained unanswered, and that bothered him.

He was determined to clear his brother's name, abso-lutely, but now he wanted even more to understand everything that had happened to the funds and who was behind the embezzlement.

Was there more he could be doing on that score? He put his head in his hands, waited for a brainstorm, for something he'd missed, but George was following up on every thread Tucker had found.

Second, Tucker wasn't going to inform the D.A. about finding Leanna Warner until he not only understood what had happened, but had evidence to back up the truth. Period. He was not going to wrench her away from Safe Haven until they had some solid information…enough, at least, to get her out of hot water and to clear Christian's reputation. He may not be able to stay with her until he and George put together a complete picture. But he had his own plane, and flying to Montana wasn't a hardship. And with telecommuting, he could work from practically anywhere.

Which reminded him that he had to call his mother in the morning, even before he called to check in with George. What Tucker wasn't sure about was letting her or Christian in on what was happening.

No, he'd stick with his decision. The fewer people who knew about Annie, the better. For now. She wasn't going anywhere. Not with a new foal coming. And she'd never desert the animals. Not unless her back was up against the wall. He'd seen how much she cared in her eyes, in her plans, in her passion. But more than that, he'd seen it in her actions.

There was so much to distrust about people. Words were easy and glib and to trust blindly was an idiot's game. Tucker might be a fool for wanting Annie so badly, but he wasn't being stupid about who she was.

He believed in her. And he would be proven right.

He opened his eyes as an idea came to him. He wouldn't

decide yet whether to act on it, but it was interesting. Very interesting.

His cell, already plugged in and charging, rang. His mother's name came up on his display, and he couldn't hit Talk fast enough. It was late, Texas time. "Mom?"

"Are you coming home tomorrow?" she asked quietly.

"No, I'm not. I'm sorry. I'm not certain when I can be back."

"I see."

Her sigh felt like a slap. The only kind she would give him, the kind that hurt deep and long. "Did you go out with Andrea tonight?"

"No." Her quiet shudder echoed in her voice. "She wanted to go for sushi and you know how I feel about that."

"I do," he said. "Did you watch a movie?"

"I think so. If I did, it wasn't particularly memorable. The house creaked a lot. I thought…"

"Were you frightened?"

"Only a little. I let Martha go home early."

Tucker stood, wishing he could do more, but he couldn't drop this thing with Annie on the off chance he could make his mother feel better. He understood that grief took all kinds of shapes, that time was relative when it came to mourning. He still felt it himself. He'd loved his father. Missed him. He could have used his old man's thoughts on this Christian business, but if Michael had still been alive, Tucker had no idea if he and his mother would be involved with Christian at all.

The thought made him ashamed, and that combined with his guilt at leaving her on her own felt like a physical weight on his back. "While I'm away, don't send the staff home early, all right? Not even Martha."

"I don't even know where you are," Irene said. "Not Dallas."

"Montana, actually."

"Do we know people there?"

"We do, but that's not why I'm here." He hesitated, knowing in his gut it wasn't a good idea to tell her anything at this juncture. She'd have too many questions he couldn't answer. But at least she'd have something to hang on to, and perhaps then he wouldn't feel so damn guilty. "Now, don't get your hopes too high, but it's possible I may have found Leanna Warner."

Her inhale stopped him. "Oh, Tucker."

"It's not certain," he said, hating the necessary lie. "Nothing is. George is working with me, and we'll just have to see how this plays out."

"But if it is her Christian will be so happy. The D.A. will leave him be. He'll be able to go back to work, wherever he chooses. He could work in Dallas. We could help him find something. You know so many people in the financial world. Oh, Tucker, this will be wonderful."

His mistake didn't take long to bite him in the ass. "Mom, I don't know if it's her. Not for sure. She *may* be the woman we're looking for. Please, don't get carried away, not yet. It's just, we can hope, right? I have to ask you not to mention this to Christian. The last thing I want is for him to—"

"Yes, yes. It's not a done deal. I'm depressed, sweetheart, not stupid. I understand completely. But thank you. I needed a bit of hope today."

"I'm sorry I'm not there."

"No. Now that I know what you're doing, I'll be fine. Whatever the outcome. You're trying. It means a great deal."

"I am trying." Out of the blue, he thought of the kiss and his chest tightened. "Look, I'll call you as soon as I can. Tomorrow, if possible."

"Be careful. I think this woman must be very clever if she could have fooled Christian. Slippery, too."

He closed his eyes at her words, wishing he could tell her everything, how she would like Annie if only she got to know her. How it would be as clear as day that there was more to the story.

Instead, he said goodbye and hung up, not dialing George right away. Annie was clever. Which was part of the reason he believed in her so resolutely.

Tomorrow afternoon he'd prove it to her.

ANNIE, HOLDING A BOX OF FILE folders, pulled open the door to the Watering Hole half an hour before the meeting would start. The jukebox was quiet, the bar deserted because it wouldn't open until four, although she knew Sadie had to be around somewhere. She didn't leave the door unlocked if she left anymore.

There'd been a rash of thefts in Blackfoot Falls last summer, which sadly had turned out to be perpetrated by locals. But it just went to show that people were people, whether they lived in New York or the wilds of Montana.

She walked across the wooden floor, her eye catching on the beautiful Wurlitzer. She wished it held more music that she liked instead of mostly country songs, but it didn't really matter since she hardly ever came in here.

Lounging around and having drinks with friends felt like something she'd read about in a book. So many things had gone away, vanished in a haze of panic and shame. A manicure would be laughable considering how she spent her days, let alone a pedicure. In Manhattan she'd often saved up for a spa day, not the high-end deals, of course, but a soothing massage, a facial. God, to be pampered like that was unthinkable now.

"Hey there, girl. Thought you'd be coming in early. Good to see you."

Annie swung around at Sadie's rusty voice. Every time Annie had seen her in the past few months, the older woman had lost a bit more weight, used a touch more makeup, including lipstick this time. "You look wonderful."

"Yeah, I'm a stunner." Sadie came up to Annie, but knowingly didn't reach out for a hug.

"Hey, none of that." Annie surprised herself and Sadie by briefly touching her arm. "I think Shea's going to be here soon, too, but the big news is that we have a potential donor coming to the meeting."

"Really? Think that's wise?"

"I've warned him. And he understands that the board members are locals doing a nice thing for the animals. I think it'll be fine. I hope. As long as Abe and Will don't get into it."

"They do and I'll knock their fool heads together. Come on, let's get these tables set up. You want something to drink?"

"No, thanks." Annie put the box on the huge mahogany bar, then helped Sadie push the small tables into a big rectangle. Halfway through moving the chairs, Shea walked in.

No hello or other pleasantry. "Is he still planning on attending?" Shea asked.

Annie nodded, while Sadie appeared unfazed. People were getting used to Shea's blunt ways.

"According to some," Sadie said, darting an amused look at Annie, "you were at Marge's last night with the best-looking man seen in Blackfoot Falls since Paul Newman visited town forty years ago."

Annie hated the fact that her cheeks filled with heat. "His name is Tucker Brennan, and don't you dare let people start rumors about him. He's rich, and he's got a foundation that could be the salvation of Safe Haven. Anything else about him is nobody's business."

"Whoa," Sadie said, holding up her hands. "I wasn't implying anything."

"I know people in this town live for gossip but I don't know what I'd do if somebody's stupid remark screwed this up."

Sadie touched Annie's shoulder. "I understand. I'll do my best to derail any talk."

After releasing her pent-up breath, Annie sighed. "Thanks. And sorry for getting worked up."

"Don't you fret." Sadie turned to greet Jesse, who'd walked in, then she herded Shea behind the bar to help fill mugs.

Beer, Annie had learned early, came automatically with all meetings that took place in the Watering Hole. Annie was used to it, but she wondered what Tucker would make of it.

Just talking about him had set her body all aflutter, and she had to tamp down her excitement. This was no time to act like a silly girl. This could be the most important few hours since she'd come to Blackfoot Falls. Something that would set her up for a future she had more than accepted. She belonged at Safe Haven, and every day spent working there chipped away at the guilt and pain of what she'd left behind.

Abe, the owner of Abe's Variety, and notorious for his unrequited crush on Sadie, walked in right ahead of Will Woodruff, who was pretty partial to Sadie himself. What they had in common did not bring the two men closer together, to say the least. Even though their scowls were a matched set.

In silence, they headed for the back room where Jesse was scrounging more chairs.

Cy Heber joined them, and he would always make Annie smile because he'd donated four acres to Safe Haven, bless him. He was an old cowboy who gave a damn, who wanted to leave something good behind, even though his own ranch was a shadow of its former self.

The door opened one more time, and Tucker Brennan walked in wearing a fine-looking Stetson along with dark pressed jeans, a pale blue Oxford shirt and a navy blazer. She bit her bottom lip, not because he filled the doors with his broad shoulders, but because of the smile that lit up his face the moment he saw her.

"Oh...okay," Sadie murmured as she put four beers down on the table. "So they weren't exaggerating."

"Hush," Annie whispered as she went to welcome him, trying her best not to mentally replay last night's kisses.

It didn't take long for everyone to take their seats and for Annie to make introductions. She sat Tucker at one end of the table, and she took her place at the other. Which might have been a mistake from the way she kept getting caught on his gaze.

But somehow she managed to begin the meeting in what was considered parliamentary procedure for Blackfoot Falls. Everybody raised and seconded everything. At least at the start.

Up until she called for new business. That's when Tucker stood. Took off his hat. Reached into his jacket pocket and pulled out a slip of paper.

"I've been spending some time at Safe Haven, and I'm very impressed with the operation. I've seen facilities with much more do a lot less. I applaud you all for doing your part for animals in need." He paused, glanced around at everyone, but settled his gaze on Annie. "This is a check.

It's not from the Rocking B Foundation. I don't make the call on who gets foundation funds. This is a personal check, one that I hope will help as you continue to develop the sanctuary. There are no strings attached—it's to be spent at your discretion."

He walked around the table and handed the check to Annie. When she looked at it, she gasped at the amount. Twenty thousand dollars. What she could do with twenty grand was more than she could comprehend. She blinked up at Tucker, then turned to the others. "We can get the engine. We can fix the tractor." She looked again at the check to make sure she wasn't crazy, then back at Tucker.

"I believe in what you're doing," he said. "I believe in you."

Annie's heart nearly stopped. His message was completely heartfelt in its honesty. She'd have been thrilled beyond measure if only he'd stopped with that first sentence. Because believing in her was believing a lie.

10

"WELL, I SAY WE USE THE REST of the money to build a quarantine barn," the gray-haired gent who owned the variety store said, his big hand almost dwarfing his beer mug.

Tucker spared him a glance, but only that. The same was true for the others. He only had eyes for one person, and it killed him that he'd had no choice but to return to his seat at the far end of the table. Since it would've been highly inappropriate to kiss her in the middle of the board meeting. He'd settle for staring into her gorgeous blue eyes.

"We should invest in some of them big internet sales things." This from another old man, Cy Heber, who looked as worn as the creaking weather vane atop the Safe Haven barn. "Those ads just keep on popping up no matter what, so they're bound to get folks' attention."

"Heber, that's spam," Jesse said, doing an admirable job of keeping a straight face. "Besides, we're already doing two internet campaigns."

Tucker watched as Annie finally put the check in her pocket and focused her entire attention on him. But instead of the heated glances from before, she seemed more confused than the money warranted. He would've liked her to smile at least, but he figured she was having mixed feelings.

He wanted her to know he was on her side. No matter what happened later with the information George gathered, where the chips fell, he needed Annie to believe that he had faith in her. That check meant something to him, as well. He never had been and never would be cavalier about his wealth, inherited or earned. Damn, he couldn't wait until there were no more secrets between them. But for now, he hoped his gesture would ease her mind in some small way.

The older cowboy, Will, said, "I think we should hire someone who can be there for Annie so that she doesn't have to work three hundred sixty-five days a year. A person needs to have some time off."

That made Annie turn. "I don't need any such thing."

Everyone started talking at once, except for Shea, who just shook her head. In fact, she'd said very little since the meeting started forty minutes ago.

Sadie slammed her hands down on the table so hard and loud she brought the chatter to a halt. "Quiet, all of you. What we're gonna do with that check is just what we've done with every other donation. Leave it to Annie. She knows better than all of us combined what Safe Haven needs. And if you don't agree, I'm bringing this meeting to a close right this second, and you can all pay for your own damn beer."

Finally, Tucker got his smile from Annie.

ANNIE WANTED TO HUG SADIE for stopping the free-for-all the board meeting had become. It was torture sitting with all these people. It was no picnic sitting across from Tucker, either.

The check and all it meant hadn't truly hit yet. Big ideas like gratitude and what she could do with so much money were right beside the echo of his words, his belief in her that made her want to weep until next week.

If he knew the truth, would he have been so quick to give her anything? No, of course not. Who would? But then, his generosity hadn't been toward Leanna Warner, and she couldn't forget that. The whole point of staying in Safe Haven was to do everything in her power to help the cause. To hide her mistakes in a coffee can under her bed, and dedicate her days and hours to something worthwhile.

The smart thing would be to continue on as if nothing had changed. In truth, nothing had. Except for the extra-large infusion of guilt.

Oh, and wanting Tucker so badly she found it hard to breathe.

She'd agonized for hours last night and before the meeting, berating herself for kissing him when there was so much at stake. Intellectually she knew that Tucker wasn't using his position to manipulate her, and she wasn't trying to use their attraction for her own benefit. But the check and the confirmation that the foundation would make an independent decision took care of any lingering doubts.

Forcing herself to tie up the meeting, to actually speak to Will and Cy and the rest of the board and really listen, put more strain on her than she'd have guessed. Tucker was there, right there, and every step closer made her want him more.

Shea and Jesse lingered after the others had left, taking the time to thank Tucker and to ask him what kind of receipt he'd like for the donation.

Annie figured that would be it. Because she had a hell of a lot to do.

"You going back to Safe Haven?" Shea asked.

Annie shook her head. "I'd like to go to Kalispell and deposit the check. Tucker's bank has a branch there. Maybe

I can keep out enough money for the engine so we can order it today. Spring will be gone before we know it."

Tucker, who'd been speaking to Jesse, joined Shea and Annie. "I could take you to the bank. Make sure you get whatever cash you need."

"No, that's okay," Annie said, ordering herself not to be nervous just because he was a foot away. "I'll have to get back to Safe Haven tonight, and you don't want to make all those trips. Not if you're leaving tomorrow."

"I'm a damn good customer of that bank. If I'm with you, they'll let you have the whole check in cash if you want." He smiled, lifted his shoulder in a casual shrug. "And hey, maybe we could even splurge and get some dinner."

Annie sighed, knowing it would be dangerous to go to Kalispell with Tucker. She'd already proven that she had no defense against this man, and God knew, she'd already broken almost every rule in her book. Still, the tractor had been sitting there for so long, and the kids had worked so hard on the project. She looked up at Shea. "Do you think you might be able to cover for me for a few hours?"

Shea smiled. "I know I can."

Jesse moved next to her. "Me, too." Then, weirdly, he nudged Shea in her side. He tried not to be obvious, but Annie saw it. Her pulse jumped when Jesse asked Tucker to join him outside.

"Maybe you should take a toothbrush with you," Shea said.

"What!" Annie groaned. Dammit, someone must've seen the kiss last night. "Are you crazy?"

Despite the flush on her cheeks, Shea took a step closer to Annie and leaned in. "Maybe get some underwear. Abe's Variety has both, you know. Then you wouldn't have to drive back to Safe Haven." Shea smiled. "Jesse and I can stay as long as you need us to. Honest."

Annie could hardly believe Shea's suggestion, and Jesse's part in this little maneuver. She wished she'd never kissed Tucker. No. That he'd never kissed her. Did everyone in the county know about it? Could a rumor spread that fast?

What was she thinking? This was Blackfoot Falls. Of course it could. Even worse, the kiss wasn't a rumor. It probably hadn't helped that she and Tucker had been ogling each other during the meeting. Jeez, she'd never live this down. Never.

Luckily, what the people of this tiny town thought of her wasn't high on her list of things she cared about. Tucker was. So was his imminent departure. God, why did she have to like him so much? Men simply did not make her heart pound anymore. Or send heat surging through her veins. But then she hadn't met anyone like him before. In her experience, rich, powerful men didn't give up their valuable time to help bring a foal into the world or get their hands dirty saving a helpless goat.

Even though she didn't deserve to be with a man like him, the fact that this was it, that they'd never see each other again once he left, was eating at her resolve faster than the summer sun melted a Popsicle. Her priorities had shifted even as she tried to reason with herself. He'd already given her a check, no strings attached, and the foundation was a separate entity. One obstacle out of the way. Was that why he'd chosen the meeting to present the check? It didn't matter. In her heart she knew… She needed tonight with Tucker as much as she needed the tractor to work.

Maybe more.

"You're right, I should duck into Abe's," she said, having trouble meeting Shea's gaze. "If you're sure."

"Please." Shea rolled her eyes. "Even I could tell you guys wanted to crawl all over each other."

Annie felt her own blush. "Oh."

"Yeah. Hurry up. I'll be talking to Tucker about when we should expect to hear from the foundation."

Annie wanted to hug her, but instead she waved at Sadie across the room, then darted out the door, ready and willing to head into a night she'd never forget. And hang the consequences.

TUCKER WAS ABOUT AS PLEASED with himself as a man could be. He had an amazing woman sitting at his side and the promise of a perfect night of nothing but spoiling her rotten in every way he could think of. Mostly, he hoped, by giving her many, many orgasms.

He'd never have asked Annie to spend the night with him. At best, he'd hoped she might ask him into her cabin after the volunteers left in the evening. But then Shea and Jesse had offered their help, and Annie had disappeared into the variety store. There were enough clues in her body language to let him know she'd picked up a few essentials. When Shea said, "See you tomorrow," the deal was sealed in his mind.

"I can't begin to thank you for the generous check, Tucker," Annie said as they merged onto the highway. "Your faith in Safe Haven won't be misplaced, I swear."

Tucker gave her a look that was a little too smug.

"I'm being sincere," Annie said.

His expression softened at her offended tone, and he realized what she must think. "Sorry. I know you are. I meant no offense. It's just…I've been caught up thinking about all the things I want to do after you take care of business. Things I want to do with you." He reached across the SUV and took her hand. "For you."

"Oh," she said, after a few seconds. "Carry on, then."

He laughed. "I intend to." After a quick squeeze, he returned his hand to the wheel because he'd been waiting for a place to pull over. There was no traffic to speak of, and he had no trouble moving onto the shoulder.

"What's wrong?" she asked. "Is it the car?"

"The SUV is fine," he said, driving onto a patch of gravel and away from the two-lane road. "What's wrong," he said, killing the engine and turning to Annie, "is that I haven't kissed you since last night."

Undoing his seat belt, he leaned over, mentally cursing bucket seats and intrusive consoles, and slipped his hand behind Annie's neck. He didn't have to pull her close; she came eagerly to meet him in the middle.

She skipped tentative altogether and went straight for mind-blowing with a quick but insistent swipe of her tongue, vanquishing any doubts he'd had about the true purpose of this escape.

He couldn't have stopped his groan if he'd tried. That he remembered her taste, that her scent had already become vital, made him glad he'd closed his eyes, because looking at her now would make him want far more than a kiss.

The moment her hand touched his chest, he gripped her more firmly, took over the kiss and slipped his tongue between her teeth. Her whimper excited his already stirring cock, and as they explored each other, the sounds of their desire filled the interior of the cab, making everything more intense.

Her roving hand reminded him that he could touch now, touch more than he'd dared last night. If the pull of actually getting her into bed hadn't been so enticing, he might have listened to the voice in the back of his head reminding him the back of the Land Rover was roomy, and how no cars had driven by since he'd pulled over.

Instead, he cupped her breast with his left hand. Over her shirt, over her bra. And learned the shape of her, the feel of her against his palm. This wasn't a grope and dash… it was a prelude, something to take the edge off until he could give her the perfect setting. Although his body wasn't too thrilled with the decision.

She drew back just as he was marveling at how hard her nipple was through two layers. "We should probably go."

Giving in, he opened his eyes, and dammit, the look of her lips, all moist and pink, was enough to make him hard. "You all right?"

"Better than all right. But I want—"

"Everything?"

She smiled, kissed him quickly on the lips, then sat back in her seat, pulling her seat belt across her chest. "Think we can do everything in one night?"

"We can sure as hell try," he said, then he put the car in gear and turned back onto the freeway, the memory of her kisses lingering like the slow, pleasant burn of twenty-year-old Scotch.

"WHEN I WAS SEVEN, I WANTED to be a fireman."

Annie immediately pictured him in one of those sexy calendars, wearing all of his gear except for his shirt. He'd have made the cover for sure. "What happened to change your mind?"

"Batman."

"Really? How's that working out for you?"

He grinned. "Great. Although the commute to Gotham is killing me."

She turned more toward him, feeling as if she were in a dream, because this was not her life. Every time she started to sink back to reality, the one she'd find soon enough in Blackfoot Falls, she snapped herself out of it. She'd have the rest of her life for regrets. But she wouldn't begin now. "I hope you brought your alter ego with you, because I'm thinking you'd look seriously hot in tights."

His laughter was deep and real and made her shiver. It also made her touch him. Her hand on his. Nothing major, no groping. The last thing she wanted was to distract him from getting them to the bank. And the hotel. She really wanted to be at that hotel.

"I can guarantee that you will never see me wearing tights. In fact, you need to stop thinking about it right now."

"Hey, tights can be very manly. All the best superheroes wear them."

Tucker looked at her. "No, some of them wear jeans and checkered blouses."

Absurdly, she looked down, although she knew what she'd put on this afternoon. "Stop it," she said, meaning it. The last thing she needed to do was get mired in her mistakes again. In fact, she wasn't going to think about herself at all. "I want to know what happened after the Batman phase."

"That's easy. Ranching. Riding. Learning the ropes. Literally."

"Did you ever try the rodeo?"

"Not for long. Being thrown off a horse hurts like a son of a bitch."

"I doubt you experienced it often."

"Not something you should bet on." His mouth twisted into a wry smile. "I preferred playing baseball. Which I did through my sophomore year in college."

"Pitcher?"

"How'd you know?"

"I'm not sure," she said. "I had a feeling, that's all."

"Well, you're right. I started out in Little League. Eventually I developed a decent arm."

He flipped his hand over hers, entwined their fingers and rubbed the skin he could reach with his thumb. A tiny movement that resonated down to her toes.

"What about you? Horses all the way?"

"Mostly. I did play basketball in school. I was tall enough to be a guard, but definitely not good enough to continue past high school. The love of my life has always been horses, though."

"No men on that list?"

She shook her head. "I lived with a guy for a few years. Thought it was love. Turned out it was more about lust and wishful thinking. Then, I don't know. Nothing major. A few mistakes. How about you?"

"I've had several relationships through the years. I expected to be married by now. I'd like to have kids. Raise them on the ranch like my father raised me. But the women that have interested me the most have had busy lives and goals of their own."

"The twain couldn't meet?"

"Five days a week I live on the ranch. I spend the weekends in Dallas. For a professional woman, that's a hard schedule to work around. And it would be difficult at the moment to give up my role at the ranch."

They were getting closer to Kalispell and traffic had picked up. She didn't want to think about him getting married and having kids. She didn't want to think of him outside of this car.

She shifted so she could see him better. "Tell me about the hotel room. Does it have a big bathtub?"

Like the gentleman he was, Tucker let the subject turn to exaggerations about the room's amenities. She relaxed against her seat, watching him as he spoke, studying that strong jaw of his before getting swept away by his cheekbones.

When the town came into view, she was a little disappointed. The ride had been the easiest stretch of time she'd had in so long. A snapshot of a life she'd never have.

FIVE MINUTES AFTER TUCKER and Annie walked into the Kalispell branch of Tucker's bank, his phone rang, and the name surprised him. He answered quickly with, "Hang on, I'll just be a minute," then turned to Annie. "I shouldn't be long, but I have to take this."

"Go ahead. If I need you to get the money, I'll wait, that's all. No problem."

He leaned over but ended up kissing her cheek instead of her mouth. She seemed as surprised as he was. He knew it was a reaction to the phone call, but he'd think about the reason later.

He didn't speak to Christian until he was in the back parking lot, away from too many passersby and far from where Annie could overhear. "What's going on, Christian?"

"That's what I want to know," his brother said.

The bite behind his words had Tucker stopping in his tracks. "You'll have to be more specific."

"Why the hell didn't you tell me you were looking for Leanna?"

"Because I don't report to you," Tucker said, instantly angry both at his impudent brother and his mother. Though he still didn't know what she'd told Christian. "Did Mom call you?"

"Yes, *Irene* called." Christian often used her name to emphasize the fact he hadn't yet forgiven her. Though he didn't mind taking her money. "She informed me you found Leanna."

"I'm not sure yet that I have. But if it is her, what are you complaining about?"

"I'm complaining because I had my own search going for her. I didn't want you involved. Leanna is a dangerous woman."

"In what way?" Tucker gritted his teeth. Getting pissed off wouldn't help. But Annie, dangerous? "You said she was a thief. That she'd taken off with the money."

Christian's huff came through as impatience, but Tucker heard more than that. Underneath the anger was panic. But over what? "Look, I didn't tell you because I didn't see the point, but there were some very shady and dangerous people in Leanna's life. People associated with the mob. Guys you don't want to get too close to, you understand? They could come after you, Tucker. And Mom."

The mob and Annie? Is that why she'd run, why she'd hidden herself away in a backwoods town near the border? Jesus, if Christian had known about it... "Why didn't you tell the police?"

"Because I didn't particularly want to die. I told you, these men are lethal. Hell, even if it is Leanna, you wouldn't be doing her any favors by bringing her in. That would be as good as signing her death warrant. Leave it alone, Tucker. This is something your big money can't fix. Trust me."

"If you'd told me the—" Tucker cut himself short. How could he blame Christian for trying to protect himself? For protecting his family? "Fine. I won't do anything to endanger you. Or her. If it is her."

"Don't say anything to anyone about this, Tucker. I'm dead serious. It won't end well."

"I understand." Tucker had walked to the side of the bank, and was headed for the entrance. He poked his head inside the door and saw Annie standing in the waiting area.

"Where are you, anyway? Mom didn't say."

Now it was Mom. Tucker wasn't sure why that rubbed

him the wrong way, but it sure as hell did. "Flying back to Dallas. I've got to run. I'll be in touch when I get home." Tucker put the phone away, more worried than ever about Annie. And Christian, yeah, but his brother seemed to be pretty good at taking care of himself.

He'd have to wait until he took Annie to order the tractor engine before he called George, see what he'd found out. Warn him. God, he hoped he hadn't sent George into danger. The thought made him so uncomfortable that after he helped Annie get her funds, he made another excuse to leave her to deal with the salesman at the machinery parts store. But she didn't just let him slip away.

"Is everything okay?"

He put on a smile, hating the subterfuge. "It's business, a fire I have to put out myself. It won't take long."

"I'll be here, and I don't mind waiting. So do what you need to." Then she pulled his head down to meet her in a kiss.

Not just a peck, either. It didn't matter that they were standing inside a busy warehouse. She took her time, and he let himself enjoy it. It hit him that he'd been one hundred percent right about her from the moment they'd met. No, from before that. He'd read her perfectly. Someone else was behind the embezzlement and had forced her hand. The only problem was, now that he understood the danger she was in, would trying to help her make things worse?

He pulled back to rest his forehead against hers, held her there for a long moment as he breathed her in, calmed himself down. There would be a solution to this. He would find one. Because anything else was unacceptable.

A few minutes later, he was on the phone with George, who delivered news Tucker wasn't prepared to hear. He found a wall to lean against. "Wait. Bookies?"

"Major bookies," George said. "These guys are affiliated with the Russian mob, Tucker. I'm sorry, but the trail is there."

"You're sure it leads to Christian?"

"No. I'm not," George said in a slow, cautious voice. "But so far, that's where things are headed."

"George, look, I appreciate everything you've done, but you need to stop now. Just back off. This is far bigger than I ever expected, and I won't have you put yourself in this kind of danger."

"You need to trust me on this, my friend. I'm not willing to get involved in anything that could get me killed. Or you, or Irene. But I've got a lifetime of sources here, and a lot of favors I've called in. I'm fine, and I'll stay fine. And I'm not stopping. If I can clear your brother, I will. But know this. I won't pull any punches."

Tucker rubbed the back of his neck. "If Irene knew, she'd be as grateful as I am. But she'd also be just as worried. No more burials, George. Not over this. Not worth it."

"I couldn't agree more. I'll get back to you."

Tucker turned off the phone, and shoved it in his pocket. Bookies. There'd been nothing in Annie's life or financial history that would tie her to gambling of any sort. Nothing. He couldn't say the same for Christian.

Jesus, what if...? No, he wouldn't jump to conclusions. The idea that Christian could be involved with the embezzlement had crossed his mind before—Tucker wasn't an idiot—but he'd dismissed the notion.

The reason for that was clear. He just hoped like hell he wasn't going to be responsible for hurting his mother even more than she was already. In the middle of forcing a deep breath, it finally struck him why he'd been annoyed that Christian switched from Irene to Mom. Subconsciously he'd recognized it had been a tactic. Pure manipulation. To tug at Tucker's emotions by upping the stakes. Even if

Tucker didn't care about himself, Christian knew he'd care about what happened to Irene. He'd back off then.

The question remained…why? Did Christian truly believe Leanna Warner was involved with the mob and feared for his life? Or was he afraid she had information that would prove his own guilt?

Damn, everything had just gotten more complicated. He should never have come to Montana. But if he'd never come, he'd have never met Annie. She wasn't the dangerous woman his brother had painted her to be. Not possible.

He walked into the store and found her by the tractors. The second she took the copy of her purchase order, he pulled her into his arms and backed her away from the counter. "I should take you to dinner. You haven't eaten for hours."

"But…?"

He looked at her, wanting to tell her everything, wanting to hide her away where no one would ever hurt her. She wasn't guilty; he still believed that with every fiber of his being, every inch of his soul. And he wanted her more than he'd ever wanted any woman. "Are you really hungry?"

"Starving," she said, a slow, sexy smile lifting the corners of her lips.

He winced, but only for a second. "Want to go find a restaurant?"

"Not a chance. Where is this hotel of yours?"

11

THE HOTEL WASN'T CLOSE ENOUGH. They had to get into the car, drive for several blocks, find a place to park. By then, Annie's focus had shifted from deposits and new engines back to sex. Sex with this man. Not only had it been ages since she'd slept with anyone, the last time she'd had sex it had been only so-so. He'd been nice, and they'd hit it off pretty well over the course of several shared meals. But in bed? They hadn't gotten in sync. She'd sworn at the time that she was done with settling, that no man would get her into bed unless there was serious heat between them.

Tucker qualified. He kept stealing glances. She kept meeting his gaze. The sizzle should have steamed up the windows.

"What are you thinking?" she asked, as they walked from the parking lot, her toothbrush and a three-pack of ugly drugstore panties safely in her purse.

"That walking in my condition is awkward and a little painful."

"Blister from your boots?"

His arm around her shoulders tightened. "Yeah. A blister."

"I might have a blister myself. Smaller than yours, though."

"I should hope so."

Her stomach grumbled. Loudly. She put her hand on her belly. "Sorry about that."

"When's the last time you ate?"

"This morning. I had breakfast."

"Which consisted of…?"

"Hey, no playing Mom."

He bumped her hip with his. "That's not at all how I'm feeling at the moment, but I have seen your refrigerator. And your cupboards."

"Fine. I had toast and string cheese."

He brought them to a halt. "I'm feeding you."

"Yes, you are. Later."

"Not later. Now. I don't need you passing out during the best part."

She turned until she stood close enough to press against his "blister." "What precisely would the best part be?"

He kissed her, then moved his lips just far enough away from her to whisper, "All of it."

She captured his lower lip between her teeth, but let him go before he could object. "The gift shop has candy bars."

His green eyes looked darker staring at her from such close range, but she liked the view. Liked the man. "I feel like I'm not taking care of you properly."

"You can fix that the minute we get into your room."

"Why are we talking? We could be buying candy right this second."

She held on to his hand as they jogged to the back entrance and found the shop. She grabbed the first chocolate bar she saw, glad to see he picked one up, as well. Neither of them wasted a moment digging in, and they crumbled the wrapping in unison before the elevator opened at his floor.

Once she got inside the suite, the memory of her old life

hit fiercely. Thank goodness she had a legitimate excuse to shut herself into the bathroom. It was huge, but even the pleasure of seeing the big tub wasn't strong enough to stop the déjà vu.

Standing still as she looked into the mirror, she saw Leanna Warner. As the emotions welled in her throat, she clamped her eyes shut. "I'm here. Right now," she whispered. "With the most amazing man I've ever met, and I've got this one chance."

After a few deep breaths, she brushed her teeth and her hair, blessed whatever gods had made her shave her legs before going to the board meeting and went out the door wearing a smile that was turned electrically real the moment she saw him standing by the bed.

Just the way he looked at her made her nipples hard.

TOSSING HIS STETSON ON THE couch, Tucker held her gaze as he slowly approached her. He wanted to watch her eyes darken the closer he got.

By the time he was a breath away, the blue of her irises had almost disappeared. "I can't decide whether I want to undress you piece by piece, or race you till we're both buck naked and panting."

"The second option gets my vote."

"Yeah?"

She nodded. Then she started unbuttoning her shirt, and the competition was on.

He won. Not the race—he'd lost that part. She was down to her underwear while he was still working on getting his boots off, but damn, the view was worth it.

"I'm pretty sure I'm the winner," she said, grinning, her thumbs hooked over the elastic of her panties.

"I could argue that." He knew she'd have great legs. "Want help?"

"No. I want to stare at you. It wouldn't hurt my feelings if you turned around a time or two."

She blushed. Pretty as a picture. The pink didn't stop with her cheeks, either. He was going to lick as much of that rosy skin as he could. Later. Taking his sweet time was for seconds. Not that he didn't want to impress her with his smooth moves, but he was already as hard as a bedpost just looking at her white cotton bra and panties.

One boot came off, and dammit, he had to focus for a minute on getting the second one loose. The moment he did, he shot to his feet and started working on his jeans.

When she did turn around, he nearly clipped himself with his zipper. Her body was even more amazing than he remembered, and he'd thought about it for two nights. Of course, he'd only seen that stretch of her back before, and now that he saw her behind, he knew he'd be dreaming of her for months, if not longer.

"Happy now?" she said, turning back to face him.

"Ecstatic," he said, and proved his point by dropping his jeans and boxer briefs at the same time. Then he realized his socks were still on, and he toed them off as fast as he was able. Almost fell over, but it was worth it.

She still laughed at him. Until he stood up tall, and then she got quiet. Seeing that look on her face as she stared down at him was a turn-on all by itself.

"Now you," he said, his voice lowering an octave.

He wanted to touch her as she reached behind her back to undo her bra clasp, but he kept his hands at his sides. Fisted, but still. His cock, not so much. The moment that bra fluttered to the floor, it jerked, tapping the flat of his stomach.

Annie was trembling slightly. Not like she was afraid. Just anxious. Her hands went to slide her panties off, and his plan to watch the whole show broke down. Before he knew he was going to do it, he hit his knees, inches away from her beautiful body.

She jumped, but didn't move back. When he looked up, he found her dark gaze and her tacit permission. He leaned forward, nestling his nose just below her indented belly button. She smelled so damn good, and she wasn't even unwrapped yet.

His fingers tugged her panties down slowly, and despite the impulse that urged him to speed the hell up, he unveiled her like a prize.

She had a perfect triangle of blond curls and once he'd uncovered her completely, he inhaled again. Nothing on earth compared to the scent of a woman, and he would swear on any book in the room that Annie had been designed with him in mind.

As gently as he could, he touched her inner thighs, hoping she'd get the hint. Bright and beautiful, she shifted her legs for him, and when he slipped two fingers just inside the barely parted lips, she was all moist heat and silk. It wasn't hard to find where she'd gotten hard, but he was careful with his touches. Still, one swipe made her grab onto his hair, a little more enthusiastically than he'd anticipated.

She let go immediately. "Sorry, I'm sorry."

Just the sound of her breathy apology got him hotter. "It's okay," he said, right before he blew a stream of air across where he'd touched.

"We need to rethink this," she said.

Talk about a cold shower. "What?"

"No...not...no. I can't do this standing up. I'm going to spoil everything if we don't get on the bed. Quickly."

Tucker obeyed like a shot. In fact, the second he was up, he had her in his arms. Not taking any chances, he swept an arm behind her knees and one across her back, lifted her up and into a kiss as they crossed the short distance to the bed. His romantic gesture crashed and burned when he had to put her down to turn back the white spread.

Not that Annie seemed to mind. When she lay down, she pulled him along and they picked up the kiss right where they'd left off.

IT WASN'T EVEN FIVE-THIRTY, the room was filled with light and precious space, and Annie had never felt more comfortable being naked with a man.

Maybe it was because he was clearly excited by her… No, that wasn't a special feat in her experience. Perhaps she'd given up being self-conscious when she'd given up everything else. Her psyche seemed to realize that there would be no return engagements.

Or it could just be that she liked him. So very much. Something had clicked from that first meeting, and it had never stopped. Despite her nerves and her secrets and her endless responsibilities, she'd found him wonderful company. His touch… God, just now he was running his palm up her side, then segueing to her breast, where he teased her nipple as if she'd given him her personal instruction manual.

She gasped, pulling away from his lips. Then they were on her throat, in that sensitive spot below her ear. He didn't just kiss, but licked and nibbled, and then when he murmured something indistinct the vibration kicked everything up a couple notches.

Easing her hand between them, she circled his length and moved to the base and back up again.

He froze. Lips parted on her skin, tongue in midswipe.

He didn't even breathe as she repeated the motion, finding a rhythm that made her own heart pound.

Tucker made a garbled noise, half word, half moan, entirely unintelligible.

"You're welcome," she whispered, grinning before she nipped him on the earlobe.

"Annie. Annie. Annie."

Her grin became a laugh. "Yes, Tucker?"

"This is going to be over very quickly if you continue doing that."

She squeezed a little harder before she pumped him again. "You mean, this?"

"Yes," he said, through clenched teeth.

She sighed. "Sure, spoil all my fun." Letting him go, she was sorely tempted to go back for one more sneaky pull, but decided the consequences might not be to her liking.

"Later you have my full permission to carry on," he said. "But for now, let's at least go for ten minutes, okay?"

"I bet we can make it twenty, if we try."

He pushed up onto his arms until he was staring straight into her eyes. "Do you want me to have a stroke? Is that the plan?"

She liked this side of Tucker. Naked and pleading looked great on him. To show her appreciation, she wrapped her left leg over his lower back.

He closed his eyes for just a few seconds, and then pretended to glare at her. "You're a devil. A stunning devil, but still. You should be careful."

"Careful? Why? What's the worst that can happen?"

The right side of his mouth quirked up in one of her favorite smiles. "I might have to ravish you again and again."

Her other leg joined the first to reinforce that she was

in favor of that outcome. She used the traction to press up against his straining erection.

Watching him throw back his head as if he was already coming made her ache along with him. "Where did you put the condoms?"

"Give me a second. And don't move."

She didn't. Not a bit. At least, not with the obvious muscles.

A moment later, he took a deep breath, turned both of them to their sides until he could reach the bedside table. His weight was just getting to be too much for her when he rolled them back to their original position.

Then he sat up, unapologetically knocking her legs away. Annie held back a laugh, then watched him get ready. Goodness, he certainly looked impatient. But then so was she.

Once the condom was on, he leaned down again, and this time, he brought her legs up toward her chest. "Next time, I swear…" He stopped to kiss the inside of her ankle. "We'll have so much foreplay we'll both be wrecks."

"Sounds wonderful. Now what are you waiting for?"

He smiled and pushed inside her, one straight shot that had her arching her back and holding on for dear life.

It wasn't the most elegant sex she'd ever had, but it was exactly what she'd needed. She touched him wherever she could reach, hoped like hell the walls were thick or the room next door was empty, because she was not quiet.

The kisses that started out hot and deep ended up pants against each other's mouths, and it turned out that was about as sexy as anything she'd ever felt.

By the time he let her right leg go, and found her clit with his thumb, she was shaking and straining so hard she thought her heart would burst. Her orgasm crested before she had a chance to warn him. All she could do was hang on, muffle her scream with his shoulder and ride the wave.

When he pushed her whole body up the bed with the force of his thrust, she pulled her head back, opened her eyes. She watched him come, the intensity in his face breathtaking. When he could relax again, he smiled down at her, then pressed a soft kiss to her shoulder.

"Hell of an appetizer," he murmured.

Which made her stomach growl so loudly they laughed even as they collapsed in exhaustion.

TUCKER ONLY OPENED his menu after Annie caught his attention. She gave him the look that meant he'd better stop staring at her. Yes, that happened a lot, but this was different. She'd been studying Louie's deli menu as if it were the Rosetta Stone, and all her questions had been answered.

"A Reuben," she whispered, in a voice that was half awe, half hunger.

"Sauerkraut have some special meaning in your life?"

She looked again at the menu, then up at him. "The highlight of my month is eating in Marge's diner. Not that Marge's isn't swell—the food is great—but I think they missed the memo on what rye bread should taste like. And I'm not going to discuss their corned beef." She looked down again. "New York cheesecake. Please let that be true. Please."

Tucker had to grin, enjoying her excitement. But it also saddened him that he wanted to use her joy over New York food to press her about her old life. See if he couldn't find out something more, anything that would allow him to help her.

He couldn't think of a way to tell her what had brought him to Safe Haven without screwing everything up. Trying to convince her that he believed she was innocent and he was on her side wouldn't be enough. She'd be furious and frightened and would probably never trust him again.

That wasn't part of the plan. Even if he explained his about-face, she'd still know he'd lied to her. If their situations were reversed, he wouldn't believe anything that came out of her mouth.

All she was doing was trying to protect herself. And she'd done it by being a selfless defender to those that couldn't defend themselves. So what the hell should he do? Damn. If Christian had told the truth, and the mob was involved, Tucker's choices had narrowed considerably. His first priority was to keep her safe. Even if it meant she'd hate him forever.

"What's the matter? Are you okay?"

Pasting on a quick grin that became genuine as soon as he saw the concern in her eyes, he nodded. "I'm fine. Too many things look good. Like the Parmesan chicken sandwich. And the Bronx Bomber."

"That's the Philly cheese steak, right?"

He nodded. "So tell me. Carnegie Deli or Katz's?"

"That's a trick question. The pickles at Carnegie and the pastrami at Katz's. And how does a cowboy from Dallas know about Katz's, anyway?"

He shrugged. "Well, shucks, ma'am. I'm not rightly sure. But I think I hopped on that there subway train from Midtown to the Lower East Side, and there she was."

She ducked her head and looked at him through her lashes. "God, you're adorable."

"It's a burden, but one I've grown to accept."

The waitress came by to take their hefty order, but Annie still made the time to ball up her straw wrapper and throw it at his head. She had damn good aim, too.

The best part of the meal was hearing her make the

sounds he hoped to duplicate when they got back to the room.

The other great thing was her laughter. She seemed like a different person, sitting across the booth from him. No wonder. This was probably her first break in years, and it had been a revelation. Seeing her shed the burden of her responsibilities gave new light to her eyes, and when she smiled…

She made him forget, for long moments at a time, that he was unsure how to help both her and his brother, that his mother was walking on thin ice, that he had grown so used to being alone he'd learned to ignore the loneliness.

"Think we could stop here tomorrow before we head back home?"

"Sure." He wanted to sit here for hours, just staring, thinking about how her eyes matched the blue of the sky. "To eat here or carry out?"

She sighed, leaning back in the booth. "I'm taking home as much food as will fit into my fridge."

"That would be what, half a sandwich?"

She glowered. "There's another fridge in the stable, you know. A big one."

"I don't think you're supposed to put the cheesecake on the same shelf as the pergolide."

"Where there's a will…as they say."

"I'd be delighted to help you improve your stash. Frozen burritos? That's just not right."

Annie leaned forward. "Guess what? You do what you have to. Money's tight. And you know as well as I do that horses are accidents waiting to happen. Not to mention goats. I swear, they should have first-aid competitions at rodeos. I can wrap a blown kneecap in under a minute when necessary. And that includes any injections."

How was it possible to become even more impressed with this woman? And how quickly could he get her back to his hotel room?

12

"LET ME HELP YOU WITH THAT," Tucker said, walking toward Annie with a wicked smile.

"You're so thoughtful." She had already taken off her boots and socks and left them in the main room. The bath was filling quickly, the scent of lilacs hinted at summer gardens and would be forever imprinted with Tucker in her memory.

Unlike the first rush to push aside anything standing in the way of sex, he took his time unbuttoning her shirt. Would she have to get rid of these clothes once he left? Hide them in coffee cans so they wouldn't torment her?

She closed her eyes, forcing herself to be present, right here, right now. Why was it so difficult to stay in the moment with him? To experience every second as it was happening instead of jumping ahead?

After her shirt fell, she took hold of him. Instantly, she felt more grounded. Of course she'd have to let him go, but for now, contact was all important.

He'd been looking down at her chest, at her ugly bra, but then he shifted his gaze to her face, to her eyes. His touch halted as they met in a kiss. It was easy and sexy, and each time they parted lips, they kept hold of each other with their warm breath, and when they came back together it was a jolt of the best kind. Again and again, as if they were near a waterfall, lying in a meadow, alone in a steamy cave, all at once while never leaving the simple, spacious bathroom in an ordinary hotel.

Both of his hands, so strong and real, went to her bare waist and she came back to earth. He undid the buttons of her jeans as if he were popping champagne corks, and the image made her laugh.

"What?"

"Nothing. You. A bubble bath."

Just his smile did startling things to her. "Exciting, huh?"

"You have no idea. I have recurring dreams of taking long, luxurious soaks in perfectly scented water."

"Did they include a devilishly handsome man tending to your every need?"

She sighed as she leaned against him. "They will from now on."

"Good," he said, his lips close to her ear. "Keep that thought." Pulling away, he turned off the water, then came back to finish his task.

"I like that look."

She shook her head, not understanding.

"You, just like that. Your jeans open, bare feet."

"My retro bra?"

"Yes, even your retro bra. I want to get my camera, take a picture. I'd put it up on the inside of my locker."

She grinned, because it was such a sweet notion. "You're a long way from locker rooms."

"I don't know. I could go to a gym. I think I'd sign up for one if you'd be my pinup."

"Those kind of lockers are temporary."

His smile changed into something else. "And you're for keeps."

She stopped. Stopped everything, including breathing, because he hadn't meant... That would be ridiculous. Turning away, not wanting to see him wince at his mistake, she finished taking off her jeans.

When she reached behind to unfasten her bra, he touched her hands, moving them down. His mouth went to the curve of her neck, where he brushed away the awkwardness with his cool lips and warm tongue.

She let her bra slide down her arms, pool at her feet. His gentle hands cupped her, teased her nipples. She cocked her head to the side to give him all the room he wanted, and he kept up his delicious assault on the sensitive skin just below her ear.

Her eyes opened—she hadn't even realized they were closed. Now she was facing the mirror, but she couldn't see herself or Tucker clearly. They were shapes in the steam, nothing specific and real, and wasn't that perfect?

Nothing real. This was the image she'd hang on to. The one that felt like a dream. Anything else was too dangerous.

Tucker chose that moment to run his hand down her belly straight into her panties. Dreams be damned. His finger found the precise spots that would give her the most pleasure, and he played her like a Stradivarius.

Part of what made her body thrum was listening to his breathing change. Deepen. Grow harsh and insistent as she trembled. Two fingers pushed inside her, though the building pressure of his circling thumb was what got to her the most.

Standing was becoming an issue. She reached behind her and grabbed what she could. Lucky for her, it was mostly his butt. God, the thickness of the denim was unfair. She wanted skin…she wanted to grip him with both hands and feel those muscles. Mark him so that later, when they were in bed, she could run her tongue where she'd scratched.

"Jesus," he whispered. The pumping stopped as he pushed his hips forward, pressing his trapped erection against her bottom. He hadn't even taken off her panties, and she was going to come.

She ground back into him, even though it cost her the pressure of his thumb, the steady buildup of intensity. Didn't matter, his groan was worth it.

He bent lower again, and this time, he wasn't teasing. Not with his fingers and not with his mouth. There were no kisses. Just his voice. Closer than anything, almost inside her head as he whispered, "Come for me, sweetheart. Come on. I want to feel you squeeze around my fingers. Do it. I've got you." His warm breath clipped her ear. "Just let go. Let go."

Every muscle strained. Then she shattered. But he was there to catch all the pieces.

TUCKER WAS ABOUT AS HARD as he'd ever been, but there was no way on this earth he was going to disrupt Annie's bliss. She could barely stand, which he took full credit for, and the bathtub was ready and waiting. He was going to massage her neck, even though there was no really comfortable place to sit. But then there didn't seem to be much comfort at all in his immediate future. Which was okay. He wasn't the one who'd had to deal with that joke of a shower in her farce of a cabin. He hadn't given up every luxury, every piece of himself, to hide from an uncertain future.

He'd tried to think what he would have done in her situation, at least what he knew of it, and he doubted strongly that he would have devoted himself to the care and feeding of abandoned animals.

"Oh, my God," she said, stirring as he pulled his hands from out of her panties. He'd made sure not to linger inside her after her orgasm, because she was sure to be sensitive and there was so much more of the night left. But it took a lot for him to stop petting her just below the line of her underwear.

"Are you ready to get into the tub?"

She nodded. Her arms dangled by her sides, her head lolled to the right. Even her eyes were half-lidded. "That was…"

"Yes," he said, kissing her lightly on the top of her shoulder. "Can you stand? Just for a minute. Let's get those panties off so you can get in the tub."

"Ohhh. The bath. Yes. Okay."

He waited for a sign she intended to move at all. Finally, just when he was planning how he could carry her into the tub without causing a horrible mess, she shifted her weight from him to her own two feet. "There we go."

"I'm perfectly capable of standing on my own," she said, awfully petulant for someone swaying as if she were drunk.

"I am very aware of that fact, Ms. Sheridan. You are capable of so much."

She sniffed, then smiled. "Are you getting in the tub with me?"

"Nope. That's all yours."

"But what about…" She turned around and put her hand directly over his cock.

He jerked back as if she'd burned him. "That's fine. We'll take care of that later. It's your turn to relax."

"That'll probably be gone by the time I'm done."

"It won't be gone for long, I promise."

She sighed, and he could see her returning from her orgasmic haze. With a two-handed push and a hip wiggle, her underpants dropped to the floor. "That was better than any massage I've ever had at any spa."

"I should hope so. Damn. What spas do you go to?"

"I wasn't being literal." She walked over to the tub and put her fingers in the water. The bubbles weren't as plentiful as they had been, but there were still enough. "Perfect."

"Good. I'll let you get settled, then come back to lend a hand."

She smiled as her eyes widened. "Like the one you just gave me?"

"I was thinking of a shoulder rub, but I aim to please."

She left her bath and circled her arms around his neck. "This is the best vacation ever. You're not what I expected."

"In what way did I disappoint?"

"Funny." She tipped her head back. "I mean. You're still here. You've been generous, and I don't mean just the check. Generous with yourself. Your time, your attention. I thought I'd show you paperwork, and take you for a tour. That would be that, and then we'd find out later whether Safe Haven made the grade. *You* were definitely a surprise."

"I guess we were both caught off guard. You're not who I pictured, either."

"I'm just a hermit who's found her calling."

He huffed. "Not even close."

She kissed him and there was no possibility his erection was going down a centimeter when he held her naked against him, when each kiss was better than the last.

When he finally pulled back, it was with great reluctance. "Your water's getting cold."

"There's more where that came from."

One more peck on the tip of her nose, and he moved

out of her arms. "Go relax. Enjoy. Soak until you're one big prune."

"Oh, that's so sweet…what an image." She laughed and stuck a foot in the water.

He left the bathroom, closing the door behind him. He rested there for a minute, waiting for his cock to settle down.

As soon as he checked his phone and saw that he had three voice mails, he cooled off. Too anxious to wait and listen, he checked the list of incoming numbers. None from George or Christian, only business associates. The pressure in his chest eased. It wasn't as if he was expecting the other shoe to drop at any second. He knew Annie was safe. So was his mother. No reason to think anyone, criminal or otherwise, was lurking in the shadows.

Only George knew Tucker had actually found Leanna and that they were in Montana. As far as Christian and Irene were concerned, they thought maybe Leanna had been located, no certainty there. He pondered for a moment, unable to recall if he'd told Irene he was in Montana. Shit. He couldn't remember. He had a feeling he had told her, but she obviously hadn't passed the information to Christian.

Restless, he picked up his iPad. The amount of work piling up and the panic he sensed in Darren's email was enough to put a damper on his mood under normal circumstances. Now it barely provided a distraction.

This wasn't like him. None of this. His original goal was met the moment he'd realized Annie was in fact Leanna Warner and found corroborating evidence. The next step should have been a phone call to the New York district attorney's office and a return trip home.

He hadn't even been gone that long, which made no sense. He felt as though he'd known Annie for weeks. Longer. The connection with her had been fast and deep, un-like anything he'd experienced before.

His unromantic soul had dismissed such a thing as pos-sible. And yet here he was, having willingly put his life on hold. He'd written her a twenty-thousand-dollar personal check. That did not happen.

He'd been raised to be cautious not only with money but with his trust, his admiration, his affection. She'd broken through all his barriers with no apparent effort.

Looking at the bathroom door, imagining her soaking in the tub, eyes closed, the water lapping at her skin, he realized he wouldn't have changed a thing. Not that there wasn't more work to do, because now that he had her, he wasn't about to lose her to false identities and an over-eager D.A.

The thing with Christian wouldn't be easy, though. Their relationship was already so muddled, and now with his mother pinning all her hopes for the future on winning her son back, Tucker had no idea what the outcome would be. It wouldn't do him any good to keep beating himself up for being so intentionally blind to his brother's connection to the embezzlement, but it was hard not to regret it. Not simply on his mother's behalf, either. He would like to have a brother again, not a memory overshadowed with guilt.

Now, all the blinders had to come off. He hoped there were extenuating circumstances and that Christian would walk away from this debacle with his reputation intact. Maybe he and Annie had both been duped somehow, or Christian had been the one coerced by bookies. What a mess.

His gaze fell on his briefcase, the files for Leanna War-ner locked safely inside. In a way, he had known Annie longer than a few days. He'd studied her past, learned who she'd been as a teenager. How honorably she'd conducted herself as an adult. He knew her better than he did Christian. Tucker wasn't wrong about her. No doubt in his mind. The woman described in those files was exactly the one behind the bathroom door. Someone like her didn't suddenly rip off charities.

She was, however, a woman to whom he'd promised a shoulder rub, and he was nothing if not a man of his word. He put away the iPad. The real world would suck them back in soon enough.

ANNIE'S IDEA OF HEAVEN was made complete when Tucker took off his clothes. She'd even made sympathetic noises when he complained about how cold the bathtub rim tiles were on his ass as he settled himself behind her, his legs in the water on either side of her arms.

But the true beauty of this moment of perfection didn't hit until he began rubbing her neck. His technique was basic and effective. Mostly just hands on skin and pressing down on parts that hurt until they stopped hurting.

Eyes closed and body floating on a sea of endorphins, she moaned as she let him have his way. It surprised her to find she'd been running her hands up and down his legs, because she didn't remember starting. It was nice, though. He had great calf muscles.

"Oh, right there," she said, as his thumb went deep right next to her spine.

"You should get more massages."

"I should also have my meals catered by Nobu, but that's not going to happen, either."

He sighed as his magic fingers continued, sometimes gently, sometimes with true commitment. "Did you grow up in New York?"

She nodded. "Queens."

"Ah."

"Lots of trains to the city."

"Huh. Where did you develop your love of horses?"

"Books first. Then a pony at a birthday party. Don't stop."

And he didn't, until he'd worked out a particularly stubborn knot at the edge of her scapula. When he was allowed to move at his own discretion again, he said, "And after the pony?"

"Central Park. They have stables. I started working there when I was sixteen."

"Wasn't that quite a commute?"

"For a guy from Dallas, you sure do know a lot about New York."

"Practically the whole world knows about New York. But I've been there quite a few times, and the foundation works with a sanctuary in Watkins Glen. I also do business with several companies that have their headquarters in Manhattan."

"Watkins Glen. I know that place." She started to twist around but he urged her to stay facing forward. "They do a great job."

"They do."

"I worked at the stables so I could ride for free. I loved it. Loved them. I knew every inch of the bridle trail."

He rested his hands on her shoulders. "I never asked about what you did before Safe Haven. Were you working with horses?"

She stilled, the euphoria of the last hour draining away, replaced with dread. "No. No horses. Just people. Who are much more complicated." Squeezing his legs, she tilted her head up. "The water's getting cold. What do you say we get warm in the shower, then crawl into that big king bed?"

His smile assured her that her distraction technique had worked. She felt sure he hadn't been snooping outside of regular curiosity. If he tried to find her on the internet, he'd find nothing—which in this day and age was suspicious in itself. The trick was to say enough without appearing cagey. She hated that she had to hide any part of herself from him.

Thank goodness for the cold, because it let her hide her discomfort behind a fluffy towel and shivering. It wasn't until he kissed her under the hot water of the shower that she was able to really relax. And to remember who she was dealing with here.

He believed in her, and if that wasn't the most amazing thing she'd ever been told, she didn't know what else could be.

She pulled him into a wet kiss, even though it turned out not to be her best idea, then continued kissing after they'd finished coughing. His hands were all over her, exactly where she wanted them, and now it was her turn. Not in the shower, though.

After he shaved, he took over drying her hair. Dressed only in a white towel, he'd sat her down on the closed toilet and rubbed her gently but thoroughly. No man outside of a salon had ever done that for her before. There were so many firsts with Tucker.

When he was satisfied, she'd run her fingers through the damp strands, knowing she would look like a scarecrow in the morning with nothing on hand to repair the damage. Not caring in the least, she led him to the bed, both of them naked and eager.

He threw back the bedding, and they burrowed into the warmth of body heat and soft sheets.

She ran her hand all the way down his chest, lingering over a nipple, his hip bone. When she moved slightly to the right, she found his hardening penis waiting.

He gasped when she ran her finger from the base to the crown.

"You were right," she said. "It didn't take long."

He rubbed his smooth, shaved jaw over her cheek. "That's completely your fault."

"Really?"

"Absolutely. I've been in trouble since we wrestled with Pinocchio. I'm sure you know that."

"I had a hint when we were patching each other up."

"Well, sure you did. We might not have smelled great, but we had chemistry from the start."

Grasping his shaft and learning the feel of him, she looked into his eyes, enjoying the effect her grip had on him. "You were very professional. Most of the time, anyway."

"Let's not use that in the testimonials, okay?"

She laughed, gave him a squeeze and slipped under the covers, wiggling until she'd lowered herself into position.

"Oh, God," he said.

His voice was muffled, but not his enthusiasm. He grew harder as she started to stroke his shaft, slowly at first, learning, memorizing. She inhaled deeply, wanting his scent to imprint, against her better judgment.

When she finally tasted him, a lick over the silky head, she felt his body jerk and heard his low moan. Another lick, and suddenly the bedding was thrown back, and he was reaching for her with one hand, trying to find a condom on the nightstand with the other.

13

TUCKER RESENTED THE BEAUTIFUL spring morning. Resented having to get out of bed, resented that she needed to get back to Safe Haven. That he had to make his own plans to return home. While they were still in Kalispell, there was no way he'd drive them back to Safe Haven before Annie had breakfast, and more. The in-room coffee hadn't been nearly enough for her. But then, the energy boost was necessary after spectacular wake-up sex.

He shook his head, dismissing the idea that what they'd experienced was just sex. He'd had that. He knew what it felt like, and what they'd done in the past couple of days was far more. Dangerously more.

He looked through the window of the beauty shop to find Annie leaning back over the deep sink where the hairdresser was washing her hair and giving her a scalp massage. Tucker had caught her cursing at her hair this morning, preparing to wet it all over again because it evidently made her look like something from a "before" photo. So he'd gotten the name of a salon from the front desk, and while he'd had to practically hog-tie Annie to agree, she'd eventually given in. But only after swearing she'd be cranky the whole ride home.

He'd deal, although he didn't honestly believe her. She hadn't been pampered in so long. She'd never indulge herself with so much as a simple professional trim, and it gave him great pleasure to be able to step in.

It also gave him some time alone. Satisfied that Annie was all set for a while, he pressed his mother's number as he walked to the hotel's parking lot.

"Tucker. I'm so glad you called. I have to leave in fifteen minutes, but I wanted to know if there's any news."

"Good morning to you, too, Mom."

He heard her tsk. "Good morning. Now, what's happened?"

"What's happened is that you told Christian. We spoke about that."

Her pause wasn't long. "I know you asked me not to, but he was so depressed. He'd just found out he hadn't gotten that job with the insurance company. The news had brightened my day so much, I simply couldn't keep it from him. Forgive me?"

He sighed, not trying to hide his frustration. "Did you mention where I am?"

"No. I didn't think that was necessary."

So Tucker had told her. He wished he hadn't. "Good. Christian doesn't need to know. We don't want him doing anything rash. Understand?"

Her silence unnerved him. "That's not quite all my news," she said, her reluctance plain.

Tucker stopped his idle pacing. "What?"

"Even though he was thrilled that you were trying so hard on his behalf I could still hear how down he sounded. There's a long road ahead, even if it turns out you have found that woman. There's a trial and evidence and his name will be suspect for who knows how long."

That wasn't his mother's reasoning. In fact, Tucker could

hear the words coming out of Christian's mouth. "How much?"

"Enough for him to take a nice vacation and to keep him in rent for a few months."

"So, what, ten thousand? More?"

"It's my money."

Who was he to talk when he'd given Annie twice that amount. "You're right. Of course. Did he say where he was going for this vacation of his?"

"Bali. Turns out he has friends there who run a hotel. He even got a deal on the flight, so that's wonderful. I think it will do him a world of good. He'll keep in touch, though. Get all the updates."

Tucker's blood chilled at her first word. Christian had left the country. Out of fear, certainly, but of what? That uncovering Leanna's whereabouts would stir up a hornet's nest? Or that Leanna coming forward would take away his scapegoat?

He supposed his brother could be telling the truth. He could very well have friends in Bali. He hadn't been able to find a job, and to the best of Tucker's knowledge Christian hadn't traveled often.

Still, Tucker couldn't deny that knowing Bali belonged to one of the few nations that didn't have an extradition treaty with the U.S. made him nervous.

"Tucker? Are you still there?"

"I'm here, Mom. You didn't tell me where you were headed this morning."

"I'm going to Dallas, where I'm shopping with Nancy Voorman and then we're having lunch before we get our nails done."

"Glad you're getting out." He glanced at his watch. George needed to know about Bali. "So I'll see you soon."

"Soon? I hope so. Your assistant has been, shall we say, pensive about your return. And I've missed you."

"I'll be back as quickly as I can."

"I suppose that'll have to do. Bye, dear."

Tucker disconnected, then moved out of the way of a car attempting to park as he tried to gather some perspective about Christian's disappearing act. He didn't have enough information to go on, that was the problem.

His palms growing clammy, he speed-dialed George. Annie had left everything she had behind. Now, so had Christian. What the hell had they gotten involved with?

George's phone went straight to voice mail, so Tucker left a message, then headed back to the salon. Annie probably wasn't ready yet. Or maybe she was. All he really cared about was that he knew exactly where she was and that she was safe.

Nothing he'd learned had changed Tucker's opinions about her. He still believed in her. Even if she'd made a mistake, he was completely convinced that she hadn't intentionally done anything malicious or underhanded.

ANNIE TURNED TO CHECK THAT THE cooler, purchased to hold all the deli treats she'd bought, was really there. Sitting on the backseat of Tucker's rented Land Rover. It was.

She thought of pinching herself as a secondary verification, but that seemed over the top. Besides, if she'd been clever enough to dream the past twenty-four hours, she'd be smart enough to include a pinch to go with it.

Instead, she looked at Tucker, remembering the feel of his dark hair through her fingers. Lord, he had a great face. The profile was rugged and handsome enough to be on a billboard. But, as with all people she grew to know, his looks had taken a minor position in her list of reasons she'd never forget him.

She wasn't immune, and she enjoyed his attractiveness, but there was so much more to him. The salon had been his idea. She couldn't think of a man in her life who would have had that kind of insight and care. "Thank you for the beauty shop," she said. "I'm surprised it occurred to you."

"I figured it had been a while since you'd taken the time to get pampered."

"You know, you're basing your assumptions on very little real evidence."

"Ah, but I have eyewitness testimony. Your friends were impressed but concerned that you don't take much time for yourself. Besides, I'm not as dumb as I look. In some circles, I'm considered astute."

She grinned, even as the guilt over her lies threatened to overshadow her glow. The battle was tough but her time with him was so short she didn't give in. "Does that kind of talk work with the ladies in Dallas?"

He shrugged. "Used to. Not so much anymore."

"Why not?"

"The women in my life, who are mostly friends, by the way, are far more impressed with substance than flash. Although come on, you have to admit, I do have a decent sense of humor."

Mostly friends? There was a thought that was being banished right that second. Of course he had women in his life. He'd told her he hadn't found the right woman. That was still true, and she'd better not forget it.

"Are you planning on leaving right after you drop me off?" she asked.

"I should, but I haven't decided if I'm flying out tonight or tomorrow morning. Tomorrow's stretching it." He reached over and squeezed her thigh. "But I'm finding it difficult to leave."

"Oh, well, that's… Yeah. Well, you're welcome to stay as long as you like."

He smiled. "Thanks."

She laughed at herself, shaking her head. She was way too comfortable with him. It was nice. Scary, too.

"Unfortunately, my staff are becoming panicked. I don't normally take such impromptu vacations," he said. Then, before she had a chance to respond, he switched gears. "What about you? You figured out how you're going to spend the rest of the money?"

"Basics, mostly. Nothing glamorous. I'll get some plans worked up for the new quarantine barn. Maybe start laying in supplies." Her brain veered toward overload and she had to rein in her thoughts. She didn't want to give up a single minute of her time with Tucker. "Depends on how much I have to spend to fix the things that have been cobbled together with duct tape and a prayer."

"I have a feeling you'll be getting more funds relatively soon."

"I thought you said that's not your decision."

"It's not. But I know what the foundation criteria are because I helped write them. Unless there's a compelling argument against Safe Haven, which I can't imagine happening, I'm confident the board will vote in your favor."

"That would be great. Wow. Better than great."

"You'll have enough to turn that mouse hole you're living in into a storage shed. Build yourself something with a bit more breathing room."

She turned to face the road ahead, leaving the subject with a quick nod. "Safe Haven, for all its trouble, is perfect for me. I'm busy all the time. I go to bed exhausted and wake up ready to go at it again. It suits me."

He touched her hand. "The work is too demanding

to come home to that tiny place. If for nothing else, you should have a decent bathtub."

She turned her hand over and threaded their fingers together. All she wanted to do was tell him the truth. Right now. Everything. Her mistakes, her naivety, how she'd gotten caught up in a lifestyle that didn't belong to her. That she'd run as much in shame as fear, and how each day compounded the pain she'd caused her family, her friends.

It wasn't the fear of losing him that stopped her, even though she was certain she would. It was losing the best chance Safe Haven had to become what the sanctuary could be. Not only a place to save so many animals, but to teach and train the next generation of caretakers.

While her life might have turned into a sordid melodrama, her legacy could still be worth something. Even though no one from her other life would know. She would. That counted for a lot. Made waking up each day a bit easier.

"You okay?" he asked.

"Fine. Sorry to see the interlude end." Squeezing his hand, she said, "I don't want to get all sappy or anything, but, well, you've been the best part of—" Her voice broke. She cleared her throat, then whispered. "Just, the best part."

PULLING INTO THE PARKING LOT at Safe Haven was bittersweet at best. Tucker got out to carry the food chest into the cabin so that Annie could decide which small items she could fit in her fridge.

Before he'd even shut the back of the Land Rover, Shea spirited Annie away, and not in the direction of the cabin. She'd given him an apologetic smile before she'd let herself be taken, anxious to find out what had gone on during her absence. It alarmed him, but Shea didn't seem off. Though with her it was sometimes hard to tell.

Jesse showed up. "Everything's fine," he said, walking with Tucker. "Doc Yardley came by and gave all the mares and foals a clean bill of health. But I suppose the ladies want to chat."

They entered the matchbox house, his mind still struggling to accept the fact that someone lived there full-time. Annie lived there. Mostly on her own. What in the hell were her winters like? They were so far up north, the snow had to be brutal. He knew the statistics about volunteers in winter. People meant well, but putting out feed during a blizzard was nobody's idea of fun. Especially when it could so easily be seen as someone else's problem.

The idea that Annie could get hurt alone in the middle of nowhere made him feel ill. He put down the ice chest and excused himself, shutting the door to the small bathroom behind him—he had to make a phone call, and it was the only remotely private place to do so.

The Annie situation had grown exponentially. It had a lot to do with the sex, of course. The intimacy between them had been as easy as taking the next breath. He wanted her all the time, his need becoming like a persistent low fever. He'd managed to wait patiently in line at the deli for her to pick out her food, and he'd only kissed her when he was sure she wouldn't be embarrassed. But dammit, the memories of their night together made it hard to think straight.

He didn't want to leave.

He had to leave.

The sooner, the better. Where the hell was George, anyway? On top of everything else, Tucker was getting worried about his friend. He was no spring chicken, although Tucker would never say that to his face. George was about ten years younger than Tucker's father…his adopted father. He'd been a police officer in Brooklyn for years, worked vice and homicide, and he'd gotten more than a few commendations. But he'd hated the bureaucratic red tape, quit the force and got his private investigator's license.

He'd met Michael Brennan during a bar fight. Neither man had meant to be in that particular bar. Just passing the time in what normally was a quiet place in Manhattan. The fight had nothing to do with them, but together they'd stopped it, not without injury. Nothing that a couple of cold ones hadn't fixed, though.

They'd stayed friends till the end of Michael's life. George had helped carry the casket. If something happened to George because of this investigation, Tucker would find it difficult to forgive himself.

He dialed the man's number again, only to have it go straight to voice mail. He left a message that was as succinct as he could make it. Seconds after he'd hung up, he heard the front door close.

Of course, Jesse had heard him. You could hear a mouse fart from upstairs in this place. At least Tucker hadn't said anything that would get him in trouble.

Leaving the bathroom, he stayed put and didn't go looking for Annie. He supposed in a few minutes he'd find Jesse, do the polite thing and socialize, but for now, he needed to sort out a few things.

First, a flight plan. He had the number for the Kalispell city airport in his wallet, and he called in for an 8:00 p.m. departure. That would give him five more hours with Annie. Which wasn't enough time, not by a long shot.

More of an issue was how in hell was he going to tell her that he was Christian's brother? Not this afternoon. Too soon, not enough information. He wasn't ready. He was scared out of his friggin' mind that she'd hate him.

He tried to imagine her reaction to his explanation, but he couldn't get past the look of certain betrayal he'd see in her beautiful blue eyes. Even if she listened to everything he had to say, she could have her own reasons for not wanting to face what she'd left behind. He wouldn't presume to tell her what she should do. A night of sex didn't give him any rights.

Except it hadn't just been sex, and that was the problem. Damn, he couldn't remember the last time he'd felt this powerless. Or this infatuated with a woman.

The cabin door opened, and Jesse stuck his head in. "Am I interrupting?"

"Nope. I'm done making belligerent phone calls."

"No problem. I'm here on a mission." Jesse snorted. "I have to get the matzo ball soup out of the cooler, put it in the dark blue bowl and leave it in the microwave."

Tucker had to laugh. "That's a pretty serious assignment you have there, son. I was there when she ordered that soup. Messing up would not be wise."

"Thanks for the heads-up."

Tucker knew which container held the soup, so he brought it out.

"I gotta say…" Jesse found the specified bowl. "That check you wrote for Safe Haven was a hell of a gesture."

"I consider it a great investment."

Jesse's faint grin spoke loudly.

"Yes, it's because of Annie." Tucker only felt defensive because he was already edgy. "She's doing an excellent job here."

"No one said you can't have more than one reason for doing something."

"Yeah, well, I suppose I asked for that." Lack of sleep was getting to him. "By taking her to Kalispell overnight. Hope that doesn't give her grief."

"Sadie will take care of any gossip."

Tucker liked Jesse and his unhurried, easygoing manner.

"I'm concerned about the winters here. Annie being alone. You have some kind of system set up to check on her?"

"Glad you asked," Jesse said, closing the microwave. "My brothers, me and several other nearby ranchers keep in touch. When it's bad, we come in shifts, so we can all take care of our own stock. It kind of depends on how many animals Annie has here. We haven't had to rescue her yet, though. She keeps up on the snow maintenance, so she has clear paths. That's one reason we need that tractor fixed. It doubles as her snowplow in winter, and we can't let her be without that."

"I've been dealing with the drought so long, I haven't given much thought to severe winter conditions. I'm glad to hear you all are pitching in."

"Winter's tricky. I'm able to fly most days. Sometimes we'll get stuck in a cycle that shuts everything down, but the airports are well maintained. If you ever want to fly back, give me a call. I'll let you know the conditions, give you the coordinates for the private airfield I use. I checked it out already. You're welcome there anytime."

Tucker leaned back against the counter. "I'll be sure and take your number. Thank you."

"She's the real McCoy, you know," Jesse said, taking a seat on one of the wooden chairs. "My…Shea has been known to keep Annie in coffee when she needs it, and food. Annie's gone without, though. Not sure how often, but more than once."

"You don't have to sell me on her. I'm going to do what I can to get some funding for this place. Steady funding."

"Good enough." Jesse kicked out a second chair. "So tell me about your plane before the women come and monopolize us. I've been meaning to ask you about it since you arrived."

14

"I DON'T HAVE THE RIGHT WORDS," Annie said softly, watching Puff, the beautiful chocolate-brown foal, find her footing with unmanageable legs.

"You're doing pretty well," Shea answered. "To be honest, I only understand because of what's happened with me and Jesse. I had no idea that people could honestly fall in love in such a short time. I'd always thought it was fiction."

Annie jerked her head up to stare at Shea. "I'm not in love with him. I didn't say *love*."

Shea pressed her lips together as she lifted her shoulders. "Sorry. I know you didn't say the word, but the way you speak about him. I guess I was wrong."

"Really? What I said made you think…?"

Nodding, Shea met Annie's gaze with the honesty she'd come to respect. "I can't tell you what you feel. In fact, I'm terrible when it comes to reading people. But your body language changed when you were telling me about the way you two talked in the car. And you just lit up about him taking you to the salon."

"Huh." Annie thought about the past twenty minutes. After being given a rundown on Safe Haven, she'd told Shea almost everything that had happened. Not the details, of course. There'd been so much else to say. His kindness. The laughter. The way she felt connected to him. Maybe Shea was right. If things were different, Annie might have let herself think it was love. But if she went there, she didn't know if she could bear him leaving. And how could she keep her secret from someone she loved?

She crossed her arms over her chest and stared down at her boots. "I want to tell him what happened. So badly, Shea, I can hardly breathe. I hate the lies and the hiding."

"Then tell him."

"I can't. I'm a criminal. I'm working under a false name. I've lied to him from the start."

"You're not a criminal. You did nothing wrong."

Annie's head came up. "I was responsible. I was an idiot. Charities lost a lot of money because I was reckless and too trusting. How is that not doing anything wrong?"

"Okay, maybe there were mistakes, but Annie, you didn't do anything illegal. That's what matters. You didn't steal a single penny. You're not a thief."

"Just a coward and a dope."

"You're not, though. You're one of the strongest people I know. Tucker seems like a smart man. Every question he asked about the foundation was astute and reasoned, and so was every question he asked about you. Give him the benefit of the doubt."

"I believed that about my associate in New York." She led Shea out of the stable. "If it was only my feelings at stake, I would talk to him. But he's basically told me he's going to champion Safe Haven with his foundation. We have so much to lose. You know as well as I do that people can forgive a lot, but being duped, being manipulated and lied to, goes straight to their pride. Believe me. I know. Tucker's a lot of things and one of them is proud."

Stopping at the doors, she looked around, made sure

no one was nearby. "He said it himself. When he handed me the check. He believes in me. After that, how can I tell him?"

Shea sighed. She looked sad and worried. "Where does that leave the two of you?"

"Nowhere. He's going home tonight or tomorrow morning. I won't encourage him to come back."

"But—"

"That's the way it is. I'll be fine." Annie didn't quite believe that, but she hoped Shea did. "Especially now that I can talk to you. Although I promise, I won't make a pest out of myself."

"You aren't a pest. You're my friend."

Those few words meant the world to Annie, and she had to take a moment to collect herself. She'd never expected another friend, not ever. No, she couldn't have the man she wanted, but she wasn't in jail, she wasn't actively on the run and she was making a difference at Safe Haven. All in all, it was more than she deserved.

"Let's go to the barn," Shea said.

Annie sighed. "What's Pinocchio done now?"

"You were only gone overnight. No one had time to do anything too terrible."

"Ha. I've been at this long enough to know that all it takes is two minutes for everything to go crazy."

"Can I just finish with one thing?" Shea asked.

"Sure."

"Actually, two things. First, I wouldn't rule out telling Tucker, because I don't think he'd renege on his promises. Second, your hair looks really pretty."

Annie wanted to believe her. The fantasy of Tucker being all forgiving and magnanimous had been floating around at the periphery of her thoughts. But every time those thoughts became too vivid, she'd shut them down.

Despite the way she and Tucker clicked, they hadn't had enough time together for a deep relationship to form, even though it felt as if it had.

Things that sounded too good to be true, were. Not remembering that basic premise had gotten her into this mess in the first place. "Thanks," she said. "I like my hair, too."

"I MEANT FOR YOU TO MICROWAVE soup for yourself, as well," Annie said. "Why don't you have this bowl, and I'll get some more out."

"I'm fine," Tucker said. "I can have a sandwich. Or a frozen burrito."

She smiled at him as she crossed the very short distance between them. "It was nice that Shea and Jesse were able to help out. But I'm glad they're gone."

The moment she was close enough, he pulled her into his arms and kissed her. It felt risky here, as if at any moment someone from town could walk in and find them. But who would come, and why would anyone care? She supposed paranoia was her natural state now.

Regardless, it felt wonderful to press up against him, to taste him, to have another opportunity to memorize all she could before he left.

The thought that this might be the very last kiss made her desperate, and with her lips and her tongue and her breath, she selfishly took all she could, but she didn't care. It terrified her to think of him fading away in her memory. Even if she took the shirt he was wearing, kept it with her always, in time the scent would go, and she'd be left with a plain white Oxford that would torment her for the rest of her days.

Her frenzy must have been catching, because he became just as ruthless, running rough hands down her back, moving his muscled thigh between her legs. The pressure made her squirm. She leaned away, looked at the stairs.

"I made arrangements to fly out at eight."

"It's only a quarter to six," she said. "We have time. If you don't mind taking your sandwich with you."

His smile did things it shouldn't have been possible to do. "I'd never eat again if it gave me more time with you."

"Oh, that is such a horrible lie. But I'll take it."

"An exaggeration, perhaps," he said, turning her around and pointing her at the staircase. "Not by much, though."

"Eight o'clock, tonight?"

"Sadly, yes. I know that doesn't give us much time, but I'd like to…"

She ran halfway up to the loft before she laughed and said, "What? What would you like to do?" She scrambled the rest of the way up when he lunged for her. "Just know you'll have to deal with the miniature shower. Say goodbye to washing anything that requires bending over."

He reached her in record time, ducking his head just enough not to get a concussion. "Speaking of bending over."

"Hmm. Normally, innuendos don't get me hot."

He paused briefly before pulling out his wallet. "I'm supposed to say something clever now, but I can't think of anything but being inside you."

She sighed, retrieved the condom packet from his fingers and tossed it on the bed. "That was better than clever. Now, kiss me and make me forget about later."

Tucker kissed her the whole time he took off her clothes, except for the removal of her shirt and her boots. Everything fell where she stood, could have disappeared from the planet for all she cared. Besides, he had more buttons to undo, which she stumbled over, before he broke down and pulled the shirt out of his jeans.

She'd finally gotten everything undone, when he stepped back. "What?"

His scowl was fierce, but he wasn't looking at her. "What the hell is it with the boots? Why don't we wear sensible shoes that we can toe off while we're walking?"

"Loafers on horseback? I don't know, I think there'd be complaints."

"Only from people who don't have a beautiful woman who is currently naked and inches from the bed."

She giggled. God, what was wrong with her? She never giggled.

He paid attention to the task at hand, while she fussed with her comforter. She remembered the fantasies she'd had about having him between these very sheets. It hadn't dawned on her that it could be something real.

She decided to appreciate the gift, and let any other expectations go. He was here. Now. And now that his frustrating boots were off, he kicked his pants so far they caught on the railing.

He swept her up, then. Onto the bed, where they touched each other with trembling fingers and eager lips. Nothing fancy happened, and that was fine with her. Great, in fact, because she wanted him inside. Deep. She wanted to squeeze his arousal, make him remember what it felt like. Not just the wet heat, but what she sounded like when she moaned, and how her hand felt in his hair as she pulled him down to kiss her.

They rattled the headboard and banged up the back wall, and if the coyotes didn't hear them when they came, the pack must have moved to Canada.

When they found their breath again, the air was filled with their mingled scents, earthy and primal, and she almost wept that she couldn't freeze the moment, keep this as the only time instead of the last time.

THE SHOWER WAS AN ABOMINATION. Annie had been right. Bending over was a joke. He supposed it beat not having any shower, although he could argue the point.

At least he was no longer sticky. Unfortunately, he also no longer smelled like sex. That wasn't something he'd ever felt bad about before. He pulled on his clothes and avoided thinking beyond the next few minutes. They'd eat, then he'd head back to Kalispell. Damn it.

After he opened a can of soda, his cell rang. He didn't even bother taking a sip because it was George. Tucker considered calling him once they'd eaten, but he couldn't. They hadn't talked all day, not since Tucker had left him a voice mail close to noon. There was too much at stake to put this conversation on the back burner. He answered, talked long enough to tell George he'd call back in three minutes, then hung up.

Annie was up next for the shower, so that would work out well. He smiled at her, aching already from missing her. "I've got to make a phone call. I'm going to step outside, but I won't be long and then we'll eat."

She pulled him into a kiss that ended too soon. "I'll be out of the shower when you get back."

He nodded, waited for her to pick up the clothes she'd stacked on the table. Once she'd closed the bathroom door behind her, he went outside. There were no volunteers at the sanctuary this evening, and after he was gone Annie would need to do the evening chores. He'd like to do them with her. Instead, he hurried behind the stable, away from the path.

When George answered, Tucker wasted no time. "You have news?"

"Yeah, I've got news."

At the tone of his friend's voice, a lump rose in Tucker's throat. "Sounds like this is going to be painful."

"You're not wrong. Christian did leave the country."

"I know. He's on vacation." This wasn't news. He'd left that information in his voice mail for George.

"I'm pretty sure that's not why he went. I'm sorry, Tucker, but he used a false passport."

"How do you know this?"

"I had someone tailing him," George said without hesitation, though Tucker's brain was on pause. How had George had the time to have someone follow Christian? "He packed heavy enough to pay over a hundred bucks in extra fees. My associate was able to get a picture of the passport, and she said it's first rate. Had to have cost Christian five grand, at least. Especially if it came with social security card and internet traceability."

"Jesus, how much money did my mother give him?"

"That kind of passport doesn't happen in a day or two. We're talking months. Many months. He's been preparing for his departure for a while."

"Since the money for the charities disappeared?"

"Possibly." George sighed. Tucker heard the sound of a pop-top opening and wished he'd brought his drink with him.

"You got my voice mail, what, around noon? You couldn't have worked that fast putting someone on Christian and finding out all this information." Tucker put the words out there, but he already knew…. He may have been myopic about Christian, but George had clearly had his suspicions.

"No," his friend admitted. "I set up a tail yesterday after I learned of the bookies." He exhaled sharply. "I really hate this. Irene is going to fall apart, Tucker. I wish we didn't have to tell her. She could just think of him taking a vacation."

"She'll find out eventually."

"His cell phone's gone dark. If you tell the authorities, they'll search his place, but they won't find a damn thing. I know. I looked. I also called an FBI agent I know in Jersey, and he hooked me up with a local agent who really knows what he's talking about. He knew exactly which bookies I meant and has a file thick as a dictionary on the way they work. They're heavily into breaking bones, kidnapping loved ones and any other kind of blackmail they can find, but they've also been linked to at least four murders. Never been convicted. No one ever testifies against them, and they don't leave a trail."

"Is there any connection you could've overlooked between them and Leanna?"

"None. In fact, the closer I've looked at her, the more I'm convinced she didn't know a thing."

"Wait," Tucker said, his pacing kicking up dust and gravel. "Just to play devil's advocate here, let me run this by you. For a minute, let's assume everything Christian told me was accurate. He had no idea about the missing money. Then the D.A. comes after him and the only thing my brother can think is that Leanna stole the profits. There's no evidence to the contrary. Nothing points to either Leanna or Christian. He hears rumors about Leanna getting tied up with some bad guys, gets scared, makes arrangements for a passport, a quick exit.

"Time goes by, nothing happens, he figures the mob has written off the loss. He can't get work, but he doesn't really need to, not after Irene gets in touch with him. Then, out of the blue, he gets word that I've located Leanna. Which scares the crap out of him, and he blows town. Takes enough money that he can make it in Bali."

George didn't say anything for a while. When he did, it was what Tucker expected to hear. "That might have made sense if this was the first time Christian's name had come up in conjunction with gambling debts."

Tucked muttered a vicious curse. This was partly his fault. He hadn't been willing to dig deep into his brother's history. If he had, this could've ended months ago. "How bad?"

"Bad enough. Not with these particular goons, no. But there's a pattern. Something he might have picked up from his old man."

"I share a biological father with Christian, remember, and I'm not a gambling man."

"No? Sounds to me like you gambled on Leanna." George hadn't meant to be cruel, Tucker was sure, but his words stung nevertheless.

"It's sure starting to look as if I backed the right horse," he said curtly, then immediately calmed down. Getting angry wouldn't help. "If I bring her back to New York, doesn't that put her in danger? Won't these bookies know Christian split, and figure she's got to know something about the money?"

"It's possible, yeah."

Tucker opened his mouth to curse as he turned, but the sight of Annie standing at the end of the building stopped him. "I'll call you back, George," he said, his heart thudding as he disconnected.

Annie was pale as a ghost, her expression one he'd seen on victims of terrible accidents. He moved toward her, taking slow, easy steps, afraid he'd spook her. She was trembling so violently that his soda, the one he'd opened, spilled over her shaking hand.

"Annie, I can explain."

She tried to respond, at least that's what it looked like, but no words came out. Finally, she seemed to snap back to herself. "You left your drink."

"I can explain."

She shook her head, still dazed, but not in complete shock. "You don't need to."

He was close enough for her to hand him the can of soda. He took it, never looking away from her eyes, dilated far more than shadows could account for. "But I do."

"It won't make any difference." She turned, headed back from where she'd come.

He wished she'd screamed at him. Cried. Run away. But her voice had sounded dead, her stride careful. He had to stop her. Let her know that he was on her side. Make her believe him.

She didn't have to forgive him, because even when his own heart was pounding like it would burst out of his chest, the most important thing was that she understood that she might be in danger. Real danger.

That he'd put her there.

15

ANNIE WASN'T SURE SHE WAS going to make it to the cabin. Her head was spinning, and she kept thinking she would throw up, but she didn't. He knew who she was. He knew about Christian. Lies. It had all been lies. It made no sense, because they'd been in bed together. She could still taste him. She'd worked so damn hard to remember everything, branding him into her being, but every sound and scent and touch had been a lie.

Somehow she was at her truck. How much gas did she have? Enough to get to the freeway. She'd go somewhere, anywhere. There were always crap jobs that nobody else wanted. She could sleep in the truck, or maybe stay at a cheap motel. That's why she had the other driver's license. To run.

Shea would take care of Safe Haven. It would all work out, except that Annie was a fool. She was so stupid it made her step falter, and she had to put her hand on his Land Rover.

Her breath caught each time, like hiccups. Her purse was inside the cabin. Her keys. God, her money. She'd only take what she'd brought with her. Nothing from Safe Haven, never. She'd just dump out her books, put some clothes in the suitcase. Why did it have to end like this? Though, what had she thought? That it would all be a fairy tale?

Her truck was so close, but her hand was sticky with spilled soda. Her things weren't here. She'd been so hungry, and now her stomach churned.

He knew who she was. He'd known who she was before he'd arrived. Was he a policeman? FBI? Or someone Christian had sent to hurt her?

Good job on that.

Broken bones would have been kinder.

"Annie!"

She winced at his voice and willed him away. The harder she tried to push herself upright, the more her legs shook. Shea. Shea would tell everyone why she left. She'd help. She was nice. Maybe. Maybe no one was nice, ever.

"Annie, please."

Lesson learned. She'd work. She'd find someplace to sleep. She'd keep to herself. No more talking to people. No more letting anyone in.

He'd lied.

Worse than that, she'd believed him.

Something gripped her wrist, and when she jerked to look, it was his hand, not cuffs.

"Please come with me to the cabin. We need to talk."

She didn't pull her hand away. She was afraid she'd fall. "There's nothing to say."

"There's a lot to say. I'm sorry you overheard that. I was going to tell you everything, but not yet. Later. When I'd fixed things."

She looked at him and it hurt. "Who the hell are you? Who sent you? I don't know anything about the money. I never did."

"I believe you."

Her laughter came out like a bark, like bile. "Liar. You planned it. All of it. The email. Everything. Is your website made up? The foundation? Who do you work for, the D.A., the police?"

"Obviously you didn't hear the part you needed to," he said quietly, his expression blank. Unreadable. But then she fooled herself into thinking she'd ever been able to read him.

She did jerk away then, and at the second pull, he let her go. "Was it funny? Did I amuse you, or was it all in a day's work? Huh? Or maybe just cruelty for the sake of it. That actually makes sense. You slept with me. You seduced me. It wasn't enough to make me trust you. You had to go the extra mile."

Closing her eyes so tightly they ached, she held back tears through sheer force of will. "The hell with you, whoever you are."

"I know you hate me right now, I do, but dammit, there was nothing funny or cruel about any of this. I had no choice."

"What?"

"You're in hiding. Living under a false name. You disappeared from the face of the earth."

He wasn't touching her, but he leaned toward her, again, his changed expression utterly new to her. Everything until now had been underlined with confidence and strength, but now he looked anxious and frightened. Not that she dared believe him.

"Look," he said, lowering his voice, as if he were afraid of scaring her. "I'm exactly who I said I was. But I'm also Christian's brother."

"Christian Andrews?" She shook her head. No, he couldn't be. Christian said he had no family. "He's your brother?"

"Yes. We share the same biological parents, but I was raised by my mother and her second husband. He adopted me."

"Well, I see lying runs in your family. You can tell your *brother* that I have no idea what happened to the money. I didn't steal it. Oh, wait…he knows already, because the thief has to be him."

"I know," Tucker said, moving closer to her. "I know."

She took a quick breath. So what if Tucker sounded sincere? He was a good actor. He'd been fooling her for days. Except the earnestness had reached his eyes, and she couldn't look there, couldn't afford to be stupid again. "What do you know?"

"Please. Come back into the house. Let me tell you everything. You need to understand what I did. Why I had to keep certain information from you."

"Nice way of putting it."

He stood straighter, frustration clenching his jaw. "What was I supposed to do? I only found you by chance. You couldn't have made yourself look more guilty if you'd tried." Tucker sighed, then gentled his voice. "If anyone should understand that sometimes lies are unavoidable, even necessary, it's you."

She inhaled and nearly choked on the breath. "The picture. It was that stupid picture from the Sundance, wasn't it?"

He nodded. "Come inside? Please? I'm not here to hurt you. I swear. I want to help." He looked down, then shook his head before facing her again. "Whatever you think of me, you need to listen because you could be in real danger. Please, Annie. I'm begging you."

God, this was so hard and, again, she'd brought this agony on herself. Was this what the rest of her life would be like? One giant mistake after the next? Because when she looked at Tucker, she saw the same man from this morning. From last night. From the bathtub in the Hilton. His eyes were pained, his brow furrowed.

And she wanted to believe him. Again.

All the energy drained out of her. Over two years of fear, of being so careful, of loneliness and regret. She'd lived a shadow life, and when she'd finally dared go into the sun, she'd been burned.

"Fine. We'll go inside." She nervously touched her hair, which brought a memory she'd now sooner forget. "I'll tell you what you want to know, but you'll be disappointed. Whatever you or Christian were hoping to find out, I don't have it. I've got nothing."

He walked with her, his hand hovering near the small of her back before he brought it, fisted, to his side. During the short trip to the cabin, he repeated the gesture three times.

She wasn't sure if she should laugh or cry. Mostly because she had no idea what it meant. Her instinct, still, was to trust him. Maybe it was some kind of reaction to his family. She'd never been attracted to Christian, not like she was with Tucker, but she'd foolishly trusted him. Christian had been clever and a smooth talker. Though they hadn't even discussed being more than business associates.

Thank God. One was more than enough.

The cabin smelled like matzo balls and chicken soup. She wanted to throw it all out, clear the air of any traces that reminded her of their night in Kalispell. Instead, she pulled out one of the wooden chairs and sat down, her hands folded on the tabletop. "What did you come here to do?"

He got out a couple of sodas and opened the cans, putting one in front of Annie. He sat close enough to see her well, probably so he could look into her eyes and figure out when she was lying. She wouldn't tell him anything but the truth, though. She was done with the secrets and lies. They'd caused her enough pain.

"I came to see for myself if you were Leanna Warner," he said. "The website photo was a bit fuzzy, and you were turned away from the camera."

"You must have confirmed it was me five minutes in. Why didn't you call the authorities?"

He shifted in his chair, drank some soda. "You didn't make sense. I was expecting someone else, even after I realized you were the woman Christian claimed ruined his life."

She blinked at the slightly disdainful way he said his brother's name. And he'd used the word *claimed*. It was nothing for her to be pleased about.... "What does that mean?"

"I was looking for an embezzler. Someone who would steal money from charities. I thought I had managed to make some pieces fit when I took into account that you'd only skimmed the profits. What kind of thief leaves the original investments? That part was confusing before I left Dallas. Meeting you, some pieces fit. But not enough."

"Maybe because I didn't embezzle anything."

"I know that now," he said, and couldn't be more matter-of-fact. "Hell, I knew before now."

"When?"

"Did I know you weren't guilty? The first day."

She shook her head. It hadn't been a trick question, but it told her that he wasn't being entirely truthful. The first day? Did he think she was that stupid? Well, yeah, he probably did, because that's how she'd played things.

"I didn't say I thought you were innocent." His brows lifted, his gaze steady. "Not guilty is different."

Annie thought for a moment. "You believed I knew something and kept quiet."

"Actually, after I met you, my theory was that you did embezzle the money, but you were coerced."

"That's still stealing."

"Yes, but with mitigating circumstances."

She broke down and picked up the can of soda he'd brought her. Her hand still shook, but her mouth was dry and she needed the liquid. Maybe he was telling the truth. He could've given her a fluffy answer.

"Look, I've had someone working on what happened to that money. He's good at what he does, and he's thorough."

"And?"

Tucker took in a deep breath, wiped his face with his hand before he let it out. "I'll tell you everything, but first, I have to understand something. Why did you run?"

Her face filled with an all too familiar heat. More than any one thing that kept her awake at night, her skipping town was the worst of it. "I didn't even know anything was wrong until I got word I was going to be subpoenaed by the district attorney. I thought it was a joke, until I checked the accounts. All the investment interest, dividends, were gone. I'd made a client's deposit the week before, and the account had been in perfect order.

"I freaked. I had raised all the original funds and made promises about the rate of returns. So I went to an attorney, an old college friend. I told him what had happened, that I had no idea how the money had been taken or by whom."

"Did you ask Christian?"

She stared at Tucker. "Of course I did. He was more freaked out than me. He told me he was calling the Securities and Exchange Commission, the trade commission, the CEO of the brokerage. He swore he'd get to the bottom of this, no matter what."

Tucker nodded slowly. "Sorry, go on."

She drank more soda and realized she wanted water,

but she couldn't seem to move. "My attorney made some phone calls. Because I hadn't been served yet, or accused of any crime, he didn't have to report me. Anyway, he told me that the D.A.'s office was out for blood because it was charity money missing. The embezzlement had even hit the papers, although it seemed everyone's attention was on Christian. He was the most logical suspect, but they didn't have an obvious paper trail.

"There was no question I would be included in the investigation. My lawyer didn't think it would matter that I had nothing to give the D.A."

"What does that mean?"

"He said that in the end, someone would go down for the crime, and if it wasn't Christian, it would be me."

"But there was no paper trail leading to you, either."

"I had no way of knowing that. By then, I was completely shut out. Christian wasn't returning my phone calls, and when I finally did get through using a friend's cell, he hung up on me. I had no access to the computers or the accounts. It was a nightmare."

Annie stood, able to move at last. Never had she hated the size of the room more. It felt too much like a cage. "It was my own fault, though."

"Wait—"

"No, let me finish." The anger in her voice surprised her. "I'd been riding high for months, doing the best work of my life. Getting into the right parties, taking meetings with people who really mattered. I should have asked more questions, been more careful. I got cocky. When the world came crashing down around me, I had no idea who had the kind of power necessary to do the job so smoothly. I couldn't go home…I couldn't bring this kind of insanity into my parents' lives. So I bolted. I cleared out my savings and took off."

"Your parents wouldn't have helped you?"

Annie's throat tightened and she couldn't breathe for a moment as she remembered the last conversation with her mom. "Yes, they would have. And it would have killed them. I knew I was the weak link. The patsy. I assumed Christian was behind everything, and if that were true, I didn't stand a chance. He had me completely fooled from the beginning."

"They couldn't convict you with no evidence."

She looked at him. "Seriously?"

Tucker waved away his comment. "Never mind."

"Anyway, if it started looking too bad for Christian, who's to say he wouldn't have created a paper trail leading to me?" She expected more reaction from Tucker. That perhaps he would leap to his brother's defense, but no. Nothing. "It wouldn't have mattered if I was convicted or not. The key to successful fundraising is credibility and integrity. No one would hire me or work with me again after they discovered the money was taken under my watch. And frankly, I was mortified. For myself and my family. I couldn't stand the thought of seeing anyone I knew. I'd been just hungry enough that no one would ever believe I was innocent."

"And what about your family? Any contact?"

"I left them a letter, and sent a few hard-to-trace postcards. I haven't spoken to them since I walked away."

Tucker's fingers touched hers as she passed his chair, making her jump. Her face flamed again, her eyes filled with tears no amount of willpower could hold back any longer. "I screwed up everything," she said. "Every part, except for one."

Now it was her hand around his wrist. As tight as she could hold on. "No matter what happens to me, you need to promise that you won't let Safe Haven suffer. I've got the rest of the twenty thousand to return to you, and I can cancel the tractor engine. But the animals, they really need this place. It's terrible here in winter. You don't know."

"I'm not taking any money back," he said, standing to face her. "Annie, I'm not here to bring you trouble. I want to help you. We can find a way to clear your name. Together. You've done wonders here. I meant what I said about the foundation. Which is real, by the way."

She sat back down in her chair, pulling her hands away from him and into her lap. "I still don't understand. Why would you want to clear my name? What about Christian? I haven't heard a single word about him since I left."

"He's in Bali."

"Bali?"

Tucker nodded. "He left the country after he discovered I'd found you."

"What?"

"He used a fake passport."

So he knew his brother was guilty. Yet he still wanted to help her? Her pulse raced out of control. "Has he been hiding the money all this time?"

Tucker shrugged. "I don't know. The private detective has uncovered some issues with gambling. Up till the day the theft was reported, he'd done well with the investments. He would have made a number of great connections, considering your donors. It doesn't make a lot of sense for a man who was trying to build a career to decide stealing would be a better plan. Especially when you consider the amount."

Thinking back, Annie shook her head. "Wait. You said real danger. What did you mean?"

DESPITE THE REASONABLE TONE of Annie's voice and the fact that she wasn't shaking nearly so hard, Tucker found it physically painful not to comfort her. He wanted so much to pull her close, to kiss her, tell her not to be afraid. It killed him that he was causing her fear.

He returned to his chair, determined to tell her every detail. He explained about the bookies, repeating his conversation with George. Especially the part where nothing pointed at her complicity in the embezzlement.

"Then I should call the district attorney's office now," she said, no longer looking at him. Her gaze had lost its sharpness as she stared at the table. "No, tomorrow morning. They won't be there now. The sooner I let them know where I am, the better."

"What, no. I haven't finished."

That got her attention again. God, this had to be so difficult. She'd been living in a cave, for all intents and purposes. Making her life as small as she possibly could. He remembered every word her friends had said about her. How she dedicated herself exclusively to the sanctuary. Now he understood that every selfless act had been one of contrition. Atonement for sins she'd never committed.

He'd pulled her out into the spotlight, unprepared, lulled into feeling safe by his attention. He wished he'd done everything differently, although for the life of him, he couldn't see what he could have done instead. "These men… These bookies have been known to go after family, after associates."

"But if Christian took the money from the accounts, why didn't he use it to pay them off?"

"For all I know, he did. He's been borrowing a lot from my mother."

"A lot."

Tucker nodded. "I can't be sure, but I think it's in the hundreds of thousands. Maybe I'm wrong. God, I don't want to be right because, as it is, he's broken my mother's heart by leaving the country. She thinks he's on vacation."

"Could he be?"

Tucker's gut tightened as he stared at her. Still so trusting, so ready to believe better of Christian. "I doubt it, considering his timing and the fact that he used a fake passport. I never knew he had a gambling problem until yesterday. I didn't understand the severity of the situation until the conversation you partially overheard."

She sat with that for a while, the quiet only broken by a nicker from outside, the chirping of birds still out at the end of the day. "Even if he's still in trouble with the bookies, why would they think I would be useful to them? I've been gone for years."

"That's the point. You need to stay gone. Until we can figure out how to take care of this mess. I know for a fact the New York police have tried and failed to get at these bastards. No one will testify. They have people terrified. Until we know what made Christian run, I can't risk you like that."

"You can't risk me."

He hadn't meant to say it like that, but he wasn't about to take it back. "You're too important to me, Annie. I'll do whatever's necessary to protect you."

Her sigh wasn't one of affection or comfort. She sounded frustrated and the look she gave him was one he never hoped to see again. "You've already helped me enough."

"I never would have—"

Annie held up her hand. "Stop. I don't want to hear it. I understand you were trying to help your brother."

"That's partly true."

Her eyebrows went up.

"I hardly know Christian. But my mother has been drowning in guilt for losing him in the custody battle.

She's been trying to make up for it since my dad died. My adopted father. He's been gone eighteen months, and the only thing keeping my mom going is the chance to make amends to the boy she gave up."

"I'm reasonably sure she has something else worth living for," Annie said, the sudden gentleness in her voice making him swallow hard.

"But I'm not a mission," he said. "She's already got me in her corner."

"I'm sorry your family's screwed up. So is mine. But my mission is to keep Safe Haven safe. What are the chances these guys will find me here?"

"I don't know. But any chance is one too many."

"So why don't you just go home? Leave here, don't come back? What do you need me for?" She stared at him, her expression flat, her hands still.

He thought he saw confusion in her eyes, but he couldn't be sure. Of anything. "I couldn't bear it if something happened to you."

"I'm not your responsibility."

The hell with giving her space. He had to make her understand, so he leaned over far enough to take her hands in his. "Yes, I knew the minute I saw you that you were Leanna. But I also knew within the hour that you weren't guilty. I didn't understand any of the connections then. Only that no one would ever convince me that you had freely embezzled that money.

"I think I couldn't exonerate you completely because I didn't want to think Christian had committed the crime and blamed you. So I stayed to make sense of things. The longer I knew you, the more convinced I became that not only were you innocent, but that I had developed feelings for you. When I said I believed in you, I meant every word. I need you safe, Annie. I need you."

He'd never looked at anyone so intently in his life. And when her eyes softened, he felt he could breathe again.

"I understand," she said. "This has been painful for you. You would drop everything to save your brother, to be a hero for your mother. But it doesn't always work out that way. You have to understand that I feel the same way toward this place. If there's a chance the authorities or these bookies can find me, I have to leave. I can't risk it."

"I'll help you—"

"By doing what? I'm not willing to run any longer. That leaves me turning myself over to the district attorney."

"No, it doesn't. At least, not yet." He pulled his chair closer to her. "Let me get my attorney on this. He's a very influential man, and he can help with the D.A. His firm is based in New York, and he's got the kind of access we need. With the new information I can give him, there's a chance we can make a difference in the case against the bookies. Can you call Shea and Jesse to come back? I have to go to the hotel and check out, get my things."

Annie stared at him for a long moment, and he didn't even try to hide his anxiety, how badly he wanted her to be safe. Without a word, she got up, went to the counter to fix a pot of coffee. After she'd turned the machine on, she said, "They don't need to come back tonight. And neither do you."

He went to the counter, needing to say this face-to-face. "I'd feel a lot better if you weren't here alone while I'm gone. As for me, I know I don't need to come back. But I'd like to."

"For all I know, you're lying about everything. You could come back with a police escort."

"You don't believe that." He rubbed the back of his neck. She stared back without so much as blinking. "I'm not lying. I'm not hiding a thing. Not anymore. Not ever again."

She continued to study him, but gave him no feedback. The past couple of years had probably taught her how to do that. To push everything down. Trouble was, he'd seen the true Annie, the joy of her, the passion.

Her gaze dropped, as did her shoulders. "I suppose I have to trust someone," she said.

Tucker wanted to kiss her as badly as he'd ever wanted anything. For now, though, he made do with a simple, "Thank you."

16

LESS THAN AN HOUR LATER, Annie explained the situation to Jesse and Shea as Tucker brewed a second pot of coffee. Before they'd arrived, he'd made sandwiches and ensured Annie ate by silently pushing food in front of her until she did something about it.

Despite the seriousness of the conversation and her own disquiet, she couldn't help but find his actions thoughtful and sweet. Each kind or protective thing he did or said kept tipping her more toward his side. The lie rankled—of course it did—but it wasn't easy to keep throwing stones from her own glass house.

"I'll be just outside," he said. "I need to make a couple of calls."

"More secrets?" The words were out before she could think, but she was still hurting and she wasn't sorry she said them.

"No, Annie." He touched her shoulder, gave it a squeeze. She felt it all the way to her toes. His pull on her was stronger than she knew how to handle. It scared her as much as it comforted. "Want me to call from right here?"

She shook her head sadly. She'd agreed to trust him.

When he closed the door, she turned to her friends. Real friends. "I'm sorry."

"For what?" Jesse asked.

"Involving you. If what Tucker believes is true, someone could come looking for me."

He smiled at her with that slow McAllister grin. "They'd have to get past a whole lot of cowboys first."

Was it foolish that her heart seemed to swell in her chest? Probably.

"You should listen to Tucker," Shea said. "Let his attorney advise you."

"I don't want to be in his debt. I'll have no way of repaying him."

"You think he'd want you to worry about that?"

The way Shea looked at her made Annie pause. When her friend was being truly herself, she hid very little. The question she asked wasn't nearly as telling as the surprise in her expression. "He's not Prince Charming, Shea. We barely know each other. Whether he worries about it or not, I pay my debts."

Shea turned to Jesse, then back to Annie. "If his lawyer didn't have New York connections, I would have suggested mine. I still might. And I wouldn't take a penny from you."

Annie didn't know what to do with herself. Friends weren't this overwhelmingly wonderful. Not in her experience. Even before all of this, she'd had girlfriends. She missed her roommate from college, and Annie had been the maid of honor at her high school BFF's wedding. This was in a different league. "Thank you," she said. "But I don't get it. None of you seem to realize that I'm in this terrible situation because I was too focused on getting ahead. Why are you being so nice?"

"Your actions," Jesse said. "Everything you've done since you came to Blackfoot Falls has been admirable.

We're not just hicks with rose-colored Stetsons." He smiled, even made her lips tilt up a little. "You made some mistakes, but you've sacrificed enough, Annie. Let us help you. Let Tucker help you. He's a decent man."

"You barely know him."

Another one of those sly grins stole over Jesse's face. "But I know people who know him. Who've done business with him. I checked him out every way but Sunday before you got to Kalispell. That wasn't just about you, either. Safe Haven means a lot to Shea. To this community."

With that little nugget, Annie was officially dumbfounded. She appreciated everything being offered to her, but she wasn't about to let their generosity make up her mind for her.

Shea and Jesse assured her they didn't mind taking care of the sanctuary until things got straightened around. They'd even promised to line up more help, swearing that everyone who knew her would lend a hand.

As for what she was going to do about lawyers and district attorneys and Tucker… She had no idea. What she wanted to do was crawl into bed and pull the covers up over her head. The problem was, she wanted Tucker to be in the bed with her.

The man himself chose that moment to come back into the cabin. "I spoke to Peter, my attorney. I'll email him what I can, but the quicker I can courier the rest of my files to him, the better. I won't be long. Maybe four hours total." He looked at Shea, then Jesse. "You guys okay with that?"

"No problem," Jesse said. "I'll call the Sundance so nobody worries."

"Great." Tucker pulled his car keys out, and Annie had about enough.

She stood, her body thrumming with electricity. "Wait a minute. Just…wait. Quit making decisions for me, all of you. I'm not a damsel in distress. I need time to think. So just quit it. I need to do my evening rounds, and I'm late for that already."

"Maybe I could do your rounds with you?" Shea asked after a very awkward silence.

Annie's self-righteous anger withered, replaced by weary confusion. "Sorry. It's just… It's a lot to take in, and the last time I made a rash decision I hurt a lot of people."

Shea nodded. "So we'll talk. As long as you want."

"I've got you covered outside," Jesse said.

Tucker moved closer to her, but he didn't touch. "And I've got to leave. Please, just hang tight. We'll work things out, I promise."

Annie thought of not saying anything, letting Tucker believe what he wanted, but she couldn't. "I'll give it twenty-four hours. You know my priorities, and if we don't have more information by then, I'm going to the D.A."

He opened his mouth, but Annie's raised hand stopped him. "I know you mean well. But this is my mess." She closed the distance between them and put her hand on his chest. "Turning myself in would solve a lot of problems. You know that."

"If Christian is at the bottom of this—"

"Then the authorities will take care of it. But I can't sit back and watch you twist yourself in knots to save my hide."

"Twenty-four hours?"

She nodded.

His pursed lips told her he didn't like it. She could tell by his jaw the moment he decided not to argue with her. When he leaned down to kiss her, the touch of his lips was as wonderful as it was puzzling. The chaos she'd created kept on growing, spreading over people she cared too much about. When Tucker pulled back it was clear he didn't want to leave. But he let her go, then held the door for Jesse.

Annie slowly turned, meaning to get another cup of coffee. Meaning to have a heart-to-heart with Shea. What she did instead was sit down on the nearest chair and fall apart.

TUCKER HATED LEAVING, BUT AT least Annie wouldn't be alone. He knew nothing was going to happen to her tonight, but that didn't lessen his worry.

"I'm sorry about your brother," Jesse said, stopping near the Land Rover.

Nodding, Tucker met Jesse's gaze, surprised at the ease between them. It felt as if time had accelerated since he'd arrived in Montana. "You know what's odd? Annie's become really important to me. I hate that my brother's involved in this, and God knows it's going to hurt like hell to tell my mother, but I need to make sure nothing happens to Annie." Exhaling, he shoved a hand through his hair. "I don't mean to sound like an uncaring bastard. My mother's been depressed since my father died, and of course I'll continue to be there for her...."

"But you keep circling back to Annie?"

"Yeah. As if we'd been together for years, not days. Listen." He looked at the cabin, then back at Jesse. "This is going to sound nuts, and I swear there isn't anything to make me believe she's in danger here, but if anything should happen while I'm gone—"

"I'll take care of it," Jesse said. "Don't worry."

"It could mean getting her out of here. Maybe all the way out. I mean, north."

"I understand. And I've got it covered. But nothing's going to happen. Do me a favor and focus on driving, huh? She needs you back here."

Tucker stuck out his hand and they shook. "Thank you. For everything."

"I'll see you later."

Tucker got in the SUV and took off. Carefully. It would defeat the purpose if he got himself killed in a traffic accident. Didn't mean he'd stopped thinking about Annie. Or his mother. With Annie it was about protection, with Irene it was concern. When he thought of his brother, there was only uncertainty. Why leave the seed money? Why not take everything? Unless he got into some trouble he couldn't get out of. He might have stolen the money as a Hail Mary pass. Which would mean he didn't go into the partnership with the intention of making Annie the fall guy.

The end result was the same, but it made it easier for Tucker to swallow. Christian was still Tucker's brother even though they'd been barely more than strangers for so much of their lives.

The drive passed more quickly than he'd assumed it would, and then he was on the phone, cursing under his breath because Kalispell was too small a town to have a courier at the ready. Something he would've anticipated if he wasn't so distracted by worry. He'd started to panic when he finally found someone who'd do it for triple pay. But it was still going to take longer than he'd like.

For a few moments he thought about flying it out himself, but that meant leaving Annie behind and he couldn't do that. Better to bargain with her to extend the deadline she'd imposed on him.

As he went through his files, he made a couple more calls. He'd already put a lot of the videos on a flash drive, so he completed the set, then went down to the hotel's business center. It was closed, but the manager opened it for him, and by the time he'd copied his case file, the courier had arrived.

George was doing the same thing with his files. There would be duplicates, but Tucker didn't care. The more information, the better. Though he worried there wasn't going to be enough time for his attorney to read through everything, let alone make any cogent suggestions.

When Tucker got back, he'd just have to make Annie see reason. Jesse and Shea were on his side. He'd shamelessly use them to make Annie listen if he had to. Especially since there was another issue besides the time constriction. It made sense for her to go back to Dallas with him. To wait there where he could keep an eye on her while the lawyers slugged it out.

The thought of her facing this alone made him irrational, so he'd have to watch his words. That's what happened, he supposed, when a man fell in love. Jesus. Somehow, he'd thought it would be simpler.

His laughter surprised him. None of this was funny. Especially that no matter what Annie decided, he wouldn't be able to let her go. Not that he'd force her into doing something she didn't want. He just knew walking away wasn't an option.

Shea had brought a roll of toilet paper and a glass of water to the table. It took Annie a minute to remember she hadn't bought tissues in a while, and that made her smile, even though she was still blubbering away.

She wiped her face, though, and looked at her uncomfortable friend. "Sorry," she said, sniffling grossly. "It's been a tough day."

"I can only imagine," Shea said. "Do you need anything?"

Annie shook her head. Blew her nose. Then sniffed again. "You were right."

"About what?"

"I'm in love with him."

"Oh."

"You can't tell him," Annie said. "I can't let my feelings for him change anything."

Shea blinked at her and frowned. "It's already changed everything."

"No. It hasn't. He's just being nice. Don't you see, he's only in this because of his brother. And his mother. I can't make him choose me over them. That would be horrible. I'd never forgive myself."

"Annie—"

"I'm serious, Shea." She pulled off another bunch of paper. "It's bad enough that I've disappointed my family. Hurt my friends and ruined my own reputation. You think I want to take him down with me? I should just leave. Go find somewhere else I can hole up. Only this time, I won't make so many mistakes."

"Like having a friend who puts your picture up on the internet?"

Annie stared. "How did you know?"

"I've been thinking about it a lot. He was very clever. If he'd approached us any earlier, it would have been obvious, but he waited a while. Remember?"

"It's not your fault."

"I know. But it's not your fault, either."

Annie shook her head, frustration making her clench her fists. "People keep saying that when it's not true. I can't sit in this cell a minute longer. Walk with me?"

"Sure." Shea got up, headed for the door, then backtracked until she could grab the toilet paper. "I'll bet Jesse is almost done. Do you want to avoid him?"

"No, of course not. Thank you, by the way, for keeping my secret. It must have been difficult."

"Not so much," Shea said, closing the door behind them.

"I can't tell him anything about my classified contract work, either. But he understands."

"Of course he does."

"Just like Tucker understands your situation."

"You may be right, but that doesn't mean I should take advantage of him."

The walk got quiet except for the sound of their boots on gravel. The crunch sounded like home to Annie. How strange. Even when she'd worked at the stables in Central Park, there hadn't been gravel underfoot like this. Home used to sound like the click of high heels on a sidewalk. Of taxis and diesel engines, and the buzz of Manhattan.

"For the first six months I was away, I dreamed about New York every night."

"The city itself?"

"Mostly streets that I knew well. Restaurants. My apartment. Things happened in the dreams—mostly I was captured or chased or thrown into oncoming traffic, but the backdrop didn't feel like part of the nightmares. I missed the rhythm of the city, as if I'd had to leave my own heartbeat behind. Now, I can't imagine myself anywhere but here."

"You'd do okay in Texas."

"I'm not going to end up in Texas," Annie said, as fast as the words would tumble out of her mouth.

Shea shrugged as they neared the barn. "How do you know that?"

"Don't. I can't go there. I can't pretend that everything's going to be all right. It'll kill me if I do. I ran from a subpoena."

"You were never served."

"That's just a technicality."

"Yeah," Shea agreed, "but it's an important one. Why do you think all those process servers have to be so tricky?

Ducking a subpoena is a cliché because it's true. You weren't served. You didn't break the law."

"I don't think the district attorney's office is going to write my disappearance off so neatly."

"Maybe not. But I doubt you'll be going to jail."

"I owe restitution," Annie said quietly. It was the one thing she tried not to think about. She'd had nothing for so long, it had been easy to ignore the pull to make things right financially. She'd certainly never raise the money by working for a nonprofit.

"That's ridiculous." Shea had never used that clipped tone before.

It stopped her. "Why?"

"You need to let go of your guilt, Annie. It's going to ruin you, and you don't deserve that."

No response would adequately convey how wrong Shea was. So Annie didn't try. They walked again, and she breathed in the smell of the place she'd carved for herself. She had trouble thinking of herself as anything but Annie Sheridan. Leanna Warner was somewhere else, gone. Buried in shame. Annie couldn't help thinking it would be better for everyone if she simply rested in peace.

TUCKER SAT ACROSS from Annie, staring into her troubled gaze. Shea and Jesse had gone home. The cabin was quiet…and after the longest day Tucker could remember, all he wanted was to take Annie to bed.

"Me going to Dallas doesn't make sense. I told you, if we don't have more to go on, I'm calling the D.A." She lifted her chin. The woman could be stubborn. "It's not a debate."

"We can work together much easier if you're with me," he said.

"Together? What am I supposed to add to this collective? If I had some information that would help, I'd have done something with it. That's the point," she said. "I don't know anything."

"I'm not doubting you, but something you may have dismissed as unimportant might be a key piece of the puzzle. Let Peter look through the files. Let him question you. He might stir a memory, remind you of a moment or an offhand remark you thought nothing of at the time."

"He can call me here. I don't like the idea of leaving Safe Haven. This place is mine. I need to be here."

Tucker wanted to throw every last piece of furniture in this cracker box outside, give them some room to work with. He kept trying to think of a way to postpone his trip home. Staying would make him feel better about her safety, but the ranch and his responsibilities at home needed his attention desperately. There were a lot of people counting on him. Especially his mother. As much as he wanted to forget about the Rocking B, he couldn't. Not without a cost he wasn't willing to pay.

"I have to go," he said, taking hold of her hand. "But leaving you…"

Annie didn't respond. Time slid by as he rubbed his thumb on the back of her hand. He ached, physically. His mother could call Christian's phone anytime. When she discovered it wasn't working, she'd worry, and then what? Lie to her? He could, but that wouldn't solve anything.

He needed to give Peter time to familiarize himself with the case. To be effective. George was still sneaking in back doors to quietly get information on the bookies and that damn account number in Annie's coffee can.

He should ask her. Just spit it out, but that would make her even more suspicious, and rightly so. And hell, he hated admitting he'd gone through her things that first day. On the other hand, he'd promised to tell her everything.

There was no winning. Nothing he could do to help the people he loved.

"This is about your mother, isn't it?"

He blinked at Annie, not able to tell how much time they'd sat in silence. "Partly, yes."

"Oh, God. You're choosing me over Christian. You realize that, right?"

"No, I'm not. He made that choice for me."

Annie's face was flushed and miserable. "She won't see it that way."

"Probably not. At least, not at first. It's going to be difficult. I'm not even sure what I should do. I thought about making something up, but then if there's proof, and I believe there will be, that Christian was involved, it's going to get out. I don't want her caught unaware."

"She needs you."

He shrugged.

"Do me a favor?"

Sitting up straighter, he curbed his instinctive nod. "What's that?"

"Come to bed with me?"

That he hadn't expected. "Yes. Of course, yes."

"You go first," she said, looking at the bathroom door. "I've got to make tomorrow's coffee."

This time he did nod, afraid if he opened his mouth he'd say something foolish and make her renege. For the first time since she'd overheard him on the phone, the world felt normal. Well, almost normal. He brushed his teeth; she counted out spoons of coffee. They passed each other on the stairs, brushing fingers and sleeves. He could see how exhausted she was, and hoped they could both find sleep.

When they were finally in bed, her in a sleep shirt she'd put on downstairs, him in a T-shirt and his boxers, they didn't touch at all.

She lay on her side facing him, and he faced her. The room was shadowed with bands of moonlight. He assumed she could see him more clearly than he could see her. But that was okay. He knew enough about what she must be going through.

There was still a matter of trust between them. Trust and a pile of guilt on both their shoulders. "I'm sorry," he whispered, as much to himself as to Annie.

"What for?"

He didn't think she was being coy, not by the tone of her voice at least. "I'm not sure," he said. "I guess I wish we'd met at another time, another place. I want to make all the bad things disappear, and I can't."

Annie sat up so quickly, it startled him. She turned the bedside lamp on, then slipped out of the bed, down to her knees. Tucker almost sat up, but then he realized what she was doing. A moment later, she sat, cross-legged, on top of the comforter, holding a coffee can.

She didn't open it immediately, and moved slowly when she did. She took out the driver's license. The roll of money, and the slip of paper with the account number written on it. Her gaze didn't leave the objects, even when she set aside the can.

"This was my exit strategy," she said. "Part of it, at least." She held up the license. "This was someone my parents used to know. She was my age, but she died four years ago. I never met her. My mother was her godmother. It was a sad story, why the license was in the attic, but I didn't think my mother would mind if I borrowed it." She put it down again, as if it were something precious, a baby blanket or a beloved garment.

Then she picked up the scrap of paper. Shook her head, and grabbed the money roll in the same hand. "These go together. One is what's left of my life savings. I had more. Twice this much, basically. A little more than twice. Enough to make it into Canada, find a place to live. Enough to give me breathing room, because I'd learned how to keep my expenses down. But then my first winter, some horses got sick. I didn't have enough to feed them and get them medicine. I dipped into the other roll."

She put the money down and stared at the paper. "This is a bank account number. A safety net. From the bank in Blackfoot Falls. My payback account. It's pitiful, and I don't think I'll ever make enough to fully repay the stolen money, but I needed to do something real. Something more. So I saved some cash from being a waitress for three months before I came here. And I made some money doing day labor. Nothing much, barely enough to eat and have a place to sleep, but I put something aside, every time. It used to be in the can, along with the rolls. But I knew if the horses needed something, or the goats or the cows, that I'd use it. So I put it away in the bank. Where it would be safe and harder to put my hands on."

She pulled the red coffee can in front of her, and put her possessions back inside. "That's it. That's everything except for this place. Do you see? I have to do what's right, now. Because I didn't before."

He wanted to argue with her. Tell her she was taking things too far. But that wasn't true. This—the coffee can, the savings account, her crusade to save all the animals— it's who she was. Maybe she hadn't been that before, but she was now. This was the woman he'd fallen in love with.

He put his hand on the can, and she nodded, giving him permission to put it down by the side of the bed. Then he helped her crawl underneath the blankets, where he pulled her into his arms. When they were entwined, he breathed again. Felt right again.

And he knew he would do whatever it took to protect her. To keep her just as she was.

"SO YOU DECIDED TO GO TO Dallas with him," Shea said, looking as if she hadn't gotten much sleep the night before. That probably had something to do with the fact that she and Jesse had arrived at six-thirty.

Annie had slept surprisingly well in Tucker's arms. In fact, all they had done was sleep. And although the day ahead frightened her to death, she felt all right. "He's put himself on the line for me," she said. "I have to give him the same courtesy."

"Have to?"

Annie smiled. "You're the slyest devil I know. No. I want to. If all the rest of this madness weren't going on, I'm pretty sure I'd be over the moon with happiness."

"People say, 'This, too, shall pass.'"

"People can be idiots. But in this case, I hope they're right. I don't want to hide anymore."

"Of course you don't." Shea nodded at the suitcase on Annie's bed. "That's all you're taking?"

"That's all I've got. I didn't leave with much to begin with, then had no place to store anything that wasn't useful."

"You should have said. I would have brought some

things for you to wear. Maybe not my clothes, because they wouldn't fit, but we could have come up with something."

"I'll be fine."

"You're right. You will be."

Annie closed the suitcase and turned to her friend. "I'm only able to do this because of you guys."

"It's everyone, Annie. We want you to be free and clear, here because you want to be. In the meantime, I've got Melanie and Levi and Kathy to help out. And Will, of course. Then there's all of them from the Sundance, and Matt's volunteered a bunch of manpower from the Lone Wolf. So don't fret. We've got it covered, no matter what."

"Just know that I appreciate it deeply. That I'd hug you so hard if we were huggers."

Shea laughed. "You are a good friend."

"Hey," Tucker called up the stairs. "You need my help?"

"Nope," Annie called back. "Fair warning, though. If there's no more coffee, you guys are toast." She picked up her suitcase and looked around the room, hoping like hell she'd see it, and the people of Blackfoot Falls, again.

DURING THE DRIVE AND ALL through the flight, they talked about school and sports and old friends and lovers. Family, too, but only about the past. Nothing about what they were facing. And they touched. A lot. After they landed in Dallas, he pointed out landmarks on the drive to his downtown condo, but she barely looked out the window, preferring to watch him.

"I'll give you a quick tour," Tucker said when they arrived, putting his Stetson on a peg by the door. It was the only overt sign that a rancher lived in his gorgeous seventh-floor condo. The motif was black and white with startling splashes of color and an ebony stone floor. It was so spacious that she could completely walk around every piece of furniture.

She lingered over the stunning view, then admired all three bedrooms and the big kitchen. It didn't hurt that he had a whirlpool tub that could comfortably hold them both.

Annie felt suspended between worlds. She'd never been to Texas, and already it felt foreign. The accents were strong, the humidity reminiscent of summertime on the east coast, but the air was different. Neiman Marcus was a hell of a lot bigger and ritzier than Abe's Variety, and while she appreciated the luxury and flash of the city, it was intimidating, as well. Dallas was a long way from the Canadian border.

Despite the lack of Western decor, Tucker belonged there. He eased her nerves with a cold beer and then made a quick call to a nearby Chinese place. She had to admit, takeout was something she'd missed a lot.

When they were unpacked in the master suite and seated at the dining room table, the reason for her visit came to roost. Made it kind of hard to enjoy the dumplings and Peking duck.

"I'll call Peter, as promised," Tucker said, "but I'm not expecting miracles. He's barely had a chance to make it through the paperwork."

She nodded. "When are you going to your ranch?"

"That depends on you. I'd like to go in the morning. It's not going to be an easy conversation, and I don't want to rush it."

"Okay, that's fair. I'll wait, then, to make my decision. But I have to warn you, as much as I appreciate your situation, I'm still having trouble seeing any other solution."

He inhaled, ready to give a speech that he clearly cut off before the first word. Several seconds passed before he began again. "You know what I know," he said. "I've already made sure that the plane is being serviced and refueled. If you want to go to New York as early as tomorrow evening, that's fine. I won't try to persuade you any more than I already have. Except for one last thing…"

She nodded, equally afraid that he'd change her mind and that he wouldn't.

Tucker put his hand on hers, and she rested her chopsticks on her plate, giving him her complete attention. "Somewhere in that mix of what you need to do," he said, "and what you want to do, and how you think this needs to play out, please consider the undeniable fact that I've fallen in love with you."

The rug swooped out from under her. Her few sips of beer seemed to have made her drunk, and she forgot, while his eyes peered into her own, that she could breathe.

A moment later, the earth turned as if it had never stopped. "Oh, Tucker," her voice shaky. "That was below the belt."

"I know. That's why I said it. I want you with me, Annie. Somehow. I don't know what it can look like yet—there's too much chaff to find the wheat—but I won't let this end without a fight. I love you."

"You can't." She adamantly shook her head. "You don't know me well enough." Of course she'd already admitted to herself and Shea that she'd gone ahead and fallen for him. But that was different. She saw so clearly the kind of man Tucker was. What woman wouldn't fall for him? He was loyal, thoughtful, smart, great looking.…

God, what was she doing here with him. No, what was he doing with *her*?

"Annie?"

"What?"

"Stop thinking so hard." He smiled when she sniffed. "Look, I have something else I need to come clean about," he said, and the fear edged back inside her. "I know you better than you think I do. The files on the embezzlement and your background that I sent to Peter? They're very comprehensive." He looked closely at her, waited while she processed what he was saying. "That's part of the reason I knew right away you weren't the woman Christian described."

"How much exactly did that private detective dig up?" She tried to remember if there was anything major in her past she should be embarrassed about.

Tucker smiled, and supporting his claim that he did know her, he said, "Don't worry. I wasn't privy to anything that would make you blush."

Annie laughed a little. "Yes, it crossed my mind."

He looked serious again. "Those files told me everything I needed to conclude you weren't a thief. You're that same woman, even after all the crap flung at you. I love you. Not just because you've changed your world to make things right in every way you could, but because I can see the strength in you. You've been forged in fire, that's for damn sure. It's made you sharp and extraordinary, and still somehow so kind."

He touched her cheek, a gentle sweep of fingers. "You're an amazing woman caught in a terrible web. Don't let it swallow you. Please. You've paid your penance."

Annie blinked back the tears only he seemed to wring out of her. "I'd hate to play poker with you. You're a ruthless man. But the truth is, I think I love you back."

His smile made her giddy inside. "You think?"

"Shea and Jesse fell in love in a week," she murmured, more for her own benefit than his.

"It happens. Not often, but it does." His calm self-assurance comforted her. Tucker wouldn't tell a woman he loved her if he had even the slightest doubt.

"It's been crazy. The past few days...life in general. I can't keep up with anything."

His steady gaze lit with a flicker of humor. "And yet some things remain consistent. For example, did you know that Chinese food heats up in a microwave, good as new?"

"Does it?"

He nodded. Rose. Offered her his hand.

Near midnight, they finally ate their reheated dinner in bed, with *Letterman* in the background. Worn out, they touched from hip to toes. All Annie could think was how incredibly lucky she was.

WHEN TUCKER ENTERED THE HOUSE, his mother was waiting in the foyer. She looked her elegant self, but he was reasonably sure she'd tried calling Christian and was concerned.

She hugged him, smiled, searched his face. "You look tired."

"It's been a long trip."

They walked to the staircase, where Tucker left his briefcase, laptop and hat, then went to the kitchen. It was just ten, and he'd skipped breakfast, knowing Irene would want him to eat with her. Leaving Annie behind had been hard, but she'd assured him she needed the time alone.

"You realize," his mother said, after they both had cups of coffee, "that you haven't told me if you found her."

Tucker looked at the spread on the table, all set out and waiting. A fresh fruit salad, all the fixings for the waffles he deduced the housekeeper had put in the oven to keep warm. Most likely next to the crisp bacon. "Let's eat," he said. "I'm starving, and it's a long story."

Irene went to the stove and pulled out the platters. He found the pitcher of orange juice in the fridge. They fixed their plates as he tried for the hundredth time to come up with an opening line that wouldn't upset her further.

Finally, after a few bites and verifying that Martha was upstairs changing linen and wouldn't overhear, he put his hand over his mother's. He hadn't realized, until Annie, that he only did that for two women. "I did find her. She was in Montana running a large-animal sanctuary."

Irene slipped her hand out of his grasp. "It took you all that time to recognize her?"

"No," he said. "It took me all that time to figure out what's been going on. I started out looking for the woman. When I got there, I knew I had to search for the truth."

Tears came to his mother's eyes. Of course she knew. Not the details, he'd have to give her those in painful doses, but Irene was an intuitive woman. Bali had likely tipped her off. "He'll never come back, will he?"

"I don't know."

"I'd hoped," she said, using the linen napkin to dab at her tears. "I wanted so much for this to be someone else's fault. But I left him with Rory, and for all that I'd once loved the man, he had his demons."

"Mom, please. You did the best you could. There's a time in every person's life where they have to stop blaming their upbringing or the circumstances and take responsibility for their actions. Christian's a grown man. He knows right from wrong. This isn't about you."

She tried to smile at him. "I'm his mother, sweetheart. I'll always be his mother. And he'll always be the child I left behind."

ANNIE HAD TAKEN A BATH, but the jetted water and the space to relax hadn't helped at all. Her thoughts were going in circles. For every argument to wait for the attorney to come up with a plan, there was a counterargument for her to cut through what would be an unknowable amount of time and take matters into her own hands.

She'd found a leather club chair that fit perfectly when she curled her legs under her, and sipped yet more coffee. The chair faced the big window in the living room, and the panorama of city life spread out before her seemed more like an art exhibit than reality.

It was odd to be alone. How had Tucker become a familiar and comforting presence in such a short time? That she missed him so much surprised and frightened her. Between each chain of thoughts about Christian and the bookies and the law were gaps filled with only one thought on a continuous loop—Tucker loved her.

That was the most astonishing thing of all. It outweighed all the fear and doubt and self-recrimination, and every time she started to think she didn't deserve him, his voice came to scold her. He was a smart man who knew his own mind. And he knew exactly who she was. All of it. All the things she'd hidden for so long.

Then she'd get back on the cycle of doubt and peddle that sucker until she ran out of steam.

In the end, the deciding factor came down to the fact that he loved her. Ironic, but that was the swing vote. Or perhaps, that she loved him. Either way, she knew what she had to do. For her, for him. For them.

She pulled out her cell, and called the number she'd looked up two years ago but never used.

TUCKER'S EVERY INSTINCT rebelled at what was happening. Ever since Annie had told him her decision to go directly to the district attorney and offer herself up as a bargaining chip, he'd had to work harder than ever to keep in mind that Annie was her own person. And she had a right to do something he considered unbelievably reckless. That was the trap he couldn't seem to escape. He, the man who would take a bullet for her, wasn't the one in control.

And now she was the centerpiece in a sting operation to blackmail the two bookies. Money in exchange for her silence. She'd give them recordings they believed Christian had made, then disappear forever this time. That's how it was supposed to work.

He'd just spent the most nerve-racking three days of his life. And Annie? Jesus, she was a rock.

"You're going to be surrounded by our people, Annie. Remember that," the FBI special agent told her.

Tucker knew Doreen Wellman believed what she said. Which didn't make it true.

Everyone else—Peter, the assistant D.A. in charge of organized crime, the supervisory special agent who ran the task force trying to nail Dave Bell and Mickey O'Brien, the bookies who'd been running roughshod across New York for over fifteen years—had cleared the room while Agent Wellman checked the wires in Annie's clothes.

It was something new, nothing like what he'd seen in the movies. This wire was literally the size of a fiber-optic strand, so slender it was sewn into Annie's bra, virtually invisible. Also untraceable by any technology out there. Or so Tucker had been told.

He wanted to sit back and let events unfold, focus on being supportive, but for Christ's sake, Annie was walking into a viper's nest.

As Annie lowered her T-shirt, Agent Wellman leaned back against the desk in the meeting room they'd taken over. "You did great on the phone call," she said. "You shocked Bell when you said Christian told you what happened to Jefferson Hope. Very few people knew they'd put a hit on their own bagman."

"If you have evidence, why not take them into custody?" Tucker had promised himself he'd keep his mouth shut. Tough. "Why Annie?"

"Because we can't use the recording of Annie's phone call in court. These guys are tricky and they've run us in circles. I'm not too proud to say that Annie stepping up now is a godsend. We need to get at least one of them to speak. We've fed Annie specific questions to ask them." She smiled at Annie. "You want to reassure your friend that you know what to say?"

Friend? The word was like a slap to Tucker. They were so much more. He saw in Annie's eyes that she was thinking the same thing.

She gave him a serene smile. "I warned them on the phone that I have a duplicate set of flash drives in a safe deposit box, and that if anything happens to me, the information will go directly to the police. I'll remind them as soon as I walk in. They know I've disappeared once and think I only came back because I'm broke. It's perfect, really."

"Believe me." Agent Wellman nodded her dark head with confidence. "They'd rather pay the blackmail than take a chance on their empire crumbling."

Screw her authoritative blue suit and her sensible black shoes and her calm demeanor. Tucker was sweating. And he had a few things to say about the "perfect, really" remark. Later. "Unless they decide she's bluffing and kill her when she walks in the door."

"If one of them lifts a weapon we'll shoot him. We have the best snipers in the country armed with infrared scopes at all windows. It doesn't matter that the drapes are closed. Right this second, we're watching them move around that old house. In fact, according to the man who's in a van a few blocks away, Mickey just went to the toilet. To pee."

Annie captured his gaze. "I can't give these people any more of my life," she said. "Neither can you. I heard Bell's doubt on the phone. I can't believe someone could be that good an actor with no warning. He was worried about what

I might have on them. He wanted more information, and I've memorized everything I'm supposed to say. I'll be out of there in the blink of an eye, and we'll be long gone before the world caves in on those bastards. It's going to be fine."

"I won't stop worrying until we're out of New York, and they're in jail. But I can't help asking one more time. Please don't do this. There has to be another way."

Annie leaned in for a kiss, and when she pulled back, her relaxed expression made him ache.

"I know you think you're doing this for all of us." He touched her hair. "But nothing is worth you getting hurt."

"I won't be hurt. When it's over, I'll have immunity. I'll be free, for the first time in over two years. And it'll open the door for Christian to come home."

"To jail."

"That's true, but at least it'll probably be at a country club prison in Dallas. For so little time, it'll give your mother a chance to get to know him before it's too late. Give you a chance, too."

"There's nothing I can do to get you to change your mind?"

She shook her head. "Just be waiting for me when I'm finished, okay?"

"I wouldn't be anywhere else."

Unfortunately, being where he'd promised turned out to be unimaginable torture. He'd suspected it would be, but waiting in the van three blocks away, putting on the headphones that let him listen to what was happening, only to pull the damn things off…and then repeating the cycle until he'd nearly ripped an ear off, was almost unbearable. It was all he could do not to run out of the friggin' van, get to her and take her away.

But that wouldn't happen. They'd reached the point of

no return, where anything he might do would put her in even more danger.

There was no doubt in his mind that if his prick of a brother ever came back to the States, Tucker would punch his lights out. How dare he put Annie in this kind of danger.

How dare Tucker let her go.

He moaned, and Agent Wellman brushed his arm in sympathy. She had no idea. None. They were all about the case, the people in the van and on the nearby rooftops of this rough neighborhood. Practically every person on the street was an undercover agent. There was more firepower on this residential street than at FBI headquarters. Or so he'd been assured.

Yes, he knew it was an exaggeration, and even though he'd wanted to deck the person who said it, he'd held his fist close to his body. Although he dared anyone to make one smart remark. He wished someone would.

He stopped breathing the second the door opened, and he could have sworn he didn't start again for the next ten minutes. He barely moved, didn't blink, thought he was going to be sick, or at the very least have a heart attack.

Annie was amazing. She played her part as if she'd rehearsed her whole life. The two men were disgusting, which wasn't a shock…that Tucker managed to not rip a seat out of the van was.

Every minute felt like an hour. Nothing had ever frightened him so deeply. He wasn't even allowed to see her, only hear her when she climbed into the back of a taxi that wasn't really a taxi.

He shook on the way back to Times Square, where Annie left the cab. She walked to a small hotel almost hidden by a huge marquee, and went up to her room.

He had to wait until the FBI was certain she hadn't been

followed. Thankfully, they'd detected no wires or bugs or worse in the bag that held the cash.

Finally, when he was about to burst out of his own skin, he was allowed into the room with her. He slammed the door behind him, locked it, bolted it, dragged Annie straight into the tiny bathroom, locked that.

Then he kissed her. Held her so tightly she almost choked, but then she laughed until he kissed her again. And again.

It took a long time for his heart to stop pounding as if it wanted to jump out of his chest.

Epilogue

Two months later...

IT WAS AMAZING TO MAKE the turn to Safe Haven. Annie was smiling like a kid, leaning forward as if she'd never seen the long dusty road.

Tucker laughed at her, but he was grinning pretty hard, himself. "You okay?"

"I think so. It feels like coming home."

"It is. But I'm hoping that it won't take you too long to feel that way about the Rocking B."

"It's an adjustment, I'll admit." She grabbed his hand as the first corral came into view. "A wonderful adjustment."

By the time they made it to the parking area, she could see the construction going on. The quarantine stable was framed, and some of the walls were up. They weren't quite as far on the new cabin, but that construction was fancier. It would be a real house, with three bedrooms and two and a half baths. Whoever ended up taking over Safe Haven for good would be happy there. She knew, because she'd seen every stage of the design.

Tucker's foundation had come through like champions. They'd hired quite a few people from Blackfoot Falls, which was fantastic for the economy, and they hadn't had to turn away nearly as many horses.

Annie couldn't wait to see Shea, who had temporarily taken over the reins but shared responsibility for decision making and managing volunteers with Melanie.

"Maybe tomorrow, when we're not so tired, we can go for a ride, check out the newly plowed field."

"Yes, absolutely. Tucker, this is so amazing."

"It's always going to be yours, you know," he said, pulling the rented truck into the expanded parking area. She jumped out before he had a chance to undo his seat belt, but she waited for him before she raced to the stable.

Sure enough, that's where she found Shea. Annie almost pulled her into a hug, but then she remembered they weren't huggers. Shea just shook her head and followed through. Somehow, Annie wasn't surprised when her friend and Tucker shook hands.

"So much is happening," Annie said, trembling with excitement.

"A lot of construction. We're sending the pregnant mares to the Sundance for the time being. Too much noise."

"How are you doing, Shea?" Tucker asked. "Is Safe Haven keeping you too busy? You know I can hire someone to come out here full-time."

"I'm fine, but I was hoping we'd take a look at hiring Kathy and Levi. I think they'd like the work, and could use the money."

Annie grinned. "That's a wonderful idea."

"Now what's all this about you starting a Safe Haven in Dallas?" It was Melanie.

Annie and Tucker turned to find her taking off her gloves as she walked into the stable.

"Yep. Tucker's dedicated two hundred acres of Rocking B land for the new sanctuary. We're designing it from the ground up. It'll be a teaching facility, as well. Just like here."

Melanie gave her hand a squeeze. "We miss you."

"I know. I miss you guys, too."

"We're not leaving the planet," Tucker said. "I do have a plane."

"Can it hold a horse?"

"No. But I'm going to build a landing strip on the edge of the property so that we can start an animal rescue co-op in central Texas."

"How long are you staying?" Shea asked.

"Just a couple of days." Annie pulled Tucker closer, and relaxed as his arm went around her waist.

"We're going to visit Annie's folks for a bit."

"You haven't seen them yet?"

He shook his head. "We did. But things were more unsettled then. They need a chance to get reacquainted."

"And to give him a proper third degree," Annie said.

"Well, as long as we have a couple of days with you, why don't you two saddle up and come see what's what?" Shea asked. "Nothing like seeing your dollars at work with your own two eyes, right, Tucker?"

He looked at Annie. She knew he was beat and so was she. They'd really intended to rest when they arrived. She shrugged. "I guess I'm not capable of saying no when I'm here. You can go on inside if you like, and we can ride again tomorrow."

"Oh, no," he said. "We'll sleep in New Jersey."

She kissed him, right in front of Shea and Melanie and all the horses in the stable. "Don't count on it."

* * * * *

MILLS_WEB